CHARLOTTE LAMB

Walking in Darkness

A SIGNET BOOK

SIGNET

Published by the Penguin Group
Penguin Books Ltd, 27 Wrights Lane, London w8 5tz, England
Penguin Books USA Inc., 375 Hudson Street, New York, New York 10014, USA
Penguin Books Australia Ltd, Ringwood, Victoria, Australia
Penguin Books Canada Ltd, 10 Alcorn Avenue, Toronto, Ontario, Canada m4v 3b2
Penguin Books (NZ) Ltd, 182-190 Wairau Road, Auckland 10, New Zealand

Penguin Books Ltd, Registered Offices: Harmondsworth, Middlesex, England

First published in Signet 1996
1 3 5 7 9 10 8 6 4 2

Set in 9.5/12pt Monotype Plantin
Typeset by Datix International Limited, Bungay, Suffolk
Printed in England by Clays Ltd, St Ives plc

Prologue

Nobody was watching the little girl as she stood on tiptoe to open the door. If they had seen her, they would have stopped her. Sophie had been waiting for hours for her chance to get out of the house, but her mother had kept her busy, offering cake to the aunts, taking home-made lemonade to her cousins, passing clean plates and carrying used plates out to the kitchen. It was getting very late when she was finally able to slip out of the back door and then she stopped dead, looking up at the sky as she realized the sun was sinking. Pink and gold streaks ran from horizon to horizon, promising a sunny day tomorrow, but they were disappearing fast and it would soon be dark. Sophie was just seven, and afraid of the dark.

She looked towards the onion dome of the village church, black against the glowing sky. Lights were coming on along the village street but the churchyard was empty and silent, and once the sun had gone down it would be as black as midnight there because there was no moon tonight.

She could go tomorrow, of course. She hesitated, wanting to run back indoors, but she had promised she would come today, and a promise was a promise.

Fingering her new crucifix on its silver chain around her neck, she poked the gritty path with one toe, staring at the white faces of the daisies by the fence, hearing the wind in the trees which crowded around the tiny village. The deepest sighs seemed to come from the great firs on the hill behind the graveyard, their tall heads bending to each other the way the old women in the village did, those old widows in black who sat at their doorsteps every day, whispering and shaking their heads at the children running by to school, who made faces back. Sophie didn't know why there were so many widows in Kysella, but they made her uneasy, just as the trees made her uneasy. At night you could almost believe the trees were closing in; you could imagine them shuffling down the hill, bowed and dark and terrifying. The village would wake up and find itself swallowed up by the forest. They might never get out . . .

Sophie shuddered at the thought. If only she had not made that promise to Anya she would have turned back. Instead, gulping hard, she began to run, holding on to the present she was taking, out through the back gate, along the unmade track towards the church. The rough flint and stone wall which ringed the graveyard was just higher than her head; she gave it a nervous glance as she got closer.

That was where the witches sat at night, all the children knew that. They whispered about it in the school playground, telling younger children that you must never go near the church once the sun had gone down or the witches would get you. Witches hated the light and loved the dark. But they wouldn't be there now, not yet, not while the sky held the last flickers of light. She just had time to get away, if she hurried.

Her white cotton skirts rustled deliciously around her bare legs. It was the first dress she had ever had made just for her and she loved it; usually she wore second-hand clothes passed on by her Aunt Anna, who lived in Prague, dresses which had belonged to her cousin Marya once and often had to be cut down for her. But for her first communion Mamma had saved up to buy material, had made the dress herself at night, on the old sewing machine. All day Sophie had been aware of wearing it, had twirled and swung, just to feel the skirts brushing around her.

Her new white shoes rubbed the back of her heel as she ran, but she couldn't slow down. She got to the wrought-iron gate and pushed it open, starting violently as it creaked. Her heart thumped inside her.

The shadows were already thickening around the old yew trees which were her landmarks whenever she came to visit Anya. They were very old, had been standing there for hundreds of years, Mamma said; their trunks rough and scaly, like lizards, their long, thin green needles pricking your finger if you tried to pick them.

Sophie took a deep breath, then darted between them and knelt by the small stone cross. It was carved with their names, Pavel Narodni, born 1946, died 1968, and Anya Narodni, born 1966, died 1968, beloved daughter of Johanna and Pavel Narodni.

She had been coming to visit them ever since she could remember. Mamma had always stopped on their way to church every Sunday to put fresh flowers in the old tin jar on the grave. She didn't visit it so often since she married Franz Michna, the schoolteacher. Sophie suspected Franz was jealous of Mamma's first husband. The photographs of Papa which had always stood around the house had all been put away, and Franz made Mamma hurry home after Mass, to cook the Sunday meal, he said; there was no time to dawdle.

But Sophie still went, in spite of Franz's frown when she got back home for lunch. 'Where have you been?' he would ask curtly, although he knew, she could tell from his face that he knew, and she would turn wide, innocent eyes on him. 'Playing,' she would say, and Mamma would come in from the kitchen and tell him quickly, 'It is Sunday, Franz. No school today.' And she would smile, soothing him, placating him. 'Are you going to read the newspaper to me while I work?' Then he would soften and forget Sophie and go into the kitchen to smoke his pipe and read from the Sunday newspaper while Mamma worked.

Sophie was lonely since Mamma married the school-

3

teacher. The other girls weren't very friendly to her any more. They said she would tell on them to her new father, they called her 'Teacher's Pet' and wouldn't let her join their games in the playground or in the village street after school. They ignored her, or ran off, giggling. She was always alone, but everyone had to have a friend, so she had begun pretending Anya wasn't dead; she talked to Anya in her head or even aloud if there was nobody else around.

'Sorry I'm late. Mamma didn't let me out of her sight all day, she was scared I'd get my new dress dirty. Do you like it? The family came, all of them, and those awful boys pulled my hair, they tried to get my wreath, but I managed to save it from them. Mamma picked the roses from the bush by the back door, the bush she said Papa planted the year they got married. Do you remember, Papa? It has grown so big, you'd be amazed if you saw it.' She laid down on the grave the wreath of little white rosebuds which she had worn on her hair for her first communion. The flowers were yellowing already, their petals withering, but their scent was sweet. She wondered if Anya could smell it in heaven.

Sophie had never known her; Anya had died before Sophie was born, of the most ordinary of childish ailments, measles. She had suddenly run a very high fever which turned to pneumonia within hours. There had been no doctor in the village then – the nearest doctor was several miles away in the next village. They had sent for him, but Anya had died before he got there. She had been two years old. There were photographs of her in the house; they had always fascinated Sophie. Anya had obviously taken after their mother. She had had Johanna's dark hair and brown eyes and Sophie had envied her for that.

Sophie was more like their father, with fine blonde hair and blue eyes. She had always been a small, thin baby, and now that she was shooting up, her legs long and knobbly-kneed, she was even skinnier. What would Anya have looked like now if she had not died?

Sophie wished she hadn't. They would have gone to school together and Anya would have played with her; they wouldn't have needed other friends. It wouldn't have mattered, then, if the other girls wouldn't play with them, they would have had each other.

'I suppose you have lots of little girls to play with in heaven, Anya, you can't be lonely, and it must be nice for you to have Papa with you,' she said, pulling a white rosebud from the wreath. Sophie kissed it, leant it up against Papa's carved name. 'This is for you, Papa.' She had been born after he was killed, the year the Russians invaded. Papa and some friends had been driving through Prague when they ran into a Russian checkpoint they hadn't known about. The soldiers had called to the driver to stop but he had panicked and driven on. He had been shot at the wheel, the car had rushed on down one of Prague's steep hills, and had ploughed into a stone wall at the bottom. It had exploded. Papa had been taken to hospital with dreadful burns, but he had died next day. Mamma had seen him and the shock had been so great that she had fainted and been put to bed so that she had not been there when he died. Sophie knew what he had looked like when he was married from the wedding photo Mamma had always kept on the mantelpiece.

The aunts were always saying that Sophie took after him, they had said it several times today, making Franz frown and shut his mouth up tight, like he did in school when he was cross with one of the children, so she had known that he was cross to hear Papa talked about.

'I had to get up very early but I couldn't have any breakfast, of course, before communion, and I was so hungry, I felt sick, but Mamma said it was excitement. I put on my new dress and then we all had to go to school, and line up,

5

to walk to church. We wore veils, too, like brides, down over our faces before we knelt at the altar rail to take communion.' She closed her eyes and remembered the long crocodile of children, the girls in white dresses, the boys in suits, walking along the street, watched by the whole village. They had sung the Latin hymn they had just learnt, and in front of them under a golden canopy some of the bigger boys carried a statue of the Blessed Virgin. 'Sister Maria said it was the most important day of our lives, our first communion. We should always remember it.' She opened her eyes and looked down, noticing that there was a dandelion growing at one edge of the grave. She grabbed it and pulled, but it didn't want to come out; the flowers and leaves tore off in her hand but the roots stayed firmly planted inside the dusty earth.

'Maybe you liked it growing there?' she thought aloud to Anya. 'It is a cheerful colour, a much brighter yellow than buttercups. I tasted a stem once, there's milk inside it but it's nasty, it might be poison. I spat it out and washed my mouth out too, and nothing happened. If I'd died, I'd have come to heaven to be with you, but I was scared. What's heaven like, Anya?' She stopped talking, stared down, sighing. 'I wish you could answer me.'

'Sophie . . . Sophie!'

For a second she thought the windblown voices came from inside the grave and all the breath seemed to leave her body.

'Sophie, where are you?' That time the voice was louder and came from behind her. She breathed normally again, realising it was Mamma's voice and knowing what that meant. They had discovered she wasn't in her bedroom. They had come looking for her.

She jumped up and began to run but her new, still shiny-soled shoes skidded on the dew-wet grass and she fell on her face, breathing in the cold of earth and moss. Before she got up her mother was there, pulling her to her feet.

'You bad girl. What on earth do you think you're doing?' She grabbed Sophie's arm and shook her furiously, glaring down into her face. 'I've been scared out of my wits. I told you to go to bed. What are you doing out here in the dark?'

Johanna Narodni had a hard hand, roughened by years of scrubbing floors for other people, reddened by years of having her hands in water and cheap soap. When she hit Sophie across the back of the head it left the child dazed, her ears ringing.

Johanna was not yet thirty, that day in 1976, a beautiful woman, with a warm, rounded figure, rich, lustrous dark hair and enormous velvety brown eyes which reminded Sophie of the centres of pansies.

'I brought my wreath for Anya,' wailed Sophie, beginning to cry.

The schoolmaster, Franz Michna, looked down at the neatly kept grave. A short, stocky man in his mid-thirties, with thick brown hair and a bristly moustache which Sophie hated to feel brushing against her when he kissed her cheek, he had taken over the village school two years ago and had married Johanna Narodni just eight months ago.

'That's nice, isn't it, Johanna?' he asked his wife softly. 'A nice thing for her to do.' He patted Sophie's blonde head and she pulled her head away, her eyes resentful even of his kindness. He had spoilt her life by marrying her mother. He couldn't get round her by being understanding. 'But you should have told us what you were going to do, Sophie. Your mother was very worried when we couldn't find you. If you had told us, we would have come with you.'

Sophie kept her eyes down, her pink mouth rebellious. She had not wanted to tell them what she was going to do. And she certainly hadn't wanted them to come with her. That was the last thing she wanted. This was just for her and Anya. Once she and Mamma had come to visit Anya, but now it was just Sophie who came and she blamed Franz Michna. Since she'd met him, Mamma no longer cared about Papa or Anya. Sophie wasn't sure Mamma cared much about her any more, either.

There was a little silence, then, putting a finger under Sophie's chin, Mamma tilted the child's head back and looked down at her with an odd expression in her eyes.

'Do you wish you still had a little sister, Sophie?' She looked up at Franz Michna and they smiled at each other while Sophie watched resentfully. Then Mamma said softly, 'Next spring you'll be getting a new little brother or sister, darling. I'm going to have a baby, and I'm going to need your help to look after it. If it is a girl we'll call it Anya, shall we?'

Sophie stared, white-faced, cold as ice. 'NO!' she yelled, and began to run.

1

Steve Colbourne first saw her on a chilly November day in a New York hotel bar; she walked in and stood just inside the door, her blue eyes carefully not lingering on anyone as she looked around, very obviously not wishing to catch the eye of any of the men jostling elbow to elbow in the room. He didn't blame her. From a girl like this the briefest meeting of eyes might be taken as a come-on – no doubt she had learnt that the hard way. Was she there to meet any of them? He looked around curiously, from face to familiar face. A number of them had also noticed her but he couldn't see recognition in any of their staring eyes. Just lust.

The Washington circus had come to New York by invitation from Senator Don Gowrie. Those of them with good expense accounts were staying here, in this hotel, which was one of the more expensive hotels in the city, and, as was their habit, had looked at once for the most congenial watering hole and taken over this dark-oak panelled bar, with its deep leather seating and polished tables, the gleaming brass along the back of the bar, as their own. Any other guests wanting a drink soon learnt to use one of the other two bars in the hotel, but the blonde, he sensed, had not wandered in here by mistake. She was looking for one of them – lucky devil.

She was quite something: hair smooth, pale gold, tall, slim, with better breasts than model girls had and terrific legs, long and shapely, but above all with skin so smooth and such a luscious texture you felt it would taste like cream, and he wouldn't mind tasting it, no, he wouldn't mind at all.

Just when he was about to go over and offer to buy her a drink, she turned and walked out. He would have gone after her, but if she was meeting some other guy it could lead to trouble and he had had enough trouble for the moment. Enough emotion, too, come to that. It interfered with your work, and left scar tissue. A year ago he had been dealt a blow that still had not healed – how could it when there were so many memories everywhere in Washington?

That was why he was glad to get out of Washington, happy to see the run-up to the primaries starting, because that was what this was all about. Don Gowrie had called a press conference two days before he was due to fly to London to begin a tour of Europe. He was going as part of a Senate commission looking into restrictive market practices which might damage the US but it was an open secret that he was using this opportunity to renew his friendships and strengthen his ties with influential people in Europe. Gowrie was throwing his hat in the ring without actually announcing the fact and he had called a press conference to deny that that was what he was doing. The political pundits had not been fooled but their votes were not what he was looking for; he was appealing to the electorate over their heads, and the voters out there in Heartland America would probably take him at his word because Don Gowrie was a charmer, a man with fireside warmth, a man who breathed sincerity.

Steve enjoyed electioneering, tramping state to state, following the politicians out into the real world, where the voters lived, where life was not as cocooned, as cosy and incestuous as it was back home in the capital. The smell of battle put a brighter light into the eyes of politicians and journalists alike.

They were all in the bar that afternoon, waiting for two o'clock when the ballroom doors would be opened for the press to rush in. Like the Gadarene swine, thought Steve, looking at their faces in the hard electric light, faces that knew everything and valued nothing, eyes that were bright and shiny and blank as if they had not yet been switched on.

They were drinking and talking, telling dirty jokes to each other, boasting about their latest lay or their handicap at golf, complaining about their wives or the alimony they paid their ex-wives, and the ones with the dreamy expressions were talking about cars. Nobody was listening to anyone else. A few were just drinking steadily, silently, almost relentlessly; they were the old hands, the soaks, remnants of years of drinking in bars while they waited for something to happen, men who didn't care anymore, just did the job and then went home to an empty apartment and drank until they passed out.

'What d'ya think, Stevie?' one of his crew shouted, leaning forward to peer at him along the bar. 'You know the guy – d'ya think he's got a bimbo stashed away somewhere, or not?'

Steve shrugged. 'I don't know him that well, Jack. He doesn't tell me his bedroom secrets, if he has any.'

'Didn't I read somewhere that you once dated his daughter?' another reporter along the bar called out.

Steve ignored him. Jack finished his beer then looked regretfully at the foam-flecked, empty glass. Steve hoped Jack wasn't going to have another drink; he had had quite a few already and in that huddle in the ballroom the cameraman was going to need a steady hand. Jack was a big guy with broad shoulders and muscles like whipcord, he could carry weights that would make most men's knees buckle, but he had a weak head where drink was concerned and Steve didn't want their picture wavering all over the place; he was hoping to get a good slot in the night news running order. You were only as good as your last story and to keep your reputation you had to keep getting your piece into the front of the news.

The TV people had all their equipment set up already in the ballroom. They always got the prime position, right up in front of the platform. TV had more influence than the rest of the media; one picture on the news at night was worth any number of articles in the press. They had left their cameras and mikes and lights under the watchful eyes of the security men. No need to be afraid someone might get at their stuff here, steal it or wreck it, in the local head-quarters of the Republican Party. There were enough security men around to stop a full-scale riot. This must be costing Don Gowrie a fortune. Steve's mouth twisted sardonically. Not Gowrie, of course, no; he was wealthy, but this campaign must be costing millions and Gowrie wasn't that rich.

No, Gowrie's father-in-law was paying for all this, old Honest John, John Eddie Ramsey, one of the most influential men along the Eastern Seaboard, whose wealth was fabulous and who came from a family which had been up to its neck in Republican politics since the early nineteenth century, one of those who still called it the Grand Old Party, and meant it.

Honest John had been bred to be a president by an ambitious father, yet he had never quite made it, somehow. He had come close several times but his chance had slipped away each time. Hard to say why. Maybe he hadn't really wanted it enough, or maybe he had had bad luck. He had certainly had no luck with his family. He had had three sons who all died, one of them fighting in Korea as a young conscript of eighteen, one of them on the hunting field when he broke his neck taking a jump too high for his horse, and Eddie Junior who had died of liver disease when he was only forty, having drunk his way steadily towards death since he was in his teens. None of them had married or had children. Old Ramsey must have thought he had made certain of having grandchildren by getting himself three sons. How could he have predicted the disasters that had overtaken them all? A funny business, life.

Honest John's one daughter, Eleanor, a pale, fragile, jumpy woman, had looked as if she was going to die a spinster. There had never been any bees around that honeypot, for all her family's money. She never learnt how to talk to people and if young men tried to chat her up she had fled, trembling. She was kept out of the political limelight, living quietly at home with her mother on the Ramsey estate at Easton, Maryland, the acknowledged social bastion along that seaboard. At thirty-three she had amazed them all by marrying Don Gowrie, a diplomat eight years her junior, good-looking and ambitious, but with very little money and no powerful family connections. The whisper around town was that her father had decided young Gowrie would make a reliable son-in-law, had put the marriage together, like a political deal, promised Gowrie his backing in the future in return for marrying Eleanor. How Eleanor felt about it nobody could guess and in those days the press did not dare ask, had never, anyway, been given an opportunity to question her. She had given no interviews. She had simply sat for photographers. In her ivory satin, lace and pearls, she had made a delicate bride, judging by the fading sepia photographs in the newspaper files Steve had seen. Whatever the truth, the two of them had finally, a couple of years later, given the old man his first and only grandchild, a girl, Catherine.

No doubt Honest John had prayed she would not take after her mother, but he must have been afraid she would. He needn't have worried.

Catherine was lovely, even as a child, when she was painted by the most fashionable portrait painter of the day, in a simple white dress. The painting had caused a sensation that year; everyone had been enchanted by the slender, black-haired little creature standing in a woodland setting with a tame deer feeding from her hand; a modern Snow White, with big dark eyes and skin like cream. She was much photographed by the press, too, at the same time: Catherine aged eight, in immaculate jodhpurs and black hat, riding her palomino pony at the Ramsey family country house; Catherine winning cups for jumping at local gymkhanas, later; Catherine in a one-piece swimsuit, her black hair tied up in a knot behind her head, down on Chesapeake Bay, with her grandfather, catching crabs at low tide and taking a bucketful back to be cooked for lunch that morning, the press story said. By the time she reached eighteen she was always in the gossip columns, tipped as debutante of the year, hotly expected to marry young because she was surrounded from the start by eligible young bachelors. It was an open secret that Honest John Ramsey doted on her, and so did her father, and as heiress to one of the biggest fortunes on the East Coast she was a prize men would fight for. But she showed no interest in marrying young, indeed as she grew up she increasingly played hostess at Don Gowrie's famous Washington dinner parties where the food was nouvelle cuisine, the talk was scintillating and the guests hand-picked. Catherine was not only beautiful, she had a shining intelligence and a sense of humour that gave her that far more elusive quality, charm.

In that, too, she took after her father. Her mother was almost never present on these evenings, or if she did appear she rarely stayed long. It was accepted that she was not strong; she had to spend most of her time in her own suite of rooms and she did not share in her husband's political life.

'Did you ever date Cathy Gowrie, Colbourne?' someone else called out, one of a group of press men who resented anyone who worked for TV, resented and were jealous of them. The other men along the bar watched Steve, some of them grinning, hoping they would needle him into showing temper, some of them just curious, not having heard the gossip before.

'Get off my back!' Steve coolly said without rising to the bait, although there was a tense line to his mouth and his jaw was tight.

'Isn't it true that his wife is a few cents short of a dollar?' Jack muttered, still trying to catch the eye of the barman.

Steve had already had this conversation with Harry Doberman, the editor-in-chief of the network, at their headquarters in New York, not a stone's throw from this hotel. Not that he would dream of telling Jack about it. Jack was a good cameraman but you didn't tell him anything sensitive, anything you did not want repeated to all and sundry the minute Jack had had a few.

'Any truth in this rumour about Gowrie's wife?' Harry had asked, and Steve had looked at him wryly, knowing that Harry knew far more about Gowrie than he did and was just throwing out feelers to see how much Steve had heard.

'Well, she seems to spend a lot of time out of sight, back home in Maryland, with her parents, and there is something a bit . . . blank . . . about her, as if she isn't listening, isn't even aware of what's going on around her, but since the election started hotting up, she's been with Gowrie all the time, and she smiles and nods, and says yes and no and maybe, so it may just be that she's bored by politics. After all, she comes from a political family – she must have had it stuffed into her all her life. Maybe she's just sick of it, but now Honest John has put it to her that it's time to do her duty and stand by her man.'

Harry had been chewing the end of his pen the way he did when he was trying to give up smoking for the umpteenth time. It made him bad-tempered and liable to blow up over nothing and he always started to put on weight if he kept it up for long.

When he was smoking he was as thin as a greyhound and twice as nervy, inclined to bite your head off if you said anything out of turn, so on the whole everyone preferred him to smoke.

Screwing up his eyes to stare at Steve, he asked, 'And what about this other dame? Is there one? Or is it just dirty minds and wishful thinking?'

Even more on the alert, Steve carefully said, 'If there is, Gowrie has done a brilliant job so far in keeping her hidden away. You know what Washington is like. You can't keep a secret for five minutes. Eyes and ears everywhere. A lot of people would pay a fortune to get the goods on Gowrie, but he seems to be as clean as a whistle.' And while he talked he was wondering if Harry knew something he could not openly pass on, was dropping him a hint to dig it out for himself.

Harry chewed on his pen some more. 'Is that a "Don't know" or a "Could be but hard to prove"?'

'Both,' hedged Steve, then, watching Harry even more closely, said, 'But I have to admit Gowrie has never struck me as having a poor libido. He's getting on for sixty, of course, but he's got a lot of buzz, and some of that energy has to be sexual. It wouldn't amaze me to find out that he had a woman somewhere, but it isn't his wife. She's older than him, for a start, and she's as plain as a horse. I don't see her being hot stuff in bed.'

Harry met his eyes, said softly, 'What about his secretary? In my experience it's often the secretary. The single ones are the most dangerous – they get possessive if the guy is the only man in their life.' His eyes glinted and he smirked. 'I've had one or two who got that way.'

Steve knew all about them; everyone had known, you couldn't hide anything in an office, any more than you

16

could in Washington. Harry had a wife and two expensive kids at good schools but that hadn't stopped him having the occasional office affair. They always ended the same way: he had to get rid of his secretary when she turned tearful and demanding.

'Gowrie's secretary is certainly devoted, runs his office like clockwork, and I wouldn't find it hard to believe she worshipped the ground he walks on – but she's no femme fatale. She wears mannish suits and shirts with ties, has horn-rimmed glasses – I don't see him having a mad affair with her.'

Harry looked disappointed. 'Well, there's someone, I'm sure of it.'

Yes, he had been told Gowrie had a woman – but was his source a good one?

'I'll keep my eyes open,' Steve had promised, but he didn't think for a second that he would catch Don Gowrie out, even if there was a woman somewhere. Gowrie was smart, and careful.

Glancing around the bar now, Steve wondered if anyone else was on to a rumour that Gowrie had a woman.

'Ready, Steve?' his producer said, appearing at his shoulder. 'I had a word with Gowrie's people, and explained we had a problem getting the tape to the studio in time for the night news, and they've shifted your interview tomorrow forward by two hours, which should be just fine.'

'I'll look forward to it,' Steve said, and meant it. He had interviewed Don Gowrie many times before, but not since Gowrie began to get his nose in front in the race for the presidency. There were other leading contenders on the Republican side, but some very big money was going on Gowrie.

By the time Gowrie showed up, the ballroom was packed to the doors and the air was rank with perspiration, bad breath, the smell of beer and whisky and the machine-oil smell of the cameras and sound equipment.

Gowrie took questions from the press in an order laid down in advance by his media people. There was no spontaneity on these occasions: too much was at stake. Any shouted, unagreed questions were ignored. There was an agreement between the sides: play ball with us, we'll play ball with you. Refuse to play the game our way and you won't get any time with the candidate, you won't get an invitation to any of the social events with which the lobby was sweethearted by the party during election year.

In his late fifties, his hair once dark, now powdered with an ashy shade, his expensive suit grey too today, his white shirt striped with a very pale blue, everything about Gowrie was discreet, elegant. There was even something faintly boyish about him – his features had a faintly haggard spareness, but they were chiselled and attractive, his eyes – a pale blue, washed out to grey – had great charm whenever he smiled that boyish smile. He was a good speaker, that came with the territory; he never made the mistake of being too clever, he talked directly, frankly, disarmingly to his audience, looking into their eyes.

Women flipped over him. Men felt they could trust him. A decent guy, they said. Not tough, maybe, but under the elegance there was a steely strength.

This was his honeymoon period with the media; he was new to this level of attention although he had been around for years, a face in the background, a useful man in his party, knowing everybody but not a leader. Now, he was suddenly hot and the press hadn't yet got around to sharpening their claws. For the moment they loved him because he was new, because he gave them something different to write about, although how long that would last was anybody's guess.

Steve was one of the first to ask a question. It had been

18

decided on by his producer, Simon, in advance, in discussion with Gowrie's people, who liked to sow the audience with friendly questions. What would the senator do about street crime in the cities? Did he favour tougher punishment or more police on the streets? Or did he think society was at fault and what could be done about that?

Gowrie went into hyperdrive on that one, talked angrily about crime and its threat to the peace of the decent people of America, said it was time America got the policing it deserved, talked of ways and means by which that could be achieved. You didn't need to be a genius to work out that that was going to be one of his campaign platforms, but then all the candidates jockeying to be picked to run as president came out with the same promises on crime. Half an hour later Gowrie's people were signalling him to leave. They all looked very satisfied, the press conference had gone well, he had answered every question ably, fluently.

As he turned to go, a voice came out of nowhere. 'Senator Gowrie, what do you believe will be the long-time effects in Central Europe of the war in the former Yugoslavia?'

Gowrie stopped in his tracks and turned back. This was one of his specialist interests; he had worked in East Europe while he was in the diplomatic as a young man and was rumoured to speak a number of East European languages. Cleverer than he looked, but good at hiding his brains, thought Steve, which made him even cleverer, because if there was one thing the voters did not like it was a clever politician. They didn't trust them.

His press officers were hurriedly searching their clipboards of agreed questions. The most senior of them leaned over the battery of mikes and said curtly, 'That question was not submitted, Miss . . .?'

'Narodni, Sophie Narodni, of the Central European Press Agency,' the blonde said, and her voice was as sexy as the rest of her, low and husky, with the faintest foreign lisp to it.

Every man in the room was staring at her by now, and they weren't thinking about politics. That was not what men thought about when they looked at this girl.

The only man in the room who wasn't goggling at her was Steve Colbourne. He had happened to be looking at Don Gowrie when he turned and had seen Gowrie's face turn stiff and white as if he was fighting with shock, frozen on the spot like someone whose worst nightmare has begun. He hadn't moved or spoken since, he was just staring at the blonde girl, and she was staring back at him.

It wasn't often that Steve Colbourne was surprised by anything. He had been a reporter for far too long in a corrupt and complex world where almost nothing was what it seemed or what people perceived it to be. He had thought himself shock-proof, but it seemed he wasn't. Jesus, it couldn't be. Could it? The air seemed to him to be charged, lightning almost visibly flashed between the two of them. His reporter's mind crawled with curiosity. Don Gowrie and this girl? It was indecent even to think it: she was young enough to be his daughter, and had that lovely, untouched wide-eyed innocence that went with blue eyes and blonde hair and a certain shape of face in the young. He could not believe she was Gowrie's mistress.

But there was something. That was for sure. Every instinct warned about that.

Then Gowrie visibly forced himself to break off from her, tore himself out of his trance, turned on his heel and was on his way, surrounded by his entourage, without answering her question. But Steve saw him turn his head to speak to a security man moving at his shoulder.

The other man nodded, spoke in turn to a couple of others, and Steve saw them spin off, and, without running or seeming in a hurry, push their way back towards the blonde girl. Steve was closer; without stopping to think about the wisdom of intervening, he moved like greased lightning to get to her before they could.

He took her elbow and began walking her out, talking rapidly, urgently, while she looked up at him in startled surprise.

'My name's Steve Colbourne, I do a weekly round-up of political news on NWTV, you may have seen me, if not I assure you I'm very respectable and trustworthy. Can I buy you a drink, or do you want those very ugly guys behind us to put an armlock on you?'

She stiffened and instinctively started to turn, but he went on softly, 'No, don't look back at them, pretend you don't even know they're there. It's called the survival instinct, animals practise it all the time. Haven't you ever seen a bird freeze and pretend to be a statue? It works, too; the psychology is shrewd. It throws a possible predator off. They aren't sure what's going on or what to do so they wait and watch, and that gives the bird time to plan its escape.'

She turned her head to look up at him, and he smiled at her. By then they were engulfed in the departing tide of media flowing through the exit; Steve held on to her arm to make sure she didn't get away. He was picking up her scent by then, a cool, light fragrance that reminded him of a spring morning. It went with blonde hair and blue eyes and long, long legs. What the hell was going on between her and Gowrie? She had something on the guy, that was certain – and she wouldn't be the first beautiful young woman to sell herself to a powerful old man. History was littered with them. Steve surprised himself by not wanting her to be one of them.

He could hear her breathing next to him. They were shoved close together by the crush of bodies moving out of the great ballroom, with its chandeliers and high, wide windows framed by heavy red velvet drapes, into the luxurious lobby of the hotel, and Steve felt the warmth of her skin under the cream silk dress she wore, almost felt he heard an over-rapid beating of her heart.

She was scared, he thought, but when he shot a sideways look her profile seemed calm, unflurried. Was she always this tranquil – or did she lose her cool in bed? He frowned, imagining her with Gowrie. Did that sleek blonde hair get rumpled and tousled? Was she hot? She didn't look as if she was highly sexed, but then with women appearances were always deceptive.

In the hotel lobby the blonde pulled free, glancing back at the same time. Steve looked back, too, and found the two security men right behind them. Their lizard eyes slithered over him, recognized his face, and then ignored him. They were only interested in the girl.

'Miss, can we have a word? You aren't wearing an official press badge, Miss . . . what did you say your name was?'

'Narodni, Sophie Narodni.' She looked at one, then the other. 'Who are you?'

'We work for Senator Gowrie, Miss Narodni. Did you say you worked for a press agency?'

'Yes, the Central European Press Agency. Have you got any identification on you? I like to know who is asking me questions.' She smiled sweetly.

'Certainly, Miss Narodni.' The taller of the two, a man with very bronzed skin, flipped back his suit collar to show a badge. She leaned forward slightly to read it. He would be getting a nostril full of her delicious scent, thought Steve, watching with amusement.

'Thank you.'

A little flushed suddenly, the guy lifted the clipboard he held, consulted the sheaf of paper clipped to it, running a finger down a list.

'Oh, yes, the agency is listed, but we have a Theo Strahov down as their representative.'

'He couldn't make it, he was taken ill, so he sent me.' She pulled out of the small cream leather purse she held in one hand a plastic-enclosed security card and showed it to them. The shorter man took it from her; both stared at it.

'You're supposed to wear this, Miss Narodni.'

'I couldn't pin it on my dress, it would have ruined the material and it is expensive.'

Her accent was a little stronger now, perhaps she was more nervous than she seemed? She gestured to her dress and the security men stared at her silk-covered breasts.

Steve had never liked private security guys; they always ended up trying to hijack police powers, believing themselves to be above the law; they were arrogant, crude-minded sons of bitches. These two were prize specimens.

Absently, without taking his eyes off her breasts, his lizard tongue flicking out to wet his lips, the taller one said, 'We should have been notified of the change. Did you show your identification to the man on the door?'

'Of course.'

They frowned; somebody was going to get into trouble for letting her in without checking her.

'We will have to have proof of your identity, Miss Narodni, and proof of your address, perhaps a letter addressed to you there? Or your driving licence?'

She went back into the purse and came up with an airmail envelope, which she handed them. They both studied the address, one of them scribbled it into a pad he took from his pocket, murmuring it aloud as he did so. Steve memorised it.

'So you live on the Lower East Side? How long have you been there?' they asked her as she took the envelope back.

'Not long. I am staying with a friend; she is the tenant of the apartment.'

'Friend's name?'

'Lilli Janacek.'

They wrote that down too. Steve was trying to work out exactly what was going on – if she was involved with Gowrie he would know all this stuff, so why were his men asking her these pretty obvious questions?

'What does she do?' they asked.

Simon, the producer, had come up, was hovering, curious and at the same time impatient. He asked through his teeth, 'What's going on? We've been waiting for you. Shall we pack up or do you want to do an intro to camera while we still have the same background?'

Speaking out of the corner of his mouth, and trying at the same time to hear what was being said by the others, Steve muttered, 'We could do a piece outside later, with the hotel façade behind me – change of background always makes a piece feel denser, gives it more variety. We might get a couple of talking heads to go with it, get some input on what New York thinks.'

Sulkily Simon nodded. He was only twenty-five, smooth-skinned, still faintly naive. He had only made producer a few months ago and was still unsure of himself, but he was touchy about his new status. He wanted to be the one who decided when they shot what, but he didn't dare argue with Steve, who had far more pull with the network.

'See you in the bar,' Steve told him, and Simon went back into the ballroom.

'You American?' the taller security guy asked the girl, who shook her head.

'I'm Czech.'

That excited him. A foreigner, that was something he could get her for. 'Have you got your visa and passport on you? How long you been in the States?'

She was still outwardly calm. Her face, her voice, had not altered under the pressure of their questions, their hard, suspicious faces. She showed them her passport, the visa in it. 'As you see, there is no time-limit on my stay here. I have

24

very good references. The agency will give you my details. You'll see their address on this envelope. It's a letter from the head of the agency. Can I have it back, please?'

The short guy reluctantly handed it back.

'Your friend, this Janacek woman – she here on a visa too?'

'She doesn't need one – she was born here, in America, right here in New York, in fact. Why are you asking me all these questions? Did Senator Gowrie send you?'

'The senator?' As if she had pressed a button they exchanged looks. The tall one said, 'Of course not, we haven't spoken to him. You weren't on our list, that's all. We had to check you out. That's our job. Well, thank you, Miss Narodni.'

They walked away towards the lifts and Steve got the impression of a tactical retreat – now why had they suddenly taken fright and left? This got more interesting by the minute.

Sophie Narodni began to walk across the lobby towards the main exit; Steve quickly caught up and fell in step with her. 'About that drink?'

She gave him a startled look, as if she had forgotten all about him. 'Oh. Sorry. I don't have the time.' He got the impression she then really noticed him for the first time. 'You're a TV reporter, aren't you? I saw you in there. You asked him a question.'

'Steve Colbourne.' He offered his hand, smiling, and after a brief pause she held out her own hand.

'Hello.' Her hand was slender, cool to the touch; she took it away almost at once. 'Do you know him? I mean, have you actually met him?'

'Do you?'

Her eyes widened, startled. 'Me? No, oh, no.'

He got the impression the question had scared her, and of course if she was Gowrie's secret mistress it would. He wouldn't find out by a frontal assault. He smiled again. 'No? Well, I do a political programme on network TV once a week. I don't know if you've ever caught it?'

Blankly, she shook her head. 'Sorry, no.'

He didn't know whether or not to believe her. But maybe she never watched TV? 'I give a round-up of life in Washington, news from Congress, gossip, interviews with major players . . .'

'Major players?' she interrupted.

'Important politicians,' he translated. 'Until recently Don Gowrie wasn't one of them. He's come up on the outside, out of the blue, surprising everybody, including me, and I've known him for years.'

Steve felt the leap of her attention; looking into her blue eyes he was certain that, whether or not she was sleeping with Gowrie, there was something going on here and he had to know what it was.

'When you say you know him . . . have you ever met his family?' she asked. 'His wife . . . his children?'

'Come and have that drink, and we'll talk,' he invited again, and knew that this time she would not turn him down.

They didn't go into the bar where the rest of the press were beginning to gather again – they walked past it, across the lobby, threading through little groups of chattering hotel guests, and went into a circular bar with smoked glass windows, low-lit, panelled, with a soothing hush that made Sophie's stretched nerves quiver with relief. She had been on edge for days, knowing what was ahead of her, and now it was over. She sat down, sighing deeply as she leaned back against yielding red-velvet cushions. She had almost forgotten the TV reporter and when he sat down next to her it made her start, her eyes jumping up to stare at his face.

Her first impression of him had been that he was a big

man with a hard face, not so very different from the security men who had been interrogating her a few minutes ago, and looking at him more closely didn't change her impression, although he was not so much big as muscular and tall. She didn't know much about men's clothes, at least in America, but even a casual glance told her that he looked expensively dressed: well-pressed dark grey suit, crisp white shirt and a discreet tie. If you were in front of a camera all the time obviously you had to look good, and he did, although the elegance of the suit did not disguise the formidable structure of the body under it.

'What would you like to drink?' he asked, watching her in his turn, and Sophie felt his curious, probing stare like a needle under her skin. It wasn't safe to relax, she thought; she still needed to be on her guard. What was this man after? Why had he come over to her like that? Why had he hung around while the security men questioned her?

Sophie's mouth went dry; she was stranded, high and dry, on the sands of shock and anxiety again. She wished she hadn't come in here with this stranger; she needed to be alone, to think. She ought to be working out what to do next. She had had one plan and one only, and now she had gone through with it. She had started something without being quite sure what would happen if she did, and she was scared. She kept remembering Don Gowrie's expression when she asked her question, the way he had swung to stare. What had gone through his mind? What was going on in his head right now?

She tried to tell herself she needn't be scared, he wouldn't dare do anything to her – but she couldn't help it, couldn't stop the jangling of her nerves. Maybe she should have gone about this some other way? Maybe she should have written to his wife? But she hadn't quite dared do that. Far too dangerous to put anything on paper. She had tried ringing his home but neither he nor his wife or daughter were ever available and the distant, icily polite voice which answered each time had scared her too much for her to risk leaving any messages.

'Can't you make up your mind what to have?' the reporter repeated and she blinked.

'Oh . . . yes . . . a glass of white wine, please.'

A young Mexican waiter in black skin-tight pants and a close-fitting waistcoast had sauntered over; he was visibly pleased with his own lithe body, walking like a matador, a look of inner attention on his face, the look of a man listening for the roar of a crowd. Sophie couldn't help smiling at him and his dark eyes glowed at her as if waiting for her to throw him a red rose.

'A glass of white wine for the lady, and a whisky for me,' the reporter said.

'Glass white wine, whisky, certainly, sir,' the waiter said in a warm, Spanish-accented voice, and sauntered away.

'Sophie . . . you don't mind if I call you Sophie? I'm Steve. Tell me about yourself,' the TV reporter said with the practised manner of one who was a professional interviewer, and she wished to God she dared talk freely to him. If only she knew someone here in New York well enough to trust them, talk to them. This city was so huge, so crowded, yet she knew nobody well enough to talk to them, but then it was nothing new to her, that feeling of isolation. Since she was very small she had been lonely, she had been cut off from other kids her age because of her stepfather's job; they didn't trust her, thought she might spy on them, tell on them. Even her mother had no time for her once she had other children. Sophie had been driven to talking to the dead because the living ignored her. That was crazy, wasn't it? Or at least not normal, talking to your dead sister because you had no one else to talk to.

When she got older she had tried to make friends, but maybe she hoped for too much, needed too much, made it all too important; her need, her air of desperation, had driven people away instead of attracting them. Even when she left the village and went to Prague to university, she had only made acquaintances; she had gone around for a couple of years in a big group, one of the crowd, but never getting very close to anyone.

The men had, it was true, wanted to date her, and didn't waste much time or finesse in trying to get her into bed. Sex seemed all they were interested in, but Sophie needed something better than sex – she wanted to be loved, but that had always eluded her.

'Everyone calls you the snow queen,' one young man had said. 'And they're right, that's what you are. Frozen from the neck down. Who wants a woman like that?'

She remembered the way she had felt as he spat the words at her, the misery that had swamped her. They had been in his car; he was driving her home from a concert. She could still hear the music they had just been listening to, light, lilting Strauss waltzes, mocking the way she felt afterwards, staying in her head for years after that night.

The very air in Prague was full of music; you could go to a different concert every night, many of them totally free, most of them offering cut-price tickets. As you walked around Prague you were always having cheaply printed flyers advertising concerts thrust into your hands. People put on concerts wherever they could, the more expensive ones in imposing concert halls or palaces in which nobody had lived for several lifetimes, some in the open air in summer, in the streets of the Old Town, in one of the many parks which threaded the city with green. There wasn't just classical music, either; there was jazz or folk music in bars, or in hotels or clubs, sung masses in churches like the church of St Nicholas, the High Baroque church, glittering with gilded cherubs, where Mozart had once played the elaborately decorated organ.

They had been parked under a lime tree just outside the grey concrete block where she lived. While he tried to kiss her, his hand had slid up inside her skirt, she had felt his fingertips stroking between her legs, soft, warm, tormenting, making her burn.

She had drunk a few glasses of wine over dinner, it must have been the heat of the wine in her veins that made her want him to go on. She had ached to let the feeling build, to let him make love to her, although she knew she wasn't even close to falling in love with him.

But he had made his move too soon. She was still sober enough to stop him, and he had lost his temper, his face red. 'What's wrong with you? What are you saving it for, you frigid bitch?'

She never went out with him again, but what he had said had really got under her skin. A year later she had gone to bed, quite deliberately, to prove to herself that she wasn't frigid, with a boy from her village, a farmer's son she had known at school. They had had a brief summer romance but it died out as suddenly as it had begun, like a passing storm over the green woods around her home. A little lightning, a little thunder, and then peace.

The TV reporter's voice interrupted her thoughts. 'Are you in trouble?'

Startled, she looked round at him, eyes wide. 'What?'

'Why don't you tell me about it? I get the feeling you could do with a friend.'

Yes, but it wouldn't be this man. After all, he was a reporter; he would use anything she told him. Why else had he come rushing over to her just now? Because he had smelt a story. Maybe she shouldn't even have this drink with him, but he knew Don Gowrie and his family – he might be able to tell her things she badly wanted to know, about Mrs Gowrie, the daughter . . . what had someone said she was called? Catherine . . . yes, Catherine. She must remember that name. There was so much she did not know. But she would have to be very careful that while she was trying to get information out of this journalist she didn't tell him anything which could be dangerous.

She had felt him staring at her while those security men were talking to her; she could see how clever he was. He had known there was something behind her question to Don Gowrie, behind the way Gowrie reacted. Her heart thumped painfully, remembering again the way Gowrie had swung round and stared at her.

She could still see his face. She wasn't sure what she had been expecting, hoping for, what reaction she had thought she would get, but she had certainly stopped him in his tracks. He had looked quite ill for a second; she could almost be sorry for him, he had gone so pale, his eyes all black and shiny, the pupils dilating with shock.

He had got away with it all this time, he must have thought he was invulnerable, as safe as houses, and then she turned up, just as he was taking his most audacious gamble, the one all gamblers dreamt about, the jackpot, the big one. If he became president of the United States he would become at once the most important man in the world. The very prospect must make your head spin. It made her breathless to contemplate what it would mean for him, and Don Gowrie must want it very badly, any man would, and she could snatch it away from him.

While she was in that room and he was up there on that platform talking she had watched him and thought: who would believe the truth about him, if she told anyone? She found it hard to believe herself.

But one thing was certain and they both knew it. If anyone found out what he had done it would blow his career sky-high, let alone ruin his private life. That powerful father-in-law would never forgive him. All that money, all that power, would be taken away from him. He would lose everything. Could she do that to him?

How much did Mrs Gowrie know, or guess? And Catherine Gowrie, how would she feel? The shock of the truth would destroy the landscape of Catherine's whole life. How would she feel, when she heard? How would all his friends, his colleagues react? Not Don Gowrie, they would think, remembering that profile, as noble and assured as the head of a Roman emperor on a thin, beaten silver coin. He wouldn't lie, cheat, conspire to deceive people who trusted him.

Sophie's mouth quivered angrily. Oh, but he would, he would, and it was time everyone knew the truth about him.

The waiter brought their drinks, making a big thing of placing them on the coasters, the supple bend of his body closer to her than was strictly necessary so that she picked up on his musky scent. 'Enjoy,' he said huskily, looking at her through his long dark lashes.

The TV reporter gave him a cold stare and the waiter sneered before sauntering away again, very slowly.

'What's it like, getting that all the time?' Steve Colbourne asked her. 'I've often wondered how women cope with men always coming on to them.'

Sophie was startled by the question. Drily she asked, 'You never come on to women, I suppose?'

He grinned. 'Oh, yes, but I hope I'm never crude or pushy.'

'Have you got a girlfriend? Have you ever asked her that question?'

His face changed, his voice grew terse. 'I'm not dating anyone just now, no. You still haven't answered my question.'

Had he just broken up with his woman? she wondered. Or was she just imagining that look of pain?

'Oh, you get used to handling men's come-ons,' she said aloud.

'Without slapping their faces?'

She laughed. 'That sometimes just encourages them. They think of a slap as a come-on.'

He gave her a sidelong glance, smiling with teasing amusement. 'I'm glad to see you have a sense of humour – you didn't seem human enough for that.'

'Thanks!' she said, bristling. 'You may get a slap yourself, any minute, if you keep up remarks like that.'

He grinned at her. 'Sorry. Tell me, what sort of outfit do you work for? This agency – is it a big one, is it independent, or government-run?'

Well, at least she could talk freely about her work; there couldn't be any risk in that. 'It's independent, founded in 1990, on a shoestring, with no capital but his brains and determination, by a Czech journalist, Vladimir Sturn.' Her voice warmed and she smiled, thinking of Vlad, a fast-talking old reporter, half-pickled in vodka after years of hanging around bars listening to gossip and whispered secrets.

He looked more like a walrus than a man, a huge, wrinkled face, mournful round eyes, a great rubbery nose above a bushy moustache, usually sprinkled with ash from the cigars he smoked all the time.

His heavy clumsy body rolled from side to side as he walked, as if he was not used to life on dry land, his hands were great paws covered in dark hair, his laughter was a rough salty bark. He was the first and only real friend Sophie had ever had; she loved him dearly and so did most people who worked for or with him.

'For the first few months he ran it singlehandedly – he couldn't afford to pay anyone else. He sat in his flat, which was his office, too, scouring foreign newspapers, listening to foreign radio stations, picking up stories he could translate into English and sell to Czech newspapers, radio, TV. He'd spent most of his career working for the state press agency; he always says he doesn't know how he stayed sane, writing lies, knowing the truth but never being able to print it or talk about it on the air. During the time Dubcek was First Secretary and everyone began to feel free to talk openly things got much better, but then . . .' She stopped, shrugging, because even now it felt odd to say the truth out loud, to say what you really thought or felt.

'Then the Russians invaded, in 1968,' Steve prompted, watching her.

'The year I was born,' she said, smiling.

'Really?' He sounded incredulous. 'Not good timing.'

'That's exactly what Vlad said when he first saw my date of birth. My God, he said, what a year to pick to be born!' Vlad had given a roar of laughter then, adding, 'I have to be worried about your timing, darling.' Then he had sobered and told her how he had felt the night the Russians invaded; the first disbelief, because none of them had believed the Russians would do it, then the panic and chaos, and then the clampdown which muzzled the press throughout the country. Everything was shut down, press, radio stations and TV, so that Vlad and his colleagues had sat there all night, helpless and gagged, while Russian tanks rolled inexorably towards Prague.

'I'm always grateful I never had to live under Communism,' Steve said, frowning into his drink. 'How do people cope with all that tension?'

'Fear becomes a way of life,' she said soberly. They were only now slowly beginning to trust in freedom, to believe they were safe in saying what they really thought.

'I guess,' Steve nodded, watching her face and fascinated by the expressions passing over it. The more he looked at her the less he could believe she had ever been Gowrie's mistress. 'So when did you join this agency?'

'I worked for Vlad part-time, doing translation, while I was at college. I did a modern languages degree and Vlad was always short of people who could read French and Italian – a lot of people in our country speak German and Russian, we've been forced to learn both, in the past, for obvious reasons. When your country is occupied by foreigners you soon realise you have to learn their language; they won't learn yours.'

Steve watched her face; not cool now, no, pulsing with feeling, her blue eyes dark with it, so that he knew what she must look like when she made love, the real woman under the ice. Ah, but how thick was the ice? How long would it take to break through the frozen surface – obviously tapping her anger about her country's history would not be the way!

'By the time I got involved with it the agency was very successful. Even Vlad was surprised by the way it took off. He couldn't go on running it alone; he needed to find staff to help him, but he couldn't pay much so he looked for students. My tutor was an old friend of his, and told me about the job. I was lucky to get it, lots of others were after it, but Vlad had known my father so he hired me. I had to comb foreign newspapers for stories he could use – it was good practice for me, helped me improve my fluency. He didn't pay much, but even so that money made my life a lot easier. Student grants are barely big enough to survive on back home. We all had to get part-time jobs. When I got my degree, I became a teacher, but I discovered I wasn't a natural teacher, I didn't enjoy the job, and the pay was poor, but then most jobs pay very low wages back home. I had to save up for weeks just to buy myself shoes.'

'I had no idea it was that bad in the Czech Republic,' Steve said, frowning.

'These days, some people do quite well, those in

35

business, but on a teacher's pay it's tough surviving, especially if you have kids.'

'Have you got kids?' he asked, and she knew he was teasing her and laughed.

'No, of course not. Have you?'

'No wife, no kids,' he shrugged. 'As my mother never stops reminding me.'

'She wants you to get married?'

'She's fixated on becoming a grandmother. Why do women get obsessed with these stages of life? First they desperately want to get married, then they want children, and as soon as the children grow up they want grandchildren – why can't women just let life surprise them?'

'We have a sense of the right order of things, I suppose,' she said, taking the question seriously. 'A sense of the natural rhythms of life.'

'But not you? You don't want marriage and children yet?'

'First I want to enjoy my job,' she said frankly. 'That's why I left teaching. I didn't like doing it, and I wanted a better life, it's so tiring being poor, really poor, never having any money left over from the bare essentials. Have you been to my country? Eaten our food? Grey slabs of meat, potato dumplings, almost no green vegetables or fresh fruit except at prices very few people can afford. And you have to ration your shampoo, can't afford to go to a hairdresser, have to keep wearing your clothes for years – it wears you down, you feel you're endlessly struggling, you get very depressed.'

'The Czechs I've met always seem very cheerful, though.'

'We're free now – of course we're cheerful and we have hope, at last. We can look forward to a better life soon. But few of us earn enough. That's why, when Vlad offered me a full-time job with the agency, working abroad, I jumped at it. He had begun to realise it was no longer enough just to take stories from other sources, he was selling the agency material all over East Europe by then and he needed his own staff out in the field finding stuff with an East European angle.'

'He sounds like a live wire. I once worked for a guy like that, the year I went into television. He was a documentary producer, Bernie Stein, he was never afraid to take chances, whatever the risk. Men like that don't come too often.'

She nodded, liking the warmth and affection in his eyes. 'Vlad is one in a million,' she agreed, and they smiled at each other, united in their feelings for these giants from their past.

'Is this the first foreign country you've worked in?'

'No, I was based in London first, for a year, but I travelled if ever a story came up elsewhere in Europe. I had my own car for the first time, too.' Her eyes were a wide, bright blue with pleasure. 'Only a second-hand Mini, it's true, but it was mine! You have no idea what that felt like, to own my own car.'

'Oh, don't I? I worked my butt off to earn enough to buy my first old banger. I was still at school and had half a dozen different part-time jobs that last year, just to save up to buy a car. I worked in a store, sweeping floors and burning trash; I cleaned houses, I washed up for a local French bistro. . .'

'Your parents couldn't afford to help?'

'They aren't rich, although we were never poor, either. But they were going to have to help me out while I was at college. I decided not to ask them for a car.'

Sophie read the stubborn lines of his mouth, the pride in the set of his head and felt a sense of kinship. Americans always seemed to her so rich and spoilt, used to getting what they wanted when they wanted it. This man was different. She could understand this man.

'You must have felt great when you finally had the money!'

His smile flashed out. 'Ten feet high. I bought an old blue Thunderbird; the chassis was beaten to hell but a friend re-tuned the engine for me and it lasted me two years. I loved that car more than any car I've had since.'

'That was how I felt seeing all the places in Europe whose names I'd heard all my life but never thought I'd ever see. After years of dreaming about Paris I finally got to sit at a table in a terrace café and drink wine while I watched the world go by, and I've floated down the Grand Canal in Venice in a gondola, although I could only afford that once, they charged me an arm and a leg. But it was worth it, to feel, just for one hour, that I was really there, looking up at those marvellous palaces and churches.'

Her breathless excitement had brought a smile into his grey eyes. 'You're making me envious! I haven't been to Europe for a long time. Although I'm going now, of course, to cover Gowrie's trip.'

She came down with a bump, her whole body jerking into attention as she remembered Gowrie. 'You're going with him?'

He was aware of her sharp interest. 'A lot of us are. If Gowrie becomes the next president, anything he thinks and says is vitally important to our country.'

Her voice was tense. 'Do you think he will become president?'

'Could be, I'm afraid.'

She watched him curiously. 'You don't think he'll be a good president?'

'We haven't had a good president for so long some of us have ceased to expect we ever will.'

'You're cynical about politicians,' she murmured. 'Me too.'

'Yeah, well, I can see how you would be,' he smiled. 'I

guess Gowrie's no worse than any of the others. He's certainly in front of the pack at the moment. A couple of years ago if he had made a trip to Europe nobody would have taken a blind bit of notice! He'd have gone alone. But he's in a new league now.'

'I didn't realise any of the press would be going with him,' she thought aloud. She must go. She had to talk to him and if she went to Europe she might get a chance. It would be an expensive trip, though, and she had to watch every cent she spent. As Vlad kept saying, the agency had to operate on a shoestring. He watched her expenses like a hawk. How could she persuade him to let her go?

What would it cost? A cut-price plane ticket from a bucket shop, a cheap hotel. She could save a lot by walking instead of taking public transport, buying cheap food to eat in her room instead of eating out. Oh, she could cut expenses to the bone. She was an expert at living on almost nothing.

'I'm a mind-reader,' Steve said and she started.

'What?'

'You mean to go on this trip, too, right?'

'If I can talk Vlad into paying for it,' she confessed. 'Which will be like talking Dracula into giving me a blood transfusion from his own veins.'

Steve roared with laughter.

In the penthouse suite of the hotel Don Gowrie was talking on the phone. 'Her passport details all check out, then? Born Prague, 1968. Parents, Johanna and Pavel Narodni. Father dead, mother remarried, now has two younger sons. Mother still alive, then?' He bit down on his lower lip. 'I see. No, don't bother with the Czech end. Leave it now; close the file.' There was a murmur on the other end of the line. 'No, I said close the file!' Don Gowrie put down the phone with a faint crash, the hand that held it slippery with sweat, picked up a decanter from the antique black-lacquered Chinese-style table and poured himself a glass of whisky, then walked over to the window of the suite to stare down, down, down at the pale grey ants flickering along the street below. From up here on the sixtieth floor you couldn't make out their sex, or what they wore, let alone their faces. It was hard to be sure they were human beings. Their life or death meant nothing at this height. If one of them suddenly fell down dead you wouldn't even notice. Would any of the others hurrying past them stop to look, or would they just step over the body and rush on?

Behind him someone asked quietly, 'Do you think she knows something that could be a problem?'

He shrugged without turning round or answering.

'How serious a problem?'

'I don't even dare ask her. That serious.' He swallowed the whisky and went back to pour himself another.

'You haven't forgotten you're speaking tonight at that dinner.'

The soft reminder made him stop pouring. He picked up the glass, swirled the whisky, holding it up in front of the Tiffany lamp on the side-table. The art nouveau glass with its metal-outlined red roses and Celtic-styled green leaves gave the whisky a deep, alluring glow, but he barely saw it. His mind was too busy, considering solutions, rejecting all of them. There was only one way out and he knew it. She had to be silenced.

Behind him, his companion was thinking along very much the same lines. 'We'll have to make sure she doesn't cause any trouble, then, won't we?'

Don turned to stare, face furrowed, pale, set.

'Be careful.'

Sophie felt the American watching her and glanced quickly at him, a frisson of warning down her spine. She must not let this man get too close, he could become a problem. She looked at her watch, ready to make her excuses and go.

'Thank you for the drink, I must –'

His voice rode over hers. 'So when did you move on to New York?'

'A couple of months ago. Vlad decided that people in East Europe were fascinated by the American political process but unless they were political students they found it all too complicated. They wanted simple explanations. Vlad had started a bureau over here, which was run by an old friend of his, Theo Strahov – Theo is an American citizen now, but he was born in Prague, worked with Vlad there before he came to America. Theo retired from full-time work some years ago, but for Vlad he came out of retirement and started the new bureau. He has been running it singlehanded ever since. But he found it more and more tiring. So Vlad sent me to help out for a while, and then last week Theo collapsed in the street. He's OK now, but the doctors say it was a stroke warning, and he must start to take it easy. So I shall be running the bureau from now on.'

She was telling him a lot, but telling him nothing, she hoped, nothing of any importance, about herself, about her life, about her world. But the cat-and-mouse game was more tiring than she had expected.

Quickly, before he could ask her any more questions, she asked him one. 'Do you know Senator Gowrie's wife? What is she like?'

'Frail, sick, a lady who doesn't always know what time of day it is.'

She already knew all that, but she pretended surprise. 'Yes? That is sad. What's wrong with her?'

'God knows. She has never been strong, I gather.'

Still casual, she murmured, 'How many children do they have?'

'Just one. Cathy.'

She noted the intimacy of the shortened name with a pang of shock. Did he know Gowrie's daughter well enough to call her that, or did the press all use her pet name?

'What's she like?' she asked, keeping her eyes down on her linked hands on the polished bar table, struggling not to betray anything by her face, by her voice, but it wasn't easy; emotion kept trying to break through.

'Beautiful,' he said with a bitter tang to his voice. She looked up then, startled, but this time it was Steve who avoided her stare, his eyes fixed on his empty glass. 'She's smart, too,' he said as if talking to himself. 'She's clever and cool-headed, a political animal. Of course, it's in her blood. She comes from a family who've been mixed up in politics for generations. She has travelled from coast to coast with her father many a time. He worships the ground she walks on, she has always been more of an asset to him than her mother, who almost never shows up. Cathy sat on platforms with him, worked on campaigns, talked to the press . . . she knew exactly how to talk to people, she could have had a career in politics any time she wanted it.'

'But she didn't?' Sophie took in everything he had said, and thirsted to hear more. She needed to know everything about this other woman whose existence dominated Gowrie's life.

He shrugged without answering. 'She may once have done, but not any more.'

Why not? Sophie wondered. What had changed? 'Does she have a career?'

He grimaced, his face sardonic. 'Several, none of them very serious. She was an interior designer for a while, she's an expert on eighteenth-century porcelain, she paints and writes articles for specialist magazines . . . she dabbles in a lot of things. I wouldn't call any of them a career. Anyway, she's married now.'

She nodded absently. 'To an Englishman. I know.'

'Why are you so interested in Gowrie?' Steve asked abruptly, and her nerves jumped.

'Well . . . obviously . . . if he should become president of the United States that would make him the most powerful man in the world.' She knew she had stammered, sounded odd, but he had taken her by surprise. He kept coming far too close. She must get away from him before he guessed too much . . .

She got up unsteadily, very pale. 'Thank you for the drink. I must go, I have copy to file,' she said in a rush, beginning to move away just as his producer appeared in the doorway, looking agitated. He didn't come over to them, but stared fixedly at Steve, held up his wrist, tapped his watch pointedly.

Steve nodded and began to walk towards him, in step with Sophie. 'Looks as if I've got to go and do some more work, too, before Simon blows his stack. Time always flies by when you're enjoying yourself. Look, could we have dinner together tonight?'

'I'm sorry,' she said, and meant it. For once she wanted to, she really did, but she couldn't. It would be far too dangerous. He was one of the most attractive men she'd ever met, and if he wasn't so shrewd and perceptive she might have taken the risk, but this was not a man it was easy to fool – she knew she would find it hard to go on lying, deceiving him, for long, if they saw each other again.

'Come on, for God's sake,' Simon grunted as they reached him, 'We're all set up outside, we've been waiting for you for ten minutes. If we miss the evening news you can explain it – I'm not taking the can for you.'

'No need to panic, we have plenty of time.'

Steve Colbourne sounded so calm and unflappable – was he always like that? Sophie envied him; she wished she could stand up to pressure that well. She tried to look and sound as cool as a cucumber, but her nerves made her stomach cramp into agony at times.

As they walked towards the swing doors leading out of the hotel, the lift doors opened and out came a massed body of men who began moving at speed in their direction, cutting a swath through the hotel guests, who fell back, parting like the Red Sea in the face of that unstoppable force. Sophie's breath caught as she saw it was Don Gowrie, flanked by security men on all sides.

Steve and his producer had already gone through the swing doors, but Sophie was too slow in following. A second later the little army of men was on her, but they didn't march past because Don Gowrie stopped, and they all stopped with him.

'Miss Narodni,' Don Gowrie said, giving her that boyish smile of his. 'Hello again. I'm sorry I didn't have time to answer your question – another time, maybe?'

His cool nerve took her breath away. She would have loved to shout out the truth, wipe that smile off his face – but she couldn't, not yet at least. She needed to meet Mrs Gowrie and Catherine, first. She didn't want to destroy their lives just because Don Gowrie was a lying, cheating bastard. Why should they pay for what he had done? She felt an intense sympathy and pity for his wife; no doubt she had known the truth all along, but the poor woman had suffered. Sophie didn't want to hurt her even more.

'Maybe you'll have time to talk to me while you're in London?' she told him, hoping she sounded as cool as he did.

She saw the flicker of shock in his eyes before he veiled them. 'So you'll be in London too?' he said. 'I'll certainly look out for you.'

Then he was gone, his entourage hiding him from her; she followed through the swing doors a moment later and saw the long black limousines driving off at speed, while

44

police held up the rest of the traffic until the limousines had got away.

While she stared, Don Gowrie's face briefly showed at the back window of the second car. He looked towards her and then he was gone.

She heard Steve Colbourne's voice from a hundred feet away; he was standing with his back to her, and the hotel behind her, recording a piece to camera, his voice confidential, smooth, accustomed.

Sophie didn't hover to listen to what he was saying. She pulled her jacket closer, and began to walk towards the subway station nearest the hotel. She had to get back to her flat and file her story with Vlad, try to talk him into letting her fly to London.

She bought a token, walked towards the turnstile, and began to push her token into the slot, conscious of a man behind her waiting for his turn. Sophie didn't look at him. She had learnt never to make eye-contact with men in the subway. She slid through the turnstile and walked on to the platform, staying where she could see the token booth; although it was daylight she still felt uneasy on the subway. There were other passengers waiting, she was not alone, but you heard such horror stories. She was relieved when another couple of women came along.

A train rattled along the tunnel and came out into the lighted station; she glanced up at the indicator board, then checked the route number, a big blue numeral, on the front of the coming train.

She was still getting used to the routes and the names of stations; she had to think for a second before she worked out that she would have to change trains at Washington Square to get to the station nearest to her flat. New York's subway system was as complicated as the underground system in London, to which she had only just become adjusted when she was transferred here.

She was so absorbed that she didn't hear a sound behind her or see anything.

She had no warning. A hand suddenly hit her in the middle of her back, right between the shoulder blades, propelling her violently forward to the edge of the platform.

2

Steve Colbourne was driving away from the hotel in a cab a quarter of an hour later when an ambulance passed him, siren going, and pulled up outside the entrance to a subway station already surrounded by a small crowd. A couple of uniformed policemen were barring entry to everyone but the medical team which jumped out of the ambulance and ran with their equipment down the stairs.

Steve was in a hurry but his reporter's instincts wouldn't let him drive on past without checking it out. He leaned forward and said to the taxi driver, 'Hey, pull over here, would you? I just want to find out what's going on.'

The driver looked round at him, shrugged, and put on his brakes. Steve leaned out of the window, and yelled to one of the policemen, 'What's happened in there?'

He got an impatient stare. 'Accident – drive on, you're holding up traffic.'

Steve pulled out his press card and held it up. 'Press. What sort of accident?'

The crowd all turned to stare at him. Before the policeman could answer, a young black guy in the crowd shouted, 'There's a girl on the line, fell under a train.'

'Dead?'

The guy spread his hands, his big shoulders moving. 'Well, they don't generally get up and walk afterwards, now do they?'

A woman hovering near the kerb complained, 'Why do they always have to do it during rush hour, huh? I got to get home. They take so long to clear the line after one of these jumpers.'

'Take the bus,' the black guy told her, and got a glare.

'Easy for you to say, you ain't got my feet.'

He looked down at her swollen ankles. 'Don't want 'em neither, lady.'

Others in the crowd began to laugh, but not the policemen. Behind the cab, traffic had now built up in a noisy log jam.

'Get going!' the cab driver was ordered by one of the policemen, who came down to the kerb to bang on the top of the cab with his night stick.

'Hey, don't damage the cab!' the driver yelled at him. The air was raucous with car horns blaring, drivers leaning out to shout insults at the cab driver, who turned to say to Steve, 'Got to go, mister. D'you wanna pay me and get out, or can we drive on now?'

Leaning back, Steve gestured. 'OK, let's go.' After all, it happened all the time, people were always throwing themselves under subway trains, although God knew why they would want so violent and painful a death, but there was nothing in it for him. It wouldn't rate more than a para in any newspaper, and, anyway, regular news wasn't his scene. He had always specialized; politics was all he had ever been interested in because, like Catherine Gowrie, he had been bred to it.

All his life, his parents had been active in neighbourhood politics: his mother was on a whole raft of committees, the local PT Association, Mother's Union, raising money for charities, and his father, a New England academic, had campaigned for his local congressman most of his adult lifetime, a stalwart Republican and boyhood friend at school of Eddie Ramsey's eldest son. Fred Colbourne had even thought of standing for Congress, himself, until a mild heart attack in his mid-fifties put paid to that idea. His doctor had warned that although he might live another twenty years if he was sensible and took care of himself, he would be asking for trouble if he didn't slow down. He certainly wouldn't be fit to cope with the tensions and strain of a political career.

'Well, that's the end of the road for me, but one day I'd like to see you in Congress, son,' he had told Steve wistfully, on his first day back home from hospital, resting on a daybed by a window downstairs in their three-bedroomed white frame Norman Rockwell look-alike house above Chesapeake Bay, Easton, a few miles from the Ramsey family home.

Steve had laughed, grimaced, shaken his head. 'I'm no politician, Dad. I've seen too much of them too close. Call me fussy, but I don't want to get my hands that dirty.'

His father had bristled. 'That isn't fair, Steve. I know plenty of decent politicians. OK, there's some corruption, there always is in government, but there are plenty of honest men in Washington.'

'Like the wonderful guys who didn't come to visit you in hospital?' Steve knew none of the politicians his father had done so much to help over the years had shown up to see him after his heart attack, and that that had hurt his father, even though he had never said a word about them.

'They're busy men. And they probably felt it was a time for family only, and didn't want to intrude. They're my friends, Steve, I know them better than you do!'

Steve had heard Fred Colbourne's voice rasp with distress and anger, and too late remembered his mother sternly warning him not to upset his father. Quickly, he said, 'I know they're your friends, and some of them are decent guys. And somebody has to do the job, like somebody has to take out the garbage. We have to be governed, but it isn't ever going to be me, Dad. Sorry to disappoint you, but keeping an eye on what they get up to is more my style.'

From his teens Steve had been out on the hoof, stuffing campaign messages into letter boxes, selling party newspapers, acting as a steward at local meetings, listening in on late-night drinking sessions where his father and various other local party bigwigs talked more freely than they ever would in public. He was disillusioned before he was twenty, and nothing he had seen since had changed his view of politicians.

His father had looked at him reproachfully, rather than angrily. 'I've never got my hands dirty, Steve.'

'No, of course not,' Steve had hurriedly agreed, his voice soothing, then went on, 'But you've had to turn a blind eye to a lot of stuff you didn't really approve of, Dad. We both know that.' Then he had leaned over to pat his father's shoulder. 'Dad, don't look that way. In the real world we all have to live with what we don't like. I do, myself – there's corruption and sleaze enough in TV, God knows. But at least nobody pretends to be perfect. It's hypocrisy I can't stand; all the sanctimonious humbug.'

From the doorway his mother had asked sharply, 'What are you talking about? I thought I told you no politics? Your father mustn't overdo things, he isn't out of the wood yet. Time he took his nap now, anyway. I've just made some coffee and hot muffins, Steve. Come back downstairs.'

She came over and made a fuss of tucking a warm patchwork quilt around his father, as if he was a child, adjusting his pillows, pulling down the blind to shut out the noonday sun, stroking back his thinning grey hair and smiling down at him maternally.

'Now, you get some sleep, you hear?'

'She finally got what she wanted, son,' his father had complained. 'I'm at her mercy, helpless as a newborn babe. Talk about politicians wanting power! It's women who're power-hungry, they're control freaks, every last one of them.'

'You hush,' Marcia Colbourne said indulgently, bending to kiss his forehead before she walked quietly back out of the room, taking Steve with her.

When she got him alone in the kitchen, she turned on him angrily. 'I won't tell you again, Steve! He may look as if he's back to normal, but he's still recovering, and I don't want him upset. Keep off the subject of politics. Talk to him about books, or the garden, or music, but no politics! And don't ever let me hear you lecturing your father again.'

Steve had been taken aback, his face flushing. His mother rarely raised her voice but when she did you knew you were really in the doghouse. 'Sorry,' he had muttered, and meant it. 'I didn't think. Stupid of me.'

'Yes, it was,' she had said, but, relenting, had poured him strong black coffee and put out a plate of blueberry muffins, his favourites, especially when his mother had made them. She was the best cook he knew; she didn't cook fussy food, only went for simple dishes, usually traditional New England fare, with home-grown herbs and vegetables, cooked perfectly. Her chowder was something to dream about and her fish melted in your mouth.

Marcia Colbourne still had the looks that had made Fred Colbourne fall for her thirty-six years ago. Until you got close to her you would never believe she was fifty-five; her skin had a smooth texture that made her look half her age, and her dark hair showed just a little elegant grey here and there.

She was as traditional in the way she dressed as she was in her cooking: in winter she wore soft pastel lambswool sweaters with pearls, in the English style, with tweed skirts; in summer she wore Laura Ashley dresses that gave her a cool, understated elegance. Slim, hyperactive, she was always on the move, cooking, working in the house, gardening, swimming, walking the beach in all weathers to hunt for bare, silvery driftwood for her famous flower arrangements.

Her artistic streak came out in many ways: she embroidered tablecloths and traycloths, made tapestry

51

firescreens, painted delicate watercolours, especially of the coast around their home, and when Steve and his sister, Sally, were kids the family often took their summer vacation at the Blackwater wildlife refuge, some twenty miles away, to sail and fish and watch birds, while their mother painted the flocks of water fowl you saw there. Steve associated those holidays with a sense of freedom, a smell of the sea, of fish they caught themselves, cooking over a makeshift barbecue on the sand while his mother threw together a salad with a dressing of lemon juice and a little olive oil.

Staring out of the cab window, Steve came back to the present with a start, realizing they had arrived in the overcrowded multi-ethnic neighbourhood of the Lower East Side, where wave after wave of new immigrants had come to rest over the years: Jews and Italians, Chinese and Poles, all washing together in a colourful mix which filled these grey streets with terrific restaurants, shops which gave off a powerful foreign smell, local markets selling everything from French cheeses to Russian icons, Polish handmade leather shoes to Chinese herbal medicines.

The cab pulled up outside a high apartment building among a row of others. After paying off the driver, Steve stood on the sidewalk, looking around in fast-falling twilight, catching sight of the East River, a bluish slate smudge between the close-set buildings opposite. You were never far from water on Manhattan: on the West Side of the city ran the Hudson, leading out eventually to the Atlantic, while the East River linked up the Atlantic with Long Island Sound.

Traffic churned past. Many shops were still open, he saw a handful of people waiting to be served at a stall selling green bananas, tied bundles of lemon grass, round bronze onions and aubergines, the colours of the vegetables still sharp in the fading light. Steve suddenly felt hungry, realising he hadn't eaten a proper meal for a day or so. He had

had coffee and orange juice for breakfast, a sandwich at lunchtime, nothing in between. He threw a glance up at the freshly painted terracotta façade of the building behind him. Iron fire-escapes gave the row of buildings a skeletal structure. Now at twilight they cast elaborate shadows on the painted walls behind them. Which floor did she live on? With his luck it would probably turn out to be the top, and there would be no lift.

Well, there were plenty of good restaurants within walking distance, he thought, if he could talk her into having dinner with him! She had told him she was living on a shoe-string, so the idea of a free meal would probably be too tempting for her to resist. He hoped.

The apartment-house lobby was dank and gloomy, as they often were in this neighbourhood. He checked out the mailboxes first and was relieved to find a first-floor flat had the name Narodni neatly printed in capital letters beside the name Janacek.

He had to ring the doorbell several times before anyone opened up, and even then the chain was left on while a face peered out through the narrow crack. It wasn't Sophie Narodni. This woman was much older; a very thin, febrile face, without make-up, faintly Oriental-looking, black eyes, slanting a little, a wide mouth and high cheekbones.

'Yeah?' Her voice was entirely American, not to say New York. Bronx-born, he decided as she added, 'Wha'd'yer want?'

'I'm looking for Sophie Narodni.'

'She's not back yet.'

'Are you Lilli Janacek?'

She gave him a suspicious look. 'What if I am? I don't know you. I'm cooking, I can't stand here talking.' The door began to close. Steve put his foot into it. The black eyes looked down at his highly polished shoe. 'I only have to press this panic button, mister, and the apartment security alarm will go off. Get your foot out of my door.'

Steve pulled out his press card, held it up. 'I'm Steve Colbourne, I work for NWTV, maybe you've seen my show? If you're interested in politics you will have. I just saw Sophie at the Gowrie press conference and wanted to talk to her about something important.'

She looked at the photo on his press card, then, closer, at him, her black, thin brows making a perfect semicircle in surprise. 'Sure. Sure, I've seen you on TV, I remember your face now.'

'Could I wait for Sophie inside, please? It's chilly enough to freeze the blood out here, and the lobby smells like a urinal.'

She hesitated, then unhooked the chain. 'I guess so, come in.'

As soon as he had walked past her she put the door back on the chain. 'I was just going to make some coffee – d'yer want some?'

'I'd love some.' He could smell something delicious; frying onions, or garlic, or both. He followed Lilli Janacek into a tiny kitchen. There was a pan on the stove. Lilli stirred its contents, poured in steaming pale golden liquid from a jug, stirred again, then turned down the heat and put a lid on the pan.

'Chicken stew,' she told Steve, turning round.

'Smells wonderful.'

She smiled. 'It's an old recipe my mother taught me.'

'Czech?'

'No, my mother was American – it was my father who was Czech. How do you like your coffee?'

'Black and strong, no sugar. Thank you. Any idea where Sophie can have got to? The press conference ended an hour ago. Would she have gone to her office?'

'What office?' Lilli Janacek asked with heavy sarcasm.

'She works from here. You don't think that old skinflint of a Czech would cough up for an office? Before Sophie came, a friend of mine, Theo, worked for Vladimir, using his own home as an office, and being paid in peanuts. The monkeys in Central Park Zoo have better pay and conditions. Every cent Sophie spends she has to account for – she can just about pay my rent and her fares. If I didn't feed her once a day, she probably wouldn't eat.'

Handing him a mug of coffee, Lilli led the way back across the little corridor into a sitting-room so small it just had room for a couple of armchairs and a TV, a dining-table squeezed into a corner with two chairs pushed under it and a set of narrow bookshelves running below the window. The threadbare carpet was a dingy beige but there were jewel-coloured little rugs scattered across it, and the walls were lit by red glass globes which gave the room a warmth and glow that made it look inviting.

'I don't allow smoking in here,' he was firmly informed.

'I don't smoke.' That got him a smile.

Steve asked her, 'What do you do? Are you a journalist too?'

'I'm an artist, but I do the odd article for trade magazines. You know the sort of thing; pieces on modern art, on New York galleries, anything to bring in some income. Every little helps.'

Sipping his coffee, Steve began to prowl along the shelves, looking at the books. Hemingway, Thurber, Wallace Stevens, Dorothy Parker, Jack Kerouac, Scott Fitzgerald.

'Are these all yours, or are some Sophie's?'

'Sophie keeps her books in her bedroom. Those are mine, and before you ask, I don't read contemporary authors, they bore me,' Lilli told him. 'Except for Toni Morrison. She's so good it hurts, but most writers today, they got no style and nothing to say worth reading.'

'Who does Sophie read?'

'Are you in love with her?'

He went red and laughed shortly, taken aback by the directness. He was used to giving out questions like knives, not getting them. 'I only just met her today.'

Lilli's smile was mocking, a little cynical. 'So what? It doesn't take but a minute to fall in love. She's quite a looker.'

'She certainly is!' Steve tried to sound very casual. 'Has she got a boyfriend?' Lilli might know about Don Gowrie, might have all the answers to the questions buzzing around his head.

Tartly, she told him, 'Ask her. I'm not gossiping about her to a guy I only just met.'

He saw he wouldn't get anything out of her. Undeterred, he asked, 'How long has she been in America?'

Lilli gave him a narrow stare. 'What is this? The Spanish Inquisition? You can ask her that, too.'

Steve shrugged and wandered over to the dining-table, stared down at a large black sheet of paper covered with white circles arranged in a wheel, a black and white image of a face in each, in the centre a lightly sketched outline of Sophie's face which had the same spectral look, and between the circles a vividly painted border in the art nouveau style. The effect was mysterious and striking. 'What's this? Did you do it?' he asked, bending to look at the circles.

'Yes, I'm doing it as a Christmas present for Sophie. I photocopied old photos she has of her family, going back a hundred years.'

'The copies are very faint,' he observed, peering at the face of an old man with a long grey beard. You could only just see his features, whereas another man, in a rather crumpled white shirt, open at the neck, could be seen quite clearly.

'They are copies of copies of copies – Sophie had

modern copies of old family photos. The originals are in the Czech Republic, in her family home. Before she went to London, Sophie borrowed them and had a photographer make copies. When I started my wheel I photocopied them, then I kept copying the copies, to make them even fainter if the person was dead.' Lilli stood beside him and put her long, slightly grubby finger on another circle. 'For instance, this is her sister, Anya, a little girl who died before Sophie was born.'

The childish face was wraithlike, fading, only just visible. 'It's extraordinary,' Steve said, oddly very moved as he stared at the child. His mother had lost a child, a little girl, before he was born, he knew, although she never talked about it.

His parents had called her Marcie; she had been pre-mature and had only survived a few days, was buried in the little churchyard half a mile from their home. His mother visited the grave now and then, and tended the tiny garden she had planted above it. It was that which had told Steve how much the dead child had meant to her.

'You know, I'm sure my mother would be thrilled with something like this,' he said slowly. 'Do you accept commissions? If I brought some photocopies of my family photos, would you do one like this for me?'

Lilli put her head on one side and considered him thoughtfully. 'I'd have to think about that. I need to know a lot about my subjects. What's your background? Where do your people come from?'

He laughed. 'Why do you need to know that?'

'People are like trees, they have deep roots; they are fed by their roots, and if they're uprooted to a new place they often die, if not in the body then in the soul.'

'Unless they're very strong, in themselves, like the people who came to the States from all over the world and found a new home here,' said Steve soberly, and Lilli nodded.

'Sure. Where they came from was so bad they would have died rather than go back. Sure. What about your people? How long they been in the States?'

'My family are New Englanders on both sides, from way back in the eighteenth century. English on both sides. On my father's side the first American was a sailor who jumped a ship bringing rum from the West Indies; on my mother's side we come from a parson with Puritan leanings who emigrated to find freedom of conscience.'

She studied him with those dark pools of eyes, frowning a little in concentration, then after a moment said slowly, 'Yes, I see both of them in your face; the courage and recklessness of your sea-going ancestor and the fanaticism and stubbornness of the Puritan parson. Interesting combination. Yes, I would like to do a study of you.'

'A study of me?' he muttered, taken aback. 'But I thought it was my family you would be studying?'

'Before I can create one of my wheels I have to know the person I'm making the wheel for, because in each of us a little of our ancestors lives, and the sum total of the wheel will be you. I shall use only pictures of your family that seem to me to explain you.' She eyed him with faint mockery. 'Do you still want one?'

'Yes,' he said, but with faint hesitation, because he wasn't sure he wanted her probing and prying, asking questions, making guesses. On the other hand, he liked to please his mother and knew she would be fascinated by one of those wheels.

Staring at Sophie's wheel, he asked, 'Tell me, does the art nouveau border have a meaning, or is it just decoration?'

'Art nouveau had a special meaning to the Czechs, it was a time of nationalist fervour, the turn of the century, and art and politics came together in a new way.' She gave him a self-mocking little smile. 'Also I love it, OK? I learnt to love it from my Czech father, I guess. And you didn't ask how much, by the way. That's the reckless sailor in you, ready to jump ship without knowing what he's getting himself into!'

He had never thought of himself as reckless and wasn't sure he liked the idea. 'I was getting round to it! So, how much?'

'Four hundred dollars.'

He was startled by the amount, but under her amused gaze he wouldn't show it. 'OK, it's a deal.' He held out his hand and she was about to take it when a telephone began to ring.

Lilli groaned. 'You know, I hate that thing. Always sounds urgent, always turns out to be nothing at all.' She walked over to the windowsill where the phone was perched on top of a book. She picked it up. 'Yeah?' Then her face changed, she went paler than ever. 'Oh. When? But how . . . Is she going to be OK? Well, can I see her? What ward?' There was a pause, then she said curtly, 'Yes, she has Medicare, of course she does. You'll get your blood money, don't worry.'

She hung up and looked round at Steve. 'God damn these people. All they care about is can she pay? Sophie can die in the street for all they care—'

'Sophie?' The name jerked out of him, shock making his voice shake.

'There's been an accident in the subway . . .'

'That was Sophie?' He thought how close he had come to finding out half an hour ago and could have kicked himself for driving away.

Lilli looked at him sharply. 'What? You heard about the accident? You know what happened? Did you hear it on the radio, or something? What did they say? The hospital wouldn't give me any details, or say how bad she was.'

He told her how he had seen the ambulance arriving. 'They said someone had thrown herself under a train.'

He felt sick as his imagination began to paint pictures of what Sophie would look like if she had been hit by a train. God, he thought, that lovely face. That body. Even if she lived, what would be left of either? 'But it never entered my head that it might be Sophie,' he muttered, his stomach churning.

'I can't understand how it happened,' Lilli said. 'She's always so careful.'

'When I talked to her she obviously had something on her mind, she was angry about something.' He glanced sideways at Lilli, wondering just how much she knew, and what there was to know. Maybe his guesswork about Sophie had been way off? After all, the gossip about Don Gowrie was vague; indeed he was sure it had started long ago, before Sophie Narodni came to America. Mrs Gowrie had been ill for a long, long time, of course – there could have been a succession of 'other women' in Gowrie's life. Sophie might just be the latest. And if she was, was she the type to kiss and tell? He didn't think she was, but women were a law unto themselves. Who knew what they would tell each other? They seemed to need to talk, to confide in each other; they were in an eternal conspiracy against the other sex. 'But I hadn't got her down as suicidal,' he said.

'Suicidal? I don't believe it. Not Sophie. Look at those faces in her wheel – the peasant strength of people who have survived the worst life can chuck at them,' Lilli said, her Oriental eyes shadow-ringed with anxiety. She sighed. 'But then what do we ever know of each other?'

She was right, Steve thought, especially where women were concerned, Steve had never yet managed to understand a woman, even when he had known her most of his life, like Cathy Gowrie. He had honestly thought he knew her as well as he knew himself, they had known each other since childhood, but how wrong he had turned out to be!

Lilli vanished down the corridor, came back wearing a

raincoat, carrying a purse into which she was pushing a blue plastic folder. 'The hospital admin people want proof that Sophie has Medicare,' she said. 'Sorry, but I'll have to rush.'

'I'm coming with you,' Steve said roughly. 'We should pick up a cab easily enough at this hour.'

Lilli gave him a sharp but unsurprised look. 'OK.' She opened the front door, then stopped, groaning. 'Oh, my stew, I nearly forgot, it would be ruined.' She hurried into the kitchen to switch it off, and Steve waited impatiently, so tense he felt as if he might come apart at the seams if he didn't get to Sophie soon. He had to know what had happened to her.

And why, he thought. Oh, yes, and why. The old joke came into his head . . . did she fall or was she pushed? Accident, suicide or . . . He shivered. My God, what was he thinking? That was crazy. Gowrie had been shaken to see her at the press conference, yes – but she couldn't possibly be that much of a threat. Could she?

Don Gowrie was dressing for a very grand dinner which would be held downstairs in his hotel, in a private dining-room glittering with crystal and silver under enormous chandeliers. Among the guests would be his father-in-law, Eddie Ramsey, who had flown in by helicopter from his Easton estate and was now resting in another suite. There would also be a whole host of other East Coast politicians, good old boys from way back who as far as the general public were concerned had apparently retired from public life yet still managed to manipulate and grease the handles of power without ever being caught doing it. Don Gowrie needed their support, their money and their influence, if he was to get his campaign bandwagon rolling fast. He had other backers; industrialists with even more money, people who wanted to be on the inside track if he did manage to get the presidential nomination – but these old men tonight were still vital to him. He needed to balance the different forces backing him; he didn't want to be in the power of any one lobby.

He stood back to look at himself in the dressing-table mirror, noting with satisfaction how good he still looked in evening dress. It suited him, the dark material, the smooth fit of that excellent tailoring. He really didn't look his age, did he? He had to work at it, of course: diet and constant exercise kept his weight down and he had inherited a good constitution. Good genes, he thought, and his eyes darkened. A pity that . . .

No, he wouldn't think about that. It was a talent he had worked on all his life – the ability to push aside what he did not find convenient to dwell upon. He shifted his feet, sighing. That tie simply didn't look right. Why the hell did he find it so difficult to tie a bowtie after all these years of doing it so often? He pulled the tie loose again just as a phone began to ring in the room behind him.

His nerves jumped. At last! He had been waiting on tenterhooks for this call.

He let go of the ends of the tie, sprinted over to the bedside table and picked up the phone, the white tie hanging loose around his neck.

'Yes?'

'Dad?' The voice was not the one he had been expecting to hear. For a second he was still, shaken, then his face lit with warmth.

'Cathy. Hi, darling.' Then anxiety came into his eyes, the old, familiar fear of one day losing her, the sense of a threat always hanging over this precious child. 'Is anything wrong?'

She was quick to reassure him, Cathy had had years of hearing that note in his voice. 'No, of course not, Dad – I'm fine. We're both fine, and looking forward to seeing you soon. I just wanted to send my love to Grandee. You're having dinner with him tonight, aren't you?'

'Yes.' Relaxing, he smiled. 'I was just trying to tie my tie when you rang.'

'Haven't you learnt how to tie a bowtie yet, Dad?'

Her laughter sounded so clearly in his ear that it was like having her in the room. When she was a baby he had felt nothing much for her except relief that he had her, that the miracle had been pulled off, he and his wife had a child against all the odds, and if it was not a boy, as he had prayed, at least he had an heir to the Ramsey fortune.

What he had not expected was that she would turn into so beautiful a girl or that he would be so proud of her. She did everything so well, she had never put a foot wrong all her life: wore her clothes with classy style, rode horses as if she had been born in the saddle, was intelligent, could talk to people at all levels of society, like a true politician, and when she chose a man chose brilliantly, a man of his own kind, wealthy, powerful, obviously ambitious and meaning to climb to the very top in his own country.

He smiled, too. 'Bowties have a life of their own! But I'll do it, if it takes me all night,' he assured her, the underlying obstinacy of his nature showing in his bony face for a second. He was a man who never gave up once he had set his mind on something.

'Where's Cope? Isn't he with you?'

'He had to have a tooth out yesterday so I sent him off to bed.' His valet had been grey with pain. Cope was nearly sixty now. He had worked for Don Gowrie for ten years, doing all the little jobs a wife normally did, taking care that Don's wardrobe was always in good shape, the suits and coats cleaned, the shirts immaculate, the shoes polished, ties pressed. He had made himself indispensable and Don had been shocked to see him look so old. If Cope retired it would disrupt his life, he would have to find someone to replace the man and he knew it would not be easy. Cope was one of a dying breed.

'You old softie!' Cathy's voice was full of affection, and Don Gowrie smiled, his face smoothing out into boyish charm once more.

'So, I'm to give your love to your grandfather? I will, but you could talk to him yourself, you know. He's resting in his own suite.'

'I don't want to over-tire him. That trip out from Easton eats into his energy, and he has to sit through a long dinner tonight. Now, Dad, don't let him drink too much or stay up too late. I know what you men are like when you get together and start talking politics. Has he got the Gorgon with him?'

'Yes, Mrs Upcher flew here with him, and whisked him off to his suite as soon as they arrived.'

'I don't know how Grandee can stand her, she's the ugliest woman I ever saw, but I have to say she does take care of him.'

'She's a good nurse,' he chided. 'And devoted to your grandfather. That he's still alive is largely down to her.'

'I know,' Cathy said, and he knew she was serious now. 'You know, I can't imagine the world without him, Dad. Can you? He's the totem pole we all live by, isn't he?'

'I'm sure he'd be thrilled to hear you say that.' The dryness escaped before he could stop it, but Cathy didn't seem to pick up on the ambivalence of his voice.

Laughing, she said, 'He's obsessed with native American culture, isn't he? I remember when I was four and he drove me along the Mohawk Trail for hours, to see the colours of the woods in the fall. He recited *Hiawatha* to me, and bought me a pair of moccasins at a trail gift shop. I grew out of them before I had worn them out. I hung them on the wall in my room.'

'They're still there, darling,' he assured her. 'We haven't done a thing to your room since you left, don't worry.'

'Really?' She sounded touched and he smiled.

'It will always be there for you when you want to come home. Sorry, darling, but I have to go and finish tying this goddamn tie or I'll be late for dinner with Grandee and then he'll have me roasted over a very slow fire. If there is one thing your grandfather cannot abide it is unpunctuality.'

'Punctuality is the courtesy of kings,' Cathy growled in a very good mimicry of Eddie Ramsey's deep New England accents. Then she said, 'Goodnight, Dad, see you soon. We can't wait to welcome you to our home again.'

'I can't wait to be there. It seems years, not months, since I last saw you,' he said, choked with sudden feeling, and heard her blow him a kiss before hanging up.

He didn't even have time to get back to the dressing-table to finish tying his tie when the phone rang again.

This time it was the voice he had been waiting to hear. 'I just heard on the local news that there was an accident on the subway this evening. A girl fell under a train.'

Gowrie hadn't expected that. He said blankly, 'Fell under a train? What girl?'

The voice was wary, no doubt remembering that there could be other ears listening to the calls he got on this line. 'The Czech reporter – Sophie Narodni.'

Cold pearls of sweat sprang out on Gowrie's pale forehead. He sat down abruptly on his bed, no longer able to stay on his feet, and gripped the phone so tightly his knuckles showed white.

'Is she dead?'

As Catherine Gowrie put down the phone, an arm came up out of the bed and pulled her back into the warmth, the crumpled sheets, where they had made love an hour ago. A

65

mouth nuzzled her neck, a hand cupped one of her naked breasts, her rounded flesh overflowing the hot crucible of fingers.

'You and your father could talk the hind leg off a donkey. I thought you would never ring off. Chatter, chatter, chatter,' Paul said. 'There are better things to do in bed than talk. Mmm . . .' His body pressed into her back, touching her from shoulder to ankle, and she felt the stirring rise of his flesh, heard his breathing quicken.

'You're insatiable,' she said, laughing, half-incredulous, but feeling her insides melt as he began moving against her with that sweet, familiar insistence.

'I can't have enough of you, sweet Cat,' he said, his lips parting on her nape, pushing aside her long silken hair, then beginning to trail down the deep indentation of her spine. He knew exactly how and where to touch her to arouse her. Shutting her eyes, she felt the rough brush of the hair on his thighs, the intimacy of his lips in the crease between her buttocks, seeking, sliding down, down, underneath and inward, until they found the heat and moistness hidden there, and she gave a groan of fierce pleasure.

'Aaah,' she moaned. 'Oh . . . yes . . .' Although they had made passionate love for half an hour so short a time ago, she was ready for him again. Her whole body was trembling, yielding, her bones waxen in her overheated flesh, as he turned her on to her back again and moved on top of her, entering her and slowly, slowly, tormentingly, began, refusing to let her hurry, rush on to the climax she was crying out to achieve.

With no other man had she ever felt anything like this wild clamouring for release to which Paul could bring her. His body had a power over hers that had become an addiction from that first night together.

They had met in Washington nearly a year ago, at a Christmas party given by a famous political hostess. Cathy

66

had known almost everyone else in the huge, glittering room and had been a centre of attention as soon as she arrived. It had been a lively, noisy occasion, everyone dressed up like Christmas trees, jewellery blinding you on every side.

She remembered the instant she first saw Paul. Their eyes had met, quite literally, across a crowded room. She had seen a tall, distinguished man with a striking, powerful face, dark eyes that seemed to pierce her to her very soul, hair still jet-black and thick. Older than her, in his late forties, she suspected, but then she liked older men. Young men were either obsessed with sex or with themselves, and bored her. She had been talking to a crowd of politicians and she had gone on talking, smiling, pretending to listen, while all the time she was only aware of this stranger on the other side of the room.

She had had no idea who he was, except that he was English. She could hear his cool, deep, cultured tones without straining although he was not raising his voice and all around them both people were talking loudly. She had loved the way he talked, she had always loved the way the English talked. It was very close to the way her own people talked in New England.

She had made no move to go over to him; she had been so sure he would come over and speak to her and she had known, even then, right from the very first, that this was going to be the most important relationship of her life.

He had detached himself from the group he was talking to and strolled calmly, without hurrying, towards her, and she had waited without looking at him, her whole body alive with excitement.

She couldn't remember what they had talked about, although they must have asked each other the obvious questions. 'Who are you? What do you do? Where do you live?' The only thing that mattered was that they had not felt like strangers; there had been something so familiar about him, as if she had known him in another life, and this was meant, intended, they belonged together.

After a while they had quietly slipped out of the party, indifferent to watching eyes or the gossip they might arouse. They were almost silent in the cab they took back to his hotel room. They had sat side by side, their bodies not even touching, from time to time looking at each other, and knowing what was going to happen as soon as they were alone.

Cathy had never before gone to bed with a stranger. She wasn't promiscuous; there had not been that many men in her life. She had twice thought she was in love. If she had not met Paul she might have married the man she had been seeing just before the night of that party. Steve would have been there with her if he had not been abroad that month.

She had known Steve most of her life. She had believed she was in love with him for a while, but at the first sight of Paul she knew the difference.

Everything she had ever felt before had been playing at love. Paul hit her like lightning striking a house, setting her on fire, and the whole landscape of her life was illuminated for her by what she felt with him. She knew she would never be the same again.

They had made love three times that night, and in the morning after sleeping a few hours they had woken up and made love again. She had been so stunned that she had said to him, 'You aren't real! Do you always do it this often?' and Paul had hoarsely laughed and shaken his head.

'Never in my life before! I can't believe it either. It's just that I haven't been to bed with anyone for a long time, and you're so bloody marvellous, I can't have enough of you. I feel like a starving man who gets his first meal for days and can't stop eating.'

It had not been a romantic declaration of love, but it had made her heart turn over. She could have told him there and then that she was in love, but she waited until Paul told her first. From the beginning she had let him set the pace, even when she was consumed with the need to know he loved her. Paul was the sort of man, she knew instinctively, who needed to be in control of everything in his life, and Cathy loved him enough to give him what he needed, whatever the cost to her.

He had proposed before he went back to England and she hadn't even stopped to think about it before accepting. Her father had known she was seeing him, but he hadn't had any idea it was serious and when she told him she was marrying Paul he had been stunned.

'But . . . Cathy . . . he's not much younger than me!' he had protested.

It was an argument she had expected. She had her answer ready. 'He's forty-eight – but so what? I'm not far short of thirty. I think that's quite a good age-gap.'

It had taken a while to talk her father round, but he had always been sensible enough to know when she was serious. And there were compensations. He couldn't deny it was a good match: Paul was a very wealthy man with a great deal of power in his own country. He not only owned an important national newspaper, but was a major shareholder in a television company, and her father could see he would be a very useful son-in-law, although he would much rather have seen her marrying an American.

Telling Steve had been far harder. She didn't like remembering his face, what he had said. She had realized she would hurt him, but not guessed how much. His feelings had been far more deeply engaged than hers. That much she had always known. It had made her uneasy at times: she felt love should be equal between lovers and ached to know a deeper intimacy than she had ever felt with Steve. In a way she knew him too well, he was more like a brother than a lover. She was fond of him rather than in love with him.

She hadn't suspected that he would be so unforgiving. She had not seen or spoken to him since. That had hurt her, because he had been her friend long before he became her lover and she missed him. She still did.

But it had been just one more thing she had had to lose for Paul. She had walked away from her country, her family, her friends – and all the sacrifices had been worth it. She didn't regret a thing. She would do it all over again.

Their wedding had been the social event of the year on the Eastern Seaboard; everyone who was anyone had been there. Cathy had refused to have her dress made by some top designer of the moment; she had delighted her grandfather by wearing the dress her grandmother had been married in, which had been put away in layers of tissue for seventy years. Cathy had loved to see it when her grandmother brought it out every spring to air in the sunshine for a day. She always imagined wearing it, had breathed in the fragrance of the pot-pourri of rose petals and lavender in little handmade gauzy bags which her grandmother scattered over it before putting it away. Full-length, with a sweetheart neckline, a tight, tiny waist and a skirt with a long train at the back, the dress had been hand-stitched in Paris in the Twenties. Ivory satin which was softly fading into cream, covered in drifts of real Chantilly lace, it had fitted her like a glove, as if it had been made for her, so she must have been exactly the same size as her grandmother on her wedding-day. Her grandfather had looked at her with tears in his eyes and said, 'If only she could have been here to see you!'

'She can see me, Grandee,' she had insisted, sure of it, feeling her grandmother's loving presence all that day while she wore the dress, like someone moving through a dream, a dream she still inhabited.

She clung to Paul's driving body, groaning in wild orgasm and hearing his deep moans of satisfaction. One flesh, she thought, consumed with pleasure; I knew, from the first time I saw him, that we were meant to be one flesh.

While Lilli Janacek gave the hospital reception the documents proving that Sophie Narodni had medical insurance, Steve talked to the doctor who was dealing with her case, a short, energetic man with the hooked nose and profile of an Aztec, and perfect white teeth which he displayed in cheerful smiles all the time.

'Very lucky, very lucky girl. Yes, you can see her, why not?' He returned Steve's grin of relief. 'Good news, huh? Pity the other woman was not so lucky.'

He had lost Steve. 'Other woman?' Steve said blankly, frowning at him.

'Your friend, Miss Narodni, trying to save herself, clutched at the woman next to her, fell sideways and hit the platform instead of falling under the train. She got some bad bruises and a minor head injury, which is the reason why we're keeping her in here tonight, for observation in case of concussion. The X-rays don't show any sign of internal damage, but you never know.'

'And the other woman?' Steve was accustomed to holding on to the main thread of a subject even when someone buried it in endless strings of words. Interviewing people required not merely patience but the ability to cut through a lot of crap without losing your temper.

Dr de Silva soberly shook his head. 'Fell under the train, I'm afraid.'

That shook Steve. 'She was killed?'

'No, and she shouldn't die, unless she develops complications . . . You know, winter is a bad time to get sick, you can develop pneumonia if you're kept bedridden for long, even with central heating and warm covers, and she isn't going to be able to move about much, not for a long while, because she broke a leg, broke both arms, and various ribs, not to mention she was knocked out by the fall, which, oddly enough, was lucky for her, because it meant she didn't try to move, and managed not to get fried alive by the electric current. They got it turned off before she recovered consciousness, which saved her life.'

Steve nodded, forehead still creased in a frown. 'That was lucky. Poor woman, though – has she got any family?'

'A husband and two sons. She works uptown, was on her way home when the accident happened.'

'Did the police give you any idea how it happened?'

Dr de Silva gave him a curious look, shrugging. 'Miss Narodni says somebody pushed her.'

Steve froze, staring at him. 'Pushed her?'

'So she says. Maybe some nut did push her, it happens, or maybe there was such a crowd on the platform that she got shoved forward.' His bleeper went and he groaned. 'Sorry, got to get that.' He rushed off, along the green-walled corridor, white coat flying.

Steve stared after him. So his first crazy suspicions hadn't been so crazy after all!

'Everything OK?' He looked up with a start as Lilli joined him. She frowned at his pale face. 'Well? What did the medic tell you?'

'Sophie is only being kept in overnight in case of concussion, but she isn't seriously injured.' He began to walk towards the elevator. 'Come on, she's on the second floor, room 323.'

Sophie was almost asleep when they walked into her room. Her lids lifting drowsily, she gazed across the room, saw Lilli first, gave a sleepy, incurious, almost childlike smile of recognition, then her eyes moved on to Steve and she drew in an audible breath of shock. At once she was wide awake.

'What are *you* doing here?'

She sounded terrified, and Lilli gave Steve a quick, narrowed look.

'Isn't he a friend of yours? He told me he was.'

Deliberately Steve said, 'Who pushed you under that train, Sophie?' and saw her eyes fill with fear.

'What the hell is going on?' demanded Lilli, looking from one to the other of them. 'Sophie? Were you pushed? What is all this?'

Sophie didn't answer her. She whispered, 'I don't know . . . I didn't see.'

'But you can guess,' Steve said. 'You know who wants you dead, and I think I know too. For your own safety, I think you should tell me everything. Once you've talked, there'll be no more attempts on your life.'

3

Sophie had been given some sort of sedative, but it hadn't made her sleep. Her body felt so heavy it was like being paralysed, but her head was tumbling with uncontrolled ideas and images. They kept jumping up like the spooks in a fairground House of Horror, leaping out of the dark, at her, glowing green, phosphorescent, eerie. Each time her mind shrieked with panic and fear, as it had when she felt the hand in the small of her back. Each time she lived it over again, falling forward, falling, falling, for what seemed an eternity, clutching at something, an arm, a body, and being thrown off in another direction, the grinding crash as she hit something hard, and then pain. There had been screaming too: herself first then someone else, another woman's voice, then others began, their cries overlaying each other in her head.

'God . . . help me . . . Jeez . . . what's happening? Oh, God . . . Look, somebody's on the line . . . somebody dead? A woman . . . on the line under the train . . . on the line . . .'

After that she couldn't remember how things had happened; she might have passed out briefly. The next thing she was looking up at a ring of faces staring down at her, and couldn't remember what had happened or where she was; her stare wandered from the circle of strangers, swung in a wild arc around the tiled walls, up to the shadowy arch of a ceiling. Lights strobed, darkness pressed in on the edge of . . . of what? Where was she? Disorientated, dazed, she heard a train shudder backwards right next to her, and knew she was in a station. Men swarmed, shouting instructions to each other. A man in uniform began pushing the crowd of people back from her.

'Get back, let the paramedics deal with her – c'mon, move back, please.'

Someone knelt beside her. 'Hi, I'm Bill. What's your name? How are you feeling? Any pain?'

A light shone in her eyes, she blinked, frowning, then shut her eyes against the intrusion and put a hand up to her head, groaning at a stab of pain.

'Don't worry about a thing, we're here to take care of you. OK, guys, on the count of three, lift.'

They took hold of her shoulders and feet and she was lifted on to a stretcher. A moment later she was being wheeled along a low-lit corridor, into a lift, out again, and then she felt cold air on her face, heard loud noises, and opened her eyes on night-time New York. She was dazed for an instant; down on the platform she had thought she was back in Prague. The underground system was much the same, indeed brighter, more modern, in Prague, whose metro had only been built in 1967, a year before her birth.

Now, staring around, bewildered, she was dazzled by the bright lights of the street, neon flashing on and off, and near by the sound of the wind in the trees in Central Park a short walk from here, the sound of rain on shop canopies and rushing in gutters, the sound of cars hooting, tyres skidding on wet tarmac, the hiss of hot air escaping from the subway up through the road.

She had really woken up then, and remembered. As they put her into the waiting ambulance she had thought: somebody pushed me, somebody wants me dead. And each time her heart raced and she couldn't breathe.

Don Gowrie . . . No, it couldn't be. But Sophie kept remembering his face when he heard her question at the conference and turned to stare with that stunned expression on his face. If she chose to she could hurt him, maybe even ruin him. He was an ambitious man, a driven man who had no scruples about doing what had to be done to get what he wanted. That much was very clear to her; and, after all, he didn't even need to get his own hands dirty. He hadn't had to do anything himself. He was rich enough to pay someone to do it for him, to hire a hitman – he need not have even met the man who was hired, he would just have put out a contract on her, wasn't that what they called it here? But whatever they called it, it was murder, plain and simple, or would have been murder, if the attempt had succeeded.

She shivered. No, she couldn't believe it – he might be a hard, ambitious man, but she hadn't got the impression that he was a cold or cruel one. He certainly wasn't without feeling or he would not have been so shaken when he heard her speaking. She had seen the shock and dismay in his face. Of course, that could simply have been fear of the threat she posed, but she couldn't believe he would go so far as to want her killed. Or would he?

Well, somebody did, she reminded herself. She hadn't imagined that hand pushing her into the path of the train. Somebody had tried to kill her – and who else had a reason for wanting her dead?

But couldn't it have been some crazy person, some total stranger, who had no motive, just wanted the kick of killing someone? Or maybe it had been an accident? Someone might have tripped and put out a hand to save himself, sending her tumbling?

No, no, it had been no accident – she was sure it had been coolly deliberate. She hadn't heard or felt anyone stumble into her. There had just been that hand coming out of nowhere. Someone had tried to kill her, and there had to be a reason. The more she thought about it, the more she had to face the fact that nobody else had a motive – it had to be Don Gowrie who wanted her dead. What on earth was she to do? He had tried, and failed – he would try again.

Her mouth dry, her skin sweating, she desperately tried to work out what to do. She could ask Vladimir to get her out of New York, send her back to London . . . anywhere, out of Gowrie's way.

Oh, but how could she just turn her back on something that meant so much? She had made promises, promises she had to keep. Emotion choked her. She was trapped by her feelings; however risky it was, she couldn't turn her back.

You couldn't turn your back on love. But oh, why did love have to hurt so much?

It should be warm and gentle. It shouldn't drive spikes into your heart whenever you thought about it.

She tried to think of something else . . . home, she thought, aching with longing; she wished she was back home, not in Prague but in her childhood home, but she could never go back there now because it no longer existed as it had in her earliest memories. The golden glow which had lit it in her first years had gone now.

When she was little the village had always seemed to be bathed in sunshine. She remembered sharp vignettes of Christmas and skating on the village pond, but mostly she remembered May, her favourite time of year, the hedges white with hawthorn in flower, purple lilac out in all the gardens, orchards white with cherry and plum trees in frothy bridal blossom. She had often lain on her back on the grass under them and stared at the blue May sky through their foaming branches.

How long ago it seemed, those childhood years, before her mother married again, while there were just the two of them, with their memories of the dead, of Papa and Anya, a gentle grief which was part of everyday life somehow and did not make her sad so much as tie her to that place, that time, woven into her heart's fibres. Then her mother married Franz and everything altered. After him came the boys, her half-brothers, who took all her mother's attention.

Sophie could no longer go out and play – she was needed at home, expected to help with the housework, help look after the babies; she was no longer a child herself. Oh, she loved them. How could she help it when she had nursed them, fed them, changed them, cared for them? She was their second mother and she missed them – but their arrival had shut her off from her childhood, all the same.

Lost in her memories of home, she jumped in shock as the door of her room opened and Steve Colbourne walked in.

Sophie was staggered to see him. What was he doing here? Had he been to her apartment? Why? What was he up to? Questions buzzed in her head like bluebottles shut up in a room, driving her crazy. Why had he made a dead set at her in the conference? Why had he come rushing over after she asked her question? Why had he been so insistent about taking her for a drink, why had he been so curious about her, asked her all those questions?

A nerve jumped in her cheek. What if . . . what if he . . . he seemed to know so much about Don Gowrie, he admitted to having known him for years – could he have been the man behind her in the subway? Had he been the one who pushed her?

Oh, for heaven's sake, she told herself – are you going crazy now? Of course it wasn't him – does he look like the sort of guy who kills people?

He had a tough face, but there was an honesty there too, and a very human warmth when his eyes smiled or glinted with amusement. She couldn't help liking him, and she couldn't believe you wouldn't know, by pure instinct, if someone was murderous. She couldn't believe, either, that a man who had already tried to kill you wouldn't betray it, somehow. The knowledge would show in his eyes, surely? Or maybe she was very naive? Maybe it didn't show in the face, the killer instinct? Maybe men who could coldbloodedly kill could also hide their thoughts, deceive even the most watchful eye.

She wished, wished desperately that she could penetrate his skull and read his mind, pierce his breast and read his heart.

Then Steve said, 'You know who wants you dead and I think I know too,' and Sophie drew breath harshly, staring, her face so tight she felt as if the bones were pushing through her skin.

'For your own safety, I think you should tell me everything,' he said then. 'Once you've talked, there'll be no more attempts on your life.'

Sophie saw Lilli's eyes fill with tears. 'Somebody tried to kill you? Oh, Sophie . . .' she whispered. 'How terrifying.' And their shared blood spoke between them, Sophie's eyes filling with tears, too.

But Lilli was American-born as well as having Czech blood. Her first instinctive helpless fear, the inbred terror of a people who had had to live in a world where a knock on the door at night could lead to someone vanishing forever, without explanation, was swamped in a rush of defiance and rage. She bristled, her face filling with furious blood.

'Have you told the police?'

'No!' Sophie and Steve both spoke at the same time, then looked at each other, knowledge leaping between them.

What does he know or guess? Sophie wondered. Don Gowrie wouldn't have talked to him – she was sure of that, certain that nobody else in this whole world knew, except maybe Mrs Gowrie, and Sophie was not sure even she knew the truth.

'Nobody would believe me,' she said to Lilli.

'They'd write her down as a crazy foreigner,' Steve agreed. 'There's no evidence.'

'I didn't see who did it,' Sophie admitted wearily. 'I just felt a hand in the small of my back, he pushed me.'

Sharply, Steve asked, 'He? You did see it was a man, then?'

'I didn't look round, there wasn't time, but it must be, a woman wouldn't have done that.' She drew a shaken breath. 'A woman . . . I grabbed at a woman . . .' Her eyes were suddenly huge, dilated, glistening with tears as she began reliving those moments again. 'Oh, God, that poor woman . . . I heard her screaming, she fell under the train, didn't she?' She swallowed visibly. 'Is she . . .? Was she killed?'

'No,' Steve said quickly. 'And she isn't going to die, either. She was injured, but it isn't fatal.'

Sophie closed her eyes, sighing deeply. 'Thank God.'

Steve moved a chair out for Lilli to sit down and sat down himself next to her. 'Now tell us about Don Gowrie.'

Her lids flew up like blinds on a wet window.

'And don't lie,' Steve said flatly. 'I know this is all about him. You've got something on him and he's scared you may go to the press with it – right?'

'Please go away,' she said, her voice rising shrilly. 'Go away, go away.'

The door opened and a nurse looked in, saw Sophie's agitation and came into the room. Her large hand clamped on the girl's wrist; she picked up the rapid pulse and frowned.

'You shouldn't be having visitors. You're supposed to be resting.' Her eyes accused Steve, instinctively fastening on him as the culprit. 'You'd better leave now.'

'Just another five minutes, it's important,' he protested, but the nurse shook her head.

'It isn't good for her to get upset. You must go now, both of you.'

Lilli bent to kiss Sophie, hugged her warmly. 'I'll come

back tomorrow morning to take you home in a taxi. Try to sleep, and don't worry, you can go and stay with my cousin in Connecticut for a few weeks. You'll be safe there.'

'I'm right,' Steve said. 'You know I am – think about it. You'll be in danger so long as you're the only one who knows.'

When she was alone she sighed, shuddering. She didn't need to think about it, she already knew he was right. She was in danger. But she had promised not to tell a living soul and she could not break that promise, not until she had talked to Don Gowrie, made him understand she did not want to threaten him – he needn't be afraid of what she might do, unless he refused to give her what she wanted.

She was given another sedative later that night, a more powerful one that almost knocked her out. Her sleep was heavy, troubled; she was back home again, seven years old, it was her first communion and she wore a long white dress, but there was blood on it, she screamed, then saw it was not blood, it was a red flower. Sophie picked it up and laid it reverently on her dead sister's grave, but a bony white hand came up out of the earth and grabbed her wrist.

She woke up screaming. The little hospital room was dimly lit; a nurse hurried in. 'Are you in pain?' she asked, bending over Sophie.

For a second Sophie didn't seem able to talk at all, then she managed to mutter, 'Sorry, I had a nightmare.'

The nurse seemed unsurprised. 'That would be the drugs,' she casually nodded. 'They can cause bad dreams if you aren't used to taking them. Would you like some warm milk? That might help. Calm you down a little, more naturally than the drugs.'

'You're very kind,' Sophie said gratefully.

In the cab driving away from the hospital, Lilli turned on Steve, eyes blazing. 'You lied to me – you aren't a friend of

81

hers, you're just a reporter after a story and you haven't any scruples about getting it, have you? You saw the state she was in – but you still kept on at her, you bastard!'

'I wasn't after a story, I was trying to save her life,' Steve said, biting the words out between tight teeth. 'You don't understand what's going on here, Lilli. Believe me, she's in danger.'

She tried to read his tense, angry face, but how could you be sure he wasn't lying? 'I wish I knew what was going on. Is she mixed up in something? This isn't spying, is it? Her country isn't in that business any more, I thought – or is it? Is this politics? The international kind? She isn't being used to get at Don Gowrie? I remember she asked me a lot of questions about him when she first arrived but I hardly knew a thing about the man. He's another guy who wants to be president, isn't he? Is that what this is about?'

'I wish I knew – you saw her reaction, there's something she isn't saying, and it scares the living daylights out of her. She's got to tell someone what she knows. Until she does there could be another attack on her at any minute, and next time they might get her.'

'Who are *they*?' cried Lilli, angry and distressed.

'Ask Sophie. You know as much as I do.'

She didn't look convinced. The cab pulled up. Lilli looked out of the window, surprised. 'Oh, we're back at my place. Well, goodnight. I'll pay the fare to here; you can take the cab on to your own place.'

'The fare is on me. I'll put it on expenses.'

'Oh, well, in that case – thanks,' Lilli said drily.

'I'm staying at the New Normandy Hotel for the night. Call me if you have any problems.'

Don Gowrie watched his father-in-law light a forbidden cigar, his eyes screwed up against the smoke but a beatific smile on his face. He was the oldest man Don knew, a living fossil, with skin like grey parchment, eyes buried in wrinkles like a tortoise, a few white strands of hair brushed across the pulsing pink dome of his bald head. Yet for all his age he was still very much all there; a shrewd old man with no illusions, an old man who held tightly to the reins of his ancient power, to his wealth and his influence in the world he was in no hurry to leave.

'Haven't had one of these for . . . oh, a year at least. Don't often get off my chain these days,' Eddie Ramsey told the other old men seated across the table from him, and they all grimaced understandingly.

'Hardly worth staying alive, the way we get treated, is it?' one of them said glumly. 'My daughter hardly lets me breathe for myself! Fuss, fuss, fuss. You wouldn't believe the time it took to persuade her to let me come tonight. If you hadn't rung her, Don, she'd never have given in, I know that.'

The old men all laughed, eyeing Gowrie half-admiringly, half-enviously.

'Sure have got a touch with women. D'you give lessons, Don?' they flattered, and Eddie Ramsey gave him a sideways look through the scented wreaths of smoke drifting between them.

'How's my daughter, Don?' he asked, swirling brandy in a balloon glass, and dropping his voice so that the mostly deaf old men shouldn't hear him.

Don was instantly wary. What had the old man heard? Keeping his own tone down, he murmured, 'No change since you last saw her, but I look after her, don't worry, Eddie.' Sweat trickled down his back, making his shirt cling to him. He could not afford to quarrel with his father-in-law; he could not afford to offend the old man's family instincts. Don's whole life depended on being married to Eddie Ramsey's only living child.

Eddie Ramsey took a sip of brandy, closing his eyes in pleasure. 'Liquid gold. Good stuff, this,' he said.

'Have another drop,' Don said, refilling the glass.

'Shouldn't, but I will. One night in the year won't hurt,' the old man said, sipped again, then held the glass, swirling the brandy and staring at it. 'Make sure you do look after Elly, Don. I had no luck with any of my children. All my boys died. Elly was the only one I was left with, and I've always had to worry about her. Maybe I shouldn't have married Matty, maybe my parents were right. They warned me against marrying my cousin, said it wouldn't do, but I wouldn't listen, thought I knew better, thought they were just old-fashioned. I loved her and I thought that was all that mattered.' He finished his brandy slowly, rolling the last drops round his mouth before reluctantly letting them trickle down his throat. 'I was wrong. D'you know the only thing that really matters, Don?'

Gowrie shook his head, knowing the question was rhetorical.

'The family, Don. The family. In the last resort we're only as strong as our family life. Which reminds me, when is that granddaughter of mine going to start a family?'

Gowrie relaxed and smiled. 'Oh, give them time – they haven't been married a year yet!'

He got another sharp, narrow glance. 'She's happy, though, isn't she? That fellow's kind to her? He's old enough to be her father, that's what worries me.'

'He worships the ground she walks on; you don't need to worry about Paul.'

'Hmm. I hope you're right.' His voice dropped almost to a whisper. 'Is he OK financially ? I mean, he's not in any trouble with his companies? The other day I heard he sailed pretty close to the wind, was over-borrowed and under-assetted. Was that just hooey or is there some truth in it?'

'Hooey, pure hooey,' said Gowrie, mentally crossing his

fingers. He knew so little about his son-in-law. When Cathy got engaged to Paul he had tried to run a thorough check on him and his finances but he had found out very little. Paul's secrets – if he had any – were well protected. Maybe it was time to try again? He had heard whispers himself. He would get on to it.

Watching him with those shrewd, disturbingly clever eyes, Ed Ramsey drawled, 'Glad to hear it. Hope you're right, boy. And I'm glad you're taking Elly with you.'

Don Gowrie met his father-in-law's eyes. For a while his wife had lived with her parents in Maryland while Don was in Washington. When she became ill, his life there had not suited her, he had been so busy. He had to work a twelve-hour day and then he was out almost every evening because it was vital to see and be seen at parties, receptions, charity functions, dinner parties, balls. It was the way Washington life worked; as much business was done over the card table, or in discreet back rooms at social events, as was done in working hours in offices.

Eleanor was better off in the peace and quiet of Easton, with the sea and the gentle landscape around her family home, with her dogs and horses. After her mother's death, though, Don had taken Elly back home with him because he could see that the strain of having her with him was too much for the old man now he was alone, and, anyway, it looked better. People were too curious about why his wife lived with her parents instead of with him. He had floated the story that she was at Easton to be with her mother during a long illness, but she couldn't stay on once her mother was dead. His public image demanded his wife should be seen with him, even if she rarely opened her mouth.

'Cathy asked me to bring her. She hasn't seen her mother since the funeral.'

Ed Ramsey sighed. Any reminder of his dead wife made

him melancholy. He had married his first cousin and lived happily with her throughout their long lives; he missed her badly, thought of her every day, looking out at the cool morning sky at Easton, remembering how she had loved mornings, winter and summer alike, the glory of pink and gold sunrises in summer, the clear, translucent colours of winter.

'She's a good girl. Well, I'll see Elly tomorrow morning before I fly back. Better have a late breakfast; not used to late nights any more. Shall need my sleep. Say ten o'clock?'

'She'll be very happy to see you.'

If she knows what's going on and recognises you, Don thought. If she isn't out of her tree, poor Elly. It came and went, her fragile sanity; sometimes she was so normal he felt he imagined those other times, those darker moments. He wished to God he did. She had turned dangerous lately; out of control she was capable of doing things he preferred to forget and would never want his father-in-law to know about. It would destroy Eddie Ramsey.

Steve had only just walked into his hotel room when the phone began to ring. Sophie! he thought at once, leaping to answer it, his heart in his mouth.

'Steve? It's Lilli. I've been burgled. The whole place has been turned over. They did a real job on Sophie's room, threw her books all over the floor. Half her stuff has been taken, even her family photos have gone.'

Steve hadn't expected it, yet he wasn't surprised. He should have guessed that would come next. Of course they would go through her room. He bet they had taken every scrap of paper they found. Letters, there would be letters – however careful they tried to be, lovers always wrote letters, they had to put it on paper, and the very risk they were running made their fever run higher.

A diary? Oh, yes, she had the look of someone who confided her thoughts and feelings, everything that happened to her, to a diary. Photos? She might even have had a photo or two of them together. In the first driven days of a love-affair a sensible man could lose all sense of caution. Love turned the head, addled the brains.

Had she been in love with Gowrie, though? Or had it all been on his side? Had he pursued her, pestered her? How had they met? How long had it gone on? Steve had so many questions and no answers at all yet. He had to persuade her to talk.

'Have you rung the police?'

'Not yet. I rang you first, you said to let you know. You guessed this would happen?'

'I guessed something would.' He had been sure they had not finished with Sophie; having failed to kill her they were bound to try again. 'Wait there, don't ring the police yet. I'm coming over.'

Lilli hadn't exaggerated; the apartment was in total chaos. Cupboards had been ransacked, their contents tipped out, shelves of books had been toppled on to the floor, a glass vase of chrysanthemums had been flung across the room, the glass had smashed and glittering shards lay in a pool of russet and yellow petals on the wet carpet.

'What a mess,' Steve said, staring around. 'Much missing?'

'A clock, a radio. I didn't have anything else worth taking.'

Steve stared thoughtfully at the TV which still stood where it had when he was in the apartment earlier.

'How come they didn't take that, I wonder?'

Lilli glanced at it, grimaced. 'I wouldn't bother, if I was a burglar. The damn thing works in fits and starts, but then I don't watch much TV. I'm too busy.'

'How did they get in?'

'Through the door, I guess; there's no sign of damage to the lock. Burglars carry skeleton keys, don't they? I don't know how else they got in.'

'Can I see Sophie's room?'

Lilli led the way and they stood in the doorway, staring at the same muddle of clothes heaped on the floor, books and tapes piled on top of them. Steve looked slowly, with distaste, around, and hating the idea of someone going through Sophie's things. An intrusion like this was always disturbing, even when it was an average burglary, but he sensed that this time the motive had been personal and someone had enjoyed wrecking the place.

'Sophie's going to hate seeing this! What has been taken exactly, do you know?'

'She didn't have much either. A cheap stereo she got secondhand from a pawnbrokers down the block, a radio alarm, her family photographs, for God's sake. Guy must have thought they were valuable frames – they were art nouveau style, but they were all reproductions, made in Prague, worth very little. And a box file of papers: articles, letters – from her family, from Vladimir, nothing valuable, as far as I know. Sophie didn't have anything valuable.'

Steve had seen enough. He turned away. 'Don't touch anything. Call the police, and when they've been here get some professional help to clear the place up, put everything to rights.'

'I'm not insured, and I can't afford to pay someone. I'll have to do it myself, and that will take time.' Lilli gave him a sharp, searching stare. 'Look, what's going on here? I'm not a fool, you know. First Sophie gets pushed under a train, then our apartment's burgled – what's this all about, and where do you fit in?'

'I'm not sure myself, I can only guess and I could be wrong, so I'd better not tell you what I think is happening.

But I blame myself for not guessing this might happen, and not taking precautions, so I'll foot the bill for a cleaner.'

'A guilt trip?' Lilli asked. 'Can you get it on expenses?'

He grinned at that. 'Good idea, I'll see if they'll wear it.' He knew they wouldn't, but if it made her feel easier about taking his help he didn't mind lying. 'I'm going to Europe day after next – but you can talk to my secretary in Washington. I'll leave instructions with her to take care of you. She'll be authorised to pay any bills for the work.'

'Well, I'm not going to argue. Fine by me. But tell me – did Sophie get pushed under a train because of something you did or said?'

That hadn't occurred to him. He thought about it, frowning. Had his intervention, when the two security guys questioned her, done some damage? Was Gowrie afraid she might sell her story to him?

'Maybe,' he said. 'I certainly didn't mean to put her in any danger. On the contrary. But you could be right.'

'I don't know what you are talking about, but you aren't making me any less worried about Sophie. The hospital said she could be discharged tomorrow – she can't come back to this mess.' Before he could answer, she took a ragged breath and harshly broke out, 'What if whoever did this tries again – comes back to get her?'

'That's why she mustn't come back here when she leaves the hospital,' Steve said quickly. 'So long as she is fit to travel, I'll take her to Europe with me.'

Lilli focused on him, breathing audibly. 'What?'

He had been thinking about it in the back of his mind ever since he saw Sophie in the hospital; he couldn't go to Europe knowing she might be killed while he was away. It had taken a while to figure out how to make sure he knew where she was all the time. He could put her on the expense sheet as a researcher. He sometimes took one with him, and Sophie said she had lived in London for a time; she knew the place well, he could easily prove a case for having her with him. He could swing it with Harry.

All he had to do was hint that she knew something about Don Gowrie's private life. Sophie must have a union card, she was, after all, a professional journalist – that qualified her to be employed as a researcher.

'But will she be safe? How do you know she'll want to go? If I was her, I'd be too scared to go anywhere.'

'Sophie isn't the type to scare easily.' He was sure of that. What little he had seen of her so far had convinced him she didn't lack guts; she would never have outfaced Don Gowrie, with all the power he could muster against her, if she were a coward. Sophie had gone up against Gowrie knowing it would make her an enemy, a dangerous one.

He looked at Lilli and shrugged. 'But I won't try to talk her into it if she is scared, don't worry.'

The attack on her had failed, but it was a warning. She might be wise to heed it.

On his way to the door of the flat he took a last look round the sitting-room and saw the edge of black paper protruding from under the table which had been thrown on to its top and lay like a stranded turtle on a wrecked beach, legs in the air. Steve bent to lift the table with one hand while with the other he drew the sheet of paper out.

Lilli came up beside him. 'Sophie's wheel!' She took it from him and held it at arm's length to stare at it. 'I didn't even dare look for it. I was so sure they'd destroyed it, like everything else.' Her face lit up. 'This is like an omen . . . they didn't manage to kill Sophie, and her wheel is OK too. D'you think it's an omen?'

'Maybe,' Steve said, and patted her shoulder comfortingly. 'It will comfort her for the loss of her family photos, anyway.' Then his eyes narrowed. 'Lilli, could I borrow this? I'll take good care of it, you'll have it back, I promise. I just want to have it photographed.'

She didn't let go of it. 'I've got a photocopier in my bedroom.'

'No, the reproduction wouldn't be good enough. It has to be done by a very good photographer. You'll have it back tomorrow afternoon, don't worry.'

She still didn't quite trust him, he saw the wary suspicion in her eyes. 'What do you want a photo of it for?'

'I'm not sure yet; I just have a feeling the wheel might be important.' It was rare for Steve to act without knowing quite why he was doing what he did, but there was so little to go on that he had to grasp at any straw he came across.

Why had they taken those framed family photographs? Lilli said the frames were practically worthless, just cheap modern reproductions – of course, the thieves might not know that and might have believed they were valuable. But Steve had a feeling those family photos could be revealing and he wanted a better look at them. Enlarged and sharpened in detail, they might tell him something.

'A hunch, huh?' Lilli smiled suddenly. 'You don't look the kind of guy who works on hunches, but they've often worked for me. Men laugh at female intuition, and then turn round and talk about gut instinct – well, let me tell you, it's the same thing. You know, I might even learn to like you, Mr Reporter.' She held out the big black sheet of paper.

'Thanks,' he said, taking it, but she didn't let go.

Her eyes held on his face. 'If you don't send it back in perfect condition I'll come after you with a hatchet.'

Steve had thought her a bit crazy when he first saw her earlier tonight, but she grew on you. Smiling he said, 'I believe you would! Don't worry, I'll look after it like a mother.'

Sophie saw Dr de Silva at nine o'clock next morning and was told she could go home at once. 'No problems in the

X-rays, just a few bruises, and you were in shock at first, but you're quite stable now.' He smiled, a short, sturdy man whose natural expression was cheerful energy, but who this morning had dark circles of weariness under his eyes because he had been up half the night dealing with emergency cases, and a hungry look, as if he never got enough to eat or enough sleep.

'And we need the bed,' he told her with a faint touch of humour, then took a sharper look at her pale face. 'You feel OK, don't you?' he demanded.

She nodded. 'I'm fine, thanks, Doctor. Everyone has been very kind, thank you.' Her voice was polite but although she smiled at him there was a blankness about her face that made him frown.

'Is there anyone at home to take care of you?'

'A friend, we share an apartment, and she works at home.'

He cheered up. 'That's great. OK, then. Get in touch if you have any serious headaches. That's the only thing to worry about. You did hit your head when you fell, but there seems to be no damage, so you probably have nothing to worry about.'

When he had gone Sophie rang the apartment but nobody answered the phone. Lilli might be out shopping, or might be on her way here. A plump black nurse, who had just begun the day shift and did not know her, brought her clothes, and Sophie got dressed while her bed was being stripped of the used bedclothes, and the plastic mattress was washed with disinfectant.

Sophie tried to ring Lilli again. Still no reply. She stood by the window, looking out at the high buildings opposite. The sky was lit with a chilly winter sunlight, but there was a lowering cloud hanging around looking as if it might pour rain down on them any minute. Sophie felt depression hanging around inside her; she wished to God she was back in Prague. She had not felt homesick all the time she was in London and Paris. She had been too excited and too busy. Oh, God, why did I go back to Prague before I came here to New York? Why did I have to go down to the village to see Mamma? If only I hadn't gone home that time. I wouldn't feel this way now.

She got hold of herself, choking down an aching need to cry. Instead, she looked round at the nurse who was dumping the bedlinen in a big wheeled basket.

'Nurse, I'd like . . . would it be OK . . .? I'd like to visit the other woman who came in with me . . . would I be allowed to see her?'

'Is she on this ward?'

'I don't know – she was more badly injured than me.'

The nurse looked dubious but shrugged. 'I don't know if they'll be letting her have visitors if she had an operation last night. It takes a while for anaesthetic to wear off. But you can try. Come on, I'll show you where to find her.'

She took Sophie to the waiting-room and left her sitting on a soft-seated chair, surrounded by soothing pale pink walls, meant to sedate the anxious into a trance, with a pile of old magazines on the central table in the room. The other people waiting looked up and stared without smiling. Some of them had the look of people who have been waiting hopelessly for a very long time; their eyes were almost dead with misery and fear. Were any of them relations of the woman she had sent plunging off the edge of the subway platform? Guilt made her stomach clench.

The door opened again and the black nurse beckoned to her. Sophie hurried out of the room. A small, thin, sharp-faced woman in white stood beside the nurse. Her grey eyes stabbed Sophie's face. 'You want to see Mrs Rogers? She's under sedation, sleeping, but you can take a peep at her, so long as you don't disturb her.'

'Is she going to be OK?' Sophie asked unsteadily, crossing her fingers.

'It will take time, and she's going to have a lot of pain,' she was told sternly. 'But with good nursing, yes, she will recover fully.'

She led the way to a room further along the corridor, opened the door and gestured. Sophie stood just inside the room. The blinds were down and the room was shadowy with pale, wintry morning light. There was just one bed; in it lay an unmoving figure, the head capped by bandages, making her face oddly mask-like, a pale, drawn set of features that expressed no character at all. Eyes closed, nose pinched, mouth pale and closed. It could be anyone. The bedclothes were draped over a support to raise them above her broken leg. Both arms were stiffly encased, and under the white hospital robe she wore Sophie could see thick bandages around her ribs.

'I'm sorry, you have to go now,' said the ward sister, and Sophie looked round at her, eyes blurred with unshed tears, wanting to sob out loud but holding back.

'Please . . .' Her voice was low and shaky. 'Please, when she wakes up, will you tell her . . . I'm so sorry, really sorry . . . it was an accident, I just grabbed at her to stop myself falling, I would never have wanted her to get hurt.'

'Sure,' said the sister with more warmth. 'Sure, she'll understand . . . accidents will happen, and look, she will get better, you know, she isn't going to die.'

It didn't help Sophie to know that; she could see how much pain the other woman was going to be in and she wished there was something she could do to help her.

She walked heavily back to her own room and with a jerk of shock saw Steve Colbourne talking to the sister. At the sound of her footsteps they both turned to stare at her; Steve looked drawn and pale but as he saw her his eyes flashed with sudden rage.

'Where the hell have you been?' he broke out in a rough, harsh voice.

Sophie didn't like being yelled at by a man she had only met yesterday. Especially in front of the sister and a couple of strange men in white coats who were walking past at that second and stared curiously at them. She glared at Steve, bristling with resentment.

'I went to visit the woman who fell under the train. Not that it is any of your business! And don't you shout at me, either. Why don't you go away? Why are you here, anyway?' Why did he keep turning up? He knew something – what? How was he involved?

The sister's bleeper sounded and she groaned. 'Sorry, I have to answer that. Miss Narodni, you have to sign out before you leave. Good luck, and remember, if you have any headaches get in touch with your doctor, or come back here, to the emergency room.'

When she had vanished back into the ward, Sophie looked coldly at Steve. 'Please go now, I'm waiting for Lilli.'

'She sent me.'

'I don't believe you.' She did a double-take, staring at him, suddenly anxious, her skin cold. 'Has something happened to Lilli? I've been ringing her for ages, and there's no reply.'

'Quiet now, don't get upset. Look, come into the waiting-room and sit down for a minute. I've got something to tell you.'

He put an arm round her and led her across the corridor to the waiting-room, and Sophie was too worried to argue.

There were a few people in the room, waiting, reading magazines or newspapers, breathing very quietly, shifting in their chairs. They all looked up and stared, then looked down again indifferently. Sophie sat down on a chair near the door and Steve sat down next to her. Lowering his voice, he said quietly, 'Sophie, your apartment was burgled last night.'

Her intake of breath made the others in the room look up again.

For a second she couldn't think straight then her mind leapt with panic. 'Lilli? Was Lilli hurt? She wasn't . . .'

'She's fine, she wasn't there,' he said in the same low, quiet voice, conscious of all the listening ears, the surreptitious glances.

Sophie closed her eyes for a second; she was very pale.

Steve went on softly, 'She discovered what had happened when she got back from the hospital last night. She called me and I went over there.'

Her brain ran with questions, doubts, suspicions. She watched him and wished she knew exactly where he fitted into all this. He knew Don Gowrie well, had known him for years, he said; was he in Gowrie's pocket? She hadn't been in New York for long, but she already realized that it wasn't just in Communist countries that some of the press were bought off, were kept on a secret retainer, to write to order, to put out what their masters wanted the public to be told. Maybe it was the same all over the world? Just the way the system worked, whatever you called it. Propaganda greased the wheels of politics and business, made the lives of the mighty easier, kept the people quiet.

'Called you? Why did she do that? Why not the police?' she asked Steve Colbourne flatly, her face hostile.

'I'd told her to ring me if anything happened. She has rung the police. They haven't been over yet. There's nothing valuable missing, nobody important involved.' His smile was cynical. 'They'll get round to it when they have time.' He looked into her eyes, his own intent and watchful. 'I'm afraid the whole place was wrecked, Sophie. They took your room apart. There wasn't much left of it.'

Her lower lip trembled. She bit down on it to stop herself

crying; she wouldn't cry, she wouldn't be scared off, he wasn't going to win by tactics like these.

'That's why Lilli isn't answering the phone. She's gone to stay with her friend Theo until the apartment can be redecorated.' Steve met her eyes and gently told her, 'They covered the walls with graffiti, I'm afraid, really smashed the place up. It isn't fit to be lived in at the moment.'

'What am I going to do?' she thought aloud. Theo Strahov's apartment was tiny, barely big enough for one, let alone Lilli too. There certainly wouldn't be room for a third person. Sophie tried to work out how much money she had in her bank account – enough to pay for a cheap lodging house for a few days? She could cable Vladimir and ask for help, for some extra money, a loan against salary.

'I'll have to find a cheap hotel,' she said.

'No, you won't,' he told her impatiently. 'You can't be left alone. Can't you get it into your head that you're in danger? They tried once. They'll try again and next time they could succeed. You're coming with me, first to stay at my hotel –'

'Isn't that where Don Gowrie is staying?'

'Safest place for you, right under his nose; as my mother always used to say, a dog never shits on his own blanket. He won't dare touch you while you're that close to him. When we go to Europe, you're coming too. I've squared it with my boss. You're coming on salary as a researcher for a week – we're paying your airfare and hotel bills. Maybe now you'll trust me enough to tell me exactly what you've got on Don Gowrie?'

'I'm not stupid. I know why you're doing all this – you just want to get a story out of me. So why should I trust you?'

Drily, he said, 'Who else do you have to trust?'

'Lilli –' she began, and he interrupted brusquely.

'If you like Lilli you'll leave her right out of it. No point in risking her life too, is there?'

Pale, she stared at him, shivering. It hadn't occurred to her until then that Lilli might be in danger too. She should have realised that. He was right, she couldn't risk Lilli's life.

'Lilli has learnt to trust me,' Steve said, and Sophie wondered how he had managed that. She gave him a smouldering, resentful look. He was too clever by half – she was beginning to find him a menace.

'You may have pulled the wool over her eyes, but you don't fool me that easily! I'm not going anywhere with you.'

'Oh, yes, you are, Sophie. Lilli gave me a case of things she thought you'd need for the next week or so. Now stop arguing. I haven't got all day to spend hanging around here.'

He took hold of her arm and propelled her firmly towards the door. For a moment Sophie meant to fight, but then she thought again and gave in, realising that it solved her immediate problems, even if it created a few more for the future. Steve Colbourne was a human steamroller. She had the feeling he was becoming a real problem for her.

4

They got a taxi to his hotel, where Steve had already booked a room for her, just across the corridor from his own. 'It would be safer if you stayed in here until we got the plane tomorrow morning,' he told her, depositing her suitcase on the luggage rack. 'If there's anything you want let me know and I'll get it for you.'

'Thank you,' she said, reluctant to be grateful but forced to it. She opened the case and looked at the neatly packed contents. 'I can't think of anything Lilli hasn't already thought of – she's one of the kindest people I've ever met. Lucky for me that Theo introduced me to her.'

'She's a one-off,' agreed Steve. He hadn't yet given her any details of the burglary. There was something far too intimate and disturbing about someone taking out their rage on her clothes, some of which had been torn to shreds. Lilli had sent what was left. 'She says she'll ring you. She packed warm winter clothes for London; sweaters and warm skirts and trousers, she said.' He looked at his watch and sighed. 'Sorry, I'm afraid I have to go to my office. But you have TV, and you can order anything you want from Room Service.' He gave her a look of concern. She was deathly pale, dark circles under her eyes. 'Try to rest. Go back to bed.'

She was standing by the window looking out at the New York skyline, the jagged battlements of grey roofs stretching into the distance. Below them were the leafless trees of Central Park, and she could see the Dakota building's eerie outline. She had visited it soon after she arrived, wanting to see where John Lennon had been shot and the Roman Polanski film 'Rosemary's Baby' filmed. Seeing the film in her early teens, Sophie had not been able to sleep, and

99

when she did had had weird dreams. It made her shiver now. There was something deeply sinister under New York's glamorous skin.

Steve wandered over to the window to look out too, without finding the vista as enthralling as she seemed to; he had known this city most of his life and preferred Washington, his chosen adopted city.

She turned her blonde head to smile at him and he felt his pulse pick up. Close to, she was even lovelier. 'You're very kind, but I'll be OK, don't worry,' she said.

He gave her an incredulous, furious look. 'Yesterday somebody tried to kill you and then wrecked your apartment – if you aren't worrying, then you should be!'

'Don't shout at me!' she burst out, her voice trembling, and he groaned.

'Sorry, sorry. I didn't mean to upset you.' Putting out a gentle finger, he stroked her cheek tentatively, then frowned. 'You're cold. Shock takes a while to wear off, you know. As soon as I've gone, go back to bed and try to sleep.'

The lingering warmth of his skin against hers comforted, was human and reassuring. When she was a little girl her mother had been very affectionate, and Sophie had often been cuddled and kissed, but after Johanna married Franz she had lost interest in Sophie and focused all her affection on the new babies that began arriving. She was the sort of woman who adored small children, especially if they were boys. Sophie had been just another pair of hands, an unpaid nursemaid, excluded from the new family circle – her mother, Franz and their two sons. The family of which Sophie had been a part was buried in the churchyard, with her dead father and dead sister.

She shivered violently and Steve watched, wondering what she was thinking about that made her eyes look so sad. Don Gowrie? What had the man done to her?

'Tell me,' he said urgently. 'Can't you see that you'd be much safer if you talked?'

She started violently at the sound of his voice. 'What? Oh . . .' She became aware of him again, picking up the scent of his aftershave, fresh, astringent, very male. It disturbed her. She didn't want to be aware of him; she had enough problems at the moment without adding a man to them. Steve Colbourne was attractive, she couldn't deny it, but she knew she couldn't trust him, it wasn't safe.

He smelt a story, and he was determined to get it out of her. The man was far too plausible, far too shrewd. She was a journalist, too; she knew how they operated, how far they would go to get a story.

The only thing she could be sure about was that he wanted to wheedle out of her whatever she knew about Don Gowrie. Everything else about him – his charm, his looks, the fact that he seemed to find her attractive – could be totally phoney. She had learnt in a bitter school that nothing was what it seemed, that even those who said they loved you could lie, that you could not trust anyone but yourself.

She looked at him, her eyes filmed with ice, and said in a chilly voice, 'I'm not telling you anything, Mr Colbourne, so stop badgering me!'

'You're a fool,' he muttered. 'Don't you realize? You're playing Russian Roulette with your own life.'

That was so true that she flinched. The stark realities of what she was doing had only just begun to dawn on her. She had not really expected her life to be in danger until the moment on the subway station. Turning away, she looked out of the window again.

'New York is breathtaking, isn't it? I still can't believe I'm really here. You said you lived in Washington, didn't you? I'm dying to see that.'

He nodded. 'That's where the centre of power is. If you

want to report on government you have to be there, and it is a fascinating place, especially for a journalist. It's a city with hidden depths. The architecture is on the grand scale – public architecture, I mean. You get the feeling at times you're back in ancient Rome or Greece. The Lincoln Memorial, all white marble columns ... the Washington Monument too ... not to mention the White House itself. The guy who designed the city, Pierre L'Enfant, wanted to awe people, impress the hell out of them, and it succeeds. But the domestic architecture is something else; you must visit Georgetown and see the restored town houses, especially in the spring, when the magnolias are out. It's like being on the set of "Gone with the Wind".' He paused, one eyebrow lifting. 'Did you ever see that film?'

'Of course I did! We do get Hollywood films in Prague, you know! It isn't the back of beyond.'

He laughed. 'Sorry, of course you do. I don't know much about life in your country. Keep filling me in, won't you?'

She softened, smiling back. 'So long as you keep telling me stuff I don't know about America, and that is a lot! I hardly know a thing yet.'

'Glad to help out,' he agreed, offering his hand.

She stared, bewildered, and he grinned at her.

'Deal?'

She understood the gesture then, and took his hand, smiling back. 'Deal.'

He didn't let go of her hand immediately; his skin was warm and firm. She liked the feel of that strength and confidence.

'Mind you, there are some spots in the States that I would feel lost in,' he said. 'I'm a New Englander, we're a different breed. We never forget that we were here first, apart from the Indian nations. You must visit my part of the country. Having spent time in England, you'll recognise something familiar. Our first towns were built by people from over there; the names, the architecture, the traditions are all very English.'

'It sounds lovely.' She pulled her hand out of his grip. 'Do your family still live there?'

'Certainly do – nothing would get my mother to leave the place, and Dad always lets her have her own way about the home and everything to do with it. Mind you, he has never shown signs of wanting to leave, although if he had got into Congress he would have had to move to Washington, of course, but she would have gone along with him in that case.'

'She's interested in politics too?'

'No, it's just that they both have old-fashioned ideas about the way marriage should work.'

Soberly Sophie said, 'If you get married you have to be together, don't you? You couldn't live in different places and expect marriage to work.'

He nodded. 'I think so, yes. Long-distance marriage is a recipe for disaster. It seems we agree on something! That's a start.'

Warily she asked, 'A start on what?'

With bland amusement he told her, 'Getting to know each other.' He looked at his watch again. 'Well, I have to get going. While I'm gone, stay here, don't go out, ring anybody, do anything. You'll be safe so long as you stay here – and don't open the door until you've had a good look through the spy hole.'

She burst out then, 'They wouldn't dare . . . in a public place like a hotel!'

But they had dared attack her in a subway, which was just as public, hadn't they?

'Who wouldn't?' Steve asked very softly and she shot him a quick, tense look. Just how much did he know? How involved with Don Gowrie was he? What did she know about this man, anyway? For all she knew it could have been him behind her in the subway station, his hand that had thrust her to the edge of the platform.

No, she couldn't believe that. He wasn't the type to kill. I'm getting paranoid, she thought – seeing dark shadows behind every face, hearing double meanings in everything anyone says to me.

At that instant there was a loud crash somewhere down the corridor and Sophie jumped about a foot in the air, gasping in fear.

'OK, OK, it's just the maids pushing a linen cart through some swing doors, I've heard them do it before,' Steve quickly said, but she couldn't stop shaking. He put his arm round her and pulled her close. 'Your nerves are shot to hell, aren't they?' he said, just above her head, one hand stroking her smooth, silky hair. He grew deeply conscious of the body he held, and his own body stirred with arousal, heat burned under his skin.

Sophie felt it, taken aback to pick up the tension of his muscles, the beating awareness inside him, and even more disturbed by an answering heat deep inside herself.

Alarmed, she pulled away, relieved when he let go of her at once and stepped back, his face flushed, his eyes restless, picked up the hotel telephone book and scribbled a number on top of it.

Without looking at her now he said, 'If you need me urgently you'll get me at this number – network head-quarters. Ask for extension 650. My secretary will know where to find me in a hurry.'

He glanced at his watch. 'Now I really must get moving. I can't be late for this meeting.'

At the door he gave her one swift backwards glance from those grey eyes. 'Come and put the chain on! And remember, don't open the door until you've checked out who's outside!' Then the door closed and he was gone, leaving her wishing he would come back, because in going he left her alone, and she was afraid of being alone.

Oh, don't be so pathetic! she told herself as she obediently crossed to the door to slip the chain through. Only a few minutes ago she had been bothered by having him touch her hair, hold her, because she couldn't cope with the way he made her feel. Now she didn't want him to go. Why couldn't she make up her mind?

She was still suspicious of him, he was far too quick to ask questions, probe, watch her every move – but the more she got to know him the more she wished she could trust him enough to confide in him. She couldn't, though. If he was being kind and sympathetic it was only because he wanted to get her to open up to him. But her natural instinct was still, disturbingly, to trust him and like him. Listening to him talking about his home and family had made her envy him. He must have had a happy childhood.

She walked back and sat down on the bed, staring around the impersonal hotel room; comfortable, pastel-painted in pale peach, with a warmer shade of apricot for curtains and bedcovers, an even darker shade for the carpet and a matching set of four rose prints, one on each wall. It could be any room anywhere in any hotel in the Western world, and normally she would have dismissed it as boring, but the very impersonality was somehow comforting at this moment.

As his secretary came into the suite, Don Gowrie was speed-reading a thick wad of documents, wintry sunlight glinting on his silver-flecked hair. Glancing up over the edge of his gold-rimmed spectacles, he smiled at her.

'Fascinating stuff, this, Miss Sanderson, especially the private backgrounds of all the British politicians I'll be meeting. I hope I shall remember it all.'

'Don't worry, sir, I'll be there to remind you of anything you forget.'

'I know you will. I rely on it.' There was a touch of glibness in his immediate response. That was what he always said and it had once been true, he had trusted her completely, but lately he was having to be careful what he said to her. He was holding back, hiding some of his thoughts; there were some things he could not risk saying to her now. To anyone, he thought, his eyes bleak. A month ago he had thought he was a happy man; he had everything, well, almost everything, he wanted in life, including ambition, an excitement at the thought of how much higher he might climb.

Now his entire life was balanced on a knife-edge, and all because of one woman. Rage surged through him. He swallowed it, controlling himself. He must keep calm.

Emily Sanderson looked down at the pad she held. 'Two messages, sir, I think you should know about. First, the governor called to say he would be a little late for luncheon, he was sorry, something urgent had come up and not to wait for him, he would skip the first course. Secondly, the British prime minister's private secretary rang to warn that he had a touch of flu and might not make the Thursday evening dinner but was sure he would be well enough to see you at lunch on Saturday at Chequers.'

Don swivelled in his chair, his face sharply thoughtful. 'That will give me an extra day with Cathy.' A free day, he thought; that could be very useful.

'Yes, sir,' she murmured unrevealingly. 'Oh, and this report just arrived.' She handed a sealed envelope to him and he slit it open, flicked his eyes down over the couple of typed pages inside. Emily Sanderson watched his face tighten, his mouth turn into a thin white line.

'Anything wrong, sir?'

He looked up, his face shuttered again, no expression visible at all.

'No. Is there a précis of these notes on the British opposition?'

'Of course – shall I get it for you?'

'Please.'

The secretary walked away without looking at him. Slim, with cropped dark hair, horn-rimmed spectacles over hazel eyes, broad cheekbones, a wide mouth, she gave an impression of cool efficiency. Her clothes emphasized that; today she wore a crisply ironed man's white shirt, with a dark blue silk tie, and a dark grey pinstripe tailored suit; a straight skirt and a fitted jacket which she wore open. She would be forty next birthday. She had been twenty-four when she came to work for Don Gowrie; he had come to trust her over the years since then so that now she knew most of his secrets. Not all of them. But it had been folly to let her know so much, he thought, frowning. It wasn't safe.

He picked up the typed report he had just received from his most trusted security man and skimmed his eye over it again. Sophie Narodni was staying here, in this hotel? That was a development he hadn't expected. What should he do about it?

Maybe he had better do nothing. Let her make her move. Once he knew what she meant to do he could decide how to silence her, and it would have to be final. He wasn't going to go on being blackmailed all his life. And even when he had dealt with her, there would still be another threat hanging over his head. Sophie was not the only one who knew his secret. How was he going to silence the other woman?

But you could always do what you had to do – all you needed was the will to do it. Ways and means were easy.

He slid the report into his inside jacket pocket. He didn't

want to leave it lying around for Emily Sanderson to see. He was going to have to be even more careful from now on.

Maybe it was time he had Jack Beverley update Emily Sanderson's security clearance. She was given a routine check once a year, along with everyone else who worked for him – but he decided to have Jack take a closer look at her. You couldn't be too careful, he was being forced to realize. He had been foolish once, had taken a stupid risk, let emotion rule his head and acted before he had thought about the possible future consequences; well, from now on he wasn't taking any more risks.

From the front steps of the great house, Cathy Brougham watched her husband's black Rolls head down the drive at the regulation five miles an hour that he, himself, had decreed for vehicles which visited the house. Any faster and the wheels churned up the gravel, depositing it on the cherished turf of his parkland.

Paul left at the same hour every morning, summer and winter alike, as regular as clockwork, after the same breakfast: prunes, orange juice and wholemeal toast with marmalade, followed by black coffee. He ate the meal in precisely ten minutes while skim-reading some of the newspapers folded beside his plate. He would finish reading the papers on his way to London and would be at his desk in his riverside offices by eight.

Cathy had a lot to do today herself, but she, too, had a routine which she was not going to vary. She hurried upstairs to change out of her ivory satin nightdress and matching dressing-gown, which she had worn for breakfast with Paul, into her smooth-fitting pale biscuit jodhpurs and a lemon polo shirt, over which she slid a warm yellow cashmere sweater. Sitting down on the bed, she pulled on her boots, then went downstairs to the back hall, where she found her riding hat on a table covered with riding accessories; she clipped the elastic under her chin, picked up her tan leather crop and went out to the stables, where Mr Tiffany was contemplating the early morning sky over the top of his half-open stable door. As he heard her footsteps on the cobbled yard, he deliberately yawned, his head back and his great yellowing piano-teeth on full display.

'No, you aren't tired, you lazy great oaf,' she told him firmly, walking past into the tack room to collect his saddle and bridle. So, it was going to be one of those mornings, was it? Every so often Mr Tiffany got up in a mood to make an issue of having to do anything other than stand in his stall and eat his beautiful, glossy head off.

As she walked back, her arms full of polished leather and jingling metal, the big chestnut backed, shaking his head, his long mane over his eyes, determined to make a fight of it, but Cathy could be just as stubborn.

'Don't even think about arguing – we are going for a ride!' she said as she approached him with his bridle. His head shot forward. He took the bridle out of her hand with his big teeth and threw it into a corner.

'You awkward bastard,' Cathy said, going to get it, and felt him lunge for her behind. His teeth grazed her jodhpurs as she jumped away. Picking up the bridle, Cathy turned round and smacked Mr Tiffany on the rump. 'Do that again and you'll be sorry!'

He laughed and she couldn't help laughing back. Paul always made fun of Cathy when she said Mr Tiffany could laugh. Horses can't laugh, Paul teased. You're sentimental where that horse is concerned! But Cathy knew she was right; when Mr Tiffany put his head back and bared his great teeth, making a low whinnying noise, he was laughing at her. He just didn't do it when anyone else was around. It was purely private – between him and her.

'You love that animal more than you love me!' Paul often said in mock grief, not believing it, and of course it wasn't true. Cathy did love Mr Tiffany and knew he loved her; it was a different sort of love, that was all. Paul was more than her love, he was her whole life.

As they rode out into the parkland around Arbory House the sun broke through low cloud, illumining the landscape: the great bare oaks, a few remaining elms, a cluster of green holly bearing glistening red berries, and, rolling away towards the iron fencing, the flat turf cropped by sheep which could be seen here and there, grazing slowly as they moved. Beyond that the green fields and woods of rural Buckinghamshire. Pied wagtails flickered among the trees; a robin was singing defiantly from a fence post; high above a hawk hung on the air, focusing downwards, watching for a movement among the grass. Cathy watched it – a sparrow-hawk? she wondered. Was that a little speck of white at the tail?

Mr Tiffany blew through his nostrils with sudden excitement at the smell of the countryside and the great, open expanse before him, then he began to canter and Cathy stroked his powerful, gleaming neck with an adoring hand.

For November, it was a beautiful morning. When Paul left it had only just been light, but now the sun was up, a fresh wind had blown the clouds away, and Cathy's heart lifted, even though the landscape was faintly elegiac, with that mournful colouring left over from autumn, before winter arrived to lay a dead hand on everything.

Her father was coming; would be here, soon, at Arbory. She wished Grandee could have come too, but the flight would be too much for him. He was so frail now. Thinking about him disturbed her. She would have to go home soon, to Easton, to see him while she still could.

She sighed with a premonition of grief to come. Oh, why did people have to get old and die? She wanted to keep them all, just as they were now, the three men she loved – her grandfather, her father, and Paul. Her life was perfect now, at this moment. She did not want anything to change. If only you could order time to stop.

She paused to look back at the house, elegant, white, a Palladian echo from the Georgian era, but designed by an eccentric architect who had let his fancy roam. As always Sophie felt a jolt of déjà vu, staring at the dome above the great library which was the centre of the house. The first time she saw it she had felt that jolt – had known she had seen it before, although she could not remember where. The memory was impossible to pin down; it came and went so fleetingly that she never had time to work out where she could have seen the dome before. Paul said it wasn't Arbory's dome she remembered – it was the domes of Brighton Pavilion, which she must have seen illustrated in a book sometime. He had driven her down to Brighton to see the Pavilion, but when she saw the Prince Regent's domed palace she did not get that immediate sense of déjà vu she got at Arbory. The mystery still nagged away at her.

When her father came, maybe he might get the same feeling? She didn't remember him mentioning it when he came shortly after their wedding, but he would have had other things on his mind, as she had had.

She had forgotten to ask him then. She must remember this time. She had very few memories of her early childhood, and those she had were very vague. Her earliest memory was of her mother crying for some reason, and holding her too close, so that Cathy got scared. She couldn't remember anything else about the occasion, only that she had begun to cry too. Her mother had probably been in one of her strange downward spirals. You never knew how she would be when you saw her; one minute she seemed perfectly normal and cheerful, the next she would either sit silent and blank-faced for hours, or would scream and turn violent.

It had made Cathy's home life uneasy and uncomfortable.

Her father had sent her off to one of the best girls' schools in New England as soon as she was old enough to go away, and although she loved her parents she had been relieved. Her life was calmer, happier, away from the unpredictable mood swings of her mother.

Later still her mother had gone to Easton to live with Grandee and Grandma, and the atmosphere at home had changed so much that Cathy had eagerly waited for vacations and a chance to spend more time with her father. With her mother at Easton, Cathy was the one who went on the campaign trail with him, canvassed, stuck up posters, sat beside him on platforms, taking her mother's place, shook hands, talked to voters. She had loved it, had talked about going into politics herself. She could remember long evenings discussing the idea with Steve Colbourne, whose family were as obsessed with politics as her own.

She frowned at the thought of Steve. He was part of a past she preferred to forget. All that was before she met Paul and discovered other dreams.

Mr Tiffany snorted and danced sideways impatiently, eager to be off again. 'OK, OK,' Cathy said, strands of her dark hair blowing across her face, and they began to gallop.

She had to get back, anyway, to make a final check on the arrangements for her father's visit. Security men had already been to inspect the security system of the estate; the electrified fence surrounding the entire park, the alarm systems on the gates and walls, the doors and windows of the house, on the stairs and corridors inside. Not a mouse could move at Arbory at night without setting off alarm bells. Paul was just as much in the public eye as her father, and just as protective of his own privacy, but, naturally, her father's staff wanted to make absolutely certain he would be safe there.

She smiled, staring at Arbory as she rode towards it. It looked so tranquil, a quiet haven of peace in this dreaming countryside. In a few days it would be alive with people, telephones would ring, faxes chatter, cars come and go, helicopters land on the immaculate turf. She still found it hard to believe that all those years of work and planning and dreaming might be about to pay off. Soon, her father could be the president of the United States, and then nothing would ever be the same again, for him or for her.

Sophie woke up, surprised to find that she had been asleep for two hours. She went to the bathroom, used the lavatory then took a leisurely shower, enjoying the warm water sluicing down her body, washing away the hospital smells, the panic and fear she had felt over the last twenty-four hours. When she stepped out, she put on a towelling robe, dried herself, lightly towelled her wet hair and went back into the bedroom to unpack. Choosing bra and panties, a pair of well-washed old jeans she had bought at Camden Market in London when she first arrived in Britain, and a thin ribbed cotton sweater she had bought a month ago at a fleamarket in Greenwich Village, she dressed, then put the rest of the clothes away and sat down to flick through Room Service. Chinese stir-fried chicken and vegetables sounded good; she rang down and ordered that, with a bottle of mineral water and a pot of coffee.

'Regular or decaff?' asked the girl who took her order, and would have begun one of those endless multi-choice questions, but Sophie interrupted. 'Regular, please. And could you send up some fresh fruit?'

'You got it,' said the girl. 'Your order should be with you in twenty minutes.'

Replacing the phone, Sophie switched on the TV and curled up on the bed to watch cartoons, but she couldn't concentrate on anything. Her mind was running along the same track all the time: Don Gowrie, her mother, the subway last night, the woman lying so still in the hospital bed this morning. Each time a new image leapt into her mind she winced and tried to think of something else. The cartoons were no help; she had to find something more interesting to watch. She flicked through the channels. Coming upon the hotel's own advertising channel she watched that for a minute. They seemed to have a whole shopping mall downstairs: hairdressing salon, news-stand, fashion boutique, gift shop, florists.

Florists, Sophie registered on a double-take. Jack-knifing upwards, she reached for the phone again, dialled the number of the florists downstairs and sent flowers to the hospital for the woman she had unwittingly pushed under the train. There was no real recompense she could make. The gesture made her feel a little better, though, lightened the burden of her guilt.

A sharp tattoo on the door made her jump. She froze, briefly, her heart running so fast it hurt.

'Room service!' a voice outside the door said, and Sophie gave a sigh of relief and hurried to let in the waiter after she had checked him out through the fish-eye spy-hole in the door. He was a small, angular Puerto Rican with a few pock-marks on his olive skin; there was nobody else around so she opened the door.

When he had laid out her meal on the table by the window she tipped him and let him out, making sure she put the chain back on the door before going back to eat. The food was better than she had hoped, the vegetables cooked crisply and quickly, the chicken tender, the sauce a mixture of honey and soy sauce. Sophie felt better when she had eaten it. She sat back to drink her strong coffee, switching the TV on again.

The news came on a few moments later, and she jumped in surprise as Steve Colbourne's face appeared, talking in that quick, super-cool, super-confident way. He was everywhere!

'With the New Hampshire primary only a few months away now, Senator Don Gowrie is gearing up for battle against the other would-be-presidents who are fighting it out for selection as future occupant of the White House. Getting yourself noticed is vital – many are called but few are chosen. Senator Gowrie had to stand out from the crowd – but with his background in international diplomacy, having represented the United States in many parts of the globe, he has many friends abroad and at home who can give him support simply by making it known how highly they value him. Most presidential candidates stay and slog it out at home, struggling to get TV and press recognition – but Senator Gowrie is not most candidates. Tomorrow he is flying to Europe to meet with the leading political figures there. He may only be a candidate so far, but Don Gowrie is already acting like a president-elect. This is a man to watch.' He paused, smiled. 'This is Steve Colbourne in New York.'

His face faded and the two newsreaders came back into shot; the woman smiled into camera. 'And on a chilly November day in New York there was a touch of spring in the air when a Brooklyn florist celebrating his golden wedding decided to give away a red rose to every woman customer who came into his shop.'

Sophie switched off the TV and sat staring at the telephone, her mind in confusion. She had made a solemn promise to her mother, a promise she could not break. You didn't break faith with someone who might die any minute. Somehow she had to persuade Gowrie to listen to her, understand what was at stake, but how? The man had so much to lose, she understood that. He wasn't going to want to talk to her – how could she make him do what she wanted?

Don't sit about brooding on it! she crossly told herself. It's time you did it. She got up and grabbed the phone, dialled the operator and asked for the Penthouse Suite, not even sure they would put her through, but they did, indifferently; she wasn't asked any questions. The phone shrilled, then a woman answered briskly.

'I would like to speak to Senator Gowrie,' Sophie tried to sound calm but was afraid her own voice was husky with nerves.

'May I ask who wishes to speak with him?'

'Sophie Narodni.'

There was an intake of air, as if the other woman was startled, then for a second or two silence before the brisk voice said, 'The senator is not available, I'm afraid.'

Sophie threw caution to the winds. She had delayed long enough; she had, somehow, to make contact. 'Please tell him I must speak to him, before he leaves for Europe. Tell him for his own sake he has to listen to me.'

The other woman's voice thickened in anger. 'Blackmail is an ugly crime. You could go to prison for a very long time and don't think he won't call the police. You aren't scaring him. He knows you don't have any evidence.'

She knows all about it! thought Sophie. He has told her! This couldn't be someone who worked for him, it had to be his wife, surely!

'Are you Mrs Gowrie?'

The voice seemed to get even angrier. 'No, I'm his secretary. Now get off this line and don't try to get in touch with him again, or you'll regret it.'

Fiercely Sophie said, 'I'm not trying to blackmail him. Tell him I just need to see her, that's all. I won't tell a living soul, so long as I can just see her.'

The phone went down with a crash and Sophie slowly replaced her own. Tears began to run down her face, blinding her.

*

Paul Brougham leaned back in his green leather swivel chair and drummed his fingertips on the matching desk, frowning as he listened to Freddy. Behind him a huge window glowed with the lights of London's riverside night scene; a helicopter flew above the skyline, watching the homeward flow of traffic out of the city. Paul heard the engine note and glanced over his shoulder, grimacing. He should be going home himself soon, he was exhausted and dying to get into a hot bath and have dinner with Cathy, but Freddy's news was too worrying. All day they had heard that there was movement in the shares, someone was buying them in large batches and the city was buzzing with curiosity.

'I'm still not sure what's going on except that the buyer is Media Inco World News,' Freddy said.

'Why are they hitting on us? They're American, for God's sakes – and big over there, too.'

'Word is they're looking around for a matching European company. I guess we'd fit their profile, and Salmond, the guy who runs them, is needy – he's hit a ceiling over here and he's looking for growth outside the US.'

That was what Paul had feared, but how far would Salmond want to take his attempt? He might back off if he met strong resistance and be satisfied just to have some sort of influence on the board. Before he talked to Salmond, Paul would like to have a clearer view of the man's financial position.

'Could you find out as much as you can about him for me?'

Freddy nodded, looking grave. 'One thing, Paul, he's solid; the man himself has a vast fortune inherited from his Swiss father. No cash-flow problems there.'

Paul met his anxious gaze and made a rueful grimace. 'You've always worried too much, Freddy. We may have cash-flow problems, but then we always have had. We've got by until now, haven't we?'

'But this time bluffing may not be enough. This time we may be up against someone with a bottomless pocket and a habit of getting his own way.'

'This time is no different from any other time. All business is based on people. I keep telling you that, Freddy. It will be me against him, whoever the guy is.'

Paul swivelled to face the London skyline, his face set. This wasn't the first time he had had to face a take-over attempt, but this time it sounded as if he might have a fight on his hands, and if it came to a showdown he would have problems fighting back. Freddy was right about that. His cash-flow was in the usual state of flux; his companies weren't nailed down, he was vulnerable and maybe this guy Salmond knew it somehow. A shrewd eye could always pick out clues from a company balance sheet.

Oh, what the hell, he had always won before. He would find a way to stop Salmond. Why did it have to happen right now, though? Now, when he had more than his usual share of worries. This had been a bad year. They had had a series of financial setbacks and he knew he hadn't dealt with them with the old force and speed. In the past they had faced far worse, and he had ruthlessly despatched any opponents, but something was different now. He had always been obsessed with the business, but since he had met Cathy . . . yes, he recognized with a drawn breath, it had been since he met Cathy that he had changed. Work didn't mean as much to him. He couldn't concentrate. The minute he thought of her everything else faded away; he felt the clutch of desire deep inside him and his insides seemed to turn to water.

If he was going to beat a take-over bid he had to get himself back in control.

'Tomorrow we'll call a board meeting,' he said to Freddy over his shoulder. 'Talk to all our friends and allies. We're going to need them now. Off you go for now, Freddy, and get a good night's rest. You're going to need it.'

When Freddy had gone, Paul looked at his watch. Before he left himself, there was a call he ought to make – would she be home by now or still in her office? If he knew Chantal Rousseau she would be at her desk.

He was right. When he rang her office she answered the phone in a voice sweet as honey and warm as Provençal sun. *'Paul, mon cher, ça va?'*

'Bien – et toi?'

'Pas mal.'

'Tu es seule ce soir?' he asked, needing to know if anyone else was with her or if she was alone, and she murmured, still in French.

'Quite alone, Paul – what do you want?'

Once upon a time, if she had asked him that question, in that melting voice, he would have felt a sensual beat start inside his body. He had never been in love with her, but she was a sexy woman, terrific in bed; their affair had gone on for quite a while. It had ended when he met Cathy.

Their public relationship had continued, of course, since Chantal was a top executive with one of his major share-holders, an important fund management company who held around a quarter of his company shares on behalf of their investors, and had been one of his chief supporters for a long time, advising on acquisitions and taking a strong interest in the running of his business.

'I'm calling an emergency board meeting,' he told her crisply, using English deliberately now, to make it clear that he was ignoring the very personal note he had heard in her voice, that soft, inviting purr he knew only too well.

She used English too then, her voice dry. 'Ah, you're taking the threat from Salmond seriously, then?'

So she already knew about it? But of course she would; everyone in the market would know by now.

'I would be a fool if I didn't. Are you free tomorrow afternoon?'

'I'll be there,' she promised, then lapsed back into French. Using French with him had always been one of the ways in which she reminded him that they were both foreigners in this very English environment, the City of London, the dull, the formal, the grey sea of English business, so different to the glamour and civilised wit of their homeland. When he dined with Chantal they ate French or Vietnamese food. She liked to go with him to concerts given by visiting French musicians, to French opera or ballet. It made their relationship special, excluded everyone around them.

Now she said, 'Why don't we have lunch first, to talk it over, Paul? There's a new French restaurant I'm dying to try. I hear it is fabulous and has a great wine list. Not the usual old plonk. Some really good stuff.'

He knew he should accept, keep her sweet, but he couldn't do it and tried to sound really regretful as he refused. 'I'd love to. Some other time, Chantal – but I'm very pressed for time at the moment with my father-in-law coming over tomorrow. I'm trying to wrap up as much as possible before he arrives. I'll see you in the board room at three, OK?'

'OK, Paul,' she said, but the sweetness had a tart edge to it.

Up in the Penthouse Suite, Don Gowrie's campaign team were in session, brainstorming ideas for the coming days in Europe. The room they sat in was crowded with chairs arranged in a circle.

His speechwriters listened to everything that was said, industriously scribbling notes, his PR people talked about the press coverage they had achieved since he got to New York and discussed the media people who were going with them to Europe to make sure the coverage continued. His campaign manager, Jim Allgood, discussed the travel and hotel arrangements for the first leg of the tour with a harrassed woman in a blue jersey suit.

The researchers passed round pages of background information on the places they would be visiting, the people they would be seeing, the issues paramount in London, Dublin, Paris, Bonn and Rome at the moment, issues he should address during his visits to those capital cities, issues which would also have an impact back home among the Americans with roots back in those countries who still kept an eye on what happened in Europe. That was the vital point to concentrate on – the reaction back home to what you said abroad. Foreigners had no vote. They didn't count.

'How do we deal with the Irish problem?' asked a speechwriter, and Jim Allgood looked up impatiently.

'For God's sake, Jeff, read your background notes once in a while! Why do you think we give them out? He has an Irish family connection, way back – ancestor left during the Famine, joined the British army and went to India, did well, got married, had a son who emigrated here in 1878. It's a good story: go big on that while we're in Dublin, don't mention while we're in London. As we go to London first, no problem. On balance the Irish vote back here is more important than the Brits, though, don't forget.'

'What about this Nato stuff the British press is banging on about?' asked a researcher, looking up from a snowstorm of press cuttings, and Jim Allgood frowned, shook his head.

'Don't touch it. We're keeping our options open on that one. If he gets hassled for some statement, he'll go for a standard response. America stands beside her friends, always has, always will, along those lines.'

'Blah, blah, blah . . .' scribbled Jeff, the speechwriter, and Allgood gave him a cold glance.

'Don't worry, he'll make it sound good, but keep it vague. Very high-minded, very serious, but no firm commitment on budget, or promises that can be thrown back at him later, OK? The world keeps changing, you never know where we'll be in a couple of years. He doesn't want to be saddled with any promises he has to break.'

A lanky, tousle-haired young man in jeans and a T-shirt which read in bright orange lettering 'Put Gowrie in the White House and Get the Job Done' said drily, 'God forbid we should do that. We wouldn't want anyone to think the man has principles or believes in what he's saying, would we?'

The other speechwriter, Jeff, grinned. Allgood didn't.

'Don't get clever, Greg,' Allgood said. 'Unless you're tired of writing for us and want to go back to writing novels that don't sell?'

'I've got too used to eating,' Greg Blake said mournfully. 'Sad, isn't it? And I don't think I'm ready to go back to sleeping in the park, either.'

'Zip it, then,' Allgood said.

Greg Blake silently mimed pulling a zip across his mouth. Jeff, beside him, zipped, too, his eyes full of amusement.

'You guys slay me,' Allgood said with no amusement whatever.

Next door Elly Gowrie was eating rainbow jelly; sunshine from the window made it flash and glisten as she carefully spooned it into her mouth with the serious concentration of a four-year-old. She watched the shimmer of it and laughed.

'Jelly,' she said.

'You love jelly, don't you?' her nurse said.

She was in one of her happy moods for the moment; she beamed. 'Elly loves jelly,' she said, and began to giggle. 'Elly loves jelly, Elly loves jelly,' she chanted, banging her spoon on the side of her bowl.

The nurse gave her a wary look, recognizing the symptoms of over-excitement which could turn into a violent rage any minute. She had had an emotional day; that always made her volatile.

She had cried earlier when her father visited her, clinging to him sobbing, 'Daddy, Daddy . . . take me home, I want to go home, I don't like it here, don't leave me with them, take me home.'

The old man had been very upset. They had had to pull her away from him; she was surprisingly strong, her arms like tentacles winding round him.

'Look, let me take her home with me. Why not let me take her home?' Eddie Ramsey had said shakily, almost in tears himself, when she had been taken away.

Don Gowrie had soothed him down. 'She'll be fine, Eddie. She was just upset, seeing you again. She'll enjoy the trip, she badly wants to see Cathy and I promised Cathy she would come with me. Cathy hasn't seen her mother for months.'

Pale and distressed, Eddie Ramsey had said, 'I know, I know, but she's always happiest at Easton. She doesn't look at all well to me. She has deteriorated since I last saw her.'

'She's sixty-five next birthday, Eddie! She's always been delicate, you know that, but I look after her and I always will.'

They had stared at each other, then Eddie had sighed. 'I'm too old to get into a fight with you, Don, but when you get back I want her to come and stay with me for a while.'

'Sure, of course,' Don had said, in quick relief, but knowing that he did not dare leave her behind or let her stay with her father once they got back to the States. He wouldn't want Eddie Ramsey to realise his daughter was very close to the edge of sanity, if she wasn't already way over it. Drugs and constant supervision kept her within limits, for the moment, but it was turning into a race between her last flicker of sanity and her father's last flicker of life. Don hoped the old man would go first; it would be unbearable for him if his last living child had to be shut away for ever in a mental hospital, for one thing, and for another Don would be safe from any prospect of Eddie Ramsey changing his will.

Steve had to attend a budget meeting that afternoon, to listen to the latest gloomy prognostications of the head accountant on the perennial problem of advertising revenue versus costs, but managed to snatch a few minutes first to take a cab to the photography shop where they had blown up individual sections of Lilli's wheel for him.

'They're very grainy, a bit scratchy, but you can see the faces a lot clearer, Steve,' the guy said, watching him peering at the glossy sheets. 'Is that OK? I can't blow them up any bigger, they'd go completely out of focus if I tried.'

'They're fine,' Steve said, shuffling them together. 'How much do I owe you?'

He paid cash and left. In the cab taking him back to the network headquarters he had another look at the blown-up copies; the faces were certainly clearer, yet even more mysterious and alien now that they were three or four times as large. Looking at them more closely, he wasn't even sure why he had had them blown up, what he had thought he might get out of them. There was nothing terribly interesting here.

They were poignant and rather pathetic, these faces – the old man in some sort of crumpled uniform, his hair oiled down, parted in the middle, a bushy moustache above his lip, a rifle propped against his shoulder – he must have lived around the turn of the century. But when had they lived, this young couple on their wedding-day? The bride looking as if she was barely out of childhood, a little girl dressing up, thick dark hair piled up behind her head, looking plump and yet childish in an old-fashioned wedding dress which might have been her mother's, it was so shapeless and yellowed, carrying a bouquet of lilies and smiling solemnly at the camera, her groom a mere boy, taller than her by a foot, dark, very thin, looking slightly dazed, in a suit which fitted him so badly it must surely have been borrowed or hired? Were these Sophie's parents – or her grandparents? He couldn't guess from the clothes.

The one face he was certain about was that of Sophie's dead sister. He briefly looked at it, oddly moved by the thought that this lovely child was dead. Well, from the age of these photos, many of these people must be dead or very old by now – yet somehow that was not as heart-wrenching.

They had lived out their span, these old people, but the baby had died before it had had a chance to live. Steve felt his throat move roughly and pushed all the photos back into the envelope.

Well, that hadn't told him anything. He had wasted his money. Or had he? Hadn't all those faces told him something about Sophie? These were her people. Part of them lived on in her. Discovering something about them was to find out more about her.

Suddenly remembering that she had not yet talked to Vladimir, Sophie rang him in Prague, got his answerphone and left a message telling him where she was staying and that she would be flying back to London next day.

'Don't worry, you won't have to pay,' she added, explaining that her trip was being paid for by the TV network. 'I'm officially going as a researcher and I'll be working for their team while I'm there, but I'll still file you stories about the political angle of the Gowrie visit.'

After she'd hung up she rang Theo's flat and got Lilli.

'Are you OK?' she was asked anxiously. 'Where are you?'

'At Steve Colbourne's hotel –'

'I hope he got you a room of your own! If he makes a pass, flatten him.'

'So far he's been a perfect gentleman. He brought me here this morning and I haven't even seen him since,' Sophie said, not adding that she had several times wished he had not left her alone like that. She needed to talk to someone.

'He's lulling you into a false sense of security, that's all!' Lilli said darkly.

Sophie laughed. 'Oh, come on, Lilli, all men aren't like that! I think he has more class than to make a cheap pass. And I thought you liked him!'

'What made you think that?'

'He did. The way he tells it you trust him completely – or why did you give him my suitcase and let him pick me up at the hospital?'

Lilli laughed. 'Well, OK, sure, I let him collect you from the hospital. He convinced me it was the safest idea, that nobody would try anything with him beside you. That's just the trouble. The guy is plausible. He can talk a good story.'

Sophie grimaced. 'Can't he just? Well, don't worry about me, Lilli, I'll be fine. I shall be off to London tomorrow. I've rung Vladimir and left a message on his answerphone. Could you do me a favour? Ask Theo to cover for me while I'm away? I'll be filing from Europe, but if anything interesting comes up here meanwhile, could he send Vlad something on it?'

'Sure. He's out shopping right now. Do you want him to ring you at the hotel?'

'If he has time, thanks, Lilli.'

'What's it like, the hotel? As luxurious as it looks from the outside? I've never been able to afford to go inside.'

'It's a palace,' Sophie told her, then started sharply as someone knocked on her door. 'Sorry . . . somebody just arrived, I'll have to go.'

'Be careful!' Lilli said, immediately anxious.

'Yes, I will, don't worry. I can see who's outside through a spyhole. I won't open the door if I have any doubts. Bye, Lilli.'

She hung up and went to the door, peered through the spyhole first. Her whole body jerked in shock as she recognized Don Gowrie standing outside.

5

He was alone; that astonished her just as much as the fact that he had come. Don Gowrie rarely made a move without being surrounded by people, but there was no sign of anyone else in the corridor. Sophie hesitated about letting him in – what if he tried to kill her again? But he wouldn't dare. It would be too much of a risk.

She took off the chain, her hands trembling a little, and opened the door. For a few seconds he didn't move or look at her; he looked past her into the room, his eyes flicking round it, checking that she was alone.

That made her smile. So he was nervous too! 'Don't worry, Mr Gowrie. There's nobody else here!'

He walked inside, their bodies almost brushing, her nostrils picking up his scent; a mix of whisky and some sort of aftershave. Had he taken a couple of drinks before he came, to get up his courage? That made him seem more vulnerable and more human, and reassured her a little. Sophie closed the door and plunged straight in to the words she had been rehearsing to say to him ever since she left Prague all those weeks ago.

'I want to see my sister, Mr Gowrie.'

'Sssh!' he muttered, and walked quickly across the room to the bathroom, glanced in there, then turned and pulled something out of his pocket, holding it up in one hand at waist level.

Sophie's heart stopped. A gun!

'No! Please . . . don't . . .' she cried in a voice that didn't seem to come from her, shrinking back against the door.

A long thin aerial, like a witch's finger, slid out of the black metal object, and Don Gowrie slowly swung round, pointing into each corner of both bedroom and bathroom. A low humming sound began and Sophie's heart beat slowed.

It wasn't a gun; it was some sort of electronic gadget. 'What . . . what are you doing?'

'Checking the place isn't bugged.'

'Bugged?' That idea had never occurred to her until that second. Her stomach clenched in sickness. What sort of world had she got herself into? Back home, as she was growing up, everyone knew they were living in an atmosphere of secrecy, spying, betrayal, but she hadn't expected to find the same fog poisoning American air.

'Colbourne is up to every trick in the book. I wouldn't put it past him to have this room bugged. This may look like a little toy but it's guaranteed to pick up the most sophisticated bug.' Sliding the gadget back into his jacket pocket, he coolly ordered, 'Close the curtains, will you?'

She stiffened. 'What?' Her skin went cold.

'Don't get ideas. I've no intention of harming you. It's another security measure. There could be someone in the building opposite with a camera with a telephoto lens trained on that window. They have equipment now which can pick up everything from half a mile away.' His mouth twisted. 'Wonderful world we live in, isn't it?' he added, oddly echoing her own thought a moment earlier.

'I'm beginning to think I hate it,' Sophie said soberly as she walked over to the window to pull the cord that drew the curtains together. The room behind her fell into shadow. She went back to the door and switched on the central light, feeling weird to be doing that in the middle of the day.

Don Gowrie sat down in the one armchair, beside the little table on which you could eat a meal sent up by Room Service. 'I've only got five minutes free. We must talk quickly.'

'I want to see my sister.' She hoped she sounded calm; in fact she was still very nervous because of what she knew about this man. He had a lot to lose and was totally without scruple. Sophie knew she would have to watch him like a hawk.

Crossing one leg over the other, he contemplated the polished black cap of a swinging shoe. 'Your mother is still in the Czech Republic. I checked.'

That was when Sophie felt a flicker of alarm for her mother. Why had he checked on her? Her mouth went dry.

'If you hurt my mother, I'll kill you myself!'

'Don't threaten me. Your mother and I had a deal. Part of the deal was that she swore never to tell a living soul. She had no right to tell you, especially now, after all these years.'

'You have a nerve! How dare you talk about her that way? You took advantage of her! You knew she was almost out of her mind over my father's death that day, that she was ill and worried, and didn't know what she was doing. She would never have let you steal her baby if she hadn't been so upset.'

His face turned dark red. 'I didn't steal Cathy!'

Sophie bristled, hating to hear him use that name. 'Don't call her that. Her name's Anya.'

'She's Cathy to me! And I did not steal her. Your mother has obviously forgotten how she felt back then. It's a long time ago. But she was desperate – the Russians had just invaded, your father had been killed, your mother was expecting any minute, she had no money, she was terrified, didn't know what to do. She begged me for help.'

'And you saw your opportunity! Your own child had died, you needed a child to take her place, so you talked my mother into letting you take Anya. She's never forgiven herself for being so weak.'

Sophie remembered her mother's face as she confessed that Anya was not dead, was alive and living in America. Mamma had blamed herself, but Sophie didn't, she blamed Don Gowrie. The sister she had mourned as dead all these years, had loved without ever knowing, who had been her comfort when she was lonely, her one real friend all her life was not dead after all. It had been like hearing the grave open.

Sophie hadn't been able to take it in at first. If she had had a sister during her childhood everything would have been so different. She would not have been so lonely, she wouldn't have felt left out of the family circle of her mother and stepfather and their boys. She would have had her sister for support. How many times as a child had she wished that Anya had not died? Having her wish come true after all those years, in such a strange way, had left her dazed.

Especially when her mother huskily went on, 'Sophie, I must see her again – you see, I'm ill, very ill . . .'

Sophie had looked at her sharply, hearing a note in her voice that sent a shiver of premonition through her.

'What is it? What's wrong with you, Mamma?'

'Leukaemia.'

Sophie had taken a shocked breath, staring at her pallor, the dark shadows under her eyes, an air of exhaustion, a lack of energy she had noticed the minute she arrived back home. Her mother had never been a big woman, but she had visibly lost a lot of weight since Sophie last saw her, she had shrunk away to nothing.

'Is it . . . serious?' she whispered, but she guessed the answer before her mother spoke.

'The doctors have given me three months.'

'Three months . . .' That was an even bigger shock.

'They said I should have seen them sooner. The illness has gone too far, there's nothing they can do for me now.'

'But surely they are trying something? Can't you have some treatment? Chemotherapy? There must be something.' Her mother's resignation made Sophie burn with rage. 'Don't just give in, Mamma. See the doctors again – make them try to help you.'

Her mother had gestured wearily, not wanting to talk about her illness. 'Never mind that, Sophie. Listen, you must find Anya, bring her back to me – I can't die without seeing her one more time, I've never forgotten her, tell her that, she was my first baby, I remember her more and more. I must see her. Promise me you'll find her and bring her back to me.'

Sophie had nodded, her eyes insistent. 'Yes, I'll promise to do that, Mamma, if you promise me you'll go to see your doctors again, at once, and ask them for treatment.'

Her mother had promised and when Sophie had talked to her again last week on the phone Mamma had said she was having fortnightly treatments at the local hospital. 'They exhaust me, I get so sick afterwards, though,' she had whispered, and Sophie had winced at the weakness of her voice.

'Don't give up going, Mamma,' she had pleaded, and her mother had promised she wouldn't.

'Have you found Anya yet?'

'I shall see Gowrie in three days' time. Don't worry, I'll soon have news for you. You'll see Anya soon, I promise.'

She had made that promise to a dying woman, but she made it for herself too. She had begun to realize that when she found her sister she could talk to the living, not the dead; could see Anya face to face, hear Anya's voice answering her.

Don Gowrie got up from his chair and began restlessly walking round and round the room, to the door and back, to the bathroom and back, like an animal in a cage. She felt the frustrated rage from him, the scent of danger, and watched him anxiously.

'Why in God's name did she tell you after all this time? Why couldn't she go on keeping her mouth shut? I kept my side of the bargain. She's had a small fortune from me over the years.'

'Is that all you think counts? Money?' Sophie felt her chest tear with contempt and anger and grief. All these years she had thought her sister was dead, and she was alive, and all this man could talk about was money. 'My mother loved Anya –' she began and he broke in hoarsely.

'I love her too, do you think I don't? Not in the beginning, OK, not then, I hardly knew her at first, but I learnt to love her as if she was my own. I forgot she wasn't. My God, this happened nearly thirty years ago.' He swung and glared at her. 'Your whole lifetime! Have you thought of that? You hadn't even been born, I've had all those years with Cathy and –'

'And we haven't!' Sophie was trembling with indignation. 'My mother hasn't set eyes on her own child all this time. I haven't seen my own sister!'

'If you care about your sister you wouldn't be here!' Don Gowrie said grimly, and Sophie froze, looking at him with pain, feeling a thorn pierce her heart.

He nodded at her. 'Don't look at me like that – you know it's true. I'm terrified for her. What do you think it will do to her, to find out she isn't who she thinks she is? You just arrive, after all these years, full of self-righteousness, talking like some avenging angel, demanding to see her, wanting her to know she is your sister – and if you tell her, you'll destroy her life.'

'My mother is dying,' Sophie said fiercely.

He stared at her, his breathing audible.

'She has leukaemia, and has been given three months to live. She wants to see her daughter again before she dies.'

'God,' he said in a low, shaken voice. 'I'm sorry. I'm very sorry, but . . . look, it isn't going to save your mother's life if she sees Cathy, but it will ruin Cathy's life. She has grown up believing herself to be my daughter, believing herself to be Eddie Ramsey's granddaughter, and his heir. Now you're going to take all that away from her.'

Sophie was icy cold now. Her knees were trembling; she sat down suddenly on the end of her bed.

He watched her stricken face, nodding. 'You're going to change the way she sees herself, her whole life, how she sees me and her mother, her grandfather, everything she has grown up believing to be her family, her history, her roots.'

Confusedly, Sophie muttered, 'But they aren't . . . she isn't . . .'

'But she believes they are! You're going to take away her past and her future.'

Sophie looked at him dumbly.

He searched her face, his own tight, sombre, angry. 'You stupid woman, you haven't even thought about what havoc you'll cause, have you? You'll bring Cathy's whole world crashing down. For a start, you don't know Eddie Ramsey. He won't leave his money to her once he knows she isn't his flesh and blood.'

'He need never know! Cathy could come and see my mother, just once, and Eddie Ramsey doesn't have to be told anything about it.'

'You talk so glibly about it all – if Cathy finds out how long will it be before she gives it away somehow? She's a woman. Women can never keep secrets.'

'You just don't know women! They keep secrets all their life. Look at the way my mother kept your secret! Nearly thirty years!'

'She should have taken it to the grave!' he snapped, then realized what he had said, looked self-conscious and plunged on, 'And then there's her marriage – what will the truth do to that? How will her husband feel when he finds out that he is married to a totally different person to the woman he thought he'd married? He's this classy Englishman, upper-class, rich, who thinks he married a girl from his own background, a girl with a huge fortune coming to her one day. He didn't bargain for waking up married to some nobody from nowhere with not a penny to her name.'

Sophie's mind clouded with doubt. She wished she could deny what Gowrie was saying, throw it back into his teeth. She wanted to see her sister face-to-face so badly that she had convinced herself that Anya would feel the same, but what if Anya refused to believe her? In her position, would anyone want to believe a story that could destroy their entire life?

Don Gowrie came and sat down next to her on the bed, took both her hands. She stiffened, pulling her hands free. He wasn't getting round her; she already knew he was a consummate politician, you couldn't take anything he said or did at face value.

'You've heard your mother's version, it's only fair you should hear mine now,' he said quietly. 'Just listen, please. It was 1968. I only arrived in Prague that summer. I was a young and ambitious diplomat, East Europe was my special interest and I was thrilled to be sent to Prague. It was an exciting city to be living in at that time. The students were always out in the streets, in the cafés, playing music, playing chess and talking politics, talking about freedom and justice and the right to determine your own fate. They made me think in a way I'd never thought before – made me realize how lucky I was, as an American, how many things I'd taken for granted. My country had never been invaded, held down, oppressed. Freedom was my birthright but I'd never even thought about it, I'd always taken it for granted, like the air I breathed. That year was a turning point in my life for many reasons.' He paused, sighing, staring at the floor, his face grim.

Sophie waited, not liking to break into his thoughts, wondering what visions of the past he saw. Not pretty ones, from his expression.

'It was a very hot August,' he slowly began again. 'Prague was crowded, the streets were cobbled, traffic made a hell of a racket on them, my wife was delicate, even then, and couldn't stand the city heat, the noise and traffic. More and more she stayed indoors, homesick, miserable – it wasn't good for her, or for our child.'

Sophie had heard her mother's version of this – Mamma had said Mrs Gowrie was highly strung, a hysteric, her moods always changing, weeping or laughing for no reason. She had spent a lot of time lying down on a sofa or not even getting up in the mornings, spending days in bed at times.

Don Gowrie sighed, his face setting into weary lines. 'I wanted to send her back to the States, and the child too, but she didn't want to go alone. She wanted me to come with her, and of course I couldn't, I had a job to do. So she wouldn't go either. I should have insisted.' He rubbed a hand across his eyes as if they were sore, and the rims were red as if he had been crying.

Sophie felt sorry for him; the charmer, the plausible politician had gone and in their place was a real man who was full of anger and pain.

'But if I talked about it she just started to cry,' he said. 'And I was afraid to let her work herself into a crying jag, that always made her worse. I'd got into the habit of giving in to her; it made life easier. So I let her stay, but it seemed better for her to be out of the city, so I looked around for a house somewhere in the country. I knew a scientist who was working in Prague at the university. He offered me his cottage in your village, Kysella. It was a small place: a couple of bedrooms, a sitting-room, a kitchen, but it had a bathroom, and there was a delightful garden; I remember a hedge of honeysuckle, the scent was overpowering on hot nights . . . and roses, old-fashioned roses, big red and pink ones, with an incredible perfume.'

His face was dreamy. Watching him, Sophie said quietly, 'It isn't there any more. My mother told me it was pulled down in the Seventies when they built a new road.'

He came out of his memories and grimaced. 'Really? That's progress for you. They tear your life up behind you as you live it. You never have time to visit your own past these days – it has usually gone when you go back there. I remember that house so well. It was a mistake for me to rent it, though. My wife wasn't strong enough to run the house herself, or even take care of our little girl – we had brought a nanny with us from the States but she got home-sick after a few weeks. She gave notice and went home. We asked the village priest to recommend someone to help out, and he suggested your mother because she was the only woman in the village who spoke any English.'

'Yes, she learnt it from my father's books – he was a linguist, you know, he could speak half a dozen languages.'

'I never met him, but I remember my wife said your mother talked about him all the time.'

Her mother had desperately wanted to keep up with him, feeling that in going away to university he was leaving her far behind. When he'd had his degree he would have been able to start a good career, earn a lot of money, so she put up with their separations for months on end, but she was conscious of the gap between them and wanted to bridge it.

Pavel Narodni had been clever and ambitious, a young man with a brilliant mind. He had had a wonderful future ahead of him, and his wife had wanted to fit herself to share it.

Lucky we can't see the future, Sophie thought; at least she had a few happy years, without any premonitions of his death during those awful days when the Russians invaded. She loved him so much – she never felt that way about Franz, I'd stake my life on it. She was fond of him, yes, but she wasn't passionately in love, the way she was with my father. Even now, when she speaks about Papa, her eyes glow.

'My wife couldn't speak Czech although she had a little German,' said Don Gowrie. 'Of course, German was the second language to most people in your part of the country. I spoke Czech but I was rarely there. I didn't know your mother too well; I interviewed her when she first started work for us and I saw her briefly whenever I came down to Kysella, but when I was there she kept out of the way most of the time to give me time alone with my wife and our child.'

'Mamma says your little girl loved to play with Anya,' Sophie volunteered.

He looked blank. 'I guess she did, but not often when I was there. But Elly started helping your mother with her English; it gave her something to do. She was lonely out there in the country, but she couldn't bear living the life of a diplomat's wife. They have a lot of socialising, you know; in foreign countries they tend to live in each other's pockets, endless parties and chit-chat. Elly hated that. She wanted peace and quiet, she went for long walks through the fields, she rambled in the woods near the village. Early nights and early mornings suited her, not parties and drinking and gossip. And she took to your mother from the start. They had more in common than you'd think. They were both mothers of little girls the same age and they both had husbands whose work took them away a lot of the time.'

And did they both feel uneasy about keeping up with a husband whose ambition drove him? Afraid that they would let him down, that his lifestyle would never suit them? Did Don Gowrie make his wife feel that, for all her family money, she was somehow a failure?

Sophie watched him, wondering what sort of man he really was behind his politician's mask, behind the charm and good manners, the carefully chosen words, the coaxing smiles. Had he loved his wife? Did he still love her? Had he loved their child, or had she only been a means to an end – the necessary child he had to have to make certain of the Ramsey fortune? If only she knew for certain, because the next obvious question was: did he love Anya? Or was she also just a means to an end? Was the Ramsey money all he had ever cared about?

'And then there was an outbreak of measles in the village,' he said flatly. 'And Cathy went down with them. My wife went into panic immediately, she always did where illness was concerned, for herself or me or the child. Elly had always been delicate herself; she was ill a good deal during her own childhood, she grew up a bit of a hypochondriac. The local doctor didn't speak English, but your mother translated for them both. The man told my wife to keep Cathy in a darkened room, to avoid problems with her eyesight, and keep her away from other children.'

'Didn't your wife send for you?'

He hunched his shoulders, frowning. 'Yes, but we were short-handed; several members of staff were on vacation and I couldn't get away.'

He's guilty about that, thought Sophie. But does he admit as much, even to himself? The man is in denial about so many things – or has he a facility for ignoring what he finds uncomfortable to remember?

'A few days later, the Russians invaded,' he said, 'and there was utter panic in Prague. I was told to get out with my wife and child. I drove down at night to get Elly and the baby. When I got there I found Elly in a state of collapse and the baby dead.'

Sophie flinched. 'How terrible.'

Without looking at her, he went on, in a flat voice, 'Your mother told me the baby's temperature had soared overnight; she had tried to get a doctor, but the local man had gone off to Prague to help in the hospital where he had trained, they were asking for volunteers because they thought there might be a lot of casualties. In fact, there were very few deaths, you know – only a handful of people were killed.' He stopped, made a face, said, 'Anyway, your mother did everything she could, but she didn't know what was wrong, she gave the baby aspirin and tried to get the temperature down by bathing her with a sponge and luke-warm water, but she couldn't get the temperature down, and an hour before I arrived the baby had died.'

He stopped talking, and Sophie was so upset herself that she couldn't look at him. She sat staring at the floor, hearing him breathe roughly.

When he started talking again it made her nerves jump like a needle on a scratchy record.

'Elly was crazy,' he said. 'Hysterical. Screaming. Your mother and I both tried to calm her down, but we couldn't get through to her. I didn't even have time to think about the baby, about the death; I was too busy trying to look after Elly and not having a clue what to do for her. Then your sister came toddling into the room and Elly gave a gasp and ran to pick her up, sat there rocking her and crying.'

Poor woman, thought Sophie.

'I tried to talk to her, but she didn't seem to see or hear me. It was as if I wasn't there. She just kept kissing the little girl, saying Cathy's name over and over again. I knew you weren't really dead, she said, I knew it wasn't true. Then it dawned on me – she thought your sister was Cathy. My wife's a hysteric, you see; and hysterics know they are half-acting, they know they could stop if they tried, but it helps them cope with what they can't bear, what they find intolerable.'

'A sort of refuge,' Sophie said, understanding. 'A sanctuary from what they find too terrifying to face.'

The more he talked about his wife the more Sophie understood how it had all happened. The woman was neurotic and out of touch with reality. What sort of marriage had it been for him? She couldn't help feeling sorry for him.

He had paid a very high price for the money and power her family could give him. He had no child of his own and his marriage must always have been a sham. She had not heard love in his voice when he talked of his wife. She had heard impatience, pity, irritation – but not love.

'Yes, I suppose that describes it,' he said, absently, as if he wasn't really listening, was still locked back there in the past. 'Elly didn't want to believe her child was dead, she knew she could never have another one and she couldn't bear to face up to what had happened. The two children were very much alike, you see; the same colouring and size, much the same age. Elly wanted to believe it was Cathy – or maybe in her state of mind she no longer knew what was real and what wasn't.'

'So you asked my mother to let you swap the children – you left her a dead child to bury as her own, and you took Anya away with you.' Sophie couldn't help the harsh, accusing tone. Her mother had been haunted all her life by what happened that day; she had lived a lie and it had festered under the skin of her mind. Sophie remembered those visits to the grave in the little church just down the road, she remembered the day her mother stopped visiting the grave, almost never went near it again. What Don Gowrie did had destroyed their family.

She had lived a lie. Perhaps it might also explain her fatal illness? She was dying with a sickness of the blood, her

141

whole body poisoned, as her mind had been poisoned with regret for so long.

Sophie had always believed her mother stopped visiting Papa and Anya's grave because Johanna had married again and wanted to forget her first husband. But it hadn't been that at all. She could not bear to remember Anya, or her own weakness in letting her child be taken away. What Don Gowrie did had destroyed their family, not the death of Pavel Narodni. When her mother married again, started a new family and deliberately turned her back on her dead first husband, her dead first child, Sophie had felt that her mother had turned her back on her, too, because she was a reminder of the wrecked family her mother wanted to forget.

If Don Gowrie had stolen Anya out of love for his wife, Sophie might forgive him, but she couldn't forget that Don Gowrie's whole future lay in having an heir to the Ramsey fortune. He had to have a child, a living child; and it obviously hadn't bothered him at all to walk away from his dead child and let her be buried in a foreign country, under a stranger's name. She did not believe he loved his wife, and he certainly had not, could not, have loved his child.

'All you thought about was yourself!' she threw at him, and he heard the contempt in her voice and went red then white.

'Don't judge me! You weren't there. Elly wouldn't let go of the child, she screamed and fought when I tried to take it away from her. I was terrified she was mad. Then your mother got the news that your father had been killed, and she collapsed, too. She begged me for help, I think she had some idea of going to America with us, but of course the Russians would never have let her leave. But she was desperate . . . that was when I thought of swapping the children.'

'You talk as if they were toys,' Sophie muttered, looking

142

at him with dislike. 'How could you do that to a woman who had just lost her husband?'

'I was doing her a favour, I was taking your sister to a life of luxury, where she would never want for anything, would be loved and cared for, and would grow up in freedom. Whatever your mother says now, she knows our bargain wasn't one-sided.'

'You pushed her into making a snap decision when she was in shock!'

'She wanted her child to have a better life than she could give it. I looked after her, and you – when you arrived. Your lives would have been very different if I had not helped you both.'

Sophie knew he was telling the truth; her mother had told her he had kept his side of the bargain, for the next few years had sent money which made it possible for them to live comfortably until she married Franz.

'Maybe that's true, but the price was too high. You could at least have let my mother know how Anya was! All these years, she was dying to know what she looked like, how she was doing at school, if you had only sent a photo once in a while. But total silence was cruel.'

'It was part of the bargain. Her child was dead, as far as everyone was concerned, and she had to keep up that pretence, had to believe it herself. I didn't want her to think about Cathy.' He stared insistently at Sophie. 'And you have to stop thinking about her, too! For her sake, as well as your own and your mother's.'

'Don't threaten me!'

'I'm just warning you . . .'

'Do you think I don't know why someone tried to push me under a train!'

He went very pale, his eyes alarmed. 'I swear on my word of honour I had nothing to do with whatever happened to you in the subway. I only heard about it afterwards.'

143

She had no doubt he was a liar, but if this was acting it was good. The best. Sophie looked at him uncertainly, wondering how she could believe him, yet half-convinced.

'But there are people who are not too happy about your interference, at this precise moment,' he said very quietly. 'There's a lot of money riding on me, you know. I have powerful friends, wealthy friends, who are prepared to back my bid for the presidency – and they are not men who have many scruples about ways and means.'

She shivered. 'You *are* threatening me.'

'A warning isn't a threat. And anyway, if you care at all about Cathy you'll leave her alone!'

'I care about my mother more than anything else. My mother needs to see her – to know that she is OK, that she's happy.'

'Of course she's happy, she's married, she loves her husband, of course she's happy! You don't know what you're doing. Go back to the Czech Republic and forget about the past. You have a life of your own to live. You're a clever girl – why not start your own business back home? I'd be happy to help you. How much would you need?'

'I don't want your money! You can't buy me!' Sophie had come here to America on a quest and she wasn't yet ready to give up that quest. It wasn't simply that she had to fulfil the promise she had made to her dying mother. The truth had changed the way she saw her life. She was in search of something indefinable; in search of that first happiness, the family she had lost all those years ago, her mother, most of all, until she had remarried and built herself a new family, and the dead father and dead sister whom death had made unchanging, who had never deserted her the way her mother had. Finding out that Anya was alive somewhere had shaken the kaleidoscope of time, whirled the coloured fragments of her life into a new pattern, strange, bewildering, making her see herself and the past in an entirely new light.

'Is there a man in your life back home? If you were thinking of getting married, you would need somewhere to live, wouldn't you? I could do a lot for you, Sophie.'

'I just want you to help me meet my sister,' she stubbornly repeated. 'I promise I won't tell her anything, not without telling you first, but I must meet her, talk to her. You owe me that.'

He lost his temper then, snarling at her. 'I don't owe you anything! Stay away from me and my family or you'll regret it!'

'You don't frighten me. I'm going to see Anya whatever you say or do – nobody is going to stop me.'

He stared at her, his face clenched in rage, then walked out, slamming the door after him.

Steve walked out of the hotel lift. Under his arm he held the big buff envelope containing the enlarged photographs of Sophie's family. He had called in on Lilli half an hour ago, given her back the big black wheel, shown her the photographs – but they had meant no more to her than the originals. He could tell from her wry expression that she thought he was barking up the wrong tree, and maybe he was. But he had this strong sense that the photos meant something – or why would the men who ransacked Sophie's room have taken them? Steve always played his hunches. In his business, instincts could mean the difference between getting a story and missing it.

On his way to his room he heard the click of a door opening. A door across the corridor from his own. His whole body jerked in alarm as Don Gowrie came out from the room, glanced quickly, almost furtively, both ways. What the hell had he been doing in Sophie's room?

At that instant a door on Steve's right opened and a

blonde swayed there, giving him the impression she was holding on to the door to stop herself falling down. A transparent black nylon négligé clung to her like a second skin, showing the whole of her full-breasted, long-legged showgirl body as if it was naked.

'Hey, bud, got a lemon?' she throatily murmured, and Steve blinked.

'Sorry? What did you say?'

The blonde gave him what was obviously meant to be a seductive smile. 'I was just going to have another gin, but I'm plumb out of lemons.' She looked him up and down through half-closed eyes with improbably long lashes. 'Hey, you're cute – come on in and have a drink with me.'

'Sorry, I'm busy just now – ring Room Service.'

'Well, fuck you,' she said, but Steve was already loping away towards Sophie's room, his heart thudding with anxiety.

There was now no sign of Gowrie. Steve banged on her door with a clenched fist and kept on banging until the door was yanked open and he almost banged on her nose.

Relief made him feel sick; his head had been full of images that terrified him, seeing her alive made him suddenly angry.

'What was he doing here?'

'Don't you yell at me!'

They were yelling at each other, neither listening to the other or answering.

'Oh, for God's sake!' Steve shouldered his way into the room, moving her bodily aside to do it.

'Get out!' she yelled.

'Not until you've told me what he was doing here!'

'Talking. We were talking.'

Suspicions began to colour his mind; he looked at her, eyes hard, angry, remembering what he had thought when he saw the way Gowrie looked at her during the press conference yesterday afternoon. So much had happened since; his first impressions had been overlaid by a hundred others, but now he said curtly, 'You are his mistress, aren't you?'

'Oh, for God's sake!' She walked away towards the window and looked out at the cloudy sky, the geometric skyline, roofs, towers, pinnacles, and between them the leafy maze of Central Park like a moving mirage.

He watched her warmly curved body and hated the thought of it in Gowrie's arms. Looking at her bed he saw the tumbled sheets and his stomach heaved. 'Have you just had sex with him?'

'You've got a nasty, dirty little mind.' She didn't turn to look at him even now, and it was beginning to annoy him, being ignored like that. She couldn't even be bothered to look at him and he wanted her to, he wanted to force her to acknowledge him. His body was throbbing with awareness of her – how could she be so totally unconscious of him?

'Something is going on between you and Gowrie. Don't bother to lie. And somebody tried to kill you yesterday. Why? And who burgled your apartment? Somebody wrecked the place, tore it to pieces. Don't try to kid me they were both coincidences.'

She turned then; he saw a shudder run down her throat. 'Wrecked the apartment?' Her face was white as scraped bone.

He wished he hadn't told her, but too late now; and maybe she should know. Shouldering out of his overcoat, he dropped it on a chair to give himself time to think what to say to her, then looked at her searchingly.

'Look, Sophie, you are fishing in dangerous waters. Gowrie is an ambitious man with a lot to lose. If you're wise you'll stay away from Gowrie. I know him, I've known him and his daughter all my life. My father's a lifelong Republican, he's worked with Gowrie for years, Dad knows what sort of guy the man is. Gowrie plays hardball.' He paused, frowning, visibly hesitating, then said offhandedly, 'For instance, I knew a guy once who was in love with Gowrie's daughter, but Gowrie didn't think he was good enough for her, he didn't have the right connections, or the money and influence Gowrie wanted for his daughter, so he saw to it that she married someone else, someone Gowrie approved of. The man's ruthless, you see. He'll stop at nothing.'

Sophie stared at him, her woman's intuition making her wonder if Steve's 'friend' had been Steve himself. There had been a harshness, an undercurrent of real bitterness, in his voice while he talked about it.

'Was your friend badly hurt? I mean . . . was he very much in love with her?' she gently asked, and saw his face tighten and turn cold.

'He felt he'd been kicked in the guts, yes.'

'It was you, wasn't it?' she whispered and their eyes met. She read the truth in his eyes, then he scowled, looking away, angry pride in his face.

'It was all a long time ago,' he bit out, his voice rough with what she suspected might be pain. Was he still in love with her? How strange, thought Sophie – he was in love with my sister, with Anya, although he doesn't know it. She felt a strange intimacy in talking to him about it while he had no idea of the true identity of Cathy – there was a surreal feel to that. Identity was so vital – if you didn't know who you were or where you belonged you would be lost, alone in a hostile universe. When she was very small she had often felt like that; afraid and isolated. She never wanted to feel that way again.

Angrily, Steve said, 'We're talking about you. Don't try to side-track me. I warned you not to open your door to anyone. Why did you let him in here?'

'He stood outside and said, "Little pig, little pig, let me in, let me in . . ."' She laughed wildly; he didn't.

'It isn't funny!' His voice rose sharply. 'Tell me the truth, Sophie. What is going on?'

'I can't tell you!'

'Why not? Is it his secret – or yours?' Steve said, still angry, and saw tears slip into her eyes, shining like a glaze over the porcelain blue.

Steve took the steps between them so fast he hardly knew he was moving, dropped the buff envelope of photos on the table and reached for her.

'Don't cry.' He put his arms round her and felt her trembling. 'What is all this? Why can't you tell me?' he murmured, his cheek against her soft hair, breathing in a fragrance that reminded him of spring, of wildflowers, sweet meadow air. She leaned on him and his heart quickened.

'I'm scared,' she whispered, looking up, her pale pink mouth quivering.

Steve kissed it, knowing he had been waiting to do that ever since he first saw her, and felt her lips tremble even more. She had her eyes shut and she wasn't pulling away, she was leaning towards him. Her breath tasted of peppermint; toothpaste, he thought, his kiss deepening, opening her mouth wider, his tongue slipping between her lips. Her body was shaking more than ever; suddenly he realized she was giving at the knees as if she was about to faint.

Steve picked her up, lifting her feet off the floor, his arm underneath her knees.

'What are you doing?' Her eyes flew open, alarm in them.

Without answering, he carried her to the bed and laid her down on it, going down with her, leaning over her to kiss her again. His face had filled with hot blood.

Desire had hit him with the force of a tidal wave, tearing him from the moorings of common sense and reason, carrying him into wilder regions than any he had ever

149

visited. He had never wanted any woman this badly, so badly he was feverish and couldn't think straight.

He shrugged off his jacket and let it fall to the floor, his hands shaking as he pushed up the thin, ribbed cotton sweater, slid his hands inside it, caressing her naked midriff, the smooth, soft skin clinging to his fingers.

'No,' she said, suddenly pushing at his shoulders. 'No.'

Steve lifted his head and looked at her, his eyes dark with need. She stared into those eyes and fell silent as she read his feelings in his face.

'The first time I saw you, I wanted to make love to you,' he whispered. 'You're beautiful, Sophie.'

'Thank you, but don't bother with the compliments,' she tartly said, wriggling from under him, sliding off the bed until she could stand up. 'Sorry, but I'm not the easy lay you seem to hope I am.'

He sat up, flushed and furious. 'For God's sake . . . what on earth gives you the idea I think that?'

'You accused me of being Gowrie's mistress. You think anyone can get me into bed.'

He was urgent to get her back into his arms, but he realized he wouldn't now and his blood began to cool. Flatly, he said, 'I never said that! I didn't think it, either.'

'Oh, yes, you did, Mr Colbourne, and I didn't like it. Get out of here, will you?' Sophie was completely in control now. She zipped up her jeans, pulling down her sweater, turning angry, darkened eyes on him. 'I shall start counting to ten – if you aren't out of here by the time I've finished I'll start screaming next.'

Steve got up reluctantly, his tie hanging loose, his shirt half-out of his trousers, and straightened his clothes. 'You're wrong about me, Sophie,' he said flatly. 'OK, I want to make love to you, but I don't think you're a push-over. Say no, if you like, but say it for the right reasons – because you don't want to go to bed with me, not because you have the wrong idea about my motives or my opinion of you.'

'Did you treat Cathy Gowrie that way? Did you try to get her into bed almost the minute you met her?' Asking that question made her realize with a shock of disbelief that she was jealous – but how could she be jealous of Anya, who she had come so far to find, had been aching to meet at last? Her own emotions bewildered and scared her. How could you feel so many contradictory reactions at once?

He slowly turned, running a hand over his ruffled dark hair, walked towards her with the silent lope of a hunter, his long body graceful and deadly.

She stiffened, alarm leaping into her throat.

He paused and looked down at her, his eyes angry. 'Forget everything I said about Cathy Gowrie – do you hear me? Forget I ever mentioned her.'

'Have you forgotten her?' she threw back with the force of the jealousy she felt, and saw his face quiver.

He stared into her blue eyes fixedly, then suddenly smiled. 'I've known Cathy most of my life, since we were both kids. I'll never forget her, how could I? I'm very fond of her. But I'm not in love with her.'

She watched him, wondering if he was lying, but not knowing because she didn't know him well enough.

He stared back at her, his face calm now, then moved away, walked over to the table and picked up the buff envelope he had dropped there. 'I brought these to show you.' He tipped them out on the polished surface; they fanned out, glossy prints, the faces grainy and surreal.

She hesitated. 'Photos? Of what?' But after a pause she joined him, picked up one of the photos with a sharp intake of air as she recognized what she was looking at.

'Where did you get it?' Her eyes flicked to the others, her face puzzled, startled. 'Are these all my family photos?'

'Yes, I had them reproduced from Lilli's wheel. Your

151

family photos were stolen from the apartment and I wondered if there was any significance in that, if there was any
reason why someone should want photos of your family to
vanish. They hadn't realized Lilli was doing this collage
thing – I found it on the floor and took it away with me,
with her permission, to have the faces blown up and
printed.'

She picked up the one of the baby, her hand shaking,
stared at it; suddenly her eyes filled with tears.

Steve wanted to put an arm round her, to comfort her,
but he didn't want her accusing him of opportunism again,
or pushing him away, so he just stood there watching her
with anxious sympathy, his own throat salting up.

Huskily he said, 'That's your little sister who died, isn't
it?'

She touched the baby face with one finger, head bent.
'Anya,' she said. 'Yes, that's her, taken on her second
birthday.'

Steve looked at the laughing little face of a child with
curling dark hair, wide-spaced eyes. He had looked at it
several times since he got the photos, but suddenly he felt
an odd flash of déjà vu, a memory he couldn't track back.
He had seen a very similar picture somewhere before. But
he couldn't remember where or when – or was he simply
remembering seeing the wraith-like photocopy set in Lilli's
wheel? Or maybe he was seeing this dead child through
Sophie's eyes by some sort of osmosis or sympathetic
magic. He seemed to himself always to be trying to understand her, work out what she was feeling and thinking –
perhaps he had begun to pick up what was happening
inside her head and heart?

It was strange, though, that she was so distressed by
seeing a picture of a child who had died before she was
born. What did the dead child mean to her to upset her like
this?

'I'm having another set of photos printed,' he told her gently. 'You can keep these. Maybe soon you'll trust me enough to tell me why the originals were stolen from the apartment.'

He waited a moment but she didn't answer or even look up, so eventually he walked away. He was almost at the door when Sophie whispered, 'I'm sorry. I do trust you . . . I think I do . . . but I still can't tell you, I can't tell anyone.'

Don Gowrie lay on his back watching the gleam of pale, pearly flesh and black lace suspenders holding up black silk stockings, as it climbed on top of him.

'She wouldn't let me buy her off, she wouldn't go back where she came from, she wouldn't swear not to tell Cathy,' he said, his voice thick with rage and frustration. 'She's going to get to her somehow, whatever I say or do. I can't stop her because I can't tell Cathy or her husband why I want to keep this girl away from Cathy. And she's going to tell her, and that will bring everything crashing down on all of us.'

A scarlet-nailed hand trailed slowly down his belly and his flesh hardened and lifted as the fingertips brushed it. 'My way is the only way, you know that. Let me deal with it.'

He closed his eyes to enjoy the sensations pulsing through him. 'You tried once and you failed. All that achieved was to make Steve Colbourne curious, the last thing I need.'

The stroking hand was joined by a hot, moist mouth; he groaned suddenly with sharp, intense pleasure.

'Good?' whispered the mouth, licking him.

Good,' he gasped. 'Ah . . . yes . . .'

'I won't fail next time. Trust me. She won't ever reach London,' the reddened, glossy lips whispered as they began to suck.

He began to pant, groaning, his mouth wide open. 'Ahhhh . . .' His mind stopped working; he gave himself up to the expert, tormenting mouth and tongue, shuddering violently, jerking, as the liquid heat finally gushed out of him.

His deep grunts of satisfaction dying away, he lay there, breathing audibly, still and flaccid, eyes shut, sated and at rest for a while. He needed the release, the letting go, the brief peace. The strain of his life was sometimes unbearable, weighing down on him until he was bowed down with it. Only this brief, ecstatic pleasure could help when it got too much.

Slowly his mind began to work again, to worry, question. 'I'm not sure. Do we have to go that far? She says she only wants to see Cathy. What if it's true? What if she doesn't mean to tell Cathy the truth? I wish I knew for certain what was best. Maybe there's some other way of dealing with this? If only she wasn't so obstinate. God, why is this happening? Why now? It's like some crazy doomsday judgment. It isn't fair. Just when I need everything to go right for me.'

'Crawling out of the woodwork like a bug.' The other body slid off the bed; gathered up clothes, a suit, a shirt, a tie. 'You know what you do with bugs. You squash them. Ruthlessly. You can't waste time arguing over the moral rights and wrongs. You just stamp on them. Isn't Colbourne going to be at this dinner tonight?'

'He's on the press guest list.'

'Then I'll deal with her tonight, while he's out of the way.'

'Be careful,' Don said, as he had said before, but with more violence. 'For Christ's sweet sake, be very careful.'

Sophie was watching TV when the phone rang, making her jump and look at it as if it was an exploding bomb. Who could that be? She wasn't expecting a call.

Then she remembered that she had rung Vladimir. She got up and ran to pick the phone up, saying breathlessly, 'Hello?'

It wasn't Vlad, it was Lilli, sounding very cheerful. 'Sophie, Theo and I are downstairs in the lobby – are you in bed, or are you up and dressed?'

'I'm up and dressed. This is nice of you. Come on up.'

'No, listen – I wondered, have you eaten? Because we thought we could eat down here. The main restaurants are out of our price bracket, but there's a trattoria in a corner of the lobby, and the menu prices aren't bad at all, for a hotel like this. Are you hungry? Will you come down and join us?'

'Give me two seconds,' she said. 'I'll see you at the trattoria.'

It took her ten minutes, in fact, because she had to wash, change into something a little more stylish than jeans and a sweater, do her make-up and hair and spray on a little perfume.

Lilli eyed her from head to foot, taking in the pretty angora pink sweater, the cheap fake pearls which still managed to gleam softly against her skin, the dark grey straight skirt, the black high heels which made her long legs look slender and graceful. 'Well, you look better than the last time I saw you, in that hospital bed,' she said approvingly.

Theo's eyes were bright with male appreciation; he bent his grizzled grey head to kiss her hand with his usual heavy Continental gallantry.

'Ah, Sophie . . . even lovelier than usual.' He straightened, almost creaking, a hand at his back. Lilli claimed he wore a corset to maintain that upright, boyish figure now that he was nearly seventy and at times Sophie believed her. 'I was sorry, so sorry to hear about your accident. I would have sent you flowers but Lilli told me you were only staying in hospital one night. No ill-effects, huh?'

'I'm fine, thanks. How are you, Theo? You look wonder-ful. Retirement obviously suits you.'

'He hasn't retired,' snorted Lilli. 'He's moonlighting with half the media in New York, working odd shifts here, odd shifts there, picking up a story here, a story there, and little crumbs of income everywhere.'

'Time enough to retire when you're put in your coffin,' agreed Theo, beaming. 'I get bored doing nothing.'

Sophie glanced into the Italian restaurant and saw that it was filling up: there were not many tables free. 'Shall we go in and eat?'

'Yes, I'm starving,' Lilli agreed, pushing open the door and leading the way. 'Have you seen much of Steve?'

'Too much,' Sophie said, then wished she had not been so unguarded as Lilli gave her an amused, intrigued glance.

'You must tell us all about it over our pasta.'

Upstairs Sophie's bed was being made, her half-eaten food taken away, the fanned photographs on the table tidied into a neat pile, her damp towels removed and clean ones hung in their place. The maid straightened the chairs, closed the curtains and left one lamp lit before going out and closing the door. She continued on to the next room, pushing her trolley, laden with sheets, towels, soap, plastic shower caps, tiny sachets of shampoo and bath foam.

It took her nearly an hour to do all the rooms on the floor. When she had vanished again, her trolley creaking to rest in the staffroom near the lifts, the corridor was quiet. Most guests were out at dinner. A few were eating in their rooms, watching TV.

A tall figure in a black jogging suit came out of the lift and walked quickly to the room next door to Sophie's, using a key card to get in, closing the door again almost silently.

Inside the room the figure moved to a door connecting

this room with Sophie's, getting a thin strip of metal from a pocket. Softly the metal slid between lock and frame, there was a click and the door opened.

Moving very fast, the intruder went into Sophie's room, then paused, flashing a rapid glance around, taking in the empty tidiness, the made-up bed, the closed curtains, the faint glow of lamplight.

Even from the other side of the room it was obvious that the bathroom, too, was empty. The door was open and no light showed, there was no sound from there, either.

Where was she? At dinner? Would she come back alone – or with someone? Was she sleeping with the journalist who had booked her in to the room? Was he just intrigued by her? Or was he in on the secret now?

The intruder walked around the room, frustrated, angry, then stopped by the table to stare down at the photos, gathered them all up to look closer. What the hell was this? The strange, grainy reproductions, all in black and white, lacking depth, took a moment to identify. Photocopies. That was what they were. Photocopies of the photographs that had been taken from the girl's apartment. They must have been taken before the burglary. But why?

Hearing a sound out in the corridor, voices, laughter, the intruder froze, listened intently, poised to act or flee. A man's deep voice said, 'Give me your key, Sophie,' and the silent eavesdropper moved hurriedly to the door leading to the other room, slid through it and closed it without making a sound. No point in hanging around here if she had company. If it was Colbourne, he might stay all night.

They would have to wait and get her in London before she could contact Cathy.

6

Sophie was astonished to discover that she and Steve and the rest of his TV crew were on the same flight as Don Gowrie and his team, not to mention a whole mob of other media people, reporters, photographers loaded down with cameras, and TV crews from other networks. The difference was that while the senator and his closest aides were in first class the press were largely in economy, except some of the higher-paid political correspondents who were in business class. Looking around the rows of seats, Sophie soon realized that most of the press seemed to know each other and were talking away. And drinking. They all had glasses in their hands most of the time.

Sophie had one glass of white wine with her very uninviting food, but otherwise drank orange juice and then mineral water. She knew the long flight would make her feet ache and her ankles swell because that was what had happened to her on her flight to New York from Prague and she didn't want a repeat performance. She didn't want a headache tomorrow, either.

'More coffee?' the stewardess asked, and she nodded, holding out her cup.

'Thank you.'

Beside her she heard an odd intake of air and looked round at Steve enquiringly. He was staring at a burly middle-aged man in a neat grey suit who was just shouldering his way past the food trolley on his way to the lavatory.

'Do you know him?' Sophie asked, and Steve frowned, hesitated, then nodded with what she saw was reluctance. Why didn't he want to talk about the man?

'Who is he?'

Steve paused, watching the stewardess pouring coffee for the row in front of them, then, as she moved her trolley on, murmured, 'Someone who means trouble,' and something in his tone made the hairs on the back of Sophie's neck rise.

'What do you mean? Who is he?'

'His name is Bross; he's in security, on the president's staff, and if he is going to London on the same plane as Gowrie you can bet your bottom dollar he's here to keep an eye on everything Gowrie does and says, and above all everyone he meets. The president must be worried about Gowrie.'

'How do you know so much?' She watched him with uncertainty, wondering again just how much she could trust this man and what his motives really were for helping her. To get the inside track on whatever she knew about Don Gowrie? Was that his only reason? Sometimes she felt it wasn't Gowrie but herself he was interested in, herself he cared about – but it was easy to fool yourself when you wanted to believe something. She hadn't known him long and she didn't know him very well. Why did she feel this strong desire to believe he cared what happened to her? Hadn't she learnt not to hope for too much where other people were concerned? They lied, they cheated, they were indifferent. You were a fool if you trusted them.

'My family has been mixed up in Republican politics all my life,' he said, staring into his drink before swallowing some. 'There isn't much I don't know about the party. And in my job I get to hear a lot of sensitive information.'

Almost angrily, Sophie said, 'Why is politics always such a dirty business, whichever country you look at?'

He laughed. 'Because politicians are human beings. There's gold in them thar hills, sweetheart, and where there's gold there is corruption.'

She shivered. 'I hate politics,' she said vehemently. 'And politicians.'

Steve picked up his glass of after-dinner brandy again. 'I'll drink to that.' He tilted the glass towards her then drank the rest of the brandy.

She frowned. 'You hate politicians, too? But then . . . why are you a political reporter?'

'Because I don't trust the bastards,' he coolly said. 'Somebody has to keep an eye on what they're up to. I wasn't going to leave that job to people who didn't hate them the way I do. If politicians had their way all reporters would be wide-eyed little optimists who take a naive view of Washington and the people who run to it. I like to keep them on their toes, make sure they know I'm watching them.'

'Can you actually tell the truth on TV, though?' she said shrewdly, and he laughed.

'Honey, you hit the button. No, not often; but now and then I can slide the truth in sideways while my bosses aren't watching.'

'You're a cynic,' she said, not accusing him but thinking aloud and shivering slightly. She was no wide-eyed optimist, herself, but cynicism was the reaction of despair, of people who had no hope, no belief, no dreams. Sophie couldn't live that way. She had to hope, to believe, to dream – why else was she here, flying to England, to look for a sister she had been told for years was dead?

'Aren't we all cynics? Reporters, I mean? We see the underbelly of society, not the glossy surface – how can we fail to be cynics? In any case, as I told you, my father was involved in politics all my life and I learnt young not to believe a word politicians said in public. They're as dishonest as salesmen trying to make a pitch. All they care about is selling the product. The truth means fuck-all to them.'

Sophie laughed abruptly at the cheerfully aggressive tone of his voice. 'I'm beginning to love America,' she said, and he looked taken aback, then grinned.

'Oh, yeah? Why, exactly?'

'I like the way you say what you really think, out loud, and don't care who's listening! You aren't afraid someone may overhear you, or that you may end up in a cell getting beaten up.'

'Well, there are parts of America where that could happen,' he drily said. 'But it's pretty safe to speak your mind in most states.'

'Even Washington?'

'Oh, in Washington they love you to speak your mind, it gives them a buzz – but not on TV, or in the press. At a dinner party you can throw caution to the wind. No voters to hear the dangerous truth in the houses of the rich and powerful.'

'If you hadn't become a TV reporter, what else might you have done?' she asked, deeply curious about him.

'Oh, when I was at university I used to act, I had brief spell of wanting to be an actor, but I wasn't able to lose myself in a part, I was too self-aware.' He leaned back and turned his head to watch her. 'My mother was relieved. She hated the idea.'

'You cared what she thought?'

He considered the question. 'I guess I must have done. I certainly listened to what my parents thought. They're not people you can ignore.'

'Your family is a close one?'

'I guess so.' His offhand tone didn't fool her. She could see he loved his parents and cared very much what they thought; she envied him. All her life she had missed that warmth and closeness.

A few minutes later she closed her eyes and felt herself slipping into a half-sleep. She had not slept well last night; she had been intensely nervous and kept waking with a start. On her return from dinner with Theo and Lilli she had had the strangest feeling that someone had been in her room. As soon as she walked into the room her instincts had quivered with warning, but nothing seemed out of place. In fact the room was neater than when she left it, so she had realized that a maid had been in there, re-making her bed, tidying the room. But what about the photographs Steve had given her? The photo of Anya as a baby had been on top of the pile. That could be sheer coincidence, of course. Maybe the maid had simply shuffled the photographs and Anya's picture had just happened to land on top.

Well, it could have happened that way. But Sophie didn't believe in coincidences that massive. She was rapidly learning not to trust anyone, or anything; even her own senses.

Don Gowrie was in conference with his people all the way across the Atlantic. First class was entirely occupied by members of his staff; the curtains had been closed off and security was stationed there throughout the flight to make sure nobody tried to eavesdrop or intrude.

'And keep an eye out for Bross,' they were told. His presence on the plane had been noticed at once.

'We must be getting to them if they've sent him to tag along with us,' Gowrie joked.

'They're worried,' his campaign manager, Jim Allgood, had agreed. 'Mr Ramsey still pulls in the party old guard, and that's a lot of money going on you.' But his face was set in a frown and he added, 'But what bothers me is this – Bross stands out like a sore thumb, we all know the guy, and they know we do. They're too smart for such an open play. So who have they got on our tail we don't know about?'

They had all looked at each other, their faces guarded, the air full of paranoia.

'Could be one of the press,' Jeff Hardy, one of the speechwriters, suggested. 'I don't trust any of the bastards further than I could throw them.'

'Not after what they said about your first novel!' Greg Blake grinned, and some people laughed briefly before a scowl from Jim Allgood stopped it dead.

'Can we not talk about your private lives, you two? And listen good, everyone – keep your eyes open for anyone who keeps turning up when you don't expect them.'

There was a silence; everyone looked sideways at someone else, their faces blank.

'Steve Colbourne's around a lot, have you noticed that?' offered Greg, not altogether seriously but just to say something. He felt compelled to rush in whenever a silence fell; silences embarrassed him. They felt unnatural.

'Are you crazy?' snapped Jack Beverley. 'The guy's a TV commentator. The more interest he shows, the better. His father's a friend of Mr Ramsey.' He looked for confirmation from Don Gowrie who nodded.

'That's right.'

'I'd forgotten that,' Greg said. 'And Colbourne is good at his job. Gets good ratings. He writes well, too. Too well. It really gets up my nose. I want to despise the media, not wish I could use words as well as they do.'

'Careful, Greg, you keep telling the truth this way and your career will be over,' Jeff said, and got another scowl from Allgood.

'Not funny, Hardy. One day you'll say that in front of someone who'll print it and then it will be you who's out of a job.'

Jeff flushed and said nothing.

Brushing his untidy hair back from his face, Greg rushed in again to cover his friend's silence. 'Who's the blonde with Colbourne today, anyone know? I noticed her at the press conference, couple of days ago. Well, I guess we all noticed her.' He grinned round at them and got some uncertain, answering grins. Encouraged he talked on fast, 'I just love those icy blondes, don't you? The kind who give you the drop-dead look if you come within a foot of them.'

'Now what does that tell us about you?' mused Jeff, having recovered his cool. 'You're a sick man, Greg. Masochism stunts your growth, remember. Sadism is the only safe sexual perversion.'

There were stifled snorts among the others.

'Hitchcock had one in every film he made,' Jeff said.

'Perversion?'

'Icy blonde.'

'You're right, I'd forgotten. The icier the better, and it isn't masochism, Jeff – guys like me and Hitchcock love to fantasize about making the ice melt.'

'Dream on, buster,' Jeff drawled, and got a big laugh from some of the team.

Jack Beverley, head of Gowrie's security people, suddenly snarled, 'Will you two, for Christ's sake, shut up? This isn't vaudeville and you aren't paid to write patter. We're supposed to be working.'

Silence fell again. Beverley tilted his bullet head downwards and ran a finger down the typed sheets in front of him. 'OK. We were talking about the speech for this dinner at the Guildhall – that's in London, right? You just say the City here, I guess you mean London?' He glared at them. 'Why the hell don't you say so?'

'Well, it is, and it isn't,' Greg said.

'What does that mean?' Beverley growled, his rocklike jaw thrust forward in aggression.

'Well,' drawled Greg, 'See, it's complicated. The City is the oldest part of London, built on the original Roman city; in the beginning it had a wall running right round it. The rest of London grew up outside the wall. That's gone now, of course, but the original city is still separate from the rest of London. It has its own by-laws and police force and Lord Mayor and Aldermen. It's the financial centre of the UK, it has the Stock Exchange, the Bank of England,

Lloyd's, all the major financial institutions. The Guildhall was where the trade guilds used to meet in medieval times.' He paused, seeing the blank faces. 'That's kind of trade unions. The old building was bombed in the war, but was rebuilt exactly as it was before, and it's still where all the big events take place in the City of London. State banquets, that kind of affair.'

'I didn't ask for a history lesson!' Beverley yelled, and Greg flinched. He hated loud aggressive men with parade-ground voices. They reminded him of his soldier father and all the reasons why he had not gone into the army himself; they made his head ache, too.

'The banquet the senator will be attending is the annual dinner of the Anglo-American Friendship Society; it will make a terrific platform for him and be widely reported back home as well as in the UK,' Jim Allgood quickly said.

'Which is why this speech you've written had better be good,' Don Gowrie told them, smiling, in an effort to improve the atmosphere. A team under stress was a team in trouble. He needed good humour and calm around him in Europe. He was already under enough stress from other quarters. 'Oh, and guys, will you keep your voices down? My wife's sleeping.'

Elly and her nurse were seated right at the front of the first-class section. Elly had eaten and taken a sleeping pill; he could see her head slumped to one side and even from this distance he could hear her soft, smothered snoring.

Everyone looked round at her. Few of them actually knew her. She no longer got involved in his political life. Luckily Elly was having one of her good days; or rather, she had been heavily sedated before they left for the airport. They could not risk a scene in public. She could be un-predictable, especially when she was with him. If she saw a beautiful woman speak to him, for instance, and got it into her head that there was something going on between him and the other woman, she could turn very nasty. He closed his eyes briefly, shuddering at memories of just how nasty she could be.

'OK?' Jim Allgood murmured, watching him uneasily.

Gowrie pulled himself together. 'Yes, sure, I'm fine. Let's hear the Guildhall speech. I want to hear reactions, then the boys can rework it before we get to London.'

Sophie slept part of the way to London, dreaming fitfully, as she had ever since her mother told her Anya was alive, not dead. The dream was always the same. She walked in darkness, looking back over her shoulder, sometimes beginning to run, her heart beating until she felt it might burst out through her chest, and heard behind her breathing, running footsteps, yet whenever she looked round there was nobody there, just the night shadows of the lane behind her home, the lane leading to the church.

That lay just ahead of her, no light in the stained glass windows, the pale onion dome glowing and mysterious, like a strange moon fallen from the sky, and the yews in the graveyard showing her where Anya waited for her.

When she got there she knelt by the grave and looked at the stone above it. Papa's name, Anya's name written underneath.

'Where are you, Anya?' she whispered, and that was when it always happened – the arm coming up from the grave, the small, pale hand grabbing her, her terror, struggling to break free, screaming.

She woke up with a stifled cry and found Steve Colbourne leaning over her, concern in his eyes.

'Did you have a nightmare? You were screaming – are you OK?'

She swallowed, fighting to shut the memory out. 'Did I . . . make a noise?' Her eyes moved, taking in the darkened cabin, the sleeping bodies on all sides, crumpled blankets roughly draped over them, heads slumped back or to one side, some of them snoring, one or two people still awake, in shirt-sleeves, a blanket draped over them, reading by an overhead light. Nobody looked back at her.

'No,' Steve said slowly, still watching her. 'No, you were just moving about, breathing in a weird way, as if you were running, and your face was . . .' He stopped and she bit her lip.

'My face was what?'

'Terrified,' he said. 'You are, aren't you, Sophie? I wish to God you'd tell me what this is all about.'

She wished she could. But she couldn't. Turning away, she closed her eyes again.

'Don't keep asking me. Go back to sleep.' That was the last thing she wanted to do herself, though. She was afraid of sleeping now; afraid of the dream coming back. The night dragged on.

It was a bitter relief when the stewardess put on the lights and everyone sat up, grey-faced, yawned and stretched, went out to the lavatories, coming back washed and shaved, hair combed and brushed. The female passengers put on their make-up; men had changed their shirts and ties. Blankets were folded and put away.

The stewards made the rounds with a trolley loaded with newspapers, and gave out cups of tea or coffee. A smell of synthetic breakfast filled the aeroplane, making Sophie feel sick.

'Sleep much?' asked Steve, inhaling the fragrance of his coffee with closed eyes.

'Not much.' Sophie smiled at the stewardess, accepted orange juice and cornflakes, took a roll and some marma-lade but rejected a cooked breakfast with a rueful shake of the head.

Flying back into London so soon after she had left gave her a sense of déjà vu. The last time she saw Heathrow it hadn't entered her head that she might be back within such a short time; she had imagined it would be years before she returned. She had not known about Anya then. It was only when she flew home for a brief visit before going to the States that her mother told her the truth, a truth which still reverberated through Sophie's life, like the aftershocks of an earthquake.

Beside her she heard Steve take a sudden, sharp breath, felt his body stiffening, and looked round at him, but he was not looking at her. Face hard and wary, he was watching a woman who had walked down the aisle and was now standing beside them.

Startled, Sophie looked up, not recognizing the smoothly made-up face, dominated by heavy horn-rimmed spectacles which balanced the formidable jaw-line. Older than herself, around the late thirties or early forties, thought Sophie; dressed to impress businessmen rather than attract them, in a pin-striped masculine suit and white shirt with a dove-grey silk tie, and yet worn with very high black patent heels, like some secret sign of femininity in direct contradiction of the rest of her clothes.

'Miss Narodni?' From behind the hornrims cold eyes inspected Sophie and were clearly contemptuous of what they saw. Without waiting for her to reply, the woman held out an envelope. Sophie stared at it and saw long, graceful fingers whose nails were pearly, showing the pink skin beneath their highly buffed surfaces, without a touch of varnish.

Taking the envelope gingerly, as if it might explode, Sophie huskily asked, 'What's this?' but the other woman had already turned on her heels and walked away.

'Who was that?' Sophie asked Steve, but had already guessed the answer before he gave it to her.

'Gowrie's secretary. The bionic woman. Scary, isn't

she?' But he was looking at the envelope Sophie held. 'Aren't you going to open that?'

She felt it crackle between her fingers. A card? She tore it open while Steve watched and took out a stiffly embossed invitation card, stared at the gold lettering on it, not quite taking it in at first. Her own name had been written on to it, in black, confident handwriting.

Steve whistled. 'Well, well – he's sent you an invitation to the Guildhall dinner tomorrow night. Now I wonder why he's done that?'

He watched Sophie's face and saw that she wondered too. He was beginning to recognize certain expressions of hers, to know when she was scared or worried, and he was sure she was both at this moment.

They both suddenly became aware that someone else had halted beside their seats and was staring fixedly at the card Sophie held.

Steve gave the newcomer a dry smile. 'Well, hello, Bross. How are you? Coming to Europe to keep an eye on Gowrie? They must be scared he might get his nose in front, right?'

'I'm not working, I'm taking a break to London, visiting old buddies, seeing the sights, that's all,' the other man said, but he was looking at Sophie not Steve and his eyes were very sharp. She felt as if she was being X-rayed, his stare piercing her to the very backbone. 'Introduce me,' he said, still not even looking at Steve, and held out his large hand, the back of it rough with thick black hair.

She couldn't refuse to take it, although it made her shudder to feel the hairs brushing against her skin.

'Sophie Narodni,' Steve reluctantly introduced. 'One of our researchers. Sophie, this is Bross. How do you describe yourself now, Bross? Private eye? Detective?'

'Investigator, I'm an investigator,' Bross said shortly, his face resenting something in Steve's tone. He turned his gaze back to Sophie. 'Nice to meet you, Miss Narodni. What's that . . . a Polish name? Russian?'

'Czech.' Sophie did not like him; there was something reptilian about him, for all his burly size and neat grey suit. His skin had a scaly texture to it, grey and large-pored, unhealthy; his eyes had a cold bloodless stare, and his bony jaw looked as if it could flap right back to allow him to swallow his prey whole.

'Czech, huh?' he said. 'Do you know the senator?'

She kept a blank expression pinned on her face.

'No, huh? Never met him?' Bross did not seem too certain he believed her. 'Been in the States long?'

'Hey, hey,' Steve interrupted, scowling. 'You don't work for the Bureau now, Bross. Lay off her.'

'Just making polite conversation.' Bross kept his snake eyes on her, smiling in a way that made the skin on her neck prickle. 'I did hear that you worked for some Czech press agency, Miss Narodni. When did you switch to working for this guy's outfit?'

Sophie was taken aback – so he already knew who she was before Steve introduced her? Again she felt that quiver of vertigo which was becoming so familiar to her – she was walking in the darkness on a taut, high wire, and every time she looked down she felt her head swim.

Smoothly Steve told him, 'She just did, OK? We needed a researcher and she's worked in Europe for a few years, she could help us out.' He stopped to listen to an announcement on the Tannoy above them, then gave the other man a cold smile. 'You heard the captain – you should be sitting down with your seatbelt fastened, Bross. We'll be landing soon.'

Bross gave them both a nod. 'Nice to meet you, Miss Narodni. I'll be seeing you.'

She shivered watching him walk away. 'I didn't like the way he said that.'

'You weren't meant to. He was just letting us know that he was on our case, hoping to surprise us into telling him something he didn't already know.' Steve seemed unbothered, though. He smiled at her. 'Don't let him get to you. Bross is harmless. It's Gowrie and his people you have to watch out for, isn't it?'

She didn't answer, turning her head to look down on grey, wintry London's familiar outlines.

'Look, there's the Thames,' she said, staring at the silvery gleam bending like a snake among the fields and houses below them.

Two hours later Cathy Brougham stood on the grand staircase at Arbory House, watching a chandelier being lowered with the utmost care into a soft nest of piled sheets. The prisms chimed and glittered in wintry sunlight as they moved. The chandelier had already been cleaned once, but that morning Paul Brougham, normally so calm and controlled, was almost jumpy with nerves over this visit, and, constantly going around the house checking that it shone with perfection, had noticed a spider's web among the long, crystal drops, and, he swore, a film of dust there too. Over breakfast he had said, 'Get it done properly this morning. We're having some very important people here over the next few days. I don't want them thinking they've come to stay with Miss Havisham.'

She had laughed. 'Well, I do still have some of our wedding-cake left – the bottom layer, darling. You're supposed to keep it for the christening of your first baby – but it isn't covered in cobwebs, it's safely wrapped in foil and put away. Of course, I could wear Grandmama's wedding dress – except that I gave it to Grandee after the wedding, and it's back at Easton now.'

'I see you're in a playful mood,' Paul said, watching her

with sensual amusement, making her pulses beat fast. 'I hope you feel the same tonight.'

She put a finger to her lips, kissed it, brushed it along his mouth in a lingering caress, her eyes smouldering. 'I will,' she promised.

The sexual excitement between them showed no signs of fading or dying down. Paul put his hand under the table and slid it over her silk-clad thigh, his fingers exploring the warmth between her legs. She closed her eyes, quivering.

Paul sighed. 'No time, got to go, darling. Hold that mood.' He stood up and kissed the top of her head before striding out.

Coming out of her sensual trance, Cathy had sighed before going upstairs to get dressed. She knew she had no time for her usual morning ride. Mr Tiffany would be petulant next time she went out to the stables, but she would take him an extra apple and maybe even a piece of the forbidden sugar he loved so much. Before she got dressed, however, she rang the housekeeper and gave the order to have the chandelier let down and cleaned.

'And this time make sure it is utterly spotless. Mr Brougham has eagle eyes, remember, he notices every detail.' And expected his orders to be followed to the letter, as every member of his staff both at home and work knew only too well.

Glancing at her watch now, Cathy smiled. Her father would have landed at Heathrow, might already be on his way into London to his hotel. As soon as he had checked in he had promised to ring her.

The servants gathered on their knees around the landed chandelier began to work with softest chamois leather, heads bent in concentration.

Cathy went back to her private sitting-room and sat down at an elegant little walnut bureau to write letters; one to her best friend from school, Bella, who was now married to a

Swiss hotelier and living in Geneva, and one to her grandfather, who liked to hear from her as often as possible, even if it was only a few lines on a postcard. Whenever Cathy visited interesting places she bought postcards to send him at some future time – postcards of Brighton Pavilion, postcards of Salisbury Cathedral, Edinburgh Castle, views of the Highlands with deer grazing, views of Paris by night, of Big Ben by day. She wouldn't get much time to herself over the next week. She could manage just half an hour now.

'Darling Grandee,' she began, and was soon deep in a detailed description of the preparations for her father's visit, aiming to make her grandfather feel he could see through her eyes. When she had addressed the envelope she reached for another sheet of headed paper but before she had taken it the phone rang, and she sighed and reached for that instead, knowing that her housekeeper would be busy with the chandelier. 'Yes?'

'Hello? I want to ... could I please speak to ... Mrs Brougham, please?' The voice was unfamiliar, husky, a little breathless.

'Who's speaking?' Cathy guardedly enquired.

There was a pause and then the voice whispered, 'Anya? Is that you?'

'What? Who's Anya?' Puzzled, Cathy listened to the breathing on the other end of the line. 'Who is this?'

The line went dead. Slowly, Cathy hung up. Now what had all that been about?

A few moments later the phone rang again; Cathy hesitated this time before picking it up.

'Yes?'

A silence, then her father's familiar voice said, 'Am I ringing at a bad time?'

'Dad! You're in London? Oh, great. Did you have a good flight? Bet you're tired. I always am after crossing the Atlantic.'

'I feel a few degrees under. We did discuss coming by Concorde, but the timings didn't work out,' he admitted. 'And we were able to work all the way coming by regular flight.'

'Oh, work! That's all you men ever think about. Paul's the same. But never mind, I forgive you both. I'm dying for you to get here, Dad, we'll go for a long ride, won't we, just the two of us, like the old days at Easton, and talk where no one can hear us? And you can tell me how you feel and all about the campaign. I miss all that, you know – the work and the excitement, and the sheer damn fun.'

'I miss you being there,' he agreed soberly. 'You were the only one I could trust to be right behind me with no hidden agendas and no secret resentments. Life's a damn sight too complicated, darling.'

She frowned, wishing she could see his face. 'You sound tired, Dad – is the pressure getting to you?'

'It was a long flight, I guess I'm tired.'

'Yes, I hate those transatlantic flights too. What about Mummy? How is she? Did she find the flight very tiring?'

His voice changed slightly, grew more careful, and she heard the neutral tone with a pang of distress. Her mother wasn't getting any better, then; getting worse, no doubt, as Paul had warned her she would as she got older. She recognized that tone in her father's voice, the will not to give anything away.

'She's borne up quite well, she slept on the plane, took a sleeping pill and zonked out, and she's lying down now, but she sends her love. She's very excited about seeing you.' He paused, then asked, 'Why did you sound so odd when you answered the phone, Cathy? Any problems your end?'

'No, no, it was just that . . . oh, some weirdo had rung and I was afraid it would be her again.'

'Weirdo?' he sharply asked. 'What kind of weirdo?'

'Some woman who asked for me and then suddenly said,

"Is that you, Anya?" I've no idea who she meant – there's nobody called Anya here.'

Silence, then, 'What did she want?' Her father sounded hoarse, as if he had got a sore throat. When you made that long flight from the States you often picked up some bug, she hoped he hadn't done that. Lately she had felt he wasn't as strong as he had been most of his life. He was the wiry type; tougher than he looked with a lot of energy burning him up so that he never put on weight.

'I don't know,' Cathy said. 'She hung up.'

'Without saying anything else?'

'Yes.'

She heard him take a long breath. 'You shouldn't answer the phone yourself, Cathy, you really shouldn't. It isn't wise, especially now. All sorts of crazies ring people in the public eye. In future, get your housekeeper to do it. Promise me you won't pick the outside phone up again until you know who's on the line?'

He was worried, really worried about her, she realized and it touched her. 'OK, Dad, I'll remember, don't worry about me. You have enough to worry about without me adding to your problems.'

'Good girl.' His voice held a smile now. 'Look, sorry, darling, I've got to go now. There's a lot to get through today. I'm meeting with some of the opposition politicians this afternoon, and I'll be seeing your husband later today. Take care of yourself, see you real soon.'

In London, Don Gowrie turned to his secretary, his face tight and pale. She was replacing the receiver of a phone on the other side of the room, having listened to the entire conversation. 'Damn it to hell. It never occurred to me that she would ring Cathy. Get me Jack Beverley on the phone, I want security tightened up around my son-in-law's place. I don't want the Narodni girl getting within a mile of the house, and I don't want her getting through to Cathy on the phone again.'

'I don't suppose she'll talk to her openly on the phone, she'll be counting on a chance to talk to her in person, face to face. And she can't do that until after the Guildhall dinner. She accepted the invitation to it, she'll be there.'

He frowned angrily. 'We can't wait another day. She has got to be dealt with, and quickly. Tonight. There's already been too long a delay. Get Jack on the phone now.'

'You couldn't tell your son-in-law the truth and what's at stake?'

Don Gowrie's fingers tightened on a pencil he had picked up; it snapped and he threw it down with a scowl.

'Too big a risk. He might divorce her if he knew there was a chance, however remote, that she wouldn't inherit.'

His secretary's eyes opened wide behind her spectacles. 'You really think so? I had the impression it was a real love-match, the way they look at each other. And he would have to pay her hefty alimony, if he divorced her for a reason like that. Not being the heir to a fortune is hardly grounds for divorce. Anyway, I thought you and he got on well.'

'I guess we do, but there's something about him that bugs me. He's very cagey; clams up if you ask questions, especially about money.'

She laughed. 'That's pretty normal with businessmen.'

'Yeah, but when she first met him I had him investigated, and my people couldn't come up with much about his early life before he left France. He came from a very remote village originally, but none of his family still lived there, and nobody remembered much about them. There were family graves in the little churchyard, his grandparents were buried there and a couple of uncles, but some sort of massacre happened there during the Second World War, and the church itself had got hit by bombs later. There were no documents surviving.'

Emily's brows rose. 'You suspect he could be lying about his background?'

Gowrie frowned, shaking his head. 'No, his name turned up in local government records – where he went to school, what exams he passed, and so on – but my guys couldn't find a living soul who remembered him.' He grimaced. 'Mind you, the French can be awkward sons of bitches, especially when they're talking to an American – my people weren't sure if they were getting the runaround or not. The French love to pretend they don't speak English. And Brougham checked out in Paris, that's for sure. A lot of people knew him there. Oh, maybe I don't trust him because he's a goddamned Frenchman. Whatever, I'm not ready to tell him the truth about Cathy. So get me Jack.'

When she had put down the phone, Cathy wrote a letter to her friend Bella, retailing some of the latest gossip about other old schoolfriends and all about her father's forthcoming visit. At the back of her mind she kept thinking about that weird phonecall, though. Who was Anya? And who was the girl who made the call? The voice had seemed familiar but she couldn't place the accent. It hadn't been an American voice, or a British one. Russian?

She had visited Russia several times and knew a few Russians, and the voice hadn't had the right intonation. East European, she thought later that morning – yes, it had been an East European voice. Her father had taken her to East Europe several times: to Poland, Hungary, both countries she had adored, and only two years ago to East Germany after the Berlin Wall fell. Her father had worked in the diplomatic service in East Europe; she had lived in Czechoslovakia with her parents as a small baby, she had been told, although she didn't remember it. On their tour of East Europe, however, her father had chosen not to revisit the

Czech Republic, although Prague was the city Cathy most longed to see.

Lots of her friends had been there. It was where American students headed in their thousands, the new Mecca, taking the place of Paris in the Twenties, when Americans saw that city as a soul city. Now it was Prague they rushed to, coming home babbling reverently of the incredibly ornate baroque architecture with its curling lines and gilding and cherubs in profusion, at the cobbled streets and art nouveau buildings, of sitting out at night drinking cheap wine out of pewter carafes in street cafés with paper tablecloths, talking about art and sex and poetry and sex and politics, and sex, while they listened with one ear to street musicians from the latest pop songs to latest pop songs to Mozart or medieval plain chant.

Cathy had felt she was being deprived, left out of a central experience of her peers; she had been furious with her father at the time, but he had pleaded lack of time.

'I prefer Hungary and Poland. We'll go there some other time.'

One day I'll get there, she thought. I'll ask Paul to take me. We could do a quick trip in the spring – that would probably be a great time of year to go. Spring is lovely in Europe, so much warmer than it is in the States.

That thought gave her a sudden visitation of childhoods at Easton in the snow; the sparkle of icy sunlight on a trackless white vista glimpsed from her bedroom window on winter mornings, woods decked out by crisp white snow which scrunched underfoot as you walked through it, and when you looked back you saw lines of footsteps following you, your own betraying imprint.

Icicles hung from branches, there was a polished gleam of frozen blue-grey lakes, through the trees. The lake surface was scratched and powdered by ducks, orange-beaked with black webbed feet, landing and taking off under a bright blue sky. If the ice seemed strong enough she was allowed to skate, wheeling and spinning on the lake, the steel runners on her skates cutting like diamond through the surface with a satisfying sound she could still hear.

She felt a homesick yearning at the memory. It was never that cold here. The English always made her laugh, complaining if a flake or two of snow came floating down the sky, stopping the buses and trains in their tracks, sending a collective shiver of dismay and incredulity through the whole of Britain – but then they had never felt the iron grip of a New England winter. What would they do if they woke up morning after morning to sub-zero temperatures and arctic blizzards and had to trek to work between head-high banks of snow? She had learnt to love it, and the mild green winters of England were too tame by comparison. Maybe instead of going to Prague she would get Paul to take her to Easton this winter? Then, frowning, she thought, I wonder why Dad doesn't like Prague? He has never talked much about his time there, has he? If you bring the subject up he's very slippery and evasive.

But then Dad was always secretive. She adored him, always had, but now and then she wondered if the man she knew was the whole man, and how much of him was hidden, like an iceberg in northern seas, beneath the surface.

Paul could be secretive, too – were all men so reluctant to talk about their past lives, before you met them? Paul said little about his home in France, his family, his childhood. He had been born in a remote village in the Auvergne, his parents were long dead and he had been an only child. He had no family left there. She kept badgering him to take her there, so that she could see where he had grown up, but Paul was reluctant – he hated the place, he said, all there was to see was a church and one dusty village street. He had spent his time there simply longing to get away.

*

In London, Paul Brougham spent the day in meetings. One of his companies was having trouble with shareholders who weren't happy with the annual profits forecast. Of course, they had no clue that it could have been much worse – Paul and Freddy had carefully moved figures around, shifted money between companies, done a clever cosmetics job on the final figure. At the shareholders' meeting that morning Paul got a rough ride. One or two of the shareholders were hard to shake off, asked far too many shrewd questions, but he managed to talk his way through the problems, promising better results the following year and a firm dividend, which was all the majority of those present wanted to hear.

Halfway through a long, complaining speech from one of the leading shareholders, Freddy leaned over and whispered in Paul's ear, 'Back row, third along . . . in tweeds . . . I know him, he's with Salmond.'

Paul looked down at the pad in front of him, scribbled one word in capitals, NAME? Under cover of doing that he glanced through his drooping lashes at the back row. The man's face meant nothing to him but he did not doubt Freddy for an instant.

Freddy wrote on the pad, 'Bennett, accountant.' He picked up the thick print-out of shareholders' names which lay on the table, skimmed through it and stopped, pointing at the name he had been looking for. Bennett was a minor shareholder; he had held shares for only a few months.

Paul nodded, tore off the top sheet of his pad and pushed it into his pocket. So, Salmond had someone planted among the shareholders of this particular company? Was that repeated over all his companies?

He murmured to Freddy, turning his head away so that nobody in the hall could lipread what he said, 'When you get back to the office, check all our companies to see how many of them have shareholders who might be planted by Salmond.'

Freddy nodded, frowning. Paul saw the alarm in his eyes. Freddy was constantly afraid that Nemesis would catch up with them.

'Stop worrying,' Paul told him affectionately.

Freddy sighed. 'Wish I could.'

Paul rushed off from the shareholders' meeting to a private meeting with the chairman of a company he was considering acquiring. Their negotiations had been going as merrily as a wedding bell until the news of Salmond's takeover bid got out, and now the other board was in a state of panic. Before the lunch, which took place in Paul's boardroom, with his private staff serving an elegant, sophisticated meal, Freddy produced a list of suspected Salmond plants among the shareholders of all the Brougham companies, which he gave privately to Paul.

'You see? Salmond is dangerous. We're in trouble.'

Giving him a reckless, dancing grin, Paul said, 'We'll chop him off at the knees, don't worry. He isn't going to win. We are.'

Telling yourself you're going to win makes it far more likely that you will; he had known that from the start of his career, but Freddy had never had that clear-sighted confidence, and he didn't have it now.

He turned that arrogant, assured smile on the chairman he was hoping to convince, and Freddy watched him with his usual mix of admiration and uneasiness. Paul always had won his battles – but Freddy was more worried than he had ever been before.

Later that afternoon, sitting at the boardroom table in wintry sunlight, Freddy still watched him with that same uncertainty. What was he thinking as he smiled at the Frenchwoman he had had an affair with last year? Freddy could never read Paul's expressions.

He had never liked Chantal Rousseau himself; she never bothered to be charming to him – she had concentrated all her allure on Paul. Had she been in love with him? Or had she just hoped to marry him? She was certainly lovely – hair like midnight, eyes as dark as coals, and a figure that promised hot nights. But there was a secrecy in her, a touch of malice, a glitter of feline spite that Freddy found unpleasant.

'We've done well for you and your investors over the past few years, Chantal, so I hope you'll be sticking with us,' Paul said softly, smiling into her eyes.

She smiled back. 'I can't give a cast-iron guarantee, Paul, you realize that? Not yet, anyway. I have to consult our board fully and see how high Salmond is prepared to go.'

The sunlight gleamed on her pale throat, and Paul was suddenly reminded of last night, of Cathy arching over him, her hair brushing his eyes, her breasts touching him. His body seemed to be boneless suddenly, he was melting with desire and tenderness.

Chantal Rousseau watched him intently, saw his throat move as he swallowed, his tongue touch his lower lip as if it was ash-dry.

At that second his secretary took a phone call and turned to whisper to him, 'Senator Gowrie, sir. He insists on talking to you.'

Paul looked round the table. 'Sorry, this won't take long.' He took the phone. 'Hello, Senator, anything wrong?'

'Hi, Paul, hope I'm not interrupting anything important, but . . . I've been thinking. The security at your place is really tight, isn't it? I know your men have checked the estate over, but I think it might be wisest if I sent some men down now, before I arrive.'

Irritated, Paul said, 'That might alarm Cathy. Don't worry, nobody is going to get in or out of Arbory without

182

the alarms going off. Keep to our arrangement, Don. Don't worry so much, this is England, not the States. I don't want Cathy getting into a panic. Sorry, sir, but I'm in the middle of a board meeting, I must get on . . . see you soon.'

He hung up and looked around the table. 'Now, where were we?'

'Yes, where were we?' Chantal Rousseau asked.

One of the board said gloomily, 'I get the impression Salmond has been planning this for months. He isn't in any hurry to make a kill because he's so damned sure he's going to get us. When he has enough of a share base, he'll offer some sort of share-for-share deal, rather than offering cash. He may have a good cash-flow, but I imagine he'd rather make a paper deal. It would make sense.'

'We have to convince our shareholders it isn't in their long-term interest to accept whatever he offers,' Paul said. Why hadn't he seen this coming long ago? But he knew why – because he had been too obsessed with Cathy to think of anything else. For years he had been steering his ship between dangerous rocks and getting away with it – but the voice of a siren had drawn him on to a fatal shore and he had a terrible feeling that he might never get off it again.

Sophie was so tired out by the long flight that she went to bed early that night and slept heavily. Next morning Steve and she had breakfast together downstairs in the hotel café; Sophie just had orange juice, coffee, rolls and a thin spreading of black cherry jam, which to her delight turned out to be from her own country, a Czech brand which she knew well, with thick real fruit embedded in every spoonful.

'Try it! It's delicious,' she urged Steve, who looked amused, but took some with his toast.

'Not bad,' he agreed, picked up the small pot and read the name of the company, the address in the Czech Republic.

'I could taste the fruit and it was thick stuff, not the thin tasteless stuff you sometimes get in these hotels.'

'My mother makes her own jam, from fruit she grows herself – apples and blackberries . . . it's even better than this!'

'My mother makes her own preserves, too – we have rows of fruit bushes and fruit trees at the far end of the yard and every autumn my mother is busy in the kitchen filling jars and stacking the shelves in the pantry with them. She's a terrific cook. When I was a kid I loved sandwiches made with a mix of jelly and peanut butter.'

She made an incredulous face. 'Sounds weird. Peanut butter AND jam? Ugh.'

'Well, I have to say I haven't eaten it in years. I'd probably hate it now – our tastebuds change over the years, don't they? Along with everything else.'

He picked up the notes she had made for him on the various English politicians who would be seeing Don Gowrie today. 'What are you going to do today? Are you coming along with us? You're invited to the dinner tonight, you'll see Gowrie then, but if you want to hang about waiting for him to come out of meetings, you're welcome to come with us.'

She shook her head. 'I thought I might go around London. I enjoyed my time here and there are lots of places I want to see again. Unless you need me?'

'No, I guess I don't need you.' He frowned at her, though. 'Sophie, don't get any crazy ideas, will you? Don't do anything stupid. Remember, somebody tried to kill you in New York – keep an eye out for anyone following you, stay out of the subways, take taxis – I'll give you some British money to pay for them, they can go on our expense sheet, don't worry. I don't want to hear you've been pushed under a London bus! Do your sight-seeing and shopping, whatever, but for God's sake keep out of trouble.'

The camera crew appeared in the doorway, gesturing urgently, and Steve sighed. 'Got to run. Now, be good, won't you? Be sensible!'

'OK, Steve,' she meekly said, but she did not intend to be sensible. She couldn't stay here in London, even though it might be safer not to go alone. Whatever her head might say, her heart spoke a different language. She had to get to Arbory House as soon as physically possible. She kept hearing Anya's voice echoing in her head.

Her whole body was shivering with the realization that for the first time she had finally heard her sister speak. It was like hearing the tomb gape open and the angels singing.

She didn't know what she had been expecting, but it didn't matter, anyway. She had loved that voice – so warm and confident, full of life and certainty – she had listened to it, and been so choked that she couldn't say any of the things she wanted so desperately to say. All she could do was whisper, 'Is that you, Anya?' At that instant she had believed, somehow, that her sister would instinctively recognize her own real name and answer, would sense, too, that it was her own flesh and blood on the other end of the line.

But Anya had just sounded startled and puzzled. Sophie had been so upset that she had hung up. That had been stupid. What on earth must Anya have thought? Shouldering into her coat, she buttoned it up with ice-cold, trembling fingers. She was not sitting around in a hotel bedroom or waiting for Steve to come with her. She had come here to see her sister, and she didn't care about the dangers she might be risking – come hell or high water she was going to see Anya and ask her to come and see their mother before she died.

There was a taxi rank right outside the main entrance of the hotel. Sophie headed for it, told the driver to take her to the main-line station from where she could get a train to Buckinghamshire.

He stared at her, scratching his chin. 'Now is that St Pancras or Euston?'

'I don't know, I thought you would.'

'Well, hop in and we'll find you the right station.'

As they drove off he started talking on his mobile phone, checking with his base office which station she would want. Sophie listened, not noticing the taxi that took off immediately after her own, or the black car parked on the other side of the road which pulled out and slotted into the traffic behind that. She got out of the taxi ten minutes later and paid the driver before walking into the busy, echoing main-line terminal, quite unaware that she was being followed.

7

Paul Brougham liked to hear the wind howling like a banshee outside the double-glazed windows of his sixtieth-floor office above the gun-metal waters of the Thames. It made it impossible for him to forget the power of nature which the grey London streets spreading in all directions shut out. Without the wind, up here it was easy to feel godlike, floating among the clouds high up above the earthbound common humanity. His offices were deeply carpeted, elegantly designed, air-conditioned, his private lift shot him up to this level in seconds. From the floor-to-ceiling windows on one wall he looked down on cars like toys and people like ants. Only the threat of the wind tugging at the walls and windows, trying to wrench them up and toss them away, reminded him that he, too, was human, and could be blown away. Paul had a superstitious streak; he was afraid of hubris, of losing touch with reality and being destroyed by it.

That morning, though, he was too absorbed in work; absorbed – and humming with the energy of someone under threat. Adrenalin was running high inside him. Salmond was on his tail and he had to shake him off somehow. He still didn't quite know how.

Running his eye down a balance sheet, he listened intently to his chief accountant. He could have sung Freddy's song for him; there was nothing Paul did not know about the financial status of his companies, but sometimes when he listened to Freddy's slow, careful expositions it helped to clear his mind and show him a way through a tangled problem.

'I'm sorry, but it can't be done,' Freddy Levinson ended.

He was a thin, grey-haired, stooping man with the expression of a solemn heron fishing in muddy waters, which they frequently had during the twenty-odd years they had worked together.

They had met in 1972 when they both worked for a printing firm in Buckinghamshire which owned a small handful of magazines and local newspapers. The chairman and managing director, William Wood, had inherited the company from his father. A methodical, unadventurous man, trained by his father to follow in his footsteps, Wood had run his company exactly as his father had ordained.

Freddy was his accountant, Paul ran the office in the printing works, but neither of them had been allowed to initiate anything. Wood did not want any innovations, thank you, he said, the first time Paul went to him with an idea for an improvement in production. He wanted a job well done; safe, not sorry, was his business motto.

In 1973 Wood had a heart attack and died. His childless, middle-aged widow had been distraught. She had never taken any interest in the business, she had simply obeyed her husband and done as he wished; now she had no idea what to do. Paul went to see her after the funeral and had no trouble at all persuading her to let him take over her husband's job. Mrs Wood, who was a well-preserved woman in her late fifties with a conservative dress sense, silvered blonde hair and a good figure, was very grateful to have someone to trust and rely on as she always had her husband. She handed over full control to Paul, and happily sank back into domestic oblivion, resuming her busy life of coffee-mornings, flower-arranging, lunches with her friends, charity work and shopping.

Paul waited a year, then went to see Mrs Wood with an excellent set of accounts, audited by the man who had always audited her husband's books, a rather dull but famously honest local accountant.

'We are doing very well, Mr Brougham,' she delightedly said, looking only at the final profit because she did not understand accounts. 'Well done. You must give yourself a rise!'

'I think we could do better, Mrs Wood,' he said, and began to explain his plans for expansion of the company, but she stopped him, shaking her head.

'Please don't explain figures to me, Mr Brougham, I never understand them.'

He eyed her indulgently. 'Well, briefly, then, I can make you far more money, if you'll trust me.'

She trusted him; she was not a clever woman in many ways, but in one sense she was very shrewd. She understood human nature and she instinctively trusted Paul, and was right to do so.

He began his new regime at once; using the company as collateral he borrowed money and began to expand.

It made Freddy's head spin to look back down the years to the beginning. Their growth had been phenomenal; at almost every stage Freddy had said, 'It can't be done, Paul!' and been proved wrong. They often had no cash in hand, and yet the business kept growing. Paul was a magician, a juggler. Even Freddy was never quite sure how he did what he did. The quickness of the hand deceived the eye. The small company had grown into a bigger one almost at once, then even bigger. Mrs Wood had died five years after her husband. She had no relatives at all, and left her shares to Paul, who had gone on to acquire most of the other shares. Now he headed a cleverly interwoven web of related companies which, together, made Paul one of the most powerful men in the media business, but with an American media company muscling in on their territory Freddy was afraid it was all going to come apart for them.

'If we shed some of the local newspaper chains, we could

raise money to improve our cash flow immediately,' Paul suggested.

Until now, he had always refused to sell, had only wanted to acquire, even though that policy had meant that they often had to juggle accounts, moving them from one company to another on paper and giving Freddy nightmares.

'Are you serious?'

'Do I look as if I'm joking?'

Freddy glanced over the balance sheets again, scratching his chin. 'Well, I'd better go over these again and see what I think we'll be able to raise. But we'll have to do this quietly, or we'll start an avalanche. We don't want people to suspect we're having problems.'

'They already do, Freddy, don't be stupid. Everybody's aware of Salmond breathing down our necks. Well, I want a lighter ship, and I want it fast.'

Salmond will think he's got us on the run, if you start selling off bits of the company,' protested Freddy.

'He isn't the target – our shareholders are. I want them to realize we're moving heaven and earth to stop him. They must be reassured that we're working hard for them. As for Salmond himself, we'll hope to make him edgy. We don't want him to think he's going to have a walk-over, do we? I always believe in attacking back hard if you come under attack.'

The phone rang. Paul picked it up and snapped, 'I thought I told you no phonecalls?' Then his face changed. 'Yes, put her through.' Looking at Freddy he said, 'My wife. OK, Freddy, get me an assessment of what we could raise and what you suggest we sell.'

Paul had been one of the most eligible bachelors in London for years. Every gossip columnist had been on his trail with stories about the various women in his life; but he had not seemed interested in getting married until he met Cathy Gowrie. Beautiful, intelligent, a good twenty years

190

his junior, she was not only the daughter of a prominent American senator but she would inherit an enormous fortune one day.

'Jammy bastard!' had said a man who had once lost out in a boardroom battle with Paul, glaring at Freddy. 'If I believed in the Devil I'd think Brougham had sold his soul to him. He never puts a foot wrong, does he? Money just showers into his lap. How does he do it, eh?'

Freddy had smiled and shaken his head without commenting. He rarely told anyone anything – that was one of the facets of his character that made him so valuable to Paul. He could be trusted implicitly; he was discreet and, Paul said, as clever as a bag full of ferrets.

Women, though, had envied Cathy Gowrie. The daughter of one of Paul's titled directors said to Freddy furiously, 'I'd kill for him, it's no secret – and I tell you, Freddy, I could kill her, walking in and snatching him from under all our noses. She's too young for him. He needs someone of his own age, not someone young enough to be his daughter.'

As for Chantal Rousseau's reaction, she was better at hiding her feelings, but Freddy suspected she was still brooding over being dumped after Paul met Cathy.

Freddy had never really understood Paul, in spite of knowing him for years, and knowing him better than almost everyone else in the world. Watching him walking a tightrope made Freddy feel sick. He had some glimpses into what made Paul tick as far as business was concerned, but what made him tick where women were concerned was another matter.

But one thing Freddy was certain of – however brilliant a catch she might be, Paul had married Cathy solely because he was in love with her. Every time Freddy saw them together he was certain of that, and he envied him. Freddy had never felt the sort of sexual passion he could see between the two of them. It seemed to burn the air; the way they looked at each other made Freddy blush.

Any day now he expected to hear that Cathy was going to have a baby. Freddy had no wife or child. He had been married but his wife had left him for another man and Freddy hadn't felt like repeating the experiment, although he was beginning to wish he had a child. He was often very lonely. He didn't envy Paul his money, his power or his wife. But he would envy him the children Cathy would, no doubt, soon start to give him. What sort of father would Paul make? Indulgent, tender, caring, no doubt – but how much time would he ever spend with his family? He might be deeply in love with Cathy, but he still spent the giant's share of his time at work; nothing had changed that. He didn't know how lucky he was, thought Freddy, sighing. The lucky ones never did.

Don Gowrie was in a meeting when the message came through. His secretary, in the conference room they had been given for a temporary office, took the call on her mobile phone. The voice at the other end was guarded, cryptic.

'Target on the move, by train. Heading for Buckinghamshire. We're right behind. Instructions still the same?'

'Until you're told different. Just stay in place. But whatever you do, don't lose her. Advise when she arrives.'

She couldn't interrupt the senator's discussions; the message would have to wait but he was going to get a shock when he heard where the girl was heading.

The meeting broke up half an hour later; Gowrie saw the British politicians to the door, shaking hands with each other vigorously, making firm eye contact, smiling, remembering their first names.

'Good to talk, John. See you again soon.' He turned the

smile on the next man. 'A very useful exchange of views, Michael.'

His secretary hovered discreetly, watching the afternoon sunlight illuminate the faint beginning of stubble on his jaw, the shadow weariness under his eyes. In that light he looked his age, but Emily Sanderson felt the usual prickle of sensual excitement as she stared at the beautiful, strong hands moving so confidently. In a year he might be the most powerful man in the world, but in secret, in bed, she could make him groan and tremble, go on his knees and beg. The very thought of that made her shudder with pleasure. There was no aphrodisiac like power.

Before she met him she had had a couple of relationships, neither of them very satisfying. Emily was very clear-sighted, even about herself; she knew she wasn't beautiful and her personality wasn't the sort that made men flock around her the way they did around some women.

It didn't bother her. She was ambitious and for that she needed independence, a freedom only earning her own money could give her. She didn't want to marry and become some man's unpaid slave. If she had had money to start with she might have gone in for politics herself, but she came from the wrong side of the tracks, quite literally, since her father had worked on the railway and the family had lived in a wood-frame shack down the line from the station where he worked. He was a large man with hard fists; he used them on his wife and child when he was angry and they did not get out of his way fast enough. They were Baptists, their home was always spotlessly clean, but cold and comfortless, and they believed in the Puritan work ethic. Emily helped her mother in the house from her earliest years. Although she was clever and her teachers begged her parents to let the girl go to college, they sharply said they couldn't afford to keep her. Did the school think they were rich folks? So Emily got her first job aged sixteen working in the booking office of the local railway station.

She was allowed to take night-school classes in book-keeping, typing and shorthand. She stayed in that first job a year, saving every cent left over after she paid her parents the sum they demanded for her keep. She never bought new clothes or make-up or perfume, none of the things her ex-schoolfriends found so necessary when they left school and started to earn their own money. At the end of the year she vanished, taking nothing with her because she had nothing worth taking.

In her bedroom she left a letter for her parents saying she wouldn't be back. She never had been. She didn't even know if they were still alive, and she didn't care. She had shed them with all the tedium and unhappiness of her early years, putting it behind her and trying to forget. She had already decided to head for Washington, the centre of power, where around half the population worked for government; Washington was a one-industry town and she wanted to get to where the power lay.

She had enough money to pay for a month's rent in a cheap boarding house, but she got a job the day after she arrived, working in a typing pool, joined the civil service, and within three years had her own tiny apartment and was earning good money.

For years she had hidden her sensuality behind the persona her work demanded: the sensible, capable, down-to-earth secretary who kept an office running smoothly and could be relied on, could be trusted absolutely. She made few friends, none of them close. She was too busy working. She had moved steadily up the career ladder until she got this job, when she was just twenty-four. She wanted Don Gowrie from the minute she saw him. He was the man she had been looking for – ambitious, clever and shrewd, a man headed for the top. She made it her business to know everything about him, his background, his wife's delicate health, his pride in his daughter Cathy, and his other women, the secret ones nobody knew about.

A secretary often knew more than a wife ever did about a man's secrets; within a very short time Emily had been familiar with all his expenses, business and personal, and knew he sometimes paid for the visits into a private apartment he kept in Washington and which few people, including Emily, ever visited.

She had dedicated her whole life to Don Gowrie from the start; she slowly became obsessed with him. She loved his looks, his deep, firm voice, the elegance of his clothes; he was always charming and courteous. He was what she knew her mother would have called 'a real gentleman'. As if her mother knew anything about it!

But he had never seemed to notice her as a woman, until one night, some eight years ago, when they were away from Washington, travelling the rural routes so that Don could meet local politicians, make speeches, make friends. In backwoods Missouri the senator's car had broken down and they had to spend a night in a cheap motel, just the two of them. There was nowhere to eat but a local cheap diner where they had huge steaks, fries and beer. Don ordered Budweiser for them both, and told her that the beer had first been brewed in Czechoslovakia, in a town called Bud-weiss, that when America began making European beers, one of those they chose to brew was a version of Budweiser.

'How do you know all that?' she had asked and he told her, then, about his years in the diplomatic, his time in East Europe.

It was the first personal conversation they had ever had; they had sat on in the diner, drinking beer, for a long time, then he drove back to the motel and walked her to her room, following her inside, letting the door slam behind him.

She remembered the way her legs had started to shake when he bent and kissed her mouth hard. This was how all her fantasies about him had started; she couldn't believe they were coming true at last.

As he lifted his head a moment later she stepped away from him a little, and he flushed, thinking she was rejecting him.

'Sorry,' he had said. 'I'm a little drunk, I guess,' and began to turn back to the door only to stop dead, his lips parted in a silent intake of air as he saw her take off her glasses and drop them on a little table before beginning to undo her silk shirt.

She could still remember the heat inside her, the fast beating of a sensual drum in her veins. She hadn't hurried, she had kept her eyes fixed on him, stripping slowly, with ritual movements, as if to music, dropping her clothes on the floor, lifting a languid hand to release her hair from the neat chignon, letting it flow down over her shoulders.

She had worn it long, in those days; she had changed her hairstyle to mislead people into believing her indifferent to men. That first night Don had stared, pupils wide and shiny, as if he was hypnotized by the body she unveiled for him – her round, firm breasts and smooth hips, her long legs and the dark curly hair between her thighs.

She had heard his thick breathing quicken as she put a hand out to his shirt and began to unbutton it. Neither of them said a word. He let her undress him; he let her make all the moves now. When she had stripped him they stood there, face to face, in silence, until she put her hands on his bare shoulders and pushed him down on to his knees.

Grabbing his hair, she thrust his head forward until his face was buried in the dark bush he hadn't been able to stop staring at. While his tongue probed her she stroked his hair, her bare thighs brushing his face, huskily groaning, 'Yes, there . . . good . . . that's good . . .'

When she had been aroused to the right pitch, she grabbed him by the shoulders again and pushed him backwards on to the floor. She remembered his incredulous face staring up at her as she mounted him, her hot, moist body sucking him into it; the high-pitched cry he gave as she began fiercely riding him, driving herself up to a frenzy of pleasure. Don had helplessly writhed under her, abandoned to her. The violent explosion of passion was brief and shattering. Afterwards she remembered they had lain on the floor like fish out of water, gasping and shuddering.

Only afterwards did she realize that she had hit upon his own secret fantasies, the first woman who ever had, but maybe he had never admitted them openly even to himself? Don, like her, had had a Puritan upbringing. He found it hard to admit what he wanted, needed. He had been as conservative in his sexual encounters as he was in the rest of his life. That night she had been so aroused that she had driven for her own satisfaction and in dominating him had discovered what turned him on. From that moment on, she had the whip-hand in their relationship. As the years went by Don had become addicted to what she did to him in bed.

Watching him with these British politicians now, her mouth was dry. She fought to keep her expression cool, but triumph glittered like jagged glass behind her eyes.

He was hers; when he was president she would rule him and, through him, the whole of America, the whole of the world. The very fact that her dominion would be a secret made it all the more satisfying. She didn't want anyone to know. She relished the shadowy nature of her power.

As the last man left and they were alone in the conference room, he turned towards her at last, one brow lifting in enquiry. Quietly she gave him the message and saw all the colour drain from his face.

'She mustn't reach Cathy,' he muttered. 'Why in God's name is she still alive? She must not reach Cathy.'

Sophie had never been to this part of England before. She had a difficult journey, having to change trains and wait for over an hour before a local stopping train arrived to take her to her final destination. It had been a very slow train too; now she stood on the platform of a small local railway station in Buckinghamshire, in cool early afternoon sunlight, and listened as the train vanished down the lines and silence returned; a silence which gradually filled with other little sounds she had not heard at first. Birds called in the fields on either side of the station; from the bare, black-boughed trees, from the dark green hollies, the tangled hedges of blackthorn. The wind blew in the trees, bent the grasses in the fields, made the station sign rattle. Another passenger had got out here, a woman in a black leather jacket and trousers, who was ahead of her, vanishing out of the station.

The ticket collector was busy outside the station, shifting heavy wooden crates from which chickens chirped and protested.

'Thanks, miss,' he said, sticking her ticket into the band of his hat.

'Can you tell me how to get to Arbory House? Is it far?'

He stared at her. 'Arbory House, is it? Well, now, that's a few miles from here, I'm afraid. You could have got a taxi, if he had been here, but our usual taxi driver is down with flu. You'll have to get the bus; there's one in ten minutes. It stops right outside, you can't miss it.'

Steve was walking through the lobby of their hotel at that moment, on the way up to his room. He stopped at the desk to pick up his key and was about to turn towards the lifts when he heard someone asking for Sophie.

'Miss Narodni?' the receptionist repeated. 'I don't think she is in, sir. I'll ring her room for you, but I believe I saw her leave the hotel several hours ago.'

'Well, maybe she's back, huh?' There was a strong foreign intonation to the voice and Steve recognized it as very similar to Sophie's accent. 'Please to try her room, OK?'

The receptionist smiled politely and turned away to dial. Steve strolled closer, studying the man's profile; a huge nose dominated it, and below that a thick moustache, grizzled with grey.

Suddenly the other man stiffened and turned to stare back at Steve with dark, melancholy eyes that held wary suspicion, the fear of being watched, being followed, that was the legacy of years of repression.

Steve handed him a friendly smile and held out his hand. 'Hello, I'm Steve Colbourne, a TV reporter – I heard you asking for Sophie. She's working as a researcher on my team.'

A big hand engulfed his and he got back an aggressive but not unfriendly grin. 'Ah, you're that guy; sure, she tells me she comes to Europe with you, she left a message on my answerphone while I was out, and I already talked to Theo and Lilli in New York and heard all about what's been bloody going on, which she should have told me herself, but she works for me, Colbourne, firstly and foremostly she works for me.'

'Of course,' Steve said. 'I know that. That is quite understood. You are Vladimir, I take it?'

The yellow walrus teeth were bared, nicotine-stained but big as piano keys.

'Good, because I made her, you know? That girl belongs to me, I gave her her first job and she works for me ever since, nuh, nuh, I taught her everything she knows. Also I have a personal interest in her, OK? I love that girl like she was my daughter. I knew her father, God rest his soul, he was a patriot, just a boy, then, one of the students in the uprising, one of the flowers of Dubcek's spring; a brave boy, clever, too. If the Russians hadn't killed him he would have been one of our great men now, I'm sure of it, because he had such drive, such fire. Why is it always the good who die young, never the rotten bastards?'

The receptionist turned back to them. 'I'm sorry, there is no reply. Would you like to leave a message?'

'Just ask her to get in touch with me as soon as she returns, please,' Steve said.

'Certainly, Mr Colbourne.'

Steve smiled at her, then turned back to Vladimir. 'I could do with a drink – how about you?'

'Always,' Vladimir enthusiastically agreed. 'Lucky we meet, Mr Colbourne . . .'

'Steve, please.'

'Lucky we run into each other, Steve. I'm very worried about Sophie, I think she could be in danger, very great danger.'

Steve steered him towards the hotel bar. 'I know she is, but keep your voice down, Vladimir. I think we may be being watched and followed.'

'You just betcha you are,' grumbled the deep voice near his ear. 'I can always smell them. You get to know, when you live in a goldfish bowl for years, if there's a cat around.' Vladimir smelt strongly of cigar-smoke and as they sat down he took out a leather cigar box and opened it, offering it to Steve, who shook his head, grimacing.

'No, thanks.' He watched the old man start the long ritual of lighting the cigar, clipping the end neatly, rolling it around his mouth, patiently holding the lit match until the tip of the cigar begin to glow red.

Steve breathed in the first fragrance of the smoke; the smell of it was nostalgic, reminding him of his father, of political dinners long ago, when the air was full of cigarsmoke and the smell of brandy.

The waiter came and took their order. When he had gone, Vladimir took his cigar out of his mouth and flicked the first tiny flecks of ash into an ashtray, staring at Steve.

'Has she told you what this is all about?'

Steve stiffened alertly – did this old man know Sophie's secret? Would he tell it? 'No,' he said carefully. 'But I guess it has to do with Senator Gowrie. Something pretty serious. Did you know someone has tried to kill her? Burgled her apartment?'

The old man grunted. 'Lilli told me, but Lilli didn't know what Sophie has on Gowrie, only that she is obsessed with getting to talk to him.' Vladimir drew on his cigar slowly, blew a smoke ring which wavered and broke up. 'As I said, I knew her father in Prague. He sighed, grimacing. 'A long, long time ago; makes me feel old just to talk about it. We were all so full of hope. Pavel was one of the student leaders; he was killed when the Russians invaded. That hit me hard. He was quite a guy. Quite a guy. Sophie was born a few weeks later.'

'Yes, she has told me all this. She obviously hero-worships her father.'

'He was a patriot, a martyr to the cause of Czech freedom. I hope she does respect him. She never knew him, of course, and I never knew her until she came to Prague, to the university, and I gave her her first job, translating for me. As soon as I heard her name I wondered if she could be Pavel's child, and when I found she was I was very moved. Ever since, I've thought of Sophie almost as my own daughter.'

'I know she's fond of you, too.'

Vladimir smiled. 'That's why, when Lilli told me what was going on here, I went to see Sophie's mother. I remembered something that I'd forgotten all about.' He fixed his dark eyes on Steve and paused with the timing of an old ham actor, smiling, knowing he was going to startle.

Steve was amused and faintly irritated by the old man's timing. 'So, what was that?'

'Did Sophie tell you that in 1968 her mother had worked as a nursery maid for Don Gowrie's wife? The Gowries were living in Czechoslovakia for a few months, they were over there for the diplomatic – what was going on excited the US government and they wanted a finger in the pie. They suddenly sent a lot of new people over to Prague to stir the pot. Of course, that was before Sophie was born.'

Steve felt as if he had picked up a live electric wire. Hoarsely he asked, 'Are you going to tell me Sophie is Gowrie's child?'

Vladimir looked startled, gave a deep roar of laughter. 'God, no. No, no. But when I remembered that Johanna had worked for the Gowries, I guessed she had to know this secret, whatever it is . . . had to have been the one who told Sophie in the first place, because Sophie never showed any interest in Gowrie before I sent her to the States. And I was right. It wasn't easy to get Johanna to talk but once I'd told her Sophie was in danger, she finally opened up and told me what she had told Sophie.'

'Which was? Come on, for God's sake . . . what is all this about?'

Across the bar a couple of men drinking beer at the counter turned to stare as they heard Steve's impatient voice; he recognized one of them as Bross. Was he in here by accident, or was Bross following him around?

'Keep your voice down,' he murmured to Vladimir. 'We've got company. Guy over at the counter; he's ex-FBI.'

Vladimir smiled. 'Sure, I spotted him. You should try living in a Communist country some day, you get that sixth sense, you know?' Lowering his voice even more, he bent his great head and began to whisper.

Sophie left the station a few minutes before the bus was due to arrive. The afternoon sunlight held no warmth but it was pleasant to feel it on her face as she looked up and down the road. The station was on the edge of a small town, she saw the roofs of new houses in an estate at a distance, but the surrounding countryside made it feel more like a village.

A black car was parked just down the street; she heard the engine start as she looked towards it, and the car began to move towards the bus-stop, picking up speed as it came, but as it came a single-decker red bus passed it and screeched to a halt. Sophie got on board, paying the driver as she entered.

'Could you let me off at Arbory House, please?'

'The Green Man stop, miss? That will be sixty pence. Do you know it? No? Well, I'll sing out when we reach it.'

'Thank you, you are very kind.'

Sophie took a seat at the front of the bus, and saw the black car passing them; the driver wasn't looking her way but Sophie had a strong sense of having seen her somewhere before. For a second she felt a flicker of panic, then she remembered the woman who had got off her train. A woman in a black leather jacket. Of course, that was it. She had to stop imagining things, seeing shadows in the dark, believing she was being followed, watched, was in danger. That way lay madness.

When the bus drew up in the village square at Arbory, the driver turned to wave at her. 'This is your stop, miss.'

'Thank you,' she smiled, and got off, finding herself standing on the forecourt of an old black-and-white timbered public house with a large sign swinging above the door. Sophie stared up at it; a confusion of green leaves out of which peered a strange, mesmeric pair of eyes that made her skin prickle with uneasiness.

If you kept staring long enough you made out the whole face; it seemed to mock you, to know you and be able to read your thoughts. It was a disturbing image.

The building looked out over a village green, a flat square of grass surrounded by trees, all of them bare of leaves now; a few elms, a weeping willow beside a small pond full of ducks and a couple of swans and a couple of horse chestnuts.

On the other side of the village green she could see an impressive pair of high iron gates, the centre of each blazoned with a coat of arms she could not quite make out at this distance. Was that Arbory House?

Sophie turned back to the open door of the pub, but found her way barred by a huge black cat the size of a small dog. It sat squarely on the mat just inside the door and filled the whole opening.

'Excuse me, I want to get in,' Sophie said, and the cat gazed at her with unreadable green eyes which were oddly similar to the eyes staring out of leaves on the inn sign. It did not budge and Sophie hesitated.

A woman opened the inner door and grinned. 'Just step over Tabitha; she thinks she owns the place but she doesn't. I do. What can I do for you? The bar isn't open yet, you know.'

'I was hoping I could get a room for the night.'

She was scrutinized thoughtfully. 'Single room? Are you alone?'

Sophie nodded. 'I have to visit Arbory House and I came without realizing how far it was from London and how difficult the journey was. So I would rather stay the night and start back in the morning.'

The landlady considered for a moment. 'Well, then,

come in and I'll show you a room – now then, Tabitha, move for the lady.'

Tabitha hunched her shoulders but clearly was not going to shift.

Sophie gingerly stepped over her and followed the land-lady up some creaking old oak stairs to a small room looking out over the village green. It was a square box with a sloping, dark-beamed ceiling, flowery chintz curtains and a matching bedspread.

'It's very pretty,' Sophie said. 'The floor creaks every time you move, doesn't it? Is there anyone sleeping under this room?'

'No, love, don't worry, this is just above the saloon bar. On a Friday or Saturday it can get a bit noisy but not this end of the week. Most of our regulars drink in the other bar. By eleven o'clock they'll all have gone home, anyway. They won't hear you. Old houses are always noisy, they're like old people, they grumble a lot.'

She tested the floorboards with one foot and smiled at the protesting creak. 'Don't worry about it, love.'

'Thank you,' Sophie said and got a shrewd look.

'French, are you, love?'

'Czech.'

It was the landlady's turn to look back. 'Czech? Well, can't say I've ever met a Czech before. Have you got any luggage?

Sophie flushed with confusion. 'No. As I told you, I wasn't expecting to be staying, I . . .'

'Not even a toothbrush!' The landlady went on staring at her, assessing her, then shrugged. 'Well, never mind, I can sell you one, and some toothpaste. I could lend you a nightie, if you want one too. Everything else you'll need is in the bathroom – soap, shampoo. Will you be wanting dinner tonight? Or are you likely to be having dinner over at the house? They often have big dinner parties, and she buys here, in the village, I'll say that for her. She doesn't go ordering all her food from London, like some. She isn't standoffish, either.'

Sophie listened intently, hungry to know more about her sister.

'Do you know her?'

'Well, not to say *know*, we're not friends, so to speak, but she often comes in here with a party of her visitors, for a drink, or some sandwiches. They like to visit a real old English pub, especially the American ones. She's American, you know, not English. She does a lot of good locally. She's always ready to help the local women's groups, she opens flower shows, and lets the pony club hold their gymkhana in Arbory grounds, and lets the vicar use the grounds, too, for the annual village fair in June. She gets us VIPs from London to open it, too. That brings the people in and raises money for the church roof fund. She's always friendly to everyone and has a smile for us if we see her. Oh, she's well liked.'

Sophie was fascinated by all this and could have listened all night, but the landlady paused, grimacing. 'Sorry, here I am chatting away, and I have a lot to do downstairs before we open. So do you want to eat here tonight?'

'Well, I'm not sure what time I'll be back after visiting Arbory House.'

'Well, you can have a bar snack if you're late – or I can give you dinner in my private dining-room, but only until nine o'clock, after that dinner is off. The main dish tonight is roast lamb, and it's good, believe me. Followed by apple and prune crumble – you'll love it.'

'It sounds delicious.'

'I'm afraid I have to ask for cash in advance, at such short notice, though. It's thirty pounds a night and a pound for the toothbrush. Did you want to borrow a nightie?'

'No, thank you, I'll manage.' Sophie got out her wallet

and paid her, glad that she had been to a bank that morning and got some English money. She was not going to spend any of the money Steve had given her; she would feel guilty, taking his firm's money and using it for her own private reasons.

Was Steve being so generous because he secretly hoped to get a story out of her eventually? A shiver ran down her spine. She didn't want to believe that. He was so cynical, though. Would he do anything to get a good story?

The landlady's smile warmed up as she pocketed the cash. 'Thanks. Here's your key. I'll leave the toothbrush and paste in the bathroom later. Let me know if you need anything else.'

Sophie moved to the window to stare out across the village green to the tall iron gates with their gilded coats of arms. 'That's Arbory House opposite, isn't it? Is it far from the gates to the house?'

'A good half-mile. Are you expected? Because the gates are always locked. You talk through some electronic contraption on the wall, give your name to the gate-keeper and he contacts the house to check they want to see you.'

Sophie hadn't expected that; had never realized how difficult it would be to get in to see Anya. It didn't put her off trying, however. She was determined to get in somehow; nothing was going to stop her seeing Anya.

The landlady left her and Sophie went into the bathroom and used the lavatory, then washed her hands and face, renewed her make-up, brushed her hair. The mirror showed her a pale, fine-drawn face with a faintly tremulous mouth, but beneath that a stubborn, determined chin, which matched eyes that were shadowed with obsession.

Ever since her mother told her that Anya was alive she had been possessed with the need to see her. She had been walking in darkness ever since, her mind troubled, aware of hostility and pursuit, knowing she was in danger, possibly risking her life. But she didn't care about any of that. The obsession which had her in its grip meant that now all she cared about was seeing her sister at last, and telling her their mother was dying and needed to see Anya at least one time before she died.

She frowned – should she ring her mother now, find out how she was today? She had spoken to her two days ago, from New York, and Mamma had sounded quite well. Maybe she should wait until she had seen Anya, and could tell her mother if Anya would come to see her.

Yes, that would be best. She had to hurry, before the sun set. She had forgotten how early the sun sank towards the horizon in England in winter. Already the sky was turning pink in the west, flame-coloured streaks running behind Arbory Woods. Soon the light would fade from the sky and it would be dark.

But first she must ring Steve at the hotel and let him know where she was before he started looking for her. He was going to be angry with her for disobeying him.

She was relieved when there was no reply from his room. She left a message with the hotel operator.

As she began to walk across the village green to the gates of Arbory House, the sun sank behind the trees of the park she could glimpse through the gates. Shadows lay in great pools under the trees on the green; there was the chill of winter in the air. She shivered as she passed the pond, whose surface rippled as the night wind blew over it, sending the mallards quacking into the cover of the bullrushes ringing the water.

Reaching the edge of the village green, she began to cross the road on the other side, and was almost at the gates when she heard a car accelerating.

Startled by how close the sound was, Sophie looked round and saw a black shape very close to her, coming at a speed that made her nerves jump. She began to run, but not fast enough; the wing of the car hit her a glancing blow and sent her flying through the air like a rag doll. She landed heavily on one side and lay, half-conscious, where she had fallen, just in front of the iron gates.

She didn't hear the car brakes scream as the driver hit them. The car zigzagged all over the tarmac, tyres spinning noisily, turned in a wide circle and slowed while the driver stared as Sophie stirred and started to struggle to her knees. Then the car engine revved, the car shot forward, driving very fast towards her. Sophie lifted her head to stare at it, her heart thudding in panic. All she could see was the black glass of the windscreen and a shape behind it in the driving seat, but she could not see a face and that scared her more than anything else.

A second later a beam of yellow headlights lit her crouching figure and she instinctively looked round towards the iron gates as they began to open electronically with a smooth humming sound for a long silvery sports car which was coming fast from the house.

It dawned on Sophie abruptly that it was coming straight for her too; that if the black car didn't hit her, the sports car would. She staggered to her feet, looking desperately around. Could she make it to the village green before either of them reached her?

As she turned to run she heard the silver car brake sharply, as if the driver had suddenly caught sight of her.

At that instant the driver of the black car must have seen the other vehicle too. Swerving out of its path towards her, the black car flashed on past, and, as it changed trajectory, went out of control. Tyres screaming, it spun across the road, hit the slight rise at the edge of the village green, turned turtle and was carried on, upside-down, at a tremendous speed over the grass.

Stunned, Sophie stood and watched, scarcely aware of breathing, as the car hit a huge oak tree near the pond. The noise was indescribable; a nightmare sound of splintering glass, imploding metal, crashing branches from the tree, ending in an explosion that deafened her, before a great wall of fire went up and engulfed the oak tree, the car and the human being that had been driving it.

Sophie had not even noticed the other car pulling up a few feet away, or realized that the other driver had got out and stood there watching, too, as appalled as herself.

Shaking and crying, Sophie began to run towards the burning car, not knowing what she was doing, not thinking, only feeling that somebody ought to do something.

'No! You can't do anything for them now!' The voice beside her made her start violently and look round, eyes dilated and full of the horror of what she had just watched.

By the orange blaze of the fire Sophie saw her, a dark-haired woman a little older than herself, in ash-grey trousers, a sweater in a paler shade of grey and a short jersey wool jacket in a warm russet shade.

When Sophie just stared, she went on, 'Are you OK? What on earth was going on? It looked to me as if that car was driving straight at you.'

Sophie's heart was beating so hard she felt sick. Even in that awful light she knew that face, those eyes. She had brought with her all the enlarged photos Steve had had made of the photocopied portraits of her family, to show her sister, but she did not need to consult them to recognize the likeness. She was looking at a younger version of her mother.

'Anya,' she said, smiling shakily, tears rising to her eyes.

Cathy Brougham let go of her and stepped back, startled, face pale. 'You? It was you who rang me this morning, wasn't it? Who are you? And who on earth is Anya?'

Sophie only heard the first few words. Shock and weariness finally engulfed her. She slumped forward in a dead faint, and Cathy caught her in her arms.

8

People came running from across the green, from up and down the village high street, shouting, their voices carrying over the roar of the burning car. Some of them tried to get closer, one man dodged in to see if whoever was inside the car could be helped, but the searing heat drove them all back.

'I rang the police and fire brigade.' The landlady of the Green Man was out of breath, her chest heaving after running across the village green. 'They should be here soon.'

'Can you help me? I'm going to put her in my car. She can't just lie here in the road.' Cathy Brougham was holding Sophie's dead weight under the arms, supporting her with her own body.

'Sure. I'll take her feet. Here we go.'

'Is she OK? That car didn't knock her down, did it?'

'I don't know what happened. She doesn't seem to be injured.'

'There's blood on her face,' said the landlady, peering closer, then she turned and stared at the burning car. 'I heard the crash – thought it was the end of the world. Terrible noise, wasn't it? I dropped the pint of beer I was pulling, all over the counter it went, glass and beer everywhere. I didn't have to go to the window to see what had happened; it lit up the windows. Lit up the sky, too, I dare say, for miles.'

'Like the Blitz,' an old man said, standing beside them, staring at the blaze like a little boy on Bonfire Night, his rheumy eyes glistening in the light. 'Reminds me of fire-watching. Terrible heat, fire has. Look at the glass melting. Won't be much left of them inside.'

'That's enough, Albert! You'll make us all ill.' The land-lady slid a look at Cathy Brougham's appalled expression.

Sophie lay with firelight shining on her lids and didn't dare to open her eyes. Her teeth were chattering, she was trembling violently and was icy cold. Why was she so cold? Where was she? What had happened? She heard the voices as if from far away, foreign, bewildering. What were they talking about?

Across the green she heard the rush and roar of the flames, branches crashing from the tree which was now on fire, too, and her memory came back. The black car driving straight at her . . . the crash . . . the explosion. Oh, God, that noise!

'Your friend's shaking like a leaf. She's staying in my front bedroom, by the way,' the landlady told Cathy. 'She didn't cause the accident, did she? She just walked out of the pub a few minutes ago, coming over here to see you, she said.'

'I think the car must have hit her, but she got up. She didn't seem seriously injured.' Cathy bent to look at Sophie. 'You're right, she's shaking badly, she must be in shock. Did you ring the doctor?'

'The police said they would be sending an ambulance.' The landlady turned to stare as a small police car drove up with siren wailing. 'What's he making that racket for? Give a man a horn and he'll blow it.'

Without answering, Cathy moved to meet the police-man. Sophie heard her voice talking quietly, heard a man's voice asking questions, then Cathy came back. 'He says it's OK for me to go back to my house and take this lady with me. There's an ambulance on the way, and he rang Dr Waring, but the doctor was out on a call. He'll be along later and can look at her then. She'll be better off lying down somewhere warm.'

Sophie could feel tears trickling down her face. She was

dizzy and disorientated. Her mind kept drifting off into confused visions: cars screamed towards her, headlights blinding, tyres spun on the road, the car slewed round and rushed towards the oak tree, she heard the crash again, endlessly echoing, the explosion with which the petrol tanks blew, saw the fireball go up into the bare black branches of the oak, orange flames climbing into the night sky.

Cathy Brougham got behind the wheel and closed her door, starting the engine. The silver car moved off through the open iron gates, drove back along the drive, over gravel, under trees which sent a strange flickering over Sophie's face, the shadows of the leaves reflected in the headlights. Her eyes opened and stared up, hypnotized.

They approached a house; she saw the black bulk of it, a front door opened and sent yellow light towards them, the car stopped outside and there were raised, startled voices.

Somebody opened the door of the car beside her and she was helped out, supported by two people, one on each side, while she staggered towards the square of light which was a door.

'In here . . .'

The light dazzled her. She swayed, and was held, was half-carried into a room and laid down on a couch. She stayed still, her eyes shut again, heard footsteps clicking on wood floors, a door somewhere near by open and close quietly.

'How do you feel?'

The voice came from right beside her and she started, opening her eyes to find herself lying flat, with a warm woollen tartan rug over her. Above her a face glowed in the firelight, soft-skinned, with wide eyes and curling dark hair.

Mamma! she wanted to say. The name came instantly to her lips but was not spoken because even as she thought it she knew that this was not her mother, this was Anya, and she remembered everything. It all came back with a rush and made her dizzy again. She couldn't believe that at last she was seeing her sister, that it was all true, Anya was alive and so strikingly like their mother that Sophie couldn't stop staring at her. If she had had any doubts at all about their mother's story, they had all dissolved. There was no shred of doubt anywhere. This was her sister, this was Anya, and she was no longer an outsider in her mother's new family, she was no longer alone, she had Anya now, even if Anya did not yet know it.

Anya might reject her. She could see that Anya was disturbed by her, thought her crazy, perhaps? And rationally, Sophie couldn't blame her.

'I'd offer you some brandy, but I'm not sure if I should give you alcohol, there's some water here, if you want it. That can't hurt you,' said the strangely American voice which should have been like her own, or like their mother's.

'Please,' she whispered, and watched her sister pick up a glass of water which looked so clear and cool her mouth thirsted for it as if she had been lost in a desert and had not drunk for days.

Cathy slid a hand under her neck and lifted her head, held the glass to her mouth; Sophie swallowed and the water flowed down her throat. Cathy lowered her again and sat down on the carpet beside the couch, her knees, in their sleek grey jersey wool trousers, bent up and her arms curled around them, hands clasped, her chin on top of them, staring at Sophie.

'When you fainted I wasn't sure what to do, so I brought you here, to my home. You didn't seem to have any serious injuries, and the nearest hospital is a very long drive away. I've sent for our doctor. He'll be able to tell us if you need hospital treatment.'

'I don't think I'm badly hurt,' Sophie said, sitting up warily to test that.

Cathy at once said sharply, 'Be careful! You ought to lie down until the doctor has seen you.'

'I'm not in any pain.' Sophie felt her arms and legs gingerly. 'No, no bones broken. A few bruises where the car hit me, or where I fell, but I expect I'm more shocked than hurt.'

'All the same you shouldn't move. Shock can be pretty devastating.'

'Yes.' Sophie lay down again and looked around the room, curious about her sister's home. Large, furnished with what she recognized as antiques, yet comfortable, a family room with a very lived-in sense. The couch was arranged in front of a huge stone fireplace which was big enough for several people to stand inside. There was a black iron basket in the centre of it, holding the great log fire which gave the room so much heat and light, scenting the air with pine, crackling as resin ran from the wood and exploded in the heat with sparks flying up the great, blackened chimney.

Sophie shivered suddenly, staring into the heart of the fire and remembering.

'Don't think about it!' Cathy Brougham said sharply, tuning into her thoughts. 'Try not to think at all.'

Sophie laughed shakily. Above it a gold clock in a glass case chimed the hour; Sophie counted the chimes and couldn't believe that it was already five o'clock. It had been morning when she left the hotel; the journey here had taken longer than she had ever guessed it might. She hoped Steve had got her message or he would be worried, finding her missing. Would the hotel remember to give it to him?

'Would you like some coffee or tea?' suggested Cathy.

'Coffee would be good,' Sophie whispered.

Cathy went to a table to pick up a telephone, pressed a button. 'Could we have a pot of coffee and some biscuits?'

she asked whoever answered. 'Thank you. No, nothing else.'

A wood-block floor gleamed in the firelight, reflecting the silver photograph frames displayed on tables, the faces in them all unknown to her except those which showed Anya, reflecting two glass vases of winter flowers, white and gold chrysanthemums, a row of dark family portraits hung on the panelled walls. Were those the ancestors of Anya's husband, Paul Brougham? Here and there the floor was laid with rugs, dark red and black, their patterns ritualized, the wavy lines representing water, the triangles trees; that much she knew from once attending a sale of rugs in London a year or so ago.

Sitting on the floor, Cathy Brougham watched Sophie, wondering what she was thinking. Who on earth was she? She was beautiful, her blonde hair silky, her skin smooth, even if it had a worrying pallor. Had the car crash put that haunted, almost hunted look in her blue eyes? Had the black car been trying to hit her? What was she doing here? Why had she rung up earlier, and asked if she was Anya – why did she keep calling *her* Anya? Who was Anya?

Cathy remembered the crash again, the explosion, the flames. Her heart raced with shock and disbelief.

'That car tried to run you down, didn't it?' she broke out and Sophie started, and looked at her, unable to hide the fear she felt.

'You saw?'

'I saw the car driving straight at you. In my headlights. I saw clearly what was happening. Before the car went into a spin and crashed.'

'Did you see who was driving?'

'There wasn't time and it was too dark, anyway. But there was just one person in the car, and I had a feeling it was a woman.'

Sophie's chest squeezed agonizingly. 'Yes, I thought it

216

was too.' Her voice sounded like dead leaves blowing down a gutter, whispering, faint.

Cathy stared fixedly at her. 'You know why she was trying to kill you, don't you? Why? Who was she? Come to that, who are you? What's this all about? And who is Anya?'

Sophie looked around wildly. 'My bag. Where's my bag? I had it with me when that car hit me, I know I did . . .'

Her voice soothing, Cathy quickly said, 'Don't worry, it's here, I saw it on the road and picked it up.' Getting to her feet she went to a table nearby and picked up the large black shoulder bag which she had found on the road beside her car. 'Here it is, you see?'

'Oh, thank you.' In her relief Sophie almost sobbed as she took it. Her hands shook as she unzipped it and pulled out the little sheaf of photographs she had brought with her to show her sister. Hunting through them, she found the photo of their mother in her wedding-dress and held it out. 'Do you recognize this?'

Frowning, startled, Cathy Brougham took it. 'What a strange picture! It looks like a photo of a ghost.' She shivered as if a ghost had in fact walked over her grave.

'It's a photocopy of a photograph; the photo was blown up to make it clearer.'

It was far from clear, thought Cathy. 'But what is it?' She found the strange black and white composition disturbing; she couldn't stop staring, though, she couldn't believe what she was seeing. Slowly she turned her head and stared into a gilt-framed Venetian eighteenth-century mirror hanging on the wall across the room. She walked over there to look closer, held the photograph up beside her own reflection, and couldn't breathe properly. It could have been a picture of her, now; yet it was clearly an old photograph, more a negative in ghostly black and white, the clothes old-fashioned, a peasant look to them that made them foreign, and yet that face was so familiar, she had seen it in her mirror a million times.

'What is this?' she whispered. 'Who is it?'

Sophie was breathless with excitement and relief because she could see that her sister had seen the resemblance, was shaken by it. 'You do recognize it, don't you?'

Cathy swallowed. 'No!' she lied. It was some trick, it had to be. Had someone taken a picture of her and stuck it on the body of someone else? Angrily she broke out, 'Who are you?'

'I am Sophie, Sophie Narodni.'

'Narodni?' The way she repeated it told Sophie that the name meant nothing to her. 'That's East European, isn't it? – where do you come from?'

'I am Czech,' Sophie said in her own language, hoping for some reaction, but Cathy looked blank, so she repeated it in English. 'I am Czech.'

'Oh. Czech.' Cathy frowned. 'What are you doing in England?'

'I am here to see you, Anya.'

A flush of anger ran up Cathy's face. 'Why do you keep calling me that? My name is Cathy, Cathy Brougham. I was Cathy Gowrie, but I have never been called Anya.' But she looked again at the photocopied face of their mother, bewilderment in her eyes. 'Who is this, anyway? It isn't me, although it looks like me. Who is it?'

'Our mother.'

Cathy Brougham felt as if she had been kicked in the stomach. She gave a shaken gasp. 'What? What are you talking about?' She almost ran over to a table and picked up a photograph in an ornate silver art nouveau frame, held it out to Sophie. 'This is me, with my mother. She doesn't look anything like this!' and she held out the photocopied photo too so that the faces were side by side.

Sophie took it eagerly and looked at the dark-haired little

girl in a cream straw bonnet and embroidered frock, un-smilingly leaning against a thin, pale woman who had a tight, possessive arm around her shoulders. So that was Mrs Gowrie? She looked neurotic, or was she simply ill?

It must have been taken shortly after they left for America; the child was the same age as the photo of Anya she had brought with her. Sophie hunted among her pile of photographs, found it and held it out.

Cathy was oddly reluctant to take it; she felt a shiver of premonition, her skin icy, and hung back, her hands by her side. She had never been prone to belief in the super-natural, in second sight or having her fortune read, she didn't believe in all that stuff, yet suddenly she was afraid, although she didn't even know what it was that frightened her, only that, although her rational mind told her that this was all nonsense, she was afraid it might be true. No. No. Sophie Narodni must be trying to play some confidence trick on her. Hoping to get money out of her?

Yet she seemed genuine enough. Indeed her face was dis-turbingly convincing. That was real emotion in those blue eyes. She's probably crazy, Cathy thought. She has to be. It isn't true, any of it, but she believes it, so she must be mad.

'Take it, Anya, look at yourself,' Sophie said gently, pushing the photo into her hands.

Cathy took one look then sat down on the floor again, her knees giving under her, her eyes wide and dark with shock as she took in the identical faces. Both herself. She couldn't deny it, but there had to be some other explan-ation, she just had to find it, and find it she would. She wasn't being taken in by some photographic trick.

She looked angrily at Sophie Narodni. 'Where did you get this picture of me? I'm not stupid, you know. I see how you played this trick – you got hold of newspaper photo-graphs, and had them photocopied then re-photographed, very enlarged. It's obvious how you did it. The press are always printing old photos from our family albums, and all my life I can remember posing for the press photographers too. This is a photo of me taken when we first came back to the States.' But her eyes went back to the photograph of the young woman in a strange, old-fashioned wedding-dress, and she frowned, unable to explain that one.

Sophie saw her glance at it and frown; and gently said, 'No, Anya, that is not you – it is our mother.' Her eyes were full of sympathy and anxiety. She had expected disbelief but she had not understood quite how much of a shock it would be for her sister. Should she have come here? Should she have told her?

But I had to – I promised Mamma I would find Anya and bring her home. I just hadn't realized what it would mean for Anya. She doesn't want a sister, she has had a whole life of which I have no share. I have thought of her all my life, I have loved her, even when I believed her dead – but Anya has not even known I existed, and can I blame her if she hates me for what I am doing?

'This is my mother.' Cathy held out the silver-framed photo in a shaking hand. Sophie looked at it and sighed.

'That is Mrs Gowrie. She may have been your mother for as long as you can remember, but she isn't your real mother, and Mr Gowrie isn't your real father.'

Cathy felt a stab of shock and pain. Her voice hoarse, she said, 'Stop telling these lies! I don't want to hear any more!'

'It's the truth. They adopted you, when you were two years old, just after this photo of you was taken for our mother. I was born a few weeks after you were taken away to America. My mother lied to me, told me you were dead, I used to be taken to visit your grave, I had no idea you were still alive until a couple of months ago when I was coming to the States and my mother told me the truth. She has leukaemia – she's afraid she'll die without ever seeing you again, and that nobody will ever know you're still alive.'

'Leukaemia?' The shock of that news froze Cathy.

'They've given her three months to live,' Sophie added.

Huskily, Cathy said, 'I'm sorry. That must be hard for you.' The more she looked at the photos, at Sophie, the more she was afraid this might all be true. Instinct kept tugging at her like an importunate hand. Every time she looked into this other woman's face she felt a pang of emotion she couldn't quite define, had never felt before.

Sophie sighed. 'Yes, it was a terrible shock when she told me, I couldn't take it in at first. It came out of the blue. She always seemed so strong, and now suddenly she is very frail, she has no energy, she is so pale and limp, I hardly knew her last time I saw her.'

Cathy stared at the photo of the young girl in the wedding-dress, moved by the thought that time had ruined both of them, girl and dress, worn down their strength and left them fading, grown thin as a yellow leaf on an autumn tree.

'I'm sorry. My own mother has been ill for a long time,' she said.

'*She* is your mother,' Sophie said fiercely, tapping the photo. 'I'm telling you the truth, Anya.'

Cathy's temper flared again. 'Don't call me that! I'm Cathy Brougham. What are you after? Money? That's what this is all about, isn't it? You want me to pay you to keep quiet. Well, you've got me wrong if you think I'll fall for this cheap blackmail, I won't pay you a cent, and when my husband finds out about this you're going to regret it. You'll end up in jail!'

Sadly Sophie said, 'I don't want to hurt you, Anya, believe me. I suppose I shouldn't have come, shouldn't have told you – but I can't let my mother die without seeing you again at least once. You don't need to be afraid, I'm not here to blackmail you or threaten you, I just needed to see you, face to face. I think I only half-believed it until now. I do understand how you feel, you see. I was incredulous at first. It's very hard to believe. But I guess that deep down I wanted to believe it. I've spent my whole life thinking about you. I used to go to the churchyard and sit by your grave and talk to you, I believed you could hear me in heaven and I needed a friend, needed someone to talk to, someone to care about.'

'Stop talking about graves! In fact, stop talking to me,' Cathy interrupted. 'Look, when the doctor has seen you, you're going, you know, you're leaving – whether you go to the hospital or just go back wherever you came from!'

'If that's what you want, I'll go. And I'm sorry if I've told you something you didn't want to hear. I thought about it for a long time, believe me, and I didn't know what I ought to do, but it had meant so much to me, finding out you were alive. I thought it might mean something to you to find out you had a sister, a family you belonged to and had never met. At the very least it might mean something to discover the truth about yourself, I thought. And I had promised our mother that I would find you. I had to do it, for her sake. I couldn't let her die without at least trying to find you. I didn't know what you were like, how you might react. But I had to take the risk of finding you and telling you, hoping you would listen.'

Cathy didn't answer, she was too busy searching Sophie's face and seeing no threat, no attempt to blackmail or terrify, just pain and deep emotion in her eyes. The silence stretched between them like a thin, shining rope, tying them together, binding them, until it was broken by a tap on the door, which opened a second or two later.

'The doctor, madam.'

Cathy slowly turned her head, blinking as if coming out of a daze. She got to her feet and forced a polite smile as a tall, attractive man in his thirties came towards them from the door. 'Good evening, Dr Waring, I'm sorry to call you out on such a raw evening. Thank you for coming so promptly.'

Don Gowrie was in his shower, his weary body relaxing under the jets of warm water, washing off the sweat and making his skin tingle. The pleasure of the exercise was broken when he heard the phone ringing. He leaned out instantly, and reached for the phone on the bathroom wall.

'Yes?' He had been waiting for a call from Emily for hours. This must be it.

It wasn't. It was Jack Beverley and he didn't waste any time with courtesies. Curtly, he said, 'I'm sorry. I have some bad news, I'm afraid, sir. Miss Sanderson has had an accident.'

Don leaned on the marble-tiled wall, feeling all his blood leave his heart. The warm relaxation was gone. 'Is she badly hurt? What happened?' His nerves chattered. Could she never do anything right? She kept failing; had she failed yet again? Had she fucked up badly? Been caught trying to kill that damned Narodni girl? If she'd been arrested . . . would she hold her tongue? What if she spilled her guts, told them . . . his mind raced ahead, imagining the worst, seeing himself arrested, charged with attempted murder.

Beverley's voice was expressionless. 'She crashed her car, sir.'

Relief made Don Gowrie sag. 'Stupid bitch . . .' he said, almost indulgently. 'I hope she wasn't hurt?'

He wasn't expecting what Jack Beverley replied. The words hit him like bullets; he jerked, stiffened, twisted in agony.

'She was doing about a hundred miles an hour when she hit a tree and the car burst into flames. She's dead, I'm afraid. I'm sorry to be the one to give you this news. Thought you'd want to hear it right away. My people had been tailing Miss Narodni, as requested. They spotted

Miss Sanderson tailing her, too, and phoned in from their mobile as soon as the accident happened.'

Don's insides caved in; he closed his eyes, swallowing bile. Emily. Damn you, you stupid bitch, what have you done?

'She must have been killed outright, sir. She wouldn't have known much about it.'

Don hadn't even noticed his teeth meeting in his lip; he was unaware of the red blood trickling down his chin. He couldn't get a word out.

Jack Beverley politely told him, 'Miss Narodni is now in Arbory House, sir.'

Finished. I'm finished, Don thought. It's over. It will all be out now. That little bitch has done for me.

'I suggest it's time you were a little more frank with me,' Jack Beverley said without emphasis. 'Not over the phone, sir. But we should talk before you go to this dinner tonight.'

'I'm getting dressed now. In ten minutes?'

'I'll be there. And, sir, I suggest a stiff bourbon, help you with your nerves. Shock plays havoc with nerves.'

Paul Brougham had been discussing circulation figures with his editor-in-chief for an hour when his eye fell on his watch. 'Christ, got to go, have to dress for this Guildhall dinner,' he groaned. He had totally forgotten about the evening in front of him; he wished he did not have to go to the dinner. He would far rather go home to Cathy.

The editor looked at his own watch. 'Is that the time? I must get changed, too. I'm dining with the French ambassador.'

'Give him my compliments,' Paul said, grinning. The ambassador was a personal friend, they watched Rugby games together whenever France played England at Twickenham, and they shared other pleasures. Until Paul met Cathy they had even shared a woman once or twice, but now their mutual interests were food, good wine, and a love of the French language. Paul's French was perfect, of course, so fluent that it would be easy to believe he had never lived anywhere else. He still went back to France as often as he could manage it, and owned a villa in the south of France, on the Côte d'Azur, not far from Cannes, his favourite place along that blue-gold coast. He disliked Nice; a beautiful but dangerous city, a glittering playground for some of the creatures that lurked in the murkier waters of French society.

When the editor had gone, Paul was about to take the lift to his penthouse flat above the newspaper, where he would change into evening dress to attend the dinner at the Guildhall at which his father-in-law was to be guest of honour, when the phone rang.

'Your wife, sir, she says it's urgent.'

'Put her through, then.' A click, then Cathy's voice, breathless, quivering.

'Paul?'

'Hello, darling – what's the problem? I was just going to get dressed.'

'Paul . . . I need you, will you come home at once, instead of going to the dinner tonight?'

'Skip the dinner?' Paul felt a leap of fear in his chest. 'Why? What is all this? Has something happened, Cathy?'

'I can't talk on the phone. I'd just like you to get here as fast as possible. Take a helicopter, don't drive home.' Her voice sounded shaky, scared. 'I don't want you hurrying on the roads tonight.'

'Are you ill? For God's sake, Cathy, what is all this?'

'I'll explain when you get here.'

'What shall I say to your father? He expects –'

'Don't tell him anything! Don't even tell him you won't be at the dinner. Just come.

The phone went dead. Paul stood there stupidly, staring at it, his mind racing with questions, with terror. Cathy had sounded so weird. Terrified, yes, she had sounded terrified. He thought of everything that could have happened to her – his imagination went crazy. Terrorists could have snatched Cathy as a hostage to use against her father, these things happened all the time. Or the Mafia could have grabbed her for ransom. Ever since Don Gowrie let them know he would be visiting England and would come to Arbory there had been an awareness of risk at the back of their minds. Why else had Gowrie's security people visited the house to check it out? They expected trouble. Paul had thought it was just the usual paranoia that hung around the American presidency like a fog, making anyone within reach of it feel threatened by invisible forces.

But maybe it wasn't. Maybe someone had got into Arbory and was threatening Don Gowrie through his daughter?

But why would someone like that let her ring him? Her father wasn't due at Arbory until tomorrow. Maybe she had had an accident. What if she was badly injured? Oh, but she had rung him herself, so she was alive, it couldn't be that serious. Maybe she had just found out that she was ill? Cancer, leukaemia, brain tumour . . . his mind was rushing with terrifying suggestions.

Icy sweat dewed his forehead; he was shivering as if in a high wind. His hand shot out to press down a key on his office console.

'Yes, sir?' his secretary asked.

'My plans have changed. I'm not going to the Guildhall dinner. Get me my chauffeur, then get me the helipad, I'm flying home right away.'

Nursing a whisky, Jack Beverley listened to Gowrie's muttered story. His face did not betray what he was thinking; his cold, shrewd eyes simply watched the other man, skewering him in his chair.

When Gowrie had finished, Beverley said, 'This is serious, sir. Well, if you aren't to walk away from the presidency, which might be the wise thing to do at this stage . . .' His eyes queried Gowrie's and the other man shook his head angrily.

'Not unless there's no alternative!'

Beverley nodded. 'OK, then we must start some immediate damage-limitation. You should have told me at once. A lot of time has been wasted. Firstly, I'm afraid you have to talk to your daughter, to Mrs Brougham.'

Bitterly, Don Gowrie said, 'You can bet that that Czech bitch is doing so right now. I wish to God I'd dealt with her myself. Or got you to do it.'

'Yes, you should have done that, sir. But there's no point in crying about spilt milk. OK, my men are outside the grounds of Arbory House at the moment. There are police all over the place, fire engines, ambulances, and crowds of people watching what's going on – my men won't even be noticed. But before the police can talk to Miss Narodni I think my men should move in to Arbory House and snatch her. We'll need a good story. My men will talk to your daughter and explain that whatever Miss Narodni has told her, the truth is that she's in the UK to cause trouble for you. She's a political extremist, dangerous – she wanted to get into Arbory House so that she could assassinate you. That should counter whatever the girl has been telling Mrs Brougham.'

With a wild leap of hope, Don Gowrie said eagerly, 'That's clever. It could work, it's convincing, Cathy knows how crazy some people can get over politics.' He began to breathe properly for the first time since he heard the news about Emily. 'How soon can your men get in there, get her away from Cathy?'

'I'll ring them back on their mobile at once and give them their orders.'

'What will you do with the girl?'

'We'll think about that later. First we must talk to her, find out exactly what she is up to, whether or not she has accomplices, who else knows the story,' Jack Beverley said. 'We must snuff this story out immediately, leave no loose ends. Ring your daughter now, explain that we're coming, don't discuss anything about Miss Narodni's story, just tell her to let us deal with Miss Narodni. Say it is a security matter you can't discuss over the phone. Then you go off to your dinner, sir, and leave this to us. You should have talked to us earlier. We are the professionals. It was unwise to let an amateur deal with the problem.'

Don Gowrie picked up the phone on a nearby table and dialled. A polite English voice answered; he asked for his daughter.

'I'm sorry, sir, she is not available.'

'What do you mean, not available? This is her father – I need to speak with her urgently.'

'Mrs Brougham is out, sir. Can I get her to ring you when she gets back?'

'Hold the line a second.' Gowrie looked at Jack Beverley. 'She's out.'

Beverley frowned. 'My men said she had gone back to her house with the Narodni girl. Maybe she went out again?'

'Shall I ask my daughter to ring me?'

'Hang on while I think.' Beverley bit on his index finger, his brows heavy. 'No, she might not ring until after you had left for this dinner. OK, leave a message for her, saying that there is a security problem. Your security people will be coming to collect Miss Narodni.'

Don lifted the phone to his mouth again and repeated this message. 'Have you got that?'

The English voice was calm. 'Yes, sir. Security people will be coming here tonight for Miss Narodni.'

'She is there, isn't she?'

'I couldn't say, sir. But I'll give Mrs Brougham that message.'

Don hung up. 'I don't like it. I didn't like that woman's tone. I'll swear Cathy was there – why wouldn't they put me through to her?'

Without replying, Beverley moved towards the door. 'Must get on, sir.' He added, with no visible sign of sarcasm, 'Enjoy your dinner.'

Gowrie stared after him. He didn't know how he was going to get through this meal. If he could have done so safely he would have pulled out of the dinner, but the Anglo-American Friendship Society was too important to be offended. Many very famous people on both sides of the Atlantic were members. Being asked to speak to them was a significant honour. He had first met his future son-in-law at one of these occasions, in Washington, around seven years ago.

No, he had to show up and give his speech, and some-how pretend everything was just fine. He wouldn't think about Emily. His skin shrivelled at the very thought of her death. No, he had no time to dwell on all that. Emily had let him down. He should never have asked her to deal with the problem. Jack was right, he should have confided in him. Well, now he had. Jack would deal with Sophie Narodni. Gowrie knew how few scruples Jack had; he was a man for whom killing was a job and he would do that job without a qualm.

Steve had been sitting in the bar with Vladimir for over an hour before he thought of trying to get hold of Sophie again. His head was ringing with the story the old Czech had told him. He felt as if he had been beaten endlessly with a brass gong, the echoes reverberating round and round his skull making him almost deaf. He couldn't think clearly about what he had heard; he just sat staring at the bristling moustache, flecked with grey ash as Vladimir drew slowly on yet another of his heavily perfumed cigars.

'Gowrie must have been crazy to take such a risk,' Steve said again, having said it a dozen times over the past hour. 'How on earth did he think he could get away with it? I mean, his wife might have blurted it out to her parents, or Sophie's mother might have told her new husband, they might have tried to blackmail Gowrie, demanding money, or wanted him to get them into the States.'

'She had begged him to do that, in the beginning, but he convinced her he couldn't get her out. I'm sure he was right – the Russians wouldn't have let Pavel Narodni's family leave at that time. He had just been killed but they probably intended to make his wife talk, give them names, tell them everything she knew. They interrogated her, on and off, for weeks; they didn't give up on her until they were finally convinced that she knew nothing at all about student polit-ics, that she was just a peasant girl. She was very young, remember; only twenty-one herself then; she'd stayed at home in her tiny village, while her husband went to university. That year he had hardly been home at all.'

'I suppose Gowrie made a dead set at him? He would have been very useful. American diplomats, like our jour-nalists, always try to get a line in to any local rebels.'

'No, Johanna claims he never met Pavel. Pavel was too busy with his political meetings to come home that summer, for one thing, and for another she never told Pavel she was working as a maid because he would have been angry if he found out. He was very proud; he wouldn't want his wife working as a servant. They desperately needed more money, but Pavel would have been furious, he would have thought it humiliating.'

'It's amazing Gowrie managed to talk her into giving up her child!'

Wryly, Vladimir said, 'Don't forget, all this happened the

week the Russians invaded; the country was in turmoil, nobody knew what was going to happen next, people were confused, terrified, and Johanna was pregnant, about to give birth to Sophie. She was in shock, too, having just heard that Pavel was dead. She was afraid for herself, too, in case the Russians came for her. And what would happen to little Anya if they did? She might end up in some state home for orphans. No, Gowrie was very lucky in his timing. He got her right at the perfect moment psychologically. She was at his mercy.'

'Poor woman. And now she's dying? Isn't there a chance she could be cured? I mean, we have very good treatments for leukaemia these days in the States.'

Vladimir shook his head soberly. 'I've seen her. She's past treatment, fading fast. She left it too late to go to the doctor. I think she's only hanging on in the hope that Sophie will find Anya and bring her home.'

Steve sighed, glanced at his watch. 'Talking of Sophie, I must talk to her. And I have to get ready. I'm going to a banquet in the City of London tonight where Gowrie is the main speaker. We'll see you tomorrow, shall we? You've got a room here?'

'I'll get one,' Vladimir said.

'We could have breakfast together.'

Steve collected his key from the desk and was handed a small yellow envelope. He ripped it open and read Sophie's message. As the words sank in, he felt as if his stomach had dropped out of him.

He ran towards the reception desk where Vladimir was handing over his credit card to the receptionist checking him into a room at the hotel.

9

The doctor finished his examination of Sophie, but gave his
views to Cathy as if Sophie, being foreign, wouldn't understand him. 'Nothing too serious – a few bruises and minor
abrasions; that's where the blood comes from. Amazing
how much blood you can get from the tiniest cut. She
doesn't have any broken bones or head injuries, her eyes
are focused; no sign of concussion. Unless something
shows up during the next few days, I think she's come off
pretty lightly.' His eyes twinkled. 'She's obviously a bit
accident-prone, of course.'

'Accident-prone?' Cathy repeated blankly.

'You didn't notice the faded bruises on the face?' He put
a hand under Sophie's chin and turned her face sideways so
that the light fell directly on to one side of her cheek.
'Under the eye, see that? And here . . .' He touched the
edge of her jaw with one light finger; he had cold skin and
Sophie did not enjoy being touched by him. 'And here, too.'
He flicked back her neckline and showed a shadowy bruise
on her neck. 'Others on her arms and legs. They're recent –
in the last few days, I'd say.' He raised an eyebrow at
Sophie. 'Not the boyfriend, I hope?'

She didn't bother to laugh at his joke, nor did she answer
his question frankly. 'I fell down.' Her eyes did not meet
his. She did not want to talk about what had happened in
the subway; it would lead to more questions and more
curiosity.

'As I said, accident-prone,' he drawled, and she knew he
did not believe her but really did not care. She did not live
here, she was only a temporary patient; it didn't matter to
him what happened to her. He might be attractive to look at

but he had cold eyes. 'Lucky young woman both times, then,' he said, opening the large black briefcase he had brought with him. 'Did you know the driver of the car, by the way?' And he shot her a quick, sideways glance as he asked, hoping, she saw, to surprise a reaction out of her.

She couldn't hide her shiver, her frown of dismay at the memory, but was able to answer honestly. 'No.' She did not know who had been driving that car, but she had her suspicions – at the back of her mind she had had a faint, fugitive impression without having time to think about it; that feeling had grown ever since. Could it have been Gowrie's secretary in that car? The idea appalled her, that Gowrie was the man behind this latest attempt to kill her; she couldn't talk about it, though, not in front of Cathy.

'Is the fire out yet?' Cathy asked him and he nodded.

'Yes, but the firemen are still working on the car.' He didn't expand on what they were doing, for which Sophie was grateful. Taking a small box out of his case, he wrote on it rapidly in an unreadable hand and held it out to Cathy. 'Give her one of these capsules with water now. It's a sedative, not a sleeping pill, but it should calm her down and help her sleep. If she needs it she can take another one in six hours; I'm only giving you enough for twenty-four hours. She must consult her own doctor or call me again if she needs any more.'

'Thank you, doctor, it was very good of you to come.'

He nodded and looked down at Sophie. 'Try to stay out of accidents, hmm?'

She felt a flare of irritation and sharply said, 'I don't enjoy having accidents, doctor!'

He raised his brows again, but said no more. Cathy saw him to the door, Sophie heard her talking quietly to him before the door closed and Cathy came back.

'He thinks you are up to talking to our local policeman

before I give you the sedative. Can I let him come in now? He needs to ask you some questions about the accident.'

A pulse of panic beat in Sophie's neck. 'Must I?' She knew she sounded childish but she couldn't help it, she was afraid of talking to the police. She always found the sight of police uniforms alarming. Right from her childhood, when Mamma had first told her about the way Papa died, giving her that vivid little picture of men in uniform appearing out of the dark, shouting to the driver of the car Papa was in to stop and then the bang, bang, bang of machine guns when the car drove on.

It must have happened just the way it did tonight; the car out of control, zig-zagging all over the place before it crashed and burst into flames.

Sophie as a little girl had listened, wide-eyed and terrified. She had taken on board then that if you didn't do what the men in uniforms ordered you were killed. All her life since she had heard similar stories from people back home: stories of police brutality, the helplessness of people confronted by the knock in the night, the disappearance of loved ones. Everyone had a story to tell. It was the commonplace of their daily lives for so many years, as she had said to Steve the other day. You had to learn to live with it.

Steve! she thought with a jab of shock – she had forgotten Steve. She must let him know what's happened, where she was.

'Don't look so scared!' Cathy knelt down beside the couch and took her hand. 'Do you want me to stay with you while Constable Hawkins interviews you?'

'Yes, please.' Sophie clutched her fingers and smiled gratefully at her. 'Oh, yes, stay, I'll find it easier if you're here. But first . . . can I make a phone call?'

The gatekeeper of Arbory House was sitting in front of his TV when, even above the noise of the chat show he was watching, he heard a loud prolonged hooting from a car outside. He reluctantly got up and went out.

A long American-style car had pulled up, headlights blazing, outside the gates.

'Hey, excuse me!' the driver called, having wound down his window electronically. 'Hey, sir! Can you open up for us, please?'

'Sorry, my instructions are not to open up for anyone but the police,' the gatekeeper yelled, from his doorstep.

He lived alone in the small stone cottage just inside the gates and with his front door open you could hear his television blaring and glimpse grainy pictures of a chat show with a permanently smiling host and a guest who was chattering inanely and gesturing far too much. The audience in the background laughed in gales; they seemed to be all teeth and big, clapping hands.

'Could you come to the gate? Don't want to shout.' The driver flapped a leather object which held a large, shiny badge. 'This is official business, sir. We're security people working for Mrs Brougham's father. We're here to check out this accident and the young lady who was involved. If Mrs Brougham wants to make sure we're who we say we are, she can ring Senator Gowrie's hotel in London, ask for Mr Beverley, the head of his security team, and he'll explain what this is all about.'

The gatekeeper lingered, giving a yearning look at his TV, then back at the waiting car; it was big and expensive and looked important. He remembered the American security men who had come a while back and gone over every inch of the grounds with a toothcomb. They had hustled him, pushed him around, with an infuriating blank courtesy that these men had, too.

Gloomily he said, 'Well, wait there. I'll have to talk to Mrs Brougham before I let you in; hold on.'

He vanished into the cottage, they caught a glimpse of

him through the open door, talking on a phone. After a minute he came back. 'Mrs Brougham would rather you waited until her husband arrives,' he yelled, and closed the front door on them with an open grin, delighted to have that message to pass on.

The engine idling, the men in the car sat staring at the locked gates, then the one in the back leaned forward and got a mobile phone out of a leather box on the floor between the front seats.

'Better pass this news on to Beverley and get new instructions. He said we had to get in there before the police, that it was urgent to snatch the girl and get away. The local cop's over there talking to the firemen, but he could go up to the house any minute.'

'We should have shot our way in!'

'Don't be dumb. In front of a limey cop? Now that would really make Gowrie happy, having two of his men shoot up an English village.'

Cathy politely left the room while Sophie made her phone call, but her discretion was not needed, because when Sophie got through to the hotel in London she was told that Steve had left an hour earlier. The switchboard operator had no idea where he had gone, offered indifferently to take a message.

Sophie left her name. 'I'm at Arbory House.' She spelt the name. 'Arbory. This is their number.' She read it off the telephone. 'Have you got that? Ask him to ring me. Please, make sure he gets it the minute he comes back to the hotel.'

She put the phone down and lay back against the couch cushions, biting her lip. Had Steve already gone to the Guildhall dinner? A big banquet with speeches would take hours, she knew those endless public functions – Steve might not get back to the hotel until very late at night. Hadn't he got the message she left earlier? That would

mean he didn't know where she was, and yet had still gone
off to his dinner. Maybe he had forgotten all about her, was
far too busy to care what she was doing or what was
happening to her?

'What's wrong? You look very unhappy,' Cathy said,
coming back into the room. 'Didn't you get through? Were
you ringing your boyfriend?'

'No, just a colleague.' Sophie forced a smile she did not
feel, but the truth was she was hurt because Steve had apparently got on with his life although she had disappeared.
It was childish to be resentful; after all, what did she
expect? They had only met a few days ago. They hardly
knew each other. Why should he drop everything and run
after her?

Watching her, Cathy said softly, 'Is that all? Are you sure?
You look as if you've lost a dollar and found a cent.'

Sophie half-laughed, very pink. 'It's just that I needed . . .
wanted . . . to talk to him, badly. I left a message for him
earlier, I thought he might come after me but he hasn't, he
has gone to this dinner at the Guildhall.'

'The one my father's speaking at?' Cathy frowned. 'Why
is your colleague going to that? He isn't in politics, is he?'

'He's a journalist.'

Cathy stiffened, her eyes chilling. 'My God, is that what
this is – a media conspiracy against my father?'

'Of course not! I only met Steve a few days ago. He –'

'Steve?' Cathy broke in, her face running with hot colour
and then as rapidly turning pale again. 'Steve who? What's
his last name?'

'Steve Colbourne,' Sophie said, then suddenly remembered Steve telling her that he knew the Gowrie family well,
and eagerly said, 'You know him, don't you? He told me he
knew your family.'

Cathy walked across the room and back again, like an offended cat swishing its tail with resentment. Her body was

stiff, her hands clenching and unclenching at her sides. She stopped beside the couch and looked angrily at Sophie.

'I can't believe he'd do anything so sneaky and vicious. OK, maybe I hurt him, but I didn't think he was deep-down serious any more than I was, and I didn't mean to hurt him, I couldn't help falling in love with another man. For him to wait all these months and then attack my father with a campaign of wicked lies and –'

'What are you talking about?' Sophie felt cold and weary. 'You and Steve . . . you were . . . lovers once?'

'He didn't tell you about us?' Cathy stared into her eyes. 'Why do you think he's doing this? Just to hammer together a story for his programme? Or did you think his motives were purely political?'

Bleakly Sophie said, 'Never mind Steve – he's nothing to do with you and me. I'm telling you the honest truth; I came looking for your father in New York because of what my mother had told me. I didn't even know Steve until I went to a press conference your father was giving in a hotel.'

'You expect me to believe that?' Cathy laughed cynically. 'I'm not that stupid.'

'It's true. That was the first time I ever met Steve, or even heard his name. I asked a question, and as soon as I said my name I saw your father's face, I looked into his eyes, and I knew my mother hadn't lied. Your father looked as if he had had a huge shock. Steve noticed your father's reaction, too, and he came over to talk to me, he asked me to have a drink with him, he was curious and asked a lot of questions.'

'And you told him?' Cathy's voice rose, shaking. 'You told him about me? You told Steve my father bought me from some Czech peasant? That I wasn't a Ramsey at all? Oh, my God.' She ran her hands through her hair. 'He'll put it on his programme. He'll broadcast your lies coast to coast and destroy my father.'

'No, I didn't tell him! Steve knows nothing, Anya.'

'Stop calling me that!' Cathy automatically said, staring at her. 'Are you telling me the truth?'

'I swear I am. I haven't told Steve anything about you. He kept asking questions but I never answered them.' Sophie stared fixedly at the familiar, bewildering face which was her sister's and yet so like the mother Sophie remembered from her childhood. Had Steve been deeply in love with her? Thinking back over everything he had said about Cathy, she realized how much emotion had charged his attitudes from the start. She had guessed when he talked about some guy he knew who had been in love with Cathy – his voice had given him away. And he had made so many odd, bitter, cynical remarks about the Gowrie family. She had assumed he was against their politics, but it had been personal all along. When Cathy married Paul Brougham, Steve had got hurt. Was he still in love with her? Looking away, Sophie stared into the fire, watching sparks flying upward, flames curling round the log. Her chest hurt. Was this strange, jabbing pain jealousy?

'He really doesn't know?' Cathy whispered.

Sophie put out her hand, seeing her sister in the glow of the fire, her dark hair aureoled in gold and her hazel eyes big and glittering with the strain of everything that had happened that evening.

'Anya, I'm not lying to you. I haven't told Steve anything. He got me a job working for his production team as a researcher –'

'Why?' Cathy sharply asked. 'Why would he do that?'

Sophie bit her lip, looking down. 'I'm afraid he suspects me of being your father's mistress. He may even think I'm trying to blackmail your father.'

Cathy was dumbstruck. 'Why on earth would he think that?' She drew a painful breath. 'Unless you were?' She turned dark red with embarrassment and shock. 'You . . .

you aren't, are you?' The idea of her father having a mistress was not new to her – she wasn't a child, she knew how little his marriage meant any more. Her mother was not a real wife, had not been one for years. But suspecting her father had other women was one thing – seeing this girl younger than herself and imagining her with Dad was something else. The very idea made her feel sick, her throat filled with bile.

'No! Of course not!' Sophie burst out, and Cathy breathed again, believing her implicitly, recognizing the look of truth.

There was a tap on the door and the housekeeper looked in: 'The policeman's at the gates asking if he can come in now, madam.'

Cathy pulled herself together. 'Are you ready to see him?' she asked Sophie, who reluctantly nodded. Cathy looked back at the housekeeper. 'He can come in, then.'

When the other woman had gone Sophie begged, 'Don't leave me alone with him, will you? I hate talking to policemen, Anya.'

'Yes, I'll stay, but for God's sake stop using that name, it is not my name.'

'It is! I can't understand how you can have forgotten it so completely. After all you were two when you were taken away – don't you remember us at all?'

'I don't want to get into an argument with you again, let's leave it for now, but I've been Cathy all my life and I don't know myself as anything else.'

'But I don't know you as Cathy, I only know you as Anya.'

'I am not Anya! Even if you're telling the truth . . . and I'm not ready to believe you are . . . but even if you were I would still think of myself as Cathy. Every day of the life that is all I remember, I've been Cathy Brougham – this girl Anya means nothing to me.'

But she glanced sideways at the table where they lay, all those eerie, pale reproduced photocopies, and frowned at the woman in the old-fashioned wedding-dress, at the face so like her own, at something even more disturbingly familiar, at an emotion she felt deep inside herself and couldn't quite pin down. What was it she felt every time she saw that face?

The telephone rang and both women jumped. Cathy leaned over to answer it. 'Hello? What? My father? Security men?'

Sophie's breathing stopped for a beat, her mouth open, in panic. Cathy looked at her, her face shaken, listening to the voice on the other end of the phone. Then she said harshly, 'No. Absolutely not. Tell them they will have to wait until my husband gets here, he is on his way, and will deal with them.'

She put the phone down hurriedly as if afraid of being talked into changing her mind. She and Sophie stared at each other.

'American security guys are at the gates, asking to come in,' Cathy said.

'They want me,' Sophie said, trembling violently.

Cathy gripped her hands tightly. 'No, of course not – I expect they just want to ask questions about the accident.'

'They're here to do the job that woman in the car didn't manage to do, they're going to kill me.'

'I won't let them in!' Cathy was surprised to hear herself say that. She hadn't meant to. Sophie's terror had startled it out of her. Cathy didn't believe what she was saying, but she was obviously scared sick, and who could blame her after the way that car had tried to run her down?

'They'll make you, they'll use force if they have to!'

'They wouldn't dare! This is England, not the States.' She was shouting. Stop shouting, Cathy told herself silently. What was she afraid of? But she knew. She was terrified that Sophie Narodni might be telling the truth. That would mean chaos, black night, the abyss of not knowing who she really was or where she belonged.

She took herself in hand and spoke more quietly, her face confident. 'They have no jurisdiction here. They have no right to bust into my house, or use any force.'

Sophie suddenly lapsed into Czech, muttering.

'What? I don't understand,' Cathy said.

'I'm so frightened,' Sophie whispered. 'Because they'll lie, invent reasons to make you give me up, and then they'll take me away and kill me!'

'I won't let them through the gates!' Cathy promised, she would have promised anything to stop Sophie looking that way, like a scared little kid, all eyes and a white face.

'They've tried to kill me twice! First in New York, in the subway, they pushed me off the platform and I was lucky I wasn't killed – that's where I got the bruises the doctor pointed out to you, the ones that are starting to fade. Then, just now, outside – you saw what happened. You can't pretend I'm imagining that, you saw with your own eyes what almost happened.'

Cathy was as white as death now, too, her mouth bloodless. 'My f. . . father wouldn't k. . . k . . .' She couldn't get the word out, it stuck in her throat like a bone, hurting her, silencing her.

'Kill?' Sophie said it for her. 'Wouldn't he? How well do you really know him? I talked to him, face to face, in New York, in the hotel, and he said to me that my mother had made a deal which included a promise never to tell anyone and she had broken that promise. He was very angry. He threatened me. He's a killer, Cathy.'

Anguished, Cathy cried out, 'Don't say that! I don't believe you. He's my father!' She loved him, she had always loved him, they had been so close throughout her life. He had kept her with him during the years when her mother was away at Easton and lost to her.

Dad had always been there for her. She thought back over all the times they had spent together, when she was a child, and later, after she grew up and before she married Paul. There had been many days on fishing trips, sailing the Ramsey yacht, or just drifting in a little wooden rowboat; summer days riding or walking in the forest, or wandering along the beach at Easton, talking politics, talking ideas, talking ways and means of making dreams reality, while they gathered clams at low tide, digging them out and taking them home in a bucket to be cleaned and cooked in a chowder by Grandee's cook. They had talked and listened to each other, argued, and agreed.

'I know him better than anyone in the world does,' she said with a faint sob in her throat. 'I always loved him better than anyone. Better than my mother, because she has had so much illness, for years we hardly saw much of her, but Dad and I were always together, he took me everywhere with him, on campaigns, all around the country, from coast to coast. Nobody knows him like I do.'

'You didn't know he wasn't your father!'

For a few seconds Cathy was silenced, staring at her with stretched, dilated eyes, then she angrily said, 'He is! He is! You're lying, I know you are.' She had to be lying, Cathy couldn't bear it to be true, everything she had thought she knew about herself was disintegrating in front of her, she was confused, watching her very identity crumbling, her memories dissolving and disappearing.

She held onto them, would not let them slide out of her fingers. 'You're lying,' she said again. 'He is my father, he loves me and I love him – and everything you've told me is moonshine.'

'Then why is somebody trying to kill me?'

The fierce question made Cathy's breath catch. 'How do I know?' she finally muttered. 'I don't know anything about you, except that you're lying.'

'Why are his security men outside the gates trying to get me?' Sophie came back without a second's hesitation, and Cathy looked wildly at her.

'I don't know!'

There was a tap on the door. They both looked at it in shock. Cathy found herself trembling a little, too, and was disturbed by that. Sophie's fear was getting to her, too. She felt it pulsing in her throat, in her ears.

'Who is it?' she called in a voice she barely held steady.

The door opened and a woman in a neat dark dress looked into the room. 'The police, madam.'

Cathy's tense muscles relaxed; she grew angry with herself now. What was the matter with her, letting herself get into such a state? As if her father would be involved in something like this! As if he would send killers to get a girl from this house. Her father spoke half a dozen languages, was highly musical, highly educated, a cultured, civilized man – not a hood. She knew what sort of man he was – why had she let herself be persuaded to doubt him?

'Show him in, please, Nora,' she said with a little sigh of weak relief, then, as the housekeeper went out again, turned to frown at Sophie and whispered urgently, 'Don't dare tell the police all those lies about my father!'

Sophie gave her a cynical look. 'If it isn't true, why are you worried?'

'Because if the press gets hold of your story it could do Dad's election prospects terrible damage.'

'Which is why he's trying to shut me up!'

'I don't believe he's doing anything of the kind. Who's behind you? One of the other Republican candidates? How much were you paid to pull this stunt?' Cathy stopped, hearing the housekeeper's footsteps outside in the hall, on the polished wood-block flooring, and even louder a man's heavy tread following.

'Constable Hawkins, madam,' the housekeeper announced and a tall broad-shouldered man in a navy-blue uniform came into the room, removing his peaked cap as he came towards them.

Cathy stood up to greet him, pulling herself together.

'Good evening, Mrs Brougham.'

'Good evening, Constable Hawkins.'

Their polite, prim voices made Sophie want to laugh hysterically. This was such a different world to the one she had been moving in over the last few days – outside in the night the dangerous animals prowled with bared fangs. In here, in this elegant room, people spoke with all the formality of dancers in a stately quadrille, showing no emotions, no fear or alarm. Death had no meaning for them; that car beyond the gates had never blazed and consumed the woman inside it.

The policeman turned to look at her, his eyes like round black currants, in his bony, weatherbeaten face, curious, but only with a calm, professional interest. 'Good evening, miss. I'm told you both saw the accident – could I ask you a few questions?'

'Sit down, Constable Hawkins,' Cathy said with a friendly smile, and the man took a brocade-seated, upright chair, placed his peaked cap on a nearby occasional table, put his black-shod feet together primly and got a little black notebook and pen out of his jacket pocket.

'Could I have your name first, please, miss?'

Half an hour later, the little police car drove back through the open gates of Arbory House. The gatekeeper stood on the doorstep waiting to close the gates, but still more engrossed in what was happening on his television, eating a sandwich with his head screwed round to stare into his living-room.

If he had been more alert he would have noticed the big, American car waiting in the shadows just to one side of the gates, he would have been in time to stop them suddenly shooting past the police car and vanishing up the drive a great deal faster than the five miles an hour requested on the signs at intervals along the way up to the house.

'Oh, no! JC and his twelve disciples!' the gatekeeper groaned, coming out to stare after the disappearing tail-lights. 'That's tore it.'

He ran back into the cottage and picked up the phone. 'Nora, trouble,' he puffed. 'Tell madam those Yanks have got past me, they went in while Hawkins was going out, I couldn't stop them, they might have mowed me down, the speed they were doing! You'd better warn her, though, and pronto. And tell her it isn't my fault, nothing I could do.'

The housekeeper made a contemptuous, disbelieving snort and hung up to hurry off to break the news to her employer.

'My husband should be here soon. You can tell him your far-fetched story,' Cathy was telling Sophie as the house-keeper knocked on the door and entered without waiting.

Flushed, Nora began at once, 'Madam, it seems the American security people have got past the gates and are on their way here. What do you want us to do? Should we let them in?'

Sophie's intake of breath was audible, her face had filled with panic. 'I knew it . . . I told you what they'd do . . . they've come to get me.'

'They'll have me to reckon with,' Cathy said with all the natural confidence of someone who has been born with a silver spoon in her mouth, educated to rule, and filled with a cool belief in her own invincibility.

The heavy doorknocker thudded sharply outside in the hall. Sophie shrank back among the cushions of the couch.

'Tell them to go away, don't let them in,' Cathy said, her chin up.

'No! Don't open the front door!' Sophie pleaded, but the housekeeper was already obeying her mistress.

They heard her voice from across the hall. 'Mrs Brougham wants you to leave imm ... Stop! How dare you, come back here!'

The heavy front door crashed shut, there was a clatter of footsteps across the wood floor and two men loomed in the doorway. Cathy recognized their look rather than their faces; she had seen it all her life, those rapidly moving, all-seeing, emotionless eyes, the faces smooth-shaven, angular, the hair very short, close to the skull, the bodies fit and yet bulky, hard with muscle, and no doubt packing guns under their expensive tailoring, the dark suits, the heavy overcoats.

'They pushed their way in, madam,' said the housekeeper.

'How dare you force your way into my house? I told you to wait until my husband arrived. He's on his way here now, he'll be here any minute.' Cathy got between Sophie and the intruders, her manner immediately becoming arrogant, high-handed. It was what they understood from people like her and her father. She knew men like this, too; it was only power they respected, a power greater than their own, and she was certain she possessed it.

'I'm sorry, Mrs Brougham, but Senator Gowrie sent us to get this young woman without delay. I'm sure you understand our position.'

The older man of the two spoke in a civil voice, smiling insincerely, his thin mouth stretched like rubber which snapped back into its usual tight line as soon as he stopped smiling. Cathy glared, disliking him and his companion

247

intensely, admitting for the first time how much she had always disliked having men like this around her and her home. They were always in the background, watching, waiting. She still had men like this around her now that she had married Paul, because although he was not a politician he was a very wealthy man with a lot of power in the media, and he needed protection too, he was always a potential target for crazy people with grievances, criminals and terrorists. OK, she knew that, she wasn't stupid, she realized she had to put up with them, but she didn't have to like these guys.

Her voice icy, she said, 'I don't believe my father told you to push your way into my home and throw your weight around!'

Softly he said, 'Your father wants Miss Narodni taken back to London. He told us to come here and get her, at all costs, so that is what we are going to do. We don't want to upset you, Mrs Brougham, but don't waste your sympathy on her. I'm sure she talks a good story, that's what she gets paid for, she's a con artist, but the truth is she was sent over to Britain to cause trouble for your father. She's part of a dirty-tricks brigade who've been following him around the States for quite a time, trying to discredit him with lies, anonymous phone calls and letters, the usual game. I'm sure you're familiar with the techniques. You've been around politics all your life, you know the way it gets done. Anything she has told you is a lie.'

This was what Cathy had been telling herself, that Sophie was lying, that this was just a con game, a dirty trick, to wreck her father's chances of nomination – but somehow when this man said it aloud she didn't believe it.

The other man had wandered behind the couch while Cathy was talking to his colleague. Before Cathy had time to realize what he was up to he was beside Sophie, grabbing her by the arm and yanking her up from the couch.

'Come along, Miss Narodni!' he said, forcing her arm up behind her back.

'Leave her alone!' Cathy said, her stomach twisting in a strange pain as she saw Sophie being hurt. At that instant she felt as if she shared Sophie's pain and fear, as if they inhabited one body, their minds linked, too.

Instinctively she ran towards them and the older man caught at her shoulder with a hand that pulled her back and made her wince and gasp in shock. She had never been manhandled that way before; she couldn't believe it was happening to her.

'If you want your father to run in the presidential race, Mrs Brougham, you'll stop making this fuss and let us take her away,' he intoned in that same cold, tight voice. 'Your father will explain what she's been up to when you see him tomorrow.'

Cathy clenched her hand into a fist and punched him angrily. 'Get your grubby fingers off me, you big ape!'

The next second she found herself falling backwards on to the couch, was stunned to realize the man had hit her, and then heard with terror Sophie screaming as she was pulled out of the room.

'Anya, Anya . . . help me . . .'

Steve and Vladimir had been lucky not to get stopped for speeding as they did a hundred miles an hour along the motorway, putting London far behind them in the race to get to Sophie, they hoped, before any of Gowrie's people caught up with her. It was a chilly night and there wasn't much other traffic around, or they might have had far less luck. The moon had risen, showing them the shadowy countryside they were driving through. The stars were white-hot points of fire high above them; frost began to make the tyres slip, and it sparkled white on the grass along the motorway verges, and into the distance the rolling English fields, backed by dark shadows of hills.

'A small country,' Vladimir said, staring. 'Very tame and domesticated, no wonder the English are so prim and two-faced. They grow up with this neat, cute countryside, like growing up in Disneyland.'

'But with far more prickles. They can be bloody-minded, too,' said Steve. 'Don't mix them up with us Yanks. We're far more conventional than they are. We find eccentricity a little worrying; the English love it.'

Vlad laughed. They drove in silence then he said, 'So, you really think Gowrie will still go to this dinner in the City of London?'

'Does the tiger turn his back on fresh meat when he's starving? Gowrie can't afford to miss it; this dinner is a biggie, a major platform for an American politician fighting for presidential nomination. With a good speech he'll make the TV news headlines back home, and all the breakfast shows, too.'

'Television has become too important; it distorts politics,' Vladimir said with heavy Slav gloom.

'It's here to stay, though. No turning our back on it, and what's coming may be worse. The technical revolution gets faster and faster. We could all be born robots in a hundred years and there may be no more humans then.'

'I wonder how many there are now? It is happening in my country now; we had the grey boredom of government lies for so long, and secretly made fun of them all, we stayed sane in a mad world that way – but now we have the gaudy colours of the rich corporations advertising every night, and nobody laughs any more! We began with such hopes for democracy, and already we follow America down the wrong roads.'

'Hell, Vlad, we all get what we say we want, that's our tragedy. No such thing as a free gift. There's always a price.

In the States we've talked endlessly of wanting democracy, praised the age of the common man. Now we've got it, we've got mindless game shows and chat shows, porn films, vacuous soaps; we've got the TV the common man wants, and the common woman, and it's no good saying you don't like it, it isn't what you meant. Democracy is the lowest common denominator and the fastest method of communication, which means TV as we know it and love it.'

'And it's what you live by,' Vlad said softly, taunting him, amused and yet cynical.

Steve grinned wickedly, angrily. 'I know, and I shouldn't bite the hand that feeds me, but, hell, owing everything I've got to it doesn't mean I can't see where we're all going, and I don't have to like it.'

'You should be in politics, yourself; you've got the gift,' Vlad said, grinning.

Grimacing, Steve told him, 'Once upon a time I might have gone into politics, but that was before I realized how low you have to sink to get anywhere in that game.' Steve stared ahead, his jaw taut. 'My father was involved in politics all his life; he had a thousand friends in the party, all good old buddies, every last man. Now he's just waiting to die and his good old guys have vanished like snow in June.'

Vlad looked at the grim face behind the wheel and then at the road and the other vehicles they flashed dizzyingly past. 'For Jesus's sake, Steve, slow down. I'm too old to die and go to hell.'

'Sorry, but I want to get to Sophie as fast as possible,' Steve said in a hard, angry voice. 'And when I get to her I'm going to bawl the shit out of her.'

Vladimir shot him another look and smiled with sudden, surprising sweetness. 'You're crazy about her, aren't you?'

Steve flushed and did not answer.

*

The angry scene inside the house, Cathy's protests, Sophie's screams, had managed to drown a sound outside the house: a helicopter landing in the dark parkland, blades whirring, the engine slowing as the great metal insect lowered itself to rest on a well-concealed landing pad among the grass. Only when the lights surrounding it were switched on could you see the pad; unless you walked right up to it, it was hidden from view by grass and shrubs discreetly planted as cover.

The occupants of the helicopter took half a minute to spring down and run, crouching, towards the house, straightening only when they were out of reach of the lethal, rotating blades.

The security men pulling Sophie out of the house walked straight into Paul Brougham and his own security men.

'What the hell is going on?' Paul rapped out, confronting the men, staring in bewilderment at Sophie. 'Who are you people, and who is this?'

The older man, who had recognized him immediately with dismay, believing him to be in London at the Guildhall dinner, in spite of Cathy telling him otherwise – but then women always lied, a wise man never believed a word they said – began a smooth, careful answer, 'Well, Mr Brougham, sir, we were sent down here by Senator Gowrie. We've been having trouble with a dirty tricks gang sent over here by one of the senator's competitors and –'

'Paul!' Cathy ran out of the house and straight at him, and Paul's arms closed round her, held her close to his heart, her head nestling against his chest so that she heard the beating of his heart right under her ear, a strong, fast beat that was the sound she went to sleep with every night, but nearer, then, because neither of them ever wore anything in bed, their bodies entwined naked under the sheets, legs tangled, arms across each other, the closer the better, one flesh, warm and relaxed after love.

'Are you OK?' he asked with fierce anxiety.

Relief was making her feel sick. She felt safe now he was here; she always did.

'Tell them to let go of Sophie,' she told him, lifting her head to glare at her father's men. 'And to get off our land!'

The older man quickly said, 'Mr Brougham, we're security men sent down here by Senator Gowrie. He wanted us to bring this girl back with us.'

'This guy manhandled me,' Cathy said, touching her upper arms and wincing. 'I've got the bruises to show for it!'

'He did what?' Paul said through his teeth, and suddenly there was danger in the air. Paul Brougham was a hard man, aggressive, if he needed to be – in fact you felt he could be violent.

'Mrs Brougham's upset, sir,' the older security man hurriedly said, 'She's exaggerating –'

'I'm not,' Cathy interrupted. 'He's a liar, don't listen to a word he says. He grabbed me and held me, and tried to railroad me into letting him take Sophie, and when I wouldn't have it he pushed me down on the couch.'

Paul made a snarling noise in his throat, like a lion, his teeth bared. 'You did, did you, you bastard?' His hand flashed out and got the older man by the throat, shook him like a dog with a rag doll between its teeth. 'You hit my wife, did you? Like hitting women, do you? They're an easy target, aren't they? Not like men.'

'No, sir, really . . . I didn't mean . . . I just . . .' The security man couldn't think fast enough and floundered helplessly. His face was drawn and afraid.

Cathy saw Sophie sagging at the knees and rushed to put an arm round her. 'Sophie? Paul, help me get her back indoors. She's as white as a ghost, and she's in shock already, she was almost killed by another of their people out there.'

She pointed towards the village at the far end of the drive, beyond the high ironwork gates.

Paul let go of the man he was shaking, turned to stare down the drive. 'What do you mean, almost killed?'

Cathy gabbled, her voice shaking. 'A car tried to run her down outside, then I drove out of the gates, and the other car went into a skid and hit a tree and exploded and the driver was killed, she must have been killed outright, I hope to God she was, anyway . . . The car burned for ages, it was terrifying, I should think you could see it for miles, half the village was out there and –'

'Who is this woman?' Paul broke in to stop her high-pitched, shaking voice, frowning at her anxiously. 'What the hell has been going on here?'

She was still supporting Sophie with one arm round her. 'Help me get her indoors first.'

Paul nodded to his own security staff. 'Take this lady into the house, will you? And be careful with her.' He turned on the other men. 'As for you – get off my land, go back to London and tell the senator that he can talk to us himself when he comes down here tomorrow. And tell him I don't take very kindly to his men manhandling my wife or busting into my home, pushing my staff around and laying down the law. Now get out of here before I really lose my temper.'

They scuttled away in a mixture of sullen resentment and relief at getting away from him. Paul watched them get back into their big American car; the engine flared, the lights came on, they reversed and drove off, their tyres screeching on the gravel and sending up a flurry of little stones.

Once they had driven out of the gates, which closed silently behind them, Paul went inside and found his wife with Sophie in the firelit room they had left earlier. Sophie was shuddering, sobbing silently, her body shaking with dry little sobs you saw but could not hear.

'Go through the house, check that there's nobody else in here, and check for bugs, too, in case they've managed to plant some,' Paul told his men. 'Check in here, first, Jock.'

One of them, a thin sandy-haired man with a bony face, pulled a box out of his overcoat and began moving quietly around the room, testing each corner of it for bugs. He had finished in a moment and walked back, shaking his head at Paul.

'Clean.'

He left, and Paul closed the door, turning to watch his wife who was bending over Sophie, pulling a tartan rug over her shivering body.

'Is she OK?' he asked her.

'Physically . . . I think so. But she's badly shocked. She ought to go to bed.'

'She's not staying here, is she?'

'She booked in at the Green Man.' Cathy came over to him and Paul put his arm round her, protective, possessive, dropping a kiss on the top of her dark head. She leaned on him, sighing. Their bodies instinctively moved together, seeking each other's warmth and reassurance.

'Oh, I'm so glad you got here, I needed you – I was scared stiff when those men broke in here.' She lifted her face and he kissed her curved pink mouth lingeringly. She put a hand to his cheek and stroked the hard angles of it, loving the faint prickling of his stubbled skin against her own. The way he looked always made her heart move with passion; he was so distinguished, every woman she knew fancied him and he was hers. Sometimes she couldn't believe it.

'I'm sorry I wasn't here when you needed me, but I'm here now, darling, you can stop worrying,' he said, smiling tenderly down at her. 'Tell me what's been going on.' He dropped his voice to a whisper again, 'And who on earth is she?' He gestured with his head. Sophie was lying with closed eyes under the rug. Her too-rapid breathing had slowed; she seemed half-asleep.

'Her name is Sophie Narodni. She claims she's my sister.'

'What? What are you talking about?' Paul looked as if she had hit him with a brick and she knew how he felt because when Sophie first talked to her Cathy had felt just the same.

'She isn't, obviously, she has to be either mad or deluded, but I don't believe she's part of a dirty-tricks gang, although that is what Dad's men said she was. I think she really believes her story. Maybe somebody has primed her, she's being used by somebody a lot cleverer than she is, but, whatever the truth, someone has convinced Sophie that my father bought me from her mother, that I am her older sister, who was supposed to be dead, a girl called Anya.'

'Anya?' Paul repeated, hoarsely as if his throat was suddenly ash-dry.

Cathy looked anxiously at him. Surely he wasn't going to believe any of this fairy story! 'Darling, it isn't true, it can't be! I'm only worried because Dad's reaction to her was so over the top. Sending those men down here to get her, and the car crash . . . I'd swear the driver tried to run her down, someone is trying to kill her, I saw that with my own eyes, and . . . well, that does make you wonder how much else is true . . . but it can't be, the idea's crazy.'

She stopped, realizing that Paul wasn't listening to her. His arms had dropped. He moved away, walked to the couch. 'Her name – what did you say her name was?'

'Sophie. Sophie Narodni.'

'Narodni,' he repeated in a voice she did not recognize, a deep, thick voice which frightened her.

Cathy looked up at him, fear in her eyes. 'Yes, she's Czech, she says she comes from a village near Prague. Her mother worked for my mother years and years ago, when my parents were living there. My father was in the diplo-

256

matic, remember? It all happened in 1968 – remember, that was when the Russians invaded Czechoslovakia. Maybe that's what gave her the idea? When people started talking about Dad as a future president she may have dreamt up this story about my parents losing their own baby, and giving my mother money to let them take her little girl away with them as their own.'

'They bought you?'

'No, of course not – Dad wouldn't do a thing like that! For God's sake, Paul! Think about it! OK, she tells a good story. The dates all fit, and she makes it sound plausible because she believes it herself, I don't dispute she believes it. She isn't a liar, but she has to be wrong. It must be a lie, Paul. Dad wouldn't have cheated Grandee that way, and my mother wouldn't have wanted somebody else's child. I mean, she wasn't sick then, she got sick later.'

Cathy hated to admit, even to herself, that her mother was not just sick, but on the verge of senility and getting worse all the time, that there was no hope of a recovery, only a slow slide into the dark.

Paul was still standing by the couch, staring down fixedly at Sophie, his back to Cathy. She saw his face in profile; every bone in it clenched, his skin ashen, his body as tense as a coiled spring.

She had expected reassurance and comfort from him, but she wasn't getting it. Paul wasn't taking it the way she had thought he would. What was he thinking?

She was suddenly afraid. She had been so sure he loved her for herself. Before she met him she had known a lot of men who were really only interested in the family she came from, the money she would one day inherit. She had learnt to pick them out on sight; the fortune-hunters, the creeps, the liars. Paul had been so different – he had his own money, he came from another, older culture, he knew very little about her family and what they meant in New

England's history. They had fallen in love at the same time, in the same place, for the same reasons.

Pure lust, he had said, once, laughing, and she had laughed, too, knowing he was joking. They had wanted each other on sight, it was true, but they had shared far more than that. They had simply known each other with total intimacy on first sight: body, heart and soul, they belonged together.

That was what she had believed. Now for the first time she wondered . . . did he really love her? What if she lost it all – the family background, the money, the social status.

What then? Would she lose Paul too?

10

Steve and Vladimir lost their way on unlit, winding English roads between the motorway and the village they were looking for, following signposts which took them round and round, it seemed to them, in ever-decreasing circles. When they finally, and quite by accident, found the right road and drove into the village, it was quiet and still. The police, the fire brigade, the people had all gone, the street was dark and the villagers had either gone to the pub or gone home. Only the burnt-out, blackened metal of the car remained to give evidence of what had happened; it still lay under the tree, the branches of which had been turned into charcoal. As Steve parked on the forecourt of the Green Man both men leaned forward to stare.

'Somebody had a nasty accident,' Vladimir murmured. 'I guess they don't survive. Nobody got out of that alive, huh?'

Steve didn't answer. Pale and suddenly haggard, he leapt out of the car and ran towards the pub. He had left the car-keys in the ignition, so before following him Vladimir removed them and locked the car. It might only be a hire car but there was no point in leaving it unlocked right outside a bar where some drunk might find it.

The brightly lit pub made Vladimir laugh aloud. 'I have seen this place on an English Christmas card!' he muttered to himself. 'All it needs is some snow, and maybe Santa Claus and his reindeer on the roof. Is real, I wonder? Or another bit of Disneyland?'

He found Steve in the oak-panelled bar, which was crowded with people drinking, the air rich with a strong smell of malt and hops, bitter English beer, which Vladimir inhaled with interest – he must try their beer while he was here although he didn't expect it to be as good as his home-brewed local beer or lager. Until Steve appeared the room had been rocking with noise, shouting, the click of darts hitting a round board, glasses clinking – Vladimir had heard all that as he got out of the car, and heard the hush that fell as Steve walked in through the door.

Now everyone was listening as the landlady answered some question Steve had asked.

'The accident? Oh, you saw the car . . . yes, terrible, it was.' She looked round the bar. 'Wasn't it?'

There was a chorus of agreement, heads nodded.

Steve said huskily, 'It certainly looks horrific – did the driver survive?'

'You must be kidding, dear – no, no, she was killed.'

'She?' Steve's voice sounded as if he was being strangled.

The landlady gave him a sharp look but answered with a shrug. 'Seems the driver was a woman. Someone saw her before she crashed.'

Very pale, Steve asked, 'Do they know who she was?'

'Not yet. The police are trying to find out. There was . . .' She paused, grimacing with a faintly sick expression because she had rarely seen anything so terrible happen in this tiny place. Most days went by without stirring the air around them, it was hard to tell one day from the next, but it would be a long time before she forgot tonight. 'There was nothing left, you know? To tell by, I mean. But they did find the car number plate, it flew off and wasn't badly burnt, they're trying to trace her from that. She was driving like a lunatic, I know that – a hundred miles an hour, I reckon. Nearly killed a young woman who's staying here in one of my bedrooms.'

Steve's haggard face sharpened into intensity, he caught her by the arm, his fingers digging into her. 'What young woman?'

The landlady unhooked his fingers with a frown, but was not unsympathetic. 'Are you looking for someone, dear? I can't remember her name just now – it will be in the guest book, she signed it. A lovely-looking girl, blonde, with a funny accent.'

'Blonde . . .' The word sighed out of Steve in deep relief. His whole body seemed to sag.

'That's right, dear.' The landlady watched him uneasily, with uncertain sympathy. 'Friend of yours, is she?'

'Is she in her room?'

'Not just now. She was knocked unconscious –'

'Is she badly hurt?' he interrupted, leaning towards her in tense anxiety.

'Oh, nothing serious, love, don't worry. She's in Arbory House, that's across the street there, on the other side of the village green. She was here visiting them, the Broughams, so they kept her there for the night. They rang to let me know. That was good of Mrs Brougham, very thoughtful. She's a lady, even if she *is* an American.'

Steve gave a bark of angry laughter. 'I'm an American too.'

She winked at her customers and smiled at him. 'Well, I did notice, dear. Get a lot of Americans here in the summer, we do. They like our olde-worlde look; we've an old church for them to visit, and a fair number of old houses. Can I get you two gentlemen a drink?'

Vladimir's eyes brightened and he leaned on the bar counter, staring along the bottles as if wondering where he might start. He beamed as he saw a row of familiar labels.

'We'll take a couple of your Budweisers,' he said. 'Did you know the original Budweisers came from Czecho-slovakia?'

'Get away.' The landlady produced two bottles for them, smiling. 'And I thought they were American. You aren't an

American, are you? Got an accent just like the young lady; she was Czech, she said.'

Vladimir nodded. 'Uh-huh, she works for me.'

'Does she now? What sort of job does she do? I thought she looked like a model. Is she?'

Vladimir laughed. 'No, no. She is a journalist. I run a news agency, covering world news for Eastern Europe.'

'Well, I'd never have guessed that, she doesn't look the type. I suppose you're here about Mrs Brougham's dad? Been reading all about him in the papers, haven't we? American politician, over here making speeches, as if we haven't got enough of that already. D'you think he's going to be president next time? That would really put the village on the map; we'd have tourists pouring in to see where his daughter lives, I reckon. I'd have some more rooms built on at the back, and maybe put in a café at the side of the pub.'

Steve forced a smile. 'I don't have a crystal ball, I'm afraid, but good luck anyway. Could you let us have two rooms for the night? We need to talk to Miss Narodni and maybe we'll have to wait until tomorrow.'

She beamed. 'Well, I am having a busy night, aren't I? Haven't had this many overnight guests since the end of August. Sure I can let you have a couple of rooms. When you've drunk your lagers I'll take you up.'

Sophie had been given the sedative left by the doctor, and was now tucked up in bed in a room at the top of the stairs. Cathy had lent her a nightie and dressing-gown, a pair of sheepskin slippers; they were very similar in size, which gave Cathy an odd feeling. She had stayed until Sophie was clearly drifting off to sleep, and then quietly went out, leaving one lamp lit by the door, with a very low wattage bulb in it, so that it would not disturb Sophie but if she woke in the night would give her enough light to see the room and remember where she was.

'Shall we have dinner?' she asked from the door, looking at Paul, sitting in his favourite chair, by the fireside, a large glass of brandy in his hand. She hoped he wasn't going to drink too much; he rarely did but when he did it seemed to plunge him into dark brooding, a heavy gloom that didn't lift until the effect of the alcohol wore off.

He didn't look round at her. 'I'm not hungry.'

'Sandwiches?'

'Later, maybe.' She watched him swirl the golden liquid in his glass, saw the firelight glinting in it; Paul wasn't looking at her, he was staring into the fire, his face still very pale and his mouth a straight, bloodless line.

'Come and sit down. Go through it again. I still haven't got it straight in my head.'

'Do we have to?' Cathy was heart-sick; wanted to cry. She had been so sure he loved her; how could that love go so quickly? Did money matter that much to him?

She wished she had never set eyes on Sophie Narodni; she had turned the world upside-down. The last couple of hours had been pure nightmare.

'It's all so far-fetched, it can't be true,' she said despairingly.

Sophie's story reminded her of fairy stories she had read as a child; tales about stolen babies, wicked magicians who wanted to be king, a quest for a long-lost princess. What was that phrase the troubadours in Provence had loved so much . . .? *La princesse lointaine* . . . The distant, long-lost princess the poets dreamed about and sang about.

'Cathy?' Paul asked sharply and she started, looked at him in confusion.

'She says her mother is dying,' she burst out, the words coming from her own pain and uncertainty.

'Dying?' he repeated as if the word was meaningless to him. 'What do you mean, dying?'

What was the matter with him? she desperately thought.

263

Paul had always been so quick-witted. His mind had worked faster than the speed of light; she had been in awe of his intelligence. Yet now, tonight, that mind of his was slow and sluggish, as if he couldn't make sense of anything she said. She hadn't expected her news to shock him this much – or was he busy thinking about something else, something he hadn't told her about? All week he had had something on his mind, he had kept drifting off into deep concentration, frowning and silent; there had been phone-calls at odd hours, business meetings in London that kept him there until very late. If their hours in bed together hadn't been so intensely passionate Cathy might have begun to suspect there was another woman, but she knew it couldn't be that. She knew better than to ask if anything was wrong – Paul never discussed business with her.

Looking at him anxiously, she said, 'She's apparently got leukaemia. Sophie says the doctors have given her three months at the outside.'

Paul walked stiffly over to the fire and leaned on the mantelpiece, his head bent down, staring into the flames.

Cathy couldn't bear any more. 'Oh, let's not talk about them, they're nothing to do with us, forget them.' Her body was throbbing with the urgent hunger she always felt when they were alone. She whispered pleadingly, 'I'm tired, I want to go to bed. Let's go to bed, make love to me, darling.'

If he would make love to her she could forget Sophie and all these doubts and uncertainties; her only real certainty would be Paul's body, her own, moving together in perfect harmony.

He didn't turn round, or look at her, but she felt the emotion in him, and had never felt anything like that from him before – a dark, brooding rage which was like a knife thrust in her.

'Don't turn away from me!' she burst out in anguish. 'It

isn't true, she was telling a pack of lies! Paul, I need you more than ever now.' She couldn't stop tears stealing down her face, her body was shaking with sobs. 'I'm frightened. I know who I am, but . . . but she's knocked me off-balance, I'm so confused and miserable.'

'You'd better go up to bed,' he said heavily. 'Go on, Cathy; get some sleep, that's what you need. Maybe you should take one of those pills the doctor gave you for her.' He sat down in one of the armchairs near the fire, still not looking at her.

'Come with me,' she begged, going over to kneel down beside him and leaning her body on his knees, clinging like ivy, putting a coaxing hand on his thigh, stroking the tense muscles under her fingers.

He pushed her away, didn't look at her, his eyes on the fire. 'I'm not sleepy, I have some work to do, too, some overseas phonecalls to make. I'll get Nora to bring me some sandwiches and coffee and work while I eat.'

The rejection made her feel sick. Humiliated, wounded, she got up, stumbled and almost fell on to the couch, knocking Sophie's photographs to the floor. They scattered like autumn leaves across the carpet, some face up, the wraith-like forms in them shimmering in the firelight. Paul turned his head to stare at them, his brows jerking together.

'What are those?'

She had forgotten them. Her throat rough with unshed tears, she muttered, 'Nothing. She brought them, claimed they were photocopies of old family photos – but they're fakes, obvious fakes.'

Paul leaned down from his chair, picked up some of the prints, straightened, holding one of them in his hands, staring at it. She saw it was the one which had startled Cathy herself; the picture of someone who looked amazingly like her, in an old-fashioned wedding-dress.

'It could be you!' Paul said in a voice that sounded as if it

265

came from the pit of his stomach. 'God, you're the image of her.'

Terrified, she argued, 'It's easy to fake a photo! All they would have to do is find a good reproduction of a photo of me in a magazine, stick my head on an old picture of someone in a wedding-dress, and photocopy that, then photograph that. Paul, can't you see what's going on? You of all people know how easy it is to fool people. It's all part of this con trick, a dirty-tricks campaign by Dad's enemies back home. Dad will deal with it when he gets here in the morning.'

But Paul wasn't listening; he was staring fixedly at that picture, his face drawn and grey. What was he thinking? If only he would talk to her, tell her how he felt, but he was shutting her out and Cathy felt so miserable she wanted to die.

'Please, Paul, come to bed.' She moved towards him again, her eyes burning with fatigue and passion. Their bodies knew each other so well, if she could only get him into bed . . . but his voice stopped her in her tracks, the tone of it harsh and hostile.

'For God's sake, do as you're told, Cathy! Go to bed and leave me alone!'

She put a hand to her mouth to stifle the sob of shock and hurt, then turned and ran out of the room just as the phone began to ring. Paul ignored it, knowing it would be answered by one of the staff.

He heard Cathy crying as she ran through the hall and shut his eyes, groaning aloud. Opening his eyes again, he looked down at the photocopies he held, made a low, bitter sound and suddenly flung all the pictures into the fire, grabbed hold of a brass poker and held them down as they crackled and blazed into flame, watching intently as the strange, eerie faces shrivelled into black ash.

Vladimir stood in the centre of the room Steve had been allocated by the landlady and experimentally shifted his feet, his bulky body swaying with elephantine grace. The floorboards creaked under his weight.

'Old, very old, this isn't Disneyland, it's real,' he said, beaming. 'I like this place – did you notice the sign saying real ale? What did that mean, I wonder? Is this an English joke? Are they telling us something? That some of their beers are not real, huh? I shall try them all, one by one, I like to do this research. When I am home I shall write an article on English beers.'

Steve wasn't listening; he sat down on his bed and picked up the phone placed on the wall beside the bed. 'I'm going to try to talk to Sophie.'

He pulled a small addressbook out of his inside pocket, flicked over the pages and then dialled. 'Hello? Arbory House? I'm told Miss Narodni is staying there – could I speak to her, please?' He listened, frowning. 'Asleep? I see. Could I speak to Mrs Brougham, then, please? My name is Colbourne – Steve Colbourne. I'm an old friend from the States. Yes, I'll hold.'

Vladimir wandered over to look out of the diamond-paned windows, stared across the village green towards the high, iron gates.

'There's a car parked over there, with two men in it,' he told Steve over his shoulder.

'And?' queried Steve, looking round at him.

'They have that look . . . you get to recognize it, all secret service men have it, they think they are above the law and it shows. I can smell them from here. The car's American.'

He had Steve's full attention now. 'What are they doing?'

'Waiting, watching. What they do best. I'd guess they're Senator Gowrie's men, watching over his daughter.'

'Or waiting to get their hands on Sophie,' Steve said grimly.

*

Cathy was almost at the top of the stairs when the house-keeper quietly said her name from the hall. Reluctantly, Cathy looked back at her.

'There's a gentleman on the phone, American, madam; a Mr Colbourne, says he's an old friend of yours.'

Cathy hesitated, then said, 'Put the call through to my bedroom, please.'

She heard a movement from the sitting-room and glanced down over the polished banisters. Paul stood in the doorway of the room she had just left; his eyes had a deep, glowing darkness like hot coals in a dying fire. He had always been jealous of Steve – he knew all about their relationship and had resented it. She looked eagerly for a betrayal of that old jealousy now, but if he was angry about Steve ringing her he didn't utter a syllable. Cathy sighed, and went on up the stairs.

As she entered her bedroom the phone beside the bed began to purr quietly; she picked it up.

'Yes? Yes, put him through.' She heard the click that meant the line had been switched through, the echoing click as her housekeeper put down the phone she was holding. Only then did Cathy say, 'Hello? Steve?'

'Yes. Hi, Cathy. How are you?'

'Fine, and you?'

The polite ritual of greeting calmed her a little. It made the unreality seem less crazy, re-established her sense of identity for the moment. That was why she had agreed to talk to him, she realized; she had known him so long, most of her life. She was sure that Steve would make everything seem normal again.

'Fine,' he said offhandedly, then plunged into staccato speech. 'Cathy, is Sophie OK?'

'Yes, she's taken a sedative and gone to bed. She needs a good night's sleep.'

'What happened here tonight, Cathy?' he urgently asked. 'Look, I'm over here at this pub . . . what the hell was it called, Vlad? Oh, yeah, the Green Man. Could I come over to talk to you, Cathy?'

Her nerves jangled. Sharply she said, 'Do you know what time of night it is? I'm just going to bed! What do you mean, Vlad? What's a Vlad?'

'Not a what – a who. He's Sophie's boss, Vladimir, he's here with me. He's worried about her, too, he flew all the way from Prague to find out what was going on.'

Why had he done that? she wondered. Did he know this story of Sophie's too? How many other people knew? And this Czech guy was a journalist, ran a news agency – how long before the story hit the newsstands in the States? Would they wake up tomorrow to find it worldwide front-page news?

Distraught, she snapped, 'Well, he can't see her tonight, either.'

'Cathy, we're anxious about her –'

'Have you put any of Sophie's garbage on tape? Have you sent the story back home?'

'No, Cathy. I'm not the gutter press. I'd want proof of what she claims before I broadcast it.'

'There won't be any proof! It's all lies – and if you attack my father I'll never speak to you again. And don't forget that my grandfather has friends in very high places.'

'Don't threaten me, Cathy – I haven't threatened you! I told you, I'm just worried about Sophie.'

'You don't need to be while she's under my roof. I'll make sure nothing else happens to her tonight. She's safe here.'

'I damned well hope she is, Cathy!' There was a brief silence, then he flatly asked, 'She told you?'

'Told me what?' she fenced.

'You know what I mean.'

'Are you in love with her?' Cathy asked instead of answering his question.

She heard Steve draw breath, then he laughed, sounding embarrassed. 'I guess,' he muttered. 'Maybe.'

Cathy gave a wry little smile. He had been in love with her for a long time, she had hurt him, made him bitter and cynical – now he was in love with this strange girl who kept insisting she was her sister. Was that why Steve had fallen for Sophie, been attracted to her? Had it seemed like fate to him? Cathy was disturbed by that, by the very idea of fate. She had lost control of her life today; once she had thought she had her life smoothly, perfectly working as she wished – all her dreams come true, this beautiful house, a man who was everything she had ever longed for. Now fate seemed to be controlling her; she felt helpless to do anything about what was happening, she didn't even know what she wanted to do, what she thought. She doubted everything she had once believed certain, including Paul. The ground was no longer solid under her feet. She had a terrible feeling that she was going to lose everything. Including Paul.

Wearily, she said, 'Come to breakfast tomorrow, Steve. I'll tell my gatekeeper to let you in – just you, not this Czech guy. He can see Sophie later.'

Vladimir and Steve sat up in a quiet corner of the bar until closing time, first eating ham sandwiches with home-baked ham and strong English mustard, served with a small salad on the side, and then drinking their way through the various beers the pub stocked. Vladimir was enjoying himself; he talked excitedly about his life, and then, encouraged by Steve, about Sophie's family, her home village, her mother, stepfather and two half-brothers.

'But it was her father I knew best – Pavel was not someone you forget. I was really shocked, huh? When I was told he'd been killed, I couldn't believe it. The Russians . . .

those bastards.' He drained his glass. 'I need another one! You, too?'

'No, thanks. This will last me for a while.' Steve didn't want to drink too much. He was beginning to get a healthy respect for Vladimir's capacity – the man could put it away faster than anyone he knew, and without showing any signs of being drunk! How many pints had he drunk so far? Old journalists were often lushes, but they usually disintegrated as the stuff got to them, but that wasn't happening with Vladimir. He still seemed as sharp as a tin-tack. He could probably write great copy after drinking everyone else under the table! Some reporters were like that. The more they drank the better they wrote. Stone-cold sober, they turned in boring garbage. Vladimir was talking a blue streak, and still making perfect sense!

Coming back with a pint of beer, Vladimir held it up to the light to inspect it. 'More real ale. You know what they call this? Thunderbox. Why? I asked the woman and she just kept laughing and wouldn't say. Well, looks good. Nice colour.' He lifted the glass to his nostrils and inhaled noisily. 'Mmm . . . smells good, too. Lots of hops, a sweetish malt. I like this smell. But let's see what it tastes like, huh?'

Smiling, Steve watched him sip, his eyes closed.

'Mmm,' he breathed, ecstatically. 'Yes, that hits the spot.'

Steve laughed. 'Where did you say you learnt your English?'

'From Americans,' Vladimir said. 'At Prague University they had an American tutor when I was young; a Communist who had come to Prague to admire our system. Ha!'

'Poor sap!' Steve said, and Vladimir grinned.

'As someone once said in an American film I saw . . . you said a cotton-picking mouthful, boy!' He drank some more, wiped the back of his hand across his foam-speckled moustache. 'The man was an idiot, but he was a good teacher; he

271

was one of the first to leave in 1968 – as the Russians came in, he left. Not quite so keen on Communism as he'd thought, nuh?'

'Fine to talk about, something else if you have to live under it?' suggested Steve cynically. '1968 was a watershed for a lot of people, one way or the other.'

Vladimir's massive head nodded vigorously. 'There are years like that, you know? 1848, now, that was a year of re-volutions in Europe – all over Europe, in Hungary, in France, there were uprisings everywhere, all at the same time. Not planned, no. It was . . . what is the word?'

'Spontaneous?'

'Spontaneous? I don't know that word. No, I meant . . . like nature, like seeds blown on the wind, carried by birds, like a forest fire, spreading too fast to stop . . . first a flame here, then a spark jumps over to there. Some years these things just happen. 1968 was one of those years, too; we had our Spring with Dubcek when it looked as if we were going to be free at last, then the Russians invaded, and the students went out on the streets to demonstrate and protest their freedom, in France, too, the students were out on the streets, and in London also, you know, demonstrating, fighting the police. But it all died out. In Czechoslovakia they clamped the lid back on and we had to wait another twenty years for freedom. Most of my life we've had to wait and now we're free I sometimes wonder what freedom actually means, whether it exists at all. Are the Americans free or are they slaves of a different sort, the slaves of the almighty dollar, nuh?'

He was getting melancholy; brooding, Slav-style, over his almost empty glass.

'Time for bed,' Steve said, realizing that this was what happened when Vladimir drank beyond a certain point, and that he might turn nasty next. You never knew with drunks. 'I have to be up early tomorrow for breakfast with Cathy and Sophie.'

'But I am not invited,' Vladimir gloomily said. 'So I shall stay down here, and have another drink.'

'Well, goodnight, then,' Steve said, and left him to it, hoping he wouldn't pick fights with anyone or break anything. It would be a nuisance if they were thrown out of here tonight.

In London Don Gowrie was drinking, and about to go to bed, too. He sat with a double brandy in his hand listening to Jack Beverley, who had laid a set of architectural plans on the table before they began talking.

'This is the layout of Arbory House. We surveyed the house as a security measure, remember, when your visit down there was first mooted, to check on any weak spots in the defences. Useful to us now. We have a clear idea where there are chinks. Here's the drive . . .' His hand followed the line of the drive on the blueprint. 'Front door. Main reception rooms. Drive curves round to the garages and stables. From back here, among these trees just beyond the park wall, there's a clear view of anyone standing in the stableyard.'

Don leaned forward to stare at the place where the stabbing finger landed. 'I remember you warned about that.'

'Exactly. Anyone who climbed one of the trees close to the wall with a rifle with a telescopic lens could pick off a target with one shot, as easy as shooting toy ducks at a fair.'

Gowrie looked nervous. 'You aren't suggesting . . . not while I'm there, for God's sake. The British police would be called, would start asking awkward questions, and I don't know how far I can trust Cathy and her husband, not any more, not after yesterday.'

Jack Beverley's face was hard with cynicism. 'No, of course not, sir. That wasn't in my mind at all. Far too risky.

I've thought all round the situation – so far, I believe the Narodni girl has only told the Broughams.'

'Unless she's told Colbourne.'

'You said she claimed she hadn't told him anything.'

'That's what she said – but who knows? She could be lying.'

'Well, we'll deal with that in a minute. But looking at Brougham himself . . . I think you can be sure of him. He's ambitious – look at the way he's climbed to the top in a very short time. He came out of nowhere, nobody knows much about him, but one thing is clear – he isn't too scrupulous. He built his business by some very dodgy methods. It's never been quite clear where he got his money from; other people, mostly, I suspect. Borrowed from Peter to pay Paul. Juggled balls in the air. I've heard whispers that he's over-committed, over-stretched.'

Gowrie was startled. 'You never told me any of this! I thought he was as solid as Fort Knox.'

'On paper, sure. But I've been digging a little deeper while I was over here. His companies all lock into each other, the money moves around from company to company, keep it moving and you never have to prove it's real money – get the picture?'

Paling, Gowrie breathed, 'My God! Are you saying he's broke?'

'Not necessarily. With these huge conglomerates it's always impossible to be sure how much of the money is real, and how much is borrowed or just on paper. We're trying to get into his main computer to find out, but it's a tough one – he has some genius on the job, locking out everyone who doesn't have the right password, and that changes all the time, probably. But it can be done, I have computer wizards on my staff too. They'll get in, if it's possible.'

Gowrie chewed on his lower lip. 'The bastard! He pulled

the wool over my eyes. Mind you, I suspected he wasn't to-tally kosher when I first met him – I had him checked out and his background sounded OK, there was no evidence it wasn't – no evidence it was, either. But he had plenty of money, and a lot of powerful friends, so I assumed he was OK. I wonder if Cathy knows?'

'Doubt it. He's too smart to tell a woman stuff like that. Wise men don't. Women never can keep secrets, and he'd be afraid she'd tell you.'

Gowrie thought of Emily; she had learnt too much about him, far more than he had ever meant to tell her. She might well have used what she knew, one day, to blackmail him. Beverley was right – you couldn't trust women.

'Having his father-in-law become president of the United States would be manna from heaven for him right now,' Jack Beverley said. 'So, when the chips are down, he'll be on your side.' Beverley gave a dry little smile. 'But it will cost you, of course – we'll have to wait to see what his demands are but you can be sure he has his price.'

Looking at him with grim cynicism, Gowrie wondered what *his* price was; what would Beverley demand in return for all this? Money, power, position? All three, no doubt. Gowrie had been in politics long enough to know that you got nothing for nothing. There was always a price. He had already had to make a string of promises to the men whose money and influence would be backing him for the nomination – they weren't backing his campaign out of patriotism or party loyalty. They had more selfish motives. Everyone always did.

Gowrie felt them all there, riding on his back, like fleas on a dog: the men he would have to pay back if he ever got to supreme power. They were vampires, they would bleed him white that day; he felt them at his throat, sucking al-ready, and was sickened by it, but he couldn't pull out of the race, now. He had to win – when he got into the White

House it would all be worth it. There was enough gravy in the gravy boat to go round, and with Emily gone that was one less vampire to feed.

'Let's hope you're right,' he agreed flatly. 'What about Cathy? She ordered your men to stay out, she wouldn't talk to me on the phone. What if she's taking the Czech girl seriously? What if she believes that little bitch, and has turned against me?'

Beverley stared into the other man's eyes, looking for pain or grief, and saw only fear and anger. Had he ever loved the girl the world thought was his daughter? Had she ever mattered to him? Or had she always been just a means to an end? Just the key that opened the door of the Ramsey family bank for Don Gowrie? The thought didn't bother Beverley, who had served too many political masters to be shocked by anything any one of them did.

He knew the men who clawed their way to top jobs. They were ruthless, amoral, self-centred, hard as nails – but they recognized fact when they saw it, which meant that Don Gowrie would pay up when Beverley put in his bill. That was all that mattered to Beverley.

'She can't be stupid enough to chuck away her whole life for some girl she only met today. After all, you're the only father she's ever known, and you've given her a wonderful life so far – she's grown up in luxury.' Beverley would have described himself as a realist; he believed only in what he could see and touch, he did not like or trust human beings. Every man had his price, in Beverley's view of life. And every woman, too. 'She'll play ball once she realizes what she'll lose if she doesn't. She's been brought up as an American, with all the good things of life on tap. Nobody would willingly throw that away just because they discovered they had another family somewhere. People are rational, deep down; they know which side their bread is buttered, you can always count on self-interest as a motive.' He believed this implicitly.

'I hope to God you're right,' Gowrie said heavily, getting up.

'I am.' Beverley had no doubts about his reading of human nature, human motivation. It never entered his head to suggest that Cathy Brougham might love the man she had called Father all her life. Love did not figure in his calculations. 'Just do as I say and we'll be OK. The important thing is to isolate the Czech girl. Get your daughter and her husband alone, talk to them, then leave it to us to deal with the Narodni girl. Once you have everyone else squared then we can take her out.'

Sophie woke up in the middle of the night, drenched in sweat, trembling. As she sat up, someone came crashing through the door and the light was switched on, blinding her.

She put both hands over her eyes with a cry of shock and fear, disorientated, not knowing where she was or what was happening.

'What's wrong? I heard you scream – was someone in here?' a voice asked, deep and cultured, very English. Anya's husband, she thought, it must be Anya's husband. She had seen him last night, but she had been so scared she hadn't really taken in much about him.

'No, it wasn't that, I'm sorry,' she whispered, still covering her eyes. 'A bad dream, that's all, I had a bad dream.'

It had been the usual dream; she had been running through the churchyard, hearing breathing behind her although whenever she looked over her shoulder there was nobody there. Reaching the grave, she knelt down and saw the names on the stone, Pavel and Anya Narodni. Suddenly the earth had bubbled up, its crust breaking, and the child's hand shot out and grabbed her.

Why did she still keep dreaming that when she knew Anya was alive?

'I thought someone must have attacked you,' said the deep voice. 'That's a relief, anyway. You're perfectly safe, don't worry, no need for bad dreams, no need to be frightened at all.' He had come over to the bed and bent over her. 'I'm very sorry to hear about . . . about your mother. But maybe something can be done to save her. Don't stay awake fretting about it, try to get some sleep.' He put a hand lightly on her shoulder, pushing her backwards, and she went obediently, lowering her hands and looking up at him.

He was wearing a heavy dark red quilted satin dressing-gown. Under the hem of it she saw matching dark red pyjama-trousers, his feet pushed into red leather slippers. He was a tall man, distinguished, still very handsome, with silvered hair and a strong face. He's much older than Anya, she thought, old enough to be her father! Why did she choose him instead of Steve? She must be crazy. I know which I would have chosen.

'Can I get you anything? A glass of warm milk? Some hot chocolate?'

She shook her head, but quiveringly smiled, liking the gentleness in his voice. You wouldn't expect it, with that tough face.

He looked startled for a second, as if her smile changed things, and smiles did, didn't they? A smile could be defensive, an attempt to placate, as well as happy.

'Sure?' he smiled back.

She nodded, recognizing then how much charm he had – maybe Anya was not so crazy, after all? He was certainly not a wallpaper person, he made quite an impact, didn't he? She could see why Anya had fallen for him.

He glanced round the room, as if he didn't know it very well, or perhaps just checking that everything was OK, then he drew her bedclothes up over her shoulders. The bed was covered with an antique American quilt; an early Homestead pattern, abstract geometric shapes in pastel pinks and greens.

'Are you quite comfortable in here?'

'Yes, thank you.' She had been too dazed last night to notice much about the room, but it was elegantly furnished, with Georgian furniture, highly polished, flowers on the dressing table, pretty pale green lamps trimmed with silk fringes. A delightful room.

He watched her intently; she was very aware of his stare although she was looking at the room – what was he thinking? That she was nothing like his wife?

'How old are you?'

She was taken aback, eyes widening. 'Twenty-eight. Why?'

'Twenty-eight?' He was frowning. 'What month were you born?'

'September. 1968.'

He sighed, met her puzzled eyes and grimaced. 'You look much younger. Well, good night, no more bad dreams.'

'I'm sorry I woke you up,' she said shyly. 'Goodnight.'

She watched him walk back to the door; he clicked off the light and closed the door behind him.

Sophie lay, frowning, in the dark, thinking that it was strange that it had been him who came when she called out. Why not Anya? Hadn't she woken up? Maybe she had taken a sleeping pill and was sleeping too heavily to be disturbed by anything short of an earthquake. Anya was unhappy and desperately worried. And it was all Sophie's fault.

She shouldn't have come here, should never have told Anya the truth, should have kept her mouth shut.

Oh, but she had promised Mamma to find Anya and talk her into going to see her before it was too late.

Her mind went round and round in circles, trying to work out what else she could have done and finding no answer.

In her bedroom, feeling cold and small and lonely in her vast kingsized bed, Cathy Brougham listened to the voices and movements, hoping Paul would come to her when he left Sophie, but silence fell and he did not come.

She had heard the scream, been on the point of getting out of bed to run to comfort Sophie, when she heard Paul's tread on the landing and a pencil-beam of yellow shone under her door as he switched on Sophie's light.

Cathy's eyes were red-rimmed with weeping, her hair tousled from tossing and turning. She did not want Paul to see her looking like that. She stayed in bed, listening, half afraid he would shout at Sophie, or bully her, yet why did she care? Sophie had ruined her life. She wished she had never even heard her name.

She heard their voices but too low to make out words until Paul's voice came again from near the door.

'Good night, no more bad dreams,' she heard him say, and then Sophie's softer, foreign-accented voice murmuring.

'Sorry I woke you . . .'

The yellow beam of light vanished; there was a click as the door shut, and she tensed, waiting to see if he would come to bed now, but his footsteps softly moved away. She tracked him like a bat tracking prey, her ears sharp as radar, identifying where he was going and understanding with a pain of the heart what it meant.

He was sleeping in the room at the end of the corridor, the room kept for unimportant visitors, a little cell of a room, barely furnished and remote.

He would not come to bed tonight. It was the first time they had slept apart since they were married, except when

Paul had to go abroad and couldn't take her. She knew it was a dangerous corner in their lives. Would he ever come to her bed again?

From Sophie's room there was silence. I hate her, thought Cathy, her teeth meeting. I wish she was dead. I should have let those men take her tonight; why did I stop them? I could kill her myself. If I killed her and we never said a word about all this, we could go back to the way it was . . . we could be happy again.

Her heart ached. She shut her eyes, wishing. We were so happy before she came. Oh, I wish . . . I wish I could have that time back, is it too much to ask?

Yet inside her head a cold, still voice asked remorselessly . . . could they? Would she ever be happy again now that she knew how much her family money meant to Paul? Had he ever loved her? Had it always been her fortune alone that attracted him? A man who was deeply in love did not change so much so fast. All this time he must have been pretending . . . lying to her, acting.

How had she been so hoodwinked, so blind to how he really felt?

11

Cathy's alarm didn't wake her because she was already awake. She had slept very little all night and was lying in bed staring bleakly at the light filtering through her curtains when her alarm shrilled. She stopped it and got out of bed, her body heavy and dull, her mind much the same. She had never felt less like getting up. This was going to be a day to be endured rather than lived through, but there was no point in hiding in bed, she had to face what was coming, so she walked like a zombie into the bathroom.

As she left her room ten minutes later she had a sudden wild hope that it had all been a bad dream, that yesterday hadn't happened, there was no Czech girl in the house, claiming to be her sister. She stopped to listen at the room next door to her own, her heart beating fast, and then shut her eyes with a muffled groan as she heard a movement.

After a long breath, she tapped on the door. 'Can I come in?'

There was a pause, as if the girl inside was startled, then Sophie said in a husky voice, 'Yes. Of course,' then, 'Good morning,' as Cathy opened the door. Sophie was out of bed, standing beside an open wardrobe in the dressing-gown Cathy had lent her. She had obviously had a shower. Her blonde hair was damp, her feet bare and pink.

'How are you this morning?' Cathy could see she looked much better than she had last night; she had some colour in her face, anyway. 'Did you sleep well?' She tried to keep the irony out of her voice but her mind was full of it.

'Yes, thank you, I hope you did.' Sophie sounded like a little girl trying to be grown-up. Had she picked up on the real feelings inside Cathy? 'I was looking for my clothes,' she went on, looking around the room. 'I can't find them.'

'Nora has washed them, they were in such a mess, damp and very muddy where you fell on the wet road last night – you couldn't have worn them. You're my size, more or less; come back to my room and pick out something to wear.'

Sophie's eyes glistened, close to tears. 'You're very kind. I'm sorry, I'm giving you a lot of trouble.'

'Yes, you are,' Cathy bluntly said, but somehow no longer wanted to shout at her, hit at her. Sophie looked so helpless; those were real tears, not pretence, and, face to face, Cathy couldn't help believing that this woman was sincere, totally genuine, was not lying. It was bewildering.

'But lending you clothes is not part of the problem,' she added. 'I have a lot of clothes, and you're very welcome to borrow some. You'd better hurry, we have a breakfast date.'

Sophie instantly paled, alarm in her eyes. 'With the senator?'

Cathy hated the fear in her face and felt a wave of anger again. She had no cause to look like that. As if Papa would . . . She flinched away from the thought of what he would or wouldn't do. Someone had tried to run Sophie down last night, she couldn't deny that, she had witnessed it with her own eyes. But what had it to do with Papa? It had probably been some total stranger, crazy or drunk, who, having accidentally knocked her down the first time, had decided to finish the job to do away with the only witness. It couldn't be anything to do with Papa.

Yet . . . why had his men burst in here last night to get Sophie? She shivered, remembering those moments before Paul arrived. She had felt so helpless.

How long had they been trailing Sophie? Had the driver of that car been one of Papa's people? What orders had Papa given them? Oh, they had claimed they were just trying to stop a dirty-tricks campaign Sophie was part of, and Cathy wanted to believe that version of events, but it wasn't easy. Once upon a time she wouldn't even have considered the idea of her father killing anyone – or ordering someone else to kill. She knew, though, that he had to be tough to survive in the world of Washington politics; weak men went to the wall. She had lived with political realities all her life – she understood. To get to the top you had to be strong, even ruthless – but murder? That was something else again.

Abruptly, she told Sophie, 'No, Steve's coming.'

Sophie instantly lit up like a Christmas tree, her eyes shining with candles. 'Steve? He's here?'

She's in love with him, Cathy thought; I knew she was, and he is obviously nuts about her, I picked that up just on the phone and he didn't deny it when I asked him. So it's mutual, and I'm not a dog in the manger. I didn't want Steve that way, so I've no right to complain if he turns to someone else – but did it have to be her? I wonder, did he fall for her *before* he heard her story about being my sister? Does he think he sees some likeness? Or am I being a simple, hometown bitch?

Irritated with herself, she said brusquely, 'He'll be here in ten minutes, which is why we have to hurry. He's staying across the road at the Green Man, he's coming across for breakfast with us. You had better come to my room and choose something to wear.'

Sophie followed her back to her own room and watched as Cathy threw open her wardrobe.

'What takes your fancy?'

Sophie hesitated, staring at the array of expensive, beautiful clothes and unable to reach out and take any of them. 'You choose for me. Just jeans and a sweater would be fine.'

Cathy ignored that, pulling out a cool almond-green wool dress with a silver belt and holding it up against her.

'This colour would suit you, it's perfect for a blonde but I always look washed-out in it. Do you like it?'

Sophie smoothed a hand over the soft material. 'I love it – are you sure you don't mind? It looks expensive.'

'I only wore it once. I'm sure it will fit you perfectly, we're much the same size. Wait a second.' Cathy hunted for lingerie; a lacy white bra, matching panties, a filmy slip in a very pale green, and dropped them all on the bed. 'I'll be downstairs, when you're ready. Don't take too long, will you?'

Before going downstairs, she paused outside the room she knew Paul had used the previous night, but there was no sound from him and she was afraid to tap on the door, afraid of how he might look at her, dreading coldness in his eyes, a distance between them growing, growing, until it became a gulf.

Had he slept much? She hadn't; she had drifted in and out of restless, uneasy, anxious sleep, in and out of dreams she didn't want to remember. She had cried a lot. Her eyes were still hot and sore from weeping so much; she had bathed them with cold water several times but it hadn't done them much good. They ached; she put a cold finger-tip on them and felt the heat radiating out from deep inside her eye-sockets.

While she was with Sophie she had relied on her long training in how to behave in public, how to keep your temper, however provoked, how to smile and smile even when you wanted to kill. So she had, somehow, been calm and polite to this girl who had come out of nowhere, without warning, and blasted her life apart the way a man with a gun blew away a pheasant.

Cathy had often gone out shooting with her father at Easton, but her attitude to the sport had changed after she spent a week with Paul at a big country house in Scotland. Each day the men had got up at the crack of dawn, while it was still dark, and vanished for most of the day. The women amused themselves at the house. Cathy had spent her time peacefully, a little bored, walking the family spaniels, playing with their hostess's baby son, daydreaming about one day having a child of her own. Just holding the baby, warm and smelling of talc and milk, made her weak with tenderness.

On the final day, the women in the party had driven across the moors in a shooting brake to join the men, taking a picnic with them. It had been a raw autumn day, a herring-bone sky, silver, glistening, with lines of cloud feathering the distance, a chilly wind carrying the scent of heather and gorse, the panic cries of unseen birds, a smell of cordite. The women unpacked the picnic baskets, the wine, the baskets of sliced French bread, the smoked salmon and smoked ham, leaving the hot chicken and pasties in a bed of straw to hold the warmth as long as possible.

Through binoculars Cathy had hunted for Paul in a line of men all dressed alike, in tweed jackets and trousers. Her heart had moved with tenderness, she had thought again about the baby they would one day have, and then he had lifted his gun and she had instinctively followed the line of it upwards, and seen the birds flying, their feathers bright amber, turquoise, black, shimmering with beauty and bright life.

She heard the crack, crack, crack of the guns. Birds stopped in mid-flight, with a jerk, their wings drooped, and they spiralled downwards into the heather. Cathy had felt sick; it had been a moment of terrible grief and pity for the bright life blown apart. It had changed her right down at her roots. She had known at that minute that she would never kill a living thing again.

That was what Sophie had done to her yesterday – she had been happy, excited about her father's visit, her sky had been blue, her wings carrying her, when suddenly she had been shot out of the sky without warning and plummeted to earth.

In his bedroom Cathy's husband lay listening to the soft, barely audible voices of the women at the other end of the corridor. What were they talking about? Cathy had been angry when he spoke to her, had claimed not to believe a word of Sophie's story, yet he had seen something very different in her face and voice last night. Bewilderment, curiosity, a protectiveness that was purely instinctive – she half-believed it, whatever she might say.

Blood talks to blood, he thought, even if you aren't aware of what is happening to you. You gave it other explanations, made up other reasons for what you felt – but it was that basic, blood calling to blood.

A shudder ran through him. Oh, Christ. Sweet Christ. He still couldn't believe it had happened to him. To them. Blood calling to blood . . . yes, and the family face . . . features so alike, instantly familiar, making the heart ache without knowing why.

He hadn't slept at all, he'd been far too shocked – yet he wasn't tired. He was wide awake, his body so tense that he felt he was on wires, like one of those puppets in old TV programmes, jerking along in slow movement, not quite co-ordinating, hands moving, then feet, mouth clacking open and shut, eyes staring this way, then that, the rest of the face all wood, flat-painted, unreal.

That was just it, he wasn't real, he was no longer living in real time, in a real place. He was out of it, in limbo, struggling to come to terms with what fate had done to him. What was he going to do? Every time he asked himself that question he felt the world spin dizzyingly around him and the words break up, sting like poisonous insects. What? What was he? What was he going to do? Over and over and over again. What was he? What was he going to do?

He heard Cathy leave the other girl's bedroom, heard her quiet footsteps, then her breathing outside his door.

He had to tell her the truth – but how? How could he? He shut his eyes, his stomach cramped; agony bled inside him, as if he'd swallowed broken glass. He had locked the door, she couldn't get in, but he couldn't bear it if she even knocked, or spoke to him through the door. Pain invaded every part of his body. He felt her out there, listening; the pulse of her came to him through the door, her body-warmth beating into him, making his body leap as it had from the first second he saw her. Sickness began to well up inside him.

Never again. He had to stop feeling like that. He must forget how he had felt once. Somehow he had to find the strength to walk away from her. Their marriage was over. He couldn't stay with her.

But his mind pulsated with images of them in bed, moving hotly, or in slow, sensuous delight . . . her mouth . . . her breasts . . . the hot, moist warmth between her thighs, into which he plunged again and again . . .

Christ, no! Don't remember. Mustn't remember. He had to leave her. But he could never tell her why. He could imagine how she would look at him if he tried to explain . . .

He couldn't bear to hurt her like that.

But he was hurting her, wasn't he? She was bewildered, unhappy, confused, and he was making it worse for her. But what else could he do? He was trapped; he couldn't see any other way out. Could she hear his breathing? Did she guess that he was awake but pretending to be asleep? Of course she did. She wasn't stupid. Oh, God, my love, Cathy . . . He hated knowing what he was doing to her, but . . . what could he say? It was over. Over.

After a long moment she walked away, and tears of ice formed behind his closed lids. They didn't fall, they merely blinded him, reminding him of snow on his lashes and in his eyes when he walked through one of the blizzards which blew, most winters, across the snowy landscapes of the Ramsey family estate at Easton, making the familiar suddenly strange, unrecognizable, taking away all the landmarks you knew, so that you lost your bearings and had no idea where you were any more, or which way to go to get home.

That was how he felt now: lost, helpless, terrified. He didn't know where he was, who he was, he didn't know anything any more; where to go, what to do, what to think.

There was a fiery image in his head, one he had first seen many years ago and never forgotten.

When he first came to London, he had visited the Tate Gallery, a grey, ornate, formal building which reminded him of Paris, and stood like one of the great buildings of Paris, on the riverside – except that this was the Thames, not the Seine. Wandering through the high-ceilinged rooms within the gallery, he had gone to look at French paintings, Impressionists, Pointillistes with their bright, coloured dots of paint giving a hazy, summery look to what they painted, because they gave him a warming injection of Frenchness, made him feel at home for a while. Those first months in England he had felt lost and lonely, and although he had good English before he came it wasn't always easy to understand what people said. Londoners had a cheerful laziness of tongue that baffled him, his first glimpse of how many varieties of English there were – from the twang of Liverpudlians to the slow brogue of country people.

Reaching a distant gallery, he came to a room full of Pre-Raphaelite paintings and sat down on a leather bench to rest before he made his way back to the door. By sheer chance he had sat down in front of one vast canvas in which a towering archangel with glowing, spread wings dwarfed the guilty, shrinking human beings crouched in front of him. He knew at once what he was looking at – Adam and Eve being turned out of the Garden of Eden by an angel with a flaming sword. The colours were magnificent, the image unforgettable.

For ten minutes he had sat and stared. When he left he took the image with him, and he had gone back many times to stare at the painting, although if you had asked him what fascinated him so much about it he would have been hard put to find an answer.

He had thought, at the time, that maybe the painting represented for him his feelings about his past, his inability to go back to places and people he loved deeply, the feelings of loss that swamped him if he ever thought about his early life. You couldn't go back; time went on, it didn't stop or reverse. Paul Brougham had come into being as the product of hard-headed common sense, the ability to face facts, a drive to survive at any odds.

What had never occurred to him until now was the possibility that you might be able to foresee your future, recognize what was to come, know your own death. Second sight? Garbage, he would have said, until now. Time flows forward – you cannot see what lies ahead.

Now that he stood on quicksands and felt the ground shifting under him, knew how perilously weak his grasp on his whole life had always been, he was no longer so sure about anything. All he knew for certain was that the archangel with his fiery sword stood between him and Cathy now and would do forevermore, and, like Adam in the Garden of Eden, he had been made aware of his nakedness and weakness, and was hiding from the Voice of God.

He had always prided himself on being able to think on his feet, fast and confidently, come rapidly to the right decisions. But now, with disaster staring him in the face, he was paralysed, unable to think at all. He had run away, locked himself in this room, alone with his pain, a pain so bad it was crippling him; he couldn't make a move in any direction, a checked king on the chessboard he had once thought he ruled.

The breakfast-room was at the side of the house with high, wide windows looking over a private walled garden which was bare of flowers at this time of year but in spring was full of purple crocus, golden daffodil, the white bells of lily of the valley. In a month or so the first green spears of the snowdrops would be pushing through the soil under the lilac trees, the buddleia, the azalea, which was already thick with tight buds.

Cathy picked up the telephone on the sideboard, rang the kitchen. 'Could I have some coffee and fresh toast, please, Nora? A gentleman is joining us for breakfast, so could you also give us some scrambled eggs, bacon, tomatoes, and mushrooms?'

She also asked her housekeeper to let the gatekeeper know that Steve was coming, then rang off and stood by the window. The shadow of the house lay against the stone wall; chimneys, roofs, windows. She loved this house, she had been happy living here, she had thought she would live here for the rest of her life. She looked away, wincing, and stared at the sky, which this morning, after last night's rain, was a newly washed blue. The sun was bright, giving an almost springlike air to the garden. Beyond the wall the tops of trees waved and birds flew from the ivy on the wall darting up into the sky. On a day like this you could believe you'd live forever. But you'd be deceiving yourself. Nobody lived forever and nothing ever stayed the same.

She turned away angrily and went out into the hall again to look for Sophie just as the doorbell rang.

'I'll get it,' Cathy told the housekeeper, who appeared at once from the baize-covered door leading into the servants' hall, and Nora vanished again while Cathy was opening the front door.

Steve looked maddeningly normal; his hair was wind-blown, his skin a fresh, healthy colour, he had obviously shaved not long ago and seemed wide awake, but she knew he was used to late nights and could function at a lower level than most people: his metabolism had been trained to cope with sleeplessness and exhaustion.

He wasn't even wearing a coat, probably because he had only had to drive such a short distance and he was used to the longer hauls of America, to New England winters, Washington winters, cruel as the grave. Under a leather flyer's jacket he wore a thick blue sweater, a blue shirt under it, jeans with a broad belt, silver-buckled, and black leather boots. He looked very American, she felt the warmth of home just looking at him, and reached out to hug him, eagerly, instinctively.

'Steve! Oh, I'm so glad you got here. Long time, no see. How are you?'

He held on to her slim waist, tilting his head back to look down at her in her warm gold and amber jersey dress, an amber necklace round her throat and gold studs in her ears.

'I'm OK, how about you?' His quizzical, searching eyes slid over her face, absorbing the pallor, the lines of anxiety and stress at eyes and mouth. She looked like a victim of shell-shock, which was probably just how she felt, thought Steve, pity jabbing in his chest. Sophie shouldn't have come here, shouldn't have told her. Hadn't he warned her she was playing with fire coming after Don Gowrie, and that was even before Vladimir told him what was behind So-phie's quest. Why in God's name was she so pig-headed?

Cathy pulled away. 'I'll live.' She forced a light laugh which made him wince at the brave pretence. 'Come in, out of this cold wind.'

'How's Sophie?' he asked, following her into the

breakfast-room which by now smelt of the coffee which had arrived, along with a rack full of perfect toast and a little row of silver dishes kept warm electronically. The housekeeper had vanished again, the room was warm and quiet and homely, and he sighed with enjoyment at the smell of real American coffee after the stuff he had been drinking ever since he hit the UK. Why couldn't the Brits make good coffee?

'She's getting dressed, she'll be down in a minute,' Cathy said, pouring him strong black coffee, remembering without needing to think about whether he took cream. She knew Steve backwards and forwards. She handed him the cup, looking at his face and suddenly thinking, Well she had thought she knew him, but what did you ever know about anyone?

She had thought she knew Paul so well; she had thought her life was based on the solid rock of his love. This morning she knew how wrong she had been. All her certainties had crumbled under her feet.

'Is she OK, though?' he insisted, staring at her stricken face and seeing far too much, things she did not want anyone to see. He had ruthless eyes; that was something she had never noticed until now.

'I'll let you decide that for yourself,' she evaded, turning her face away from that steely probe. 'Can I get you cooked breakfast? Eggs, bacon?'

She lifted the silver lids and he peered at the contents and was startled to feel his stomach clench in hunger at the smell of the beautifully cooked food. 'A little of everything, please,' he said, watching her spoon out scrambled egg, lift several rashers of bacon on to the plate.

'Hungry?' she asked, and he laughed wryly.

'I'm starving. We only had sandwiches last night, and far too much to drink. God knows when Vladimir will wake up, and when he does he'll have the hangover to end all

293

hangovers. That man could drink the Pacific dry. Could I have two tomatoes, please? I love them. Plenty of mushrooms, yes, thanks.'

Cathy placed his generous plate of food in front of him. 'Help yourself to toast.' She moved the toast, the butter and a yellow glass bowl of thick home-made marmalade to his elbow, then went out into the hall, hearing footsteps.

Sophie was wandering about, looking into rooms like a lost child. Her face brightened as she saw Cathy.

'Oh, there you are! I didn't know where to go – this house is so enormous!'

'We're in here.' Cathy stood back to gesture her into the room, and followed, watching as Sophie stopped, her breath catching, as she saw Steve at the table.

He got up at once, scowling. 'So there you are at last! I ought to slap you stupid for going off like that, without even telling me what you were planning! Didn't I tell you not to take risks? You could be dead this morning – do you realize that, you silly bitch?'

'I know,' she said submissively. 'I'm sorry.'

'Huh!' he snorted. 'You don't fool me with that sweet, feminine stuff.' But his face had softened, and he was looking her over with hunger, taking in every inch of her warm, feminine body in the almond green dress, her blonde hair gleaming in the morning sunlight. 'You look good anyway. How do you feel?'

'Good,' she said, and they smiled at each other, the atmosphere suddenly dancing with sexual awareness.

Cathy knew what a gooseberry felt like; she was prickling with tiny hairs of irritation and felt distinctly green. For so long Steve had been *her* property; now he only had eyes for Sophie, he had forgotten *she* was in the room. Stop it! You're being ridiculous! she told herself but the feeling didn't go away, it lurked at the bottom of her heart, an ugly black sediment she couldn't identify and was ashamed about.

She was deeply in love with her husband, she didn't love Steve, or want him back – why was she reacting like this? Why?

The question was rhetorical because she knew the answer even as she asked the question. She was unhappy and frightened and needed reassurance; she wanted the stability and certainty of her childhood and Steve meant that. Steve meant a lot of other things too: he stood for her own country, for America, for home, Easton, New England, for comfort and kindness. He had been there for as long as she could remember: when hadn't she known Steve? He was as solid and real as Thanksgiving and Christmas, summer camp, beach parties, all the memories of her childhood and adolescence, everything in her life that had once mattered so much. Steve was bound up with it all.

Oh, she wasn't in love with him but she was fond of him, it had made her heart lift to see him standing at the front door.

When he hugged her she had almost burst into tears of gratitude because he was just the same, he hadn't changed towards her. Steve knew about Sophie's allegations – but it hadn't changed him, he obviously didn't care whether or not she was rich or came from a famous old family. He had smiled at her and hugged her with the old cheerful warmth, and that had made her heart lift.

Now, seeing him with Sophie, she was childishly jealous. She wanted to shout at Sophie, Get away from him, he belongs to me! Because he did, in the way that Papa had always belonged to her, and Grandee, and the dogs and ponies, everything at Easton, all the things that she loved. Love made them hers.

Cold reason sank through her mind then, told her that

she had to face the truth – none of them belonged to her. Papa was not her father, Grandee was not her grandfather, and Easton would never now belong to her. She might still love them, but love gave you no hold on anything.

'Your breakfast is getting cold,' she told Steve sharply, but didn't meet the surprised look he gave her, flushing because she knew she was behaving badly. She went over to the sideboard and gestured to the food. 'Sophie, do you like eggs, bacon?'

Sophie joined her and looked at the scrambled eggs as Cathy lifted their silver lid. Steve sat down again and picked up his knife and fork, but was more interested in watching them together.

'I can see the likeness now,' he said as they turned to come back to the table, and they stood stock-still, startled, turning to look at each other. Standing so close, one to the other, in profile the resemblance was even more striking, and Steve breathed, 'My God, yes! The shape of your faces . . . the angle of your cheeks, same nose, same jawline, same mouth.'

Cathy said angrily, 'I don't see any similarity at all! I'm dark, she's blonde!'

He made an impatient gesture. 'That's just surface – your colouring is so different it deceives at first, but the bone-structure underneath the skin is identical, Cathy.'

Cathy looked at Sophie's face, not wanting to see any likeness, but seeing it, all the same. She didn't want to believe it, but the bewildering sense of recognition kept growing. My sister? she thought. My sister?

Sophie thought that too, in an echo of Cathy's thoughts but without the question mark. My sister. My sister.

'You see, Anya? I'm not crazy. Steve sees it, I see it,' she said with a face like morning sunshine.

'I'm Cathy,' the automatic reply came, but Cathy was thinking: Anya? Is that really my name? It was even beginning to sound familiar. She was beginning to like it. More than she had ever liked Cathy.

What's in a name? she angrily thought. Everything, it seemed. Anya Narodni was a very different person from Cathy Brougham. Changing her name changed everything.

'Anya, look at me!' Sophie eagerly said, staring into the mirror. She took hold of Cathy's chin and turned her face forward. Cathy gazed at her own reflection, then at Sophie's, and Sophie breathed huskily, 'You see? We both get our bone-structure from Mamma, but you're more like her, she always said I was like Papa, although I never saw it in the photos of him. I brought some with me – where did I leave my photos? I had them with me last night.'

'They're in the sitting room,' Cathy said. 'You can look for them after breakfast.' She felt too tired and miserable to talk any more. She pulled her chin out of Sophie's fingers and turned away. 'Please sit down, Sophie, and eat your food before it gets cold.'

She poured coffee, sat down, too, and ate half a slice of toast and marmalade while the others ate their cooked food.

'Where's your husband?' asked Steve.

'In bed asleep. He's very tired.' Cathy tried not to sound defensive, not to betray her anxiety, but Steve knew her too well. His narrowed eyes probed her averted face.

'Does he know about Sophie?'

She nodded without looking up. She did not want to talk about Paul; Steve was far too shrewd, his prescience disturbed her.

Sophie was staring at Steve fixedly. 'I just realized . . . I didn't tell you about Cathy, about us being sisters . . . how do you know?' She looked at Cathy. 'Did you tell him?'

'No, of course not!'

'Vladimir,' Steve said, swallowing a bit of bacon.

'Vlad?' she gasped. 'But Vlad doesn't know either. I never told him, I didn't tell anyone!'

'You underestimate your friends,' Steve drily said. 'Apparently you left him a message to say you were coming to London, so he rang Lilli at Theo's apartment, and Lilli told him what happened in the subway, and about the burglary. Vladimir was worried about you. He's a born newspaperman, he couldn't rest until he knew what was behind it all, so he went to see your mother.'

'He didn't tell her people had been trying to kill me?' Sophie had gone very pale, her eyes wide and full of distress. 'Oh, why did he have to do that? She'll be so scared. I wish Vlad would for goodness' sake mind his own business! I've a good mind to ring him up and tell him so! Wait till I see him!'

'You won't have to wait very long.'

'What?'

'He's here, with me, staying at the Green Man. When your mother told him about Don Gowrie he flew over to London to find you. He reckoned you'd need help. He'll be along later to see you.'

Sophie's lips quivered into a half-tearful smile. 'That's so kind of him . . . typical Vlad! But all the same, I wish to God he had not told my mother about the accident in New York.'

'It was not an accident, Sophie. Someone tried to kill you and they've tried again since then,' Steve said flatly. 'Wake up to the danger you're in! These people are not going to give up – they'll try again.'

'Not under my roof,' Cathy said, and winced as Steve looked at her with irony and pity.

'You're almost as naive as your sister!'

My sister, she thought, looking at Sophie, and Sophie smiled at her.

'My sister,' she said, echoing Cathy's thought again. She

was still having trouble believing that this was Anya, not dead, but alive.

The village was busy with traffic and people shopping when Don Gowrie's helicopter appeared on the horizon. Villagers halted in the street to watch briefly as it flew towards them, then hovered over Arbory House, but they were used to seeing Paul coming and going by helicopter and soon went about their business. The rotating blades on the chopper made it impossible for Gowrie to hear the faintly cracked note of the church clock when it chimed ten o'clock, but looking down into the village he got a clear view of the warm, golden stone of the houses, the grass, the trees, the blackened, twisted metal shape of the car in which Emily had died.

Having caught one glimpse, he looked away, his face stiff and cold as a carved statue. He wouldn't think about her. It wasn't his fault she had been killed – she had been the one who crashed that car, not him. In the office she had been a miracle of efficiency. Why, when it came to killing Sophie Narodni, had she failed again and again? He couldn't understand it, unless she had not really wanted to kill the girl at all.

Or maybe it had been a run of bad luck. He had been having a run of bad luck ever since that damned girl showed up in the press conference.

Luck was something you couldn't manipulate or bribe. It had its own rules and its own logic. Random, unpredictable, blind – it struck out of the blue.

In his mind's eye he saw the remains of the car again – had they got Emily out yet, or was there nothing left to . . .?

He shivered. He wouldn't think about that – there was too much on his mind, far more important things to think about; he had no time to dwell on her death. First, he had to survive, end Sophie Narodni's threat to him. After that he could think about . . . about other things.

He glanced over his shoulder at Jack Beverley, who was as calm as a bowl of milk. Gowrie envied him his temperament. But then, what had he to lose?

In the house they all heard the sound of the chopper coming down to land.

'He's here,' Cathy told Steve, who nodded, watching Sophie, who had turned pale and was trembling a little. Paul had not put in an appearance, but none of them had mentioned him. They had left the breakfast-room and gone into a small, sunlit sitting-room with a view of the landing pad and had been listening for the chopper while they sat around the fire in ancient, sagging leather armchairs.

'Maybe I should go back up to my room? If the senator finds me here he'll be very angry.'

Sophie was white with nerves. She was terrified of seeing Don Gowrie again. Last night was still alive in her memory. The way the car had come out of nowhere and hit her; climbing on to her knees just as it turned and drove straight back at her; then the driver swerving away and hitting the tree, the explosion, the roar of flames, the great red light illumining the darkness. In her dreams she had heard the woman in the car screaming; but that had not happened, she had not heard that. Or had she? She didn't want to remember if she had.

Steve saw the fear in her eyes, and put his arm round her. 'You're safe with me, don't worry. He won't dare touch you under this roof. He'd have to kill all of us. And even Gowrie hasn't got the neck to try anything like that. No, he's stymied, and he knows it. I'm just curious to know how he's going to handle all this. What sort of excuses is he going to come up with? I wonder, has he got his speechwriters to write that script? Or has he worked it up by himself?'

The sarcasm and contempt made Cathy flinch, and the sight of Sophie in Steve's arms angered her too. She needed his comfort too, but he was only concerned with Sophie, it seemed.

Fiercely, she burst out, 'Once word of these accusations leaks out – and it will, gossip like this always does – he's finished as a politician, he may even have to face some sort of proceedings. He certainly won't get the presidential nomination. The money men will desert him. Grandee will be so furious he won't want to know him either.'

'Don't waste your pity on him.' Steve's face turned grim and scathing. 'Can't you see yet what sort of cold-hearted bastard he is? He deserves everything that's coming to him. And it will come, Cathy. Sooner or later someone will launch an investigation into what he's been up to, and I just bet they find all sorts of skeletons buried in his backyard. Somebody once said that Washington is filled with two kinds of politicians – those trying to get an investigation started, and those trying to get one stopped. But once a can of worms is opened you can't get the worms back into the can.'

Cathy was white, her eyes shadowed with dark rings. 'For God's sake, you're talking about my father!'

'No, that's the whole point. I'm not,' Steve curtly said. 'Your father is dead, and Gowrie took you away from your mother just when she needed you most, needed you to hold on to. What if she had lost the baby she was expecting? She'd have been left alone with nothing in the world to love. God knows what would have happened to her then.'

Cathy stared at him, realizing that the sick, sad woman she had called 'Mother' all her life was, perhaps, not her mother at all, that the strange distance between them which Cathy had felt all her childhood, could be because they shared no blood, were not mother and child at all. She had thought it was because her mother was always sick that she had not really loved her. She had felt guilty because she didn't care for her mother the way other people seemed to love their parents. She could remember many times when she had watched Steve with his mother, seeing the warmth between them, the easy, relaxed affection, and envying him.

Somewhere in a strange country she had never visited there was this other woman who might be her real mother. What was she like, this other mother? How would it feel to see her, get to know her?

'It's time you faced all that,' Steve said, more gently, seeing the haunted look in her face and intensely sorry for her. 'You have a lot of re-thinking to do, Cathy.'

Yes, he was right – if Sophie's story was true her whole life had been a lie and it would take her a long time to think it through, come to terms with it. She would be losing everything she had ever thought so secure.

If it was true. If it was true.

Sophie's voice made her start. 'What will happen to him?' Sophie was feeling guilty. She had set out on this quest with a driven instinct to find her sister, to rebuild the family shattered even before she herself was born, and above all to bring Anya home to their mother before she died. She had not meant to ruin Don Gowrie's chances of becoming president, she hadn't meant to tear Cathy's whole world apart. She should have stopped to think all round the situation before she made a single move, but she hadn't, and now it was too late to say, Sorry, I didn't mean this to happen, this wasn't what I meant.

She looked at Steve miserably. 'They won't send him to prison, will they?'

Cathy broke out in a shaken voice, 'What charge could they bring? I mean . . . he's done nothing illegal.'

'Only committed fraud,' said Steve in that cool, contemptuous voice she hated. 'He passed you off as the heir to the Ramsey fortune, remember? He passed you off as his

302

child, used his real, dead child's passport to smuggle a Czech girl into America as an American. That's two very serious counts, to start with, and I can't see him getting out of either of them.'

Cathy put a trembling hand to her mouth. If all this was true . . . she wasn't even an American. She was Czech. The implications of Sophie's story were only just beginning to dawn on her.

'If it's true!' she threw back at Steve. 'I don't believe it, any of it!'

12

Up in his bedroom, Paul Brougham was just dressing when he heard the chopper engines, the whirr of the blades. He crossed softly to the window, pulled the curtains back and looked up into the sky, watched the machine slowly descending, the down-draft blowing the grass back and forth.

Gowrie had arrived. Paul's eyes burnt with hatred. He had never quite trusted the man, but he had liked him well enough once, perhaps because he wanted to like him. Cathy's family had become his family; he had been careful to weave himself into them and some of them he liked a hell of a lot. Old Ramsey, for instance, he was quite a guy; tough, yes, as old shoe-leather, but a man you respected all the same. He had principles, he believed in something; you knew that once his word was given you could trust him.

Paul had never really respected Gowrie. The man was a typical diplomat, all surface and no depth. He was smooth, far too agreeable to be true; an oily, deceptive, devious man, and Paul had always suspected he had no heart. Now he was sure of it.

But Cathy loved her father. She had been close to him all her life; he had taken care to keep her close, and Paul had taken that to prove the man loved her, but now he could see how she had been used, manipulated. Gowrie had used her to buy himself golden opinions – as a good father, a good family man, a man you could rely on. Now it would reap him dividends. How could she turn against the man she had loved all her life? However angry she might be, however disillusioned, hurt, bewildered . . . he was still the man she thought of as her father, wasn't he? You couldn't just discard the feelings of years like a shed snake-skin.

He heard the muted voices below him as they also stood by the window on the floor below, watching the helicopter descending. Paul recognized Cathy's husky tones, picked up the familiar notes of Steve Colbourne's voice, jealously resenting his presence here at Arbory.

Colbourne had never been here before, had not been welcome in Paul's home. He wasn't welcome now. Paul wished he could go down and throw him out, but he had too many other things to worry about. He couldn't waste his time on minor irritations.

The third voice was Sophie's, but sounded as at ease with the others as if they had known each other all their lives. The intimacy between them hurt him, made him feel excluded.

Gowrie had ruined all their lives with his self-seeking ambition, his total lack of scruples, and now he had been found out the bastard was trying to wriggle out of the consequences, ready to kill to save himself. It was pure luck that he hadn't already killed Sophie.

Gowrie had to be stopped before he did more harm. He had done Cathy a terrible injury; she didn't know yet just how much harm Gowrie had done her, done both of them. Paul closed his eyes, shuddering at the thought of how she would feel if she ever found out the truth. He couldn't tell her. He would do anything to make sure she never found out.

He walked soft-footed down the stairs to his study without anyone hearing him, opened a drawer in his desk, pushed aside a false bottom and got out the hidden contents: a handgun and some ammunition in a box.

He loaded the gun with deft competence; he had learnt years ago how to do it quickly although he had never yet used the gun against a human being. Slipping it into his inside jacket pocket, he felt it, heavy and cold, against his heart, but that was nothing new – his heart had been cold and heavy all night.

He had felt like this before, he knew the bitter chill of grief and loss, the ache of the inevitable, the pain of unbearable choice. He had had to leave them behind once before, those he loved, his family, wife and children – leave them not knowing if he would ever return. It had been one of those life-or-death choices; well, he hadn't really had much choice at all, unless he was ready to die, and he hadn't been.

He had been young then, though, a man at the very beginning of his life with hope and possibility inside him.

God! He wished he were that age now; could still run and start again somewhere else, but last night something had broken inside him, some vital spring without which he could not move.

They met Gowrie as he arrived at the front door, surrounded by security men who fanned out with watchful, skimming eyes, their jackets unbuttoned and their fingers splayed across their waistcoats, ready to draw at the first hint of danger.

Cathy was white, drawn. 'I don't want those men in my house! They pushed me around enough last night – in my own home! They aren't doing that again.'

Jack Beverley coolly answered before Gowrie could open his mouth. 'I'm sorry, Mrs Brougham, but I've had to advise the senator not to enter your house until we've had an opportunity to check it out for listening devices.'

'You aren't checking my house for anything!' Cathy snapped at him. 'You and your men can stay out!'

Gowrie said, 'We have to talk though, Cathy. Look, why don't we go for a walk around the grounds? Get your coat on, it's cold out here.'

'Not until these men have all been withdrawn. And I mean all, Mr Beverley. You included. Get yourselves back in that chopper and get out of here.'

Beverley gave one of his cold sneers. 'I'm here to protect the senator! And I'm going to do my job. Your husband no doubt has his security men here! How do we know we can trust them?'

It was stalemate. They stood there staring angrily at each other. Steve said curtly, 'You either trust us or you don't, Senator. Cathy wouldn't bug her own house, for God's sake.'

Gowrie quietly said, 'Look, why don't we take a walk, Cathy? I'd like to see your stables. I can have a look at Mr Tiffany.' He glanced at Beverley. 'The stables are a safe, enclosed spot, Jack. No hidden surveillance out there. Your men can withdraw to the helicopter while we have our chat, OK?'

Steve frowned. 'She isn't going anywhere alone with you.'

'Watch yourself, Colbourne! Who the hell do you think you are, talking to the senator like that?' Beverley snapped, but Gowrie intervened in his best diplomatic tone, smooth as cream.

'You come too, Colbourne, if you're worried, but for heaven's sakes ... d'you really think I'd hurt my own daughter?'

Tears stung Cathy's eyes. She swallowed, her face averted. All the years of growing up rushed into her head in a swarm of memories.

'I love Cathy,' Gowrie said in a deep, moved voice, and it was impossible to believe he was lying.

Sophie moved closer to Steve, and he looked down at her. 'Sophie comes too,' he said, seeing the anxiety in her face. 'We're not going with you and leaving Sophie alone with your thugs. They'd have her in that chopper and away before we knew what was happening.'

'Oh, very well, all three of you, then,' Gowrie said, as if he was reluctant – but he had meant to talk to them all together. His apparent surrender was purely tactical, part of his negotiating strategy. If you had 'given in' on one point, your opponents could be made to feel obliged to give in to you later over something more important.

In the house, Paul had come down the stairs and noticed the open front door. He was walking slowly towards it when the phone in the hall began to ring just as he was passing it. On a reflex instinct he picked it up. His voice was curt. 'Yes? What? Mr Colbourne's colleague is here to join him?' For a second his eyes flashed with rage. So Colbourne had started inviting people to the house now, had he? Could they expect a camera crew next, complete with soundmen and electricians? Oh, yes, they would come – and the rest of the media. They would all come, crowding in on the scene like some Greek chorus, to stare and be amused, to make their comments and pass judgement on people whose lives they had envied until now, and, above all, to talk pityingly yet with hidden glee, glad that, after all, they were not them, but led quiet, safe, unremembered lives out of the sight of the gods.

He stared into the ornate gilt-framed eighteenth-century Venetian mirror hanging on the wall in front of him. His white face looked back at him, haggard with pain, convulsed with anger. Fate played strange games. Why was Colbourne involved in this? Another of fate's little jokes? If he, personally, had not been so closely involved, Paul might even have found the irony amusing – but it hurt too much for him to summon a smile.

Colbourne, of all people. Paul had always been jealous of Colbourne. Cathy had once been close to marrying him, whatever she said now. She had sworn that she had never been in love with Colbourne, but they had been lovers, she admitted that, and Paul hated to know it; couldn't stop his imagination picturing them together.

And now it was Colbourne who was the instrument of fate; Colbourne who had brought this calamity down on their heads.

'Ask him to wait,' he said bleakly into the phone and hung up. He would like to have said: tell him to get lost! But there was no point in taking such a position. He might as well face facts.

Once before he had been faced with disaster and had refused to accept his fate, had escaped – but he knew now with all the fatalism of his race, the melancholy acceptance which had always been there in his blood, behind his confidence and drive, that this time he was finished.

He had thought himself in the very middle of his life with much still to do; he had dreamt of all sorts of futures for himself and Cathy, not least a dream of having children. Thank God – at least they had been spared that.

He walked into the breakfast-room and found it empty, the table already cleared of their breakfast remains. As he hesitated he heard voices outside in the stable yard, recognized Gowrie's voice, then Cathy's. She sounded distraught. His forehead tightened in anxiety and pain.

He wasn't hungry but he needed some hot, strong coffee before he went out to face her. He rang for the housekeeper.

Gowrie said nothing as they walked slowly along the gravelled terrace running round the house past the small, formal box trees in square white-painted pots which gave the house such a French air, reminiscent of Paris parks where nurserymaids walked their charges and lovers met under the blue summer shadow of plane trees. All this had been designed by Paul himself; he had deliberately brought memories of his homeland into this very English setting, and it gave the old house a very different personality, a foreign look which was nevertheless graceful and charming, and suited the eighteenth-century formality of the building.

Sophie murmured something about it to Cathy. 'Very French, like the dècor in your house. Did you choose it? It's lovely.'

Cathy smiled. 'We love it,' then her breath caught, and she huskily corrected herself, 'Loved it.'

Steve shot her a quick, sharp look, noting the past tense, as they entered the beautifully kept stable yard. She might deny that she believed Sophie, but obviously she did. A groom was curry-combing Mr Tiffany, who immediately on seeing Cathy showed his yellow piano-teeth in that grin of mingled pleasure and mischief, toss-ing his head, his long chestnut mane gleaming in the sunlight.

The groom said, 'Morning, Mrs Brougham.' Taking in the fact that she was not wearing jodhpurs or boots, he asked politely, 'Shall I get Mr Tiffany saddled, or would you like me to bring out any of the other horses?'

'No, just leave that for now. Go and have a cup of tea, would you?'

He nodded and led the chestnut back into his stall, closed the half-door on him and walked away towards the house.

As he vanished indoors, Cathy turned to look directly at Gowrie, seeing the long-loved familiarity of his face and hurting because she had never really known him after all, he had lied to her all her life. Behind that familiar face lived a stranger. 'It's true, isn't it?'

'Cathy –'

Angrily she stopped the words rising to his tongue. 'Don't lie, not this time.'

'Cathy, darling,' he quickly said, moving to put an arm round her, but she immediately stepped back, shaking her head.

'It will be easy to prove the truth, you know. I only have to have a blood test. There's no arguing with DNA.'

He had never thought of that before. No, there was no arguing with DNA. Blood didn't lie.

'But I don't even need to wait for the test results to know the truth,' Cathy said, pain in her eyes because she had loved him all her remembered life and been cheated by him. Bleakly, she said, 'I'm not your daughter, I'm Sophie's sister, and you smuggled me out of Czechoslovakia and into the States on the passport of your own child who was dead, was buried as me. That is the truth, isn't it?'

'You put it very harshly. It wasn't quite like that, Cathy – at least give me a chance to explain.' He looked down at her, his eyes pleading. They had been so close, closer than most fathers and daughters. How often had Cathy shared his campaign trail, sitting up with him in smoky rooms discussing tactics, knocking on doors, shaking hands in crowded campaign halls, beside him all the way. She had always been Daddy's girl. He couldn't believe he had lost that hold on her. 'For heaven's sake, Cathy, how can you doubt I've always loved you? Whatever they've said to you, you've always been my little girl, and I've done my best to make you happy, haven't I?'

He saw the hesitation in her eyes, the struggling feelings. She might be fighting it, but she still loved him.

In a gentle voice, he said, 'I won't lie to you, Cathy. But you have to understand why I did it! You've listened to them – aren't you going to listen to me? Don't you think you owe me that much?'

She sighed, nodded. 'OK, I'm listening.'

'Thank you, darling,' he said in a soft, humble voice.

Steve picked up that note and gritted his teeth. God, he'd like to smack the lying, manipulative bastard in the teeth. Why couldn't Cathy see through him? But then Gowrie had had her on his team all her life. She was bound to him by old affection and loyalty. It must be very hard for her to turn against him now.

'Despite what Colbourne says, it wasn't for the money,' Gowrie said, his voice ringing with conviction.

Oh no? thought Steve, acid in his smile.

Gowrie looked away, into the distance of the park beyond the stable yard, the wintry trees, skeletal and dark against the sky, but his face had an even more remote look, as if he was seeing another place, another time. 'You'd have to have been there to understand how it happened. I had got out of Prague on a back road, into the hills. The Russians were across the border and advancing fast. Their collaborators in the Czech army and government had already shut the airport and the border posts but we thought they wouldn't dare stop us leaving – even the Russians respect diplomatic immunity. But I had to move fast. I wanted to pick up my wife and child and get the hell out of there. But when I arrived . . .' He broke off, swallowing as if there was a lump in his throat.

Cathy was moved by the huskiness in his voice. He couldn't be pretending; nobody could sound like that if they didn't mean it.

'That was when I heard . . . found . . . that . . . that our baby had died,' he said in a husky, stammering rush. 'She had been so special, little Cathy, I couldn't take it in at first, I guess I was out of my mind with grief, so was your mother . . .' He met Cathy's eyes and said angrily, 'Well, I'm too used to calling her that to change now! She has been your mother, most of your life . . . just as I've been your father!'

'I didn't say anything,' she said in a placating voice. She had heard this story from Sophie; hearing it from him made it seem somehow different, gave her a new idea of how it had been. Sophie had left out his feelings, hadn't seemed to realize he had had any, but of course he must have been shattered. It had been his child that died, after all. He was

only flesh and blood. She found it hard, that was all, to realize that he had been the father of another child. His image
kept shifting in her head, spinning like a kaleidoscope into
new patterns. She was so confused. Her own image was
fragmenting, too: who was she? The person she thought
she was had never existed, then – so who was she? She
couldn't relate to this Czech girl, Anya – that girl had
ceased to exist in 1968, she had died.

I am not that girl. I am not Czech. I am not Anya. I do
not have a sister or a family in a foreign country.

But who am I, then?

'I didn't know what the hell to do,' Gowrie was saying,
and she looked at him, blankly – who was he? Not her
father, not her father.

He said, 'Your mother . . .' then stopped, meeting her
wounded eyes and looking away quickly, frowning. 'My
wife,' he substituted, as if she had spoken. 'My wife . . . was
in a bad way; she had always been highly strung, and this
had pushed her right over the edge. She was so desperate I
thought she might kill herself. Then you toddled in.' Again
he stopped and looked at her then away again. 'The Czech
maid's little girl,' he added, and the pain inside her grew
worse. That was what she was to him had always secretly
been. The Czech maid's child.

'I didn't even know who you were or where you had
come from,' he went on. 'Only that you were the same sort
of age as my own daughter, with the same colouring – one
two-year-old is much like another.'

Steve made a muffled sound, like laughter, but when
Cathy looked at him she saw rage in his eyes. He turned his
head to look at her as he felt her gaze, and she felt his sympathy, knew he was sorry for her, had to look away because
she was afraid she might start crying and that was the last
thing she wanted to do, break down in front of him and
Sophie.

313

'My wife ran at you, sobbing,' Gowrie said. 'She picked you up and wouldn't let go of you. She thought you were her own baby, she kept calling you Cathy, and that was what gave me the idea. I had to get her out of the country, safely back home, I was scared what might happen to her if she was trapped there, couldn't get out. She would never have recovered from that double shock. I couldn't let that happen to her. She needed to get home, back to the States. I admit I used you, Cathy . . . yes! I used you, you see I don't deny it.' His eyes were liquid with emotion, with pleading, coaxing her to see the story his way, to be convinced. Words were his stock in trade, he lied easily, without thinking. 'But only to save her sanity. You know she's been balanced on a knife-edge all your life, anything could have tipped her over at that moment. She needed you, Cathy, and I was ready to grab at anything that helped her.'

Cathy looked back into her childhood and remembered her mother's good times and bad times – the increasing strangeness of her weeping and laughing, the hysteria, the frightening outbursts when she threw her arms round Cathy, clutched her, covered her face in kisses, held her too tightly, scaring her silly. The sinking into silence and staring, her thumb in her mouth, rocking back and forth in her chair, while five-year-old, six-year-old, eight-year-old Cathy watched and wanted to cry, wanted to get away from this strange, scary mother who was unlike the mothers of any of her friends.

'But why keep it up once you were back in the States?' Steve asked coolly. 'Why not tell Mrs Gowrie's father what had happened? Because you didn't, did you? He has no idea that Cathy is not his granddaughter.'

Gowrie looked into Cathy's eyes and spoke to her, answering Steve. 'Your mother needed you so badly, I couldn't do that to her. If I had told Grandee I was afraid he wouldn't let her keep you. Cathy, be honest with yourself – was what I did so terrible? If I hadn't taken you to the States you would have grown up in the most abject poverty – your real mother had nothing. She would barely have been able to feed you, she couldn't offer you much of a future. I was doing her a favour, taking you off her hands; she was half crazy after losing her husband.'

Sophie angrily burst out, 'You're twisting the truth! Yes, she'd lost her husband and she was desperate – so what did you do? You took away the only thing she had left that she cared about. Her baby. And you left her feeling guilty. Isn't that crazy? She lost her husband and her child on the same day, and ever since she's felt she was to blame.'

'She was looked after,' Gowrie defensively said. 'And so were you. She had plenty of money from me. If she felt that badly, why did she accept it?'

Flushing, Sophie said, 'Because she was terrified to say anything! She was afraid of what might happen to her, and to me, too. You know what life under Communism was like – she was afraid she'd be accused of collaborating with the enemies of the state. Taking money from an American spy . . . she thought they might shoot her.'

'You're making my case for me!' Gowrie told her, then looked at Cathy, 'You see what I saved you from? It wouldn't have been much of a life. Even now, they're living on a very basic level.' He looked at Sophie. 'That's true, isn't it?'

She nodded, her face tense. How could she deny it when she had struggled and fought to escape from that poverty trap, from having to scrimp and save every cent just to buy clothes or shoes for herself.

Gowrie gave Cathy an insistent stare. 'There you are – even she admits it! Instead of living on the breadline and going without all the things that make life pleasant, even bearable, you were brought up as an American "princess". You had everything a girl could want – lovely clothes, dogs, ponies, the best education money could buy.' He stopped and gave her a pleading smile. 'And you were loved, you can't deny you were loved. By me, by your mother, when she wasn't sick, by Grandee. You had a happy childhood, Cathy. And if you tell the world what you've found out, if you insist on ruining everything I've tried to do for you, Grandee will disinherit you and your mother will lose any chance she has of recovering her sanity, because whenever she remembers anything she wants to see you.'

Her mother occasionally came out of her long retreat from reality and was pitifully herself for a while, clinging to Cathy as if she were the child and Cathy the adult.

Cathy bit her lip, and Gowrie went on soberly, 'And as for you yourself, Cathy, don't you realize that you'll probably lose your American citizenship and have to go back to Czechoslovakia? God knows what the legal implications will be – for me, as well as you. I may go to prison for fraud – is that what you want to happen to me, Cathy?' His eyes reproached, glazed as if with tears. 'Do you hate me that much?'

'No, of course not!' Cathy was distraught; there was a dull thudding in her head, an aching in her heart. She didn't know what to think or feel. 'It's all so complicated,' she muttered. 'But I don't hate you, Dad – I couldn't, how could I?' Her eyes slid to Sophie and Steve. 'How could I?' she repeated to them, begging them to understand. 'It's true, all of it – I had the happiest childhood, I loved him, and Grandee . . . we were a happy family.' She had even loved that strange, remote, scary figure she had thought of as Mother, felt guilt and pity and uneasiness about her, but a sort of love, too.

'I know,' Sophie said in a comforting voice, putting a hand on her arm. 'Of course you did, nobody says you didn't.'

Gowrie was quick to see his advantage and rush in, 'I just

wish I had been the one who told you the truth – but I never felt I could, it was never the right time – but at least I wouldn't have hurt you like this.' He looked at Sophie with accusation in his eyes. 'Why the hell did you come here and break it to her the way you did? I suppose you wanted to get some sort of spiteful revenge on me? And on her, too! Oh, I know you keep saying you have a noble reason for doing this . . . because your mother is dying, and because you wanted to see the sister you'd thought was dead. But the truth is you've already gone a long way to destroying her life. When her husband finds out, do you think he's going to stay married to some Czech peasant girl who has no money or background?'

Cathy was white, her very lips bloodless. So he thought that too – he suspected what she did, that Paul would turn against her now, would no longer want a woman who wasn't the woman he thought he was marrying.

Sophie flinched and angrily said, 'I don't want to hurt her. I just wanted to find her, for my mother's sake – why should my mother die without ever seeing her own child again? You have no right to quarrel with that! You've already deprived my mother of Cathy since she was a baby; surely to God she can see her now, even if it is only for a last time? I couldn't just forget it, once my mother had told me the truth. I thought Anya was dead, then I was told she was alive, and I had to find her, I had to.'

'Even if it wrecked her life?' Gowrie's voice was loaded with scorn. 'Believe me, she'll hate you for this one day, when she realizes what you've done to her. If you really care about her you'll tell her to be sensible and forget she ever heard your name! And then you'll vanish again to wherever you came from, and stay away. You owe her that – and me, too.'

'She doesn't owe you a thing!' Steve bit out. 'I haven't forgotten the attempts on her life, even if she has.'

317

Gowrie kept his temper, but his voice was thick and his cheekbones carried a dark red stain. 'I don't know exactly what your game is in all this, Colbourne – but I suppose you're after the story to use in your TV programme. That's all you really care about, isn't it? You used to care for Cathy, though – until she married someone else. Is this your revenge for her preferring another man?'

'You have a low, dirty mind, Senator,' Steve ground out between his teeth. 'I'm not here as a reporter, and I'm not the vengeful type, although I guess you are. I don't want to hurt Cathy. I'm here because I care about Sophie, and for no other reason.' He put his arm around her and Sophie gave a little sob and turned her face into his chest, leaning on him. Steve began to stroke her hair comfortingly, feeling her quiver against him.

Cathy watched them, envying their intimacy, the closeness between them. If only Paul would come, would put his arm around her, the way Steve was holding Sophie. If only she could be sure he wouldn't turn away from her now – she had been so sure he loved her once; why was she no longer sure? Why had this great abyss opened up between them?

Gowrie saw he had made a psychological error, and hurriedly said, 'OK, I see . . . Look, I swear to you, Colbourne, it was my secretary who tried to kill Sophie. She wasn't too balanced, she must have had some sort of brainstorm. She knew Sophie was causing a problem for me, she wanted to help me – but I had no idea what she was up to.' He gave Cathy a sideways look, then said in a low voice, 'I suppose I'll have to tell you. I'd been having a . . . a relationship . . . with her for some time. She was in love with me, and I found her very attractive. I haven't had a real marriage for so long.' He looked at Cathy again, begging her to sympathize. 'You know that, Cathy. I've been very lonely at times, especially after you got married. My wife hasn't been a real wife to me for years, I needed some sort of companionship and love. Emily threw herself at me, and I . . . I'm human, I was tempted. I wish to God, though, that I'd never got involved with her. She was no more balanced than my wife, as it turned out.' His voice roughened, took on a slur of rage. 'Why do I keep getting women like that? Why always the screwballs?' Then he stopped, reddening as he saw how they all looked at him, and hurriedly added, 'If I'd known what she was planning I'd have stopped her, but she was acting on her own initiative – she thought she was saving me from ruin. When she told me what she had done I was appalled.'

'But you didn't stop her trying again, did you?' Steve sardonically pointed out.

'I tried to stop her! I told her to leave Sophie alone, I told her I didn't want her to hurt Sophie, but last night –' He broke off, shuddering, lost all his colour, a dew of perspiration bursting out on his forehead, above his mouth. He pulled a handkerchief from his pocket and passed it over his pale, sweating face. 'Well, you know what happened last night. I can't bear to think about it, about what she tried to do, how she died.'

He wasn't lying now, thought Cathy. Even a career diplomat trained to lie with total plausibility could not control his bodily functions, make himself sweat, make himself go pale or shake like that. No, this was a real reaction.

Had he been in love with that woman? It didn't surprise her to know he had had an affair; she had often suspected he might have other women, although she couldn't actually remember anyone in particular. She had never thought much about his sexual needs or tastes – you never did, where your own father was concerned, did you?

But she knew he was a man who feared pain – he always had, as long as she could remember. Once when they were fishing from a boat off the bay near Easton he had got a hook embedded in his palm and had gone white and looked sick. He had told her to row back to shore while he sat there nursing his hand, the blood welling up around the buried hook, and he couldn't even look at it, he hadn't watched while a doctor extracted the hook and put some stitches into his palm.

She wondered if it was Emily Sanderson's death he found painful – or the way she had died, the image of that death, which must be burnt on his mind's retina, indelible, like the ghost of a word forever there on a computer screen left switched on too long.

Gowrie took a deep breath and pushed his handkerchief back into his pocket, looked from one to the other of them, dwelling longest on Cathy. 'The bottom line is . . . if this gets out we'll all suffer. It won't just be me. Cathy will possibly lose everything, maybe even her home here and her husband, and you, Sophie, you may well lose her, once she realizes who is to blame for blowing her life to pieces – which, if you really care about Sophie, Colbourne, isn't going to be good news for you either. On the other hand, if nobody talks, and I become the next president, then we'll all benefit.' His eyes moved from one face to the other again. 'I would be a very powerful friend for all of you. Colbourne, you'd have the inner track at the White House; I'd make sure your career went sky-high. You and Sophie would have a great future together. Cathy's marriage wouldn't fall apart. Nobody will lose, everyone will benefit. All we have to do is make sure our secret never gets out.'

All three of them stared at him in silence; then into the stillness a footstep fell and they swung round to find Paul standing there, his eyes implacable.

'Making deals, Gowrie? You left me out of your conference, didn't you? What's on offer for me to keep my mouth shut?'

Cathy's heart had leapt at the sight of him, but at the sound of his voice all the hope left her. She knew at that instant that it was over. She was going to lose him. She had known it last night, but in some corner of her mind a tiny, fugitive hope had lingered and now it died, and it hurt more than she could bear.

She had to get away. She ran past him without looking at him, out of the stable yard, along the gravelled terrace.

'Cathy, wait!' Sophie pulled herself free of Steve and hurried after her. Paul turned hurriedly, too, as if to go after her too, his face marble, stiff and white and without any visible humanity, but then he stopped dead, his hands hanging by his sides, changing his mind.

Gowrie quickly said, 'Just name your price, Paul. We're men of the world, we both know it's always possible to make a deal. Tell me what you want and I'll make sure you get it. I know about your money problems; I wouldn't insult you by suggesting you married Cathy for her money, but clearly you need financial help with your companies and you wouldn't get it from the Ramsey family trust if they ever found out Cathy wasn't really a Ramsey, wasn't my wife's child. They'll disown her once they know that. It can't possibly be in your interests for them to find out.'

Paul stared at him and laughed shortly. 'You evil little man.'

Steve's eyes widened in surprise and interest. The tone was filled with such loathing. He knew how Paul felt, he felt the same; yet he was surprised by the sheer depth of the hatred. He had thought Paul was the type to take a shock like this in his stride. The man had always seemed so cool, so civilized, a typical drawling Englishman with ice-water in his veins. Obviously he had been completely mistaken about the guy.

Gowrie flushed. 'There's no need to be so insulting. I

may have made mistakes . . . but I'm not evil! When I brought Cathy out of Czechoslovakia I did it to save my wife's sanity, but you must see that it was good for Cathy too; she had a much better life with us than she would have had if I had left her in her own home. And if we are all sensible and keep our heads nobody need ever know.'

Paul stared at him oddly, rubbing a hand over his temples as if he had a bad headache.

'Nobody need ever know,' he repeated thickly, in a voice which was different suddenly.

Gowrie's eyes glittered. 'Nobody, Paul. We can keep it to ourselves. None of us would lose out. You won't regret it if you support me now, Paul. I can be a big help to you. Even if I don't get the nomination, don't make it to the presidency, I'll still be a very wealthy man, and Cathy would still be the heiress to the Ramsey money. So long as nobody ever finds out, we're safe.'

Paul gave him a twisted little smile. 'Offering me all the kingdoms of the world, Gowrie? I'm tempted, Satan, I admit I'm tempted, but you're wasting your time – too many people already know. Have you forgotten Sophie's mother, the woman in Czechoslovakia? I had, but she is still there, still alive, still able to testify and blow your clever schemes to kingdom come. And who else has she told? How many people know and could come crawling out of the woodwork?'

Gowrie looked confused, taken aback, then visibly pulled himself together. 'Don't worry about the Narodni woman – she won't dare risk talking. She has too much to lose, and, anyway, you heard Sophie . . . she's dying.'

'And when she comes to her last confession on earth – you think she won't tell the priest?' Paul drily asked. 'She's a devout Catholic. She'll confess all her sins on her deathbed.'

'Priests can't repeat what they hear under the seal of confession,' Steve reminded him. 'But she's told one other person, to my knowledge.'

'Shit!' Gowrie burst out, his face crimson with temper. 'Who? Has he talked? To you? And to who else? How many others am I going to have to square?'

Steve almost felt sorry for him – he looked demented. Almost sorry for him but not quite, because every time Steve thought about what Gowrie had done to Sophie, to Cathy, he wanted to strangle him. Gowrie deserved the torment he was going through now.

'You won't know him, but he's a decent guy,' Steve said sarcastically. 'If you remember what that is! He wouldn't do anything to harm Sophie, or Cathy, for any money.'

Paul gave him a cynical look. 'I hadn't imagined you would be so naive! Haven't you learnt yet that you never know with people? They keep surprising you, and it's rarely a pleasant surprise, in my experience.'

'Not this guy. He's a one-off. I only met him yesterday but I'd trust him with my life. But if Mrs Narodni has told him and Sophie, she might have told others, and when she's dying who knows who she might not talk to?'

Gowrie was breathing thickly, his body tense, hands screwed at his sides.

'I'll deal with it,' he thought aloud. 'I'll find a way. They aren't stopping me getting there, I'm not giving up, I'm going on somehow, anyhow.'

The other two men contemplated him with a mixture of horror and awe, like people watching the undead walk. Steve almost believed, at that instant, that, in spite of everything Sophie had revealed about his past, Gowrie wasn't finished, would go on with his campaign, might still make it to the presidency.

And God help America that day, he thought.

★

As Sophie re-entered the house, she heard Cathy running up the stairs, and followed, hearing a door slam shut before she reached the first floor. Sophie slowed as she got to the top of the stairs and stood there, irresolute, hearing wild sobbing from Cathy's bedroom. Guilt made Sophie hesitate about going in – all this was her fault, she wouldn't blame Cathy if she screamed at her to get out, leave her alone.

She must hate me. In her place I would. Poor Cathy. She's undergone so many shocks over the past twenty-four hours, God knows what is going on inside her now.

The weeping went on and on, and Sophie felt tears spring to her own eyes. All my fault, she thought. This is all my fault.

The Latin words she had learnt as a child, in the little village church in whose graveyard her father had been buried, beside the body of Don Gowrie's baby daughter, came back to her now. *Mea culpa* . . . Out of the past; it came like a ghost from the past – Don Gowrie's sins, ambition, greed, selfishness had been the first cause, the original sin, but she had been the one who resurrected the buried secret.

My fault. *Mea culpa*. Words no longer used in the mass, but still so powerful, resonant with centuries of use, full of contrition and guilt, welling up in her mind like tears. *Mea culpa, mea culpa* . . . My fault, my most grievous fault. She should never have come looking for her dead sister, she should have forgotten her mother had ever told her.

She pushed open the door, and Cathy's crying was stifled at once, as if she had put a hand over her mouth to hold back the sound. Across the elegant bedroom, Sophie saw her lying face down on the bed. Her body was shaking violently. The sobbing was silent now, but had not stopped.

Sophie ran over and sat down on the bed, close to her, put a hand on her shuddering shoulders.

'I'm sorry, I'm so sorry, this is all my fault, please stop crying, I can't bear it.'

'*You* can't!' Cathy's bitterness was like a blow in the face. Sophie winced.

'Go away,' Cathy said, then. 'Leave me alone.' The words were barely audible. Sophie had to bend to hear them.

Miserably Sophie said, 'I can't leave you like this.' She pushed the tumbled hair back from Cathy's face, touched her cheek, her skin chill as death under Sophie's fingers. 'Oh, you're so cold,' Sophie whispered. 'I'll get a quilt for you, shall I?'

'I don't want one.'

'Can I get you a hot drink then?'

'No! For Christ's sake, just go away, will you?'

'I want to do something for you.'

'You've done enough.'

'I know! Do you think I don't realize what I've done? I wish to God I could undo it.'

If she had the chance to live this last week over again, she would do everything very differently. She wouldn't come looking for Anya. Or would she?

She just didn't know.

Cathy's crying had stopped. She was listening, silent, unmoving, but listening.

'I'm so sorry, I feel terrible . . . I should never have come,' Sophie said, tears trickling down her face, the saltiness of them in her mouth, sounding in her voice.

'Yes,' Cathy said in that muffled voice, still face down on the bed. 'Yes, you had to . . .'

She turned over and sat up, her beautiful face pale and ravaged, her skin blotchy, her hair dishevelled, her eyes drowned in tears, but looking at Sophie directly, wide and blazingly honest.

'You had no choice. I don't really blame you, I'm just angry. I've been hurt, and I want to hurt someone back.' She laughed raggedly. 'Not a very nice motive. I'll get over

325

it. I shall have to learn to live with what I've found out about myself. It's like being born all over again, I suppose.' She put her hands over her face. 'Oh . . . I wish to God I could believe you were lying, but wishing never changes anything, does it?'

Sophie put both arms around her, rocked her gently as if she were a child. 'Wishes do come true sometimes.'

'Not this time. I've been living a lie all my life without knowing it. Well, now I know the truth, I have to come to terms with it.' She pulled away from Sophie. 'I don't think I'll have any choice, anyway – I think Paul . . . my husband . . .' Her voice shook and a tear spilled from her eyes, ran down her cheek. 'He doesn't want me now.'

'Of course he does!' Sophie was appalled. 'He loves you, I could see that the minute I saw him with you, and he's a nice man – I liked him a lot, he was kind to me when I had a bad dream last night. You don't need to be afraid he'll stop loving you just because you aren't Gowrie's daughter.'

Cathy quivered, listening to that reassurance, wanting to believe it but deep inside herself aware of a chilling change in Paul's response to her. Until last night they had been so intensely aware of each other every minute of the day and night. Even across a room full of other people they had always been in silent, sensual contact, their eyes meeting, their bodies aching to touch, their hearts beating in unison, their blood pulsing at the same fevered pace.

Or that was what she had thought. *She* had felt that way, at least. She had believed he did.

Now she no longer knew. Had he ever really loved her? You couldn't switch off that sort of feeling in a flash, could you?

'I think he's in some sort of money trouble,' she whispered. 'He needs the Ramsey money. And now he knows I'm not a Ramsey, won't be able to help him out, I'm no use to him any more.'

All her perceptions of herself were undergoing radical surgery. Once she had believed her father loved her – now she had been forced to recognize how he had used her, right from her earliest years. She had been a pawn in his power game, of no more importance to him than that.

She had thought Paul loved her, too. Now it seemed that he had married her for her family money, and he didn't want her if she was likely to lose it.

'Your father is busy persuading everyone not to tell,' Sophie wryly said. 'And I won't, so don't worry – I think you'll still get that money, and I don't believe for an instant that your husband will leave you, or doesn't love you. I'll go back to the States with Steve in a few days, and you'll go on with your life here. Everything will be back to normal.'

Cathy gave a long, slow, agonized sigh. She turned her head and stared at the dressing-table, her own reflection. How could everything go back to normal? She no longer knew who she was – and even if nobody ever told the world the truth, how could she go on living a lie? And how could she ever be happy with Paul again?

She ran her hands over her wet eyes, pushed back her hair. 'I look a mess. I must wash my face, put on make-up, do my hair. I might feel better then,' she said brightly.

She got off the bed and went into her bathroom and Sophie wandered around the room, picking up silver-framed photographs, staring at them, recognizing Gowrie in some, with Cathy, Paul with Cathy in others. Like the photographs downstairs, these showed Cathy at all ages: a little girl in jeans, carrying a fishing-net or riding a pony, a teenager in tennis gear, holding a silver cup, on a platform with her father, and in frothy, foaming white, a bride on her wedding-day, standing between Paul and Gowrie, her face alight with happiness.

All those memories had just been blasted to kingdom come.

Mea culpa, my fault. All I thought about was my mother, dying, so thin and pale and weak . . . so little time left for her, I would have done anything to make her better. I just wanted to find Anya and bring her home, I never really thought of what I would do to Anya. Obsessed, stupid, thoughtless, selfish – I hate myself for what I've done to Anya.

The bathroom door opened again and Cathy came out, face enamelled, doll-like in its perfection, hair brushed until it shone, her mouth bright and smiling, wearing the armour of outward appearances.

Sophie looked at her uncertainly, guiltily. This Cathy was harder to talk to, to approach. The walls were up; you couldn't get near her.

Falsely cheerful, she said, 'Let's go down and have some coffee, I'm dying for a cup of good strong coffee, I don't know about you.'

'I'd love some.'

Downstairs, Cathy rang for the housekeeper and ordered a pot of coffee. They sat down in the drawing-room and drank it, black, sweet.

'What made you become a journalist?' Cathy asked conversationally, with a stilted little smile.

Sophie gave her a wry look but recognized the sense of trying to put everything on a calmer footing, so she told her about her years at university, in Prague, how she had worked part-time, translating for Vladimir, to help pay her way through college, and then she talked about her brief attempt at school-teaching, her problems with her students, her boredom and the difficulty of living on a low salary in Prague.

'You have to save up to buy clothes or shoes, or anything expensive, like electrical equipment – your salary just about pays rent, and for food and the usual household bills. We're beginning to be more prosperous, especially people who work in tourism, in the hotels, or restaurants. Things get better all the time. But it is still a pretty tough life for most people.'

'Very different from mine,' Cathy thought aloud.

'Yes, you owe Gowrie that,' Sophie gently said. 'He was right, he did give you a wonderful life, and I'm sure he cared for you. He couldn't keep up that sort of lie for so many years.'

'God knows! I don't. I can't think straight at the moment, I no longer know what I . . . I don't know anything, even who I am.' Cathy's emotion welled up to the surface again. The tears weren't far away.

Sophie put down her coffee-cup and moved to sit beside her chair, on the floor.

'You're you, that's all – you're the person inside your head, not a name . . . not Cathy Gowrie, or Anya Narodni – just YOU. You're the person you've always known you were, the person your life happened to! This is just another part of your life, don't you see? I realize you feel confused, even lost – but in a day or two everything will settle down again.'

'And then what? Who will I be then?' Cathy angrily demanded, looking down at her. 'Cathy or Anya? American or Czech? Paul's wife or . . .' She broke off again, sobbing. 'Can't you see? I don't know what's going to happen next and I'm scared!'

Sophie quickly knelt up and put her arm round her. 'I'm sorry, Cathy, I'm so sorry. I wish I could undo what I've done. I didn't mean to hurt you, that was the last thing I wanted to do. When I heard you were alive the only thing I could think of was finding you – I didn't stop to think what I would do to your life. Don't hate me, please don't hate me.'

Cathy put her head down on Sophie's shoulder. They sat there quietly for several minutes, then Cathy moved away, got out a handkerchief and wiped her eyes, blew her nose.

'Tell me more about your . . . our . . . mother,' she said, getting up and going to the window to curl up in a windowseat.

Sophie gave a little exclamation. 'Of course, yes, but first . . . could I please . . . would you let me use your phone? To ring Mamma? After what Steve said about Vladimir telling her someone had tried to kill me, I must talk to her, reassure her, or she'll make herself ill worrying.'

Cathy nodded. 'Of course, use the phone there now, if you like.'

Sophie got up eagerly. 'Will you talk to her? Anya? Will you, please?'

Cathy looked horrified, shaking her head. 'I don't know her, what could I say? I can't talk to her, I really couldn't.'

Sophie turned pleading eyes on her. 'She's dying, Anya, and she desperately needs to hear your voice.'

'I can't!' Cathy refused fiercely, and didn't move as Sophie sighed and went over to the phone. The sad, reproachful eyes made her uneasy, yet she resented Sophie's insistence. It was so easy to make judgements from outside but when it was happening to you it wasn't a simple matter.

This strange woman was dying and Cathy was expected to feel deeply about that, to be sad, grief-stricken, to feel all the emotions a bereaved daughter should feel. But how could she? She hadn't even known this woman existed. She had never seen her, she didn't know anything about her. She still wasn't certain she believed that Johanna was her real mother. Oh, she accepted all the evidence now, but knowing with your mind was one thing – feeling it in your heart was something very different, and her heart was not ready to believe.

She heard Sophie's soft, husky voice talking into the

phone in her own language. Cathy didn't understand Czech, couldn't follow a word of what Sophie said until she lapsed into English, which Cathy realized was done for her own benefit.

'And guess who is with me? Anya.' She laughed, looking at Cathy. 'Yes, really, Mamma – I've found her, talked to her, I told her everything. Yes, she's here, hold on . . .'

Sophie turned and held out the phone, her eyes begged. 'Please,' she whispered.

Cathy sat stiffly, unable to move.

'She's dying, Cathy,' Sophie whispered, covering the mouthpiece of the phone so that her mother shouldn't hear. 'This may be the only chance she has of hearing your voice, and you don't have to say anything much, just hello and ask how she is – that will be enough for her, to hear your voice.'

Cathy swallowed, unable to make up her mind, then she slowly got up and unsteadily walked over to take the phone.

Sophie gave her a quick, warm hug. 'Thank you.'

Cathy held the phone to her mouth. 'Hello?' she said in a voice that wavered.

There was a silence at the other end and then a woman's voice breathed. 'Anya . . . my Anya . . .'

13

Cathy put down the phone a few minutes later and turned away quickly before Sophie could see her face; she stood by the window, staring out, her back to the room. Sophie waited, watching her with sympathy. How did you talk to a woman you had never met but discovered was your mother? What did you say? The gap was so enormous; a whole lifetime. Everything Cathy knew had happened since she was taken away; she didn't remember anything about the years before that day, the baby years. They were strangers who yet had the most intimate of relationships – mother and child. And what could you say to each other?

Cathy had said very little. She had listened and murmured a few comforting words now and then, in the spaces when there was no whispering, sobbing voice at the other end.

'Yes. Yes, Sophie told me. Yes, I know. I understand how it happened. No, I don't blame you, of course I don't. Please, don't upset yourself. Don't cry, please. Yes, I forgive you. I do. I'll try to come soon, I promise I'll try. Yes, soon. As soon as I can, I promise.'

Sophie had felt tears in her own eyes and had brushed them away. All the years those two had lost, mother and daughter, so long apart that they couldn't even talk to each other now. Don Gowrie had boasted of having given Cathy a wonderful life, the life of a princess – but did it really make up for what he had taken from her?

She watched Cathy struggling to deal with it all, and wished there was something she could say or do to help.

'Thank you for talking to her,' she said at last, and Cathy found an angry noise.

'Thank you for talking to my own mother?'

'It was tough, I know it was hard for you.'

'Not as hard as it was for her.' Cathy took a deep breath. 'She kept crying. I wished she would stop; her English isn't very good and when she kept crying it was harder to understand and I was embarrassed. I was embarrassed talking to my own mother!' Her hands were clenched into fists, as if she wanted to hit something or someone.

'Not surprising, after so many years,' Sophie said gruffly. 'She wouldn't blame you. She understands how hard this must be for you.'

'Does she? I wonder –'

The telephone began to ring and they both started violently.

'Shall I answer that?' offered Sophie.

'Would you?' Cathy said huskily without looking round.

Sophie picked up the phone. 'Hello?'

'Mrs Brougham?'

Sophie opened her mouth, but before she could say she wasn't Cathy the man's voice at the other end went on, 'I've still got Mr Colbourne's colleague waiting down here at the gate, ma'am – he's getting impatient, shall I let him through now?'

'Wait a minute.' Sophie turned to Cathy. 'I think Vladimir is here – can he come up to the house? Is that OK?'

Cathy nodded. 'Why not?' she said indifferently, then suddenly wheeled and began to walk to the door. 'I have a headache, I'm going to take a pill and lie down for a while.'

Sophie told the man at the gate to let Vladimir through, then hung up and ran after Cathy, called after her.

'Can I get you anything? Do anything?'

'No, I just want some peace and quiet,' Cathy said, vanishing up the stairs without looking back.

Sophie stood in the magnificent hall, listening to the

solemn ticking of the tall grandfather clock, watching wintry sunlight strike the polished floors, striking fire out of some bronzed branches of beech which stood in a tall urn near the hearth. Such a calm, ordered atmosphere. Her eye travelled upwards to admire the great chandelier hanging overhead. Had Cathy been happy here? Of course she must have been – she had had everything anyone could want, and she must have thought her life would always be like that.

The front door stood partly open; through it she heard the men's voices and the sound of their feet crunching on the gravel. They were returning to the house. Had they made the deal Don Gowrie wanted? Want to bet? she asked herself, mouth twisting.

He had the measure of every one of them, knew exactly what to offer as a bribe or use as a threat. Politicians always did. Human beings were their stock in trade; they bought and sold them, manipulated and cheated them, used them without scruple. Somehow or other Don Gowrie would have cobbled together some sort of agreement with Steve and Paul.

Above their voices rose the sound of a vehicle. Was that Vlad? Sophie pushed the door wider and watched a Land-Rover parking right outside. Vlad stumbled from it, dishevelled as ever, brushing ash off his ancient tweed jacket and shabby raincoat. The man driving the vehicle drove off again and Vlad looked round, orientating himself, saw her, and held out his arms, grinning from ear to ear.

'Sophie! Girl, I've been worried sick about you!'

She felt her spirits lift. Smiling as she ran, she threw herself into his waiting arms.

'Vlad! Oh, Vlad, it's so good to see you!'

He held her away after a warm hug and stared down into her face, searching her eyes, noting her pallor, her quivering lips.

'You OK?' His heavy features were anxious, concerned.

She made a face, shrugged. 'I'll survive.'

He hugged her again. 'That's my girl.'

Paul and Steve stood watching; she didn't look their way because Steve's shrewd eyes saw too much, she was afraid of what he would read in her eyes, and she didn't want to give anything away to Paul, either.

In the house the phone began to ring again, rang on and on, and Paul turned his head to stare through the open door.

'Where is everyone? Why doesn't somebody answer that? Damn the thing! I'd like to have it cut off.'

The ringing stopped. They heard footsteps and the housekeeper came to the open front door. 'It's for you, sir. Mr Levinson.'

'I'll take it in my study,' Paul said curtly. He glanced at the rest of them. 'Sorry, excuse me.'

He vanished into the house and Vladimir turned to stare after him. 'Is that the husband? The guy who married little Anya? I didn't get a chance to take a good look at him. What do you think? Is he OK for her? Do you like him?'

Sophie nodded, ruefully smiling. 'He has been very kind to me. Very sympathetic.' She couldn't betray her sister's confidences, tell them that Cathy wasn't certain of Paul, was afraid he might leave her now. Cathy might be way off the mark, her imagination working overtime. She was too upset to be able to think properly.

'Where is she?' Vlad demanded. 'I am dying to see her. Last time I saw her she was a baby, just born – Jesus, that was a long, long time ago. Another world, nuh? This is going to make me feel very, very old.'

'You are very, very old,' Steve joked, and they grinned at each other.

Sophie was startled but loved the easy familiarity between them. How had they become friends so fast? But then they had so much in common: they were both

335

newsmen, both cynical, hard-boiled, humorous, capable of great tenderness.

'Anya is upstairs lying down,' she said, then looked behind them. 'Where's Gowrie?'

'He walked over to the helipad to talk to his security people,' Steve told her drily. 'He will be leaving soon, I gather.' His eyes glinted with anger and contempt.

'Having made a deal with you?' She stared into those eyes, wondering why he had agreed to accept Gowrie's terms. He was ambitious, but she couldn't believe he would sell her and Cathy out just to help his own career.

'Oh, yes, he got what he wanted, so he's ready to leave. He says he wouldn't feel safe here unless his men can stake out the house, and Paul won't have that, he doesn't want them around, so Gowrie is going. But first he says he'll come to say goodbye to Cathy. He wants her to drive up to London to see his wife; they didn't bring her with them in the chopper. In case something went wrong, Gowrie said, but he meant in case she overheard anything, picked up what was really going on here. The last thing he wants is for her to remember that Cathy isn't . . .' He broke off, gesturing.

'Isn't her Cathy,' Sophie murmured, pitying the woman she had never met, a woman who had deferred her child's death by nearly thirty years, yet had never been a real mother to Cathy, never close to her, because she had been in flight from herself and the truth, drifting between illusion and reality.

'Could we have something to drink?' Vlad asked wistfully. 'I've been hanging about outside the gates for hours, they wouldn't let me in for some reason. That wind is icy and I'm freezing.'

'I'll ask the housekeeper to make us some coffee,' Sophie said, and he grimaced.

'I was thinking of something stronger, nuh?'

★

336

Paul walked into his office, closed the door and sat down behind his desk. The telephone was already ringing; his housekeeper had switched the call through.

'Hello? Freddy?'

'Yes. Paul, I –'

'I hope this is important. I'll be back in town in a couple of hours. Can't it wait?'

'I saw Salmond last night,' Freddy abruptly said, and Paul stiffened, his knuckles turning white as he gripped the phone. What was Freddy going to tell him? Had he sold out? Had Salmond bought him? Then he thought: no, not Freddy, Freddy wouldn't rat on me, he never has and he never will. He's been loyal to me from the beginning. Loyalty is his middle name. What the hell is the matter with me? I've been spending too much time with shits like Don Gowrie.

'I was having dinner with my cousin and his wife last night,' Freddy was saying. 'Celebrating their wedding anniversary. I was paying, my present to them – she wanted to go to the Primavera, that new Italian place that's all the rage at the moment, she's that sort of woman, you know, loves to be in the latest fashion and –'

Paul erupted. 'Freddy, for God's sake – never mind your bloody family – what about Salmond?'

'Sorry, I'm in quite a state this morning. Can't think straight. I almost rang you last night, but we drank too much over dinner, you know how it is, cocktails, then wine, then brandy afterwards, and I don't usually drink, as you know and –'

'Get to the starting-price, damn you, Freddy!'

He audibly swallowed. 'Yes. Sorry. I saw Salmond as we walked into the restaurant. He was at a corner table; he was having dinner with . . . you'll never guess, I couldn't believe my eyes –'

'I don't have time for guessing games, Freddy. Just tell

me, will you?' Paul was on tenterhooks waiting for the crunch – why wouldn't Freddy spit out whatever bad news he had to tell?

'Chantal Rousseau,' Freddy gabbled out, and Paul jerked as if someone had kicked him in the guts.

'What?'

'I couldn't believe it, either, when I saw them – I didn't even know she knew the guy, after all he lives in the States, I had no idea . . .'

'Salmond's trying to persuade her to sell her shares to him, of course,' Paul thought aloud.

'That was the first thought I had. But I sat there for two hours and watched them,' Freddy told him grimly. 'And they never even noticed me, never once looked round, they were too engrossed in each other. There was no two ways about it, they kept touching hands, looking into each other's eyes, I could even see under the table, their knees touching . . . he was moving his leg against hers. Paul, they're having an affair.'

'Shit,' Paul said thickly. 'That bitch, that two-faced bitch. Sweet as honey to me on the phone the other day, when all the time . . . She's going to sell me out.'

Freddy sighed. 'I remembered after a while that she had been going over to the States regularly over the last six months; her firm are associated with some American firm now, aren't they? That's how she and Salmond must have met. But of course that doesn't mean she'll sell him our shares. Well, we can't be sure she'd do that. I mean, she wouldn't confuse her private life with her business – she's quite a cold-headed bitch, isn't she? That was the impression I always had of her.'

'I wouldn't be surprised to find out that it was her who suggested he targeted us,' Paul said flatly. 'Chantal has always been one of those people who enjoys revenge served cold. She's never forgiven me.'

'She must have been crazy about you to feel that bad,' Freddy said, sounding pitying, and Paul laughed angrily.

'It was her ego not her heart that got hurt, Freddy! Don't be so sentimental. Everyone knew we'd been dating; she felt I'd humiliated her. If she had had any warning she'd have publicly dumped me first, but I was over in the States when I met Cathy, and half the gossip columnists had the story before I got round to ringing Chantal. She never forgives an injury. Oh, she's put on a good act this past year, pretending to be very friendly whenever we met, but she must have been waiting her chance to hit back at me, and when she met Salmond she had the idea of plotting with him to take my firm away from me.'

Freddy groaned. 'What are we going to do, Paul?'

'There's nothing we can do. Her people hold a quarter of our shares – that, combined with what Salmond has already acquired, will give him control.'

'We can't just sit here and wait for the blow to fall!' Freddy broke out.

'What do you suggest we do, Freddy? Oh, use your head. Salmond knew he would win before he went public with the bid. They've just been having fun with me. It's a foregone conclusion. We'll go ahead with the shareholders' voting, it will give us time to work out our next move, but we've already lost, take it from me.'

'I can't believe you're taking this so calmly!'

Paul laughed shortly. 'I'm not calm, Freddy. I'm shellshocked, believe me, but facts are facts and there's no point in hiding our head in the sand.'

'But there must be something you can do! You always have in the past. Couldn't you talk to her? Persuade her not to sell?'

'Persuade a shark to give up the body it has between its teeth, you mean? What do you think? She has the taste of my blood now. She won't let me go until she has the rest.'

'But we'll still have our own shares, Paul. If we sell those to Salmond we'll release all that money, we can start again.' Freddy tried to sound optimistic, daring, but that had never been his nature. It had always been Paul who was the high flyer, the reckless one.

'I'll come back to London at once, Freddy. We'll talk then,' Paul said.

Cathy was almost asleep when she heard the soft footsteps outside her door. They paused. She heard muffled breathing and lay with closed eyes, suddenly knowing it was Paul. Her heart began to beat fast and hard; shaking her body. Was he going to come in? But after a moment he walked on, past her room, and opened his dressing-room door.

Was he changing his clothes? She lay still, listening, and heard him getting down a suitcase from the top of one of the long wardrobes which ran the length of the narrow room. As if she were in the room with him, she could see what he was doing, heard him snap open the case, heard the rattle of hangers as he took down clothes, shirts, jackets, suits.

Why is he packing? What is he packing? He had clothes in London, in the penthouse flat he used when he could not get home. He had everything he might need there.

Why was he packing all that stuff? More rattling of hangers; other clothes going in, and now he was opening drawers, getting out socks, underwear, pyjamas. How many cases was he taking, for God's sake?

Cathy sat up, trembling, stumbled off the bed, tying a dressing-gown around her; she had taken off her clothes so that she could sleep. Under the dressing-gown all she wore was a silky slip, bra and panties.

Paul was so intent on packing that he didn't hear her open the door into his dressing-room. He was closing the lid, locking the case, his head bent; the wintry sunlight striking his hair made it look quite white. With a shock Cathy thought, He looks . . . old. Overnight he had begun to look his age. His face was so gaunt, so haggard, and the silvery hair had no life in it at all.

He straightened to shut the wardrobe door, and saw her. They stared at each other without speaking; the abyss between them had been growing ever since he had discovered that she was not Don Gowrie's daughter. Now it was so wide, so deep, she felt she would never be able to reach him again.

'What are you doing?' she stupidly asked, wanting to howl and scream like a wounded animal. How was it possible to feel such pain but talk in such a normal voice?

'Packing a case.' His face moved, then, with some thought she saw but could not identify – what was he thinking? His bones had tightened as if he was in pain, but his eyes stared at her from that terrible distance.

'I can see that. Why? Why are you going? Where are you going?'

'Back to London. I'll be staying at the flat there for a while, I've got problems to deal with . . . it looks as if we can't be at Salmond, I'm probably going to lose the company.'

'Oh.' It was another shock; the news shook her. 'Oh, God, Paul, I'm so sorry.' What did that mean? For them? If he lost the company would he leave her? Or not? 'Can't my father . . .?' She stopped, shivering, at having used that word – she couldn't stop thinking of him as her father yet, she didn't know how else to think of him. She needed time to get used to the real truth. 'Can't he help?' she huskily finished.

Paul shook his head. 'Nobody can help. It's all over, bar the counting.'

'What happened? I thought various of your shareholders had pledged their votes to you.'

'They changed their minds.'

'Why?'

He shrugged. 'They just did.'

'Talk to me, Paul! Tell me what is going on!'

'I haven't got time now. I have to go.'

'Why don't I come with you?' she pleaded. 'Let me come! You shouldn't be alone with all these worries, let me come.'

'No!' He took a long, rough breath, shuddering with it. 'I'm sorry, no.'

A chill certainty seeped into her. 'You're leaving me,' she half accused, half stated. 'You aren't coming back, are you?'

He looked away, his face stiff and set, nodded. 'I'm sorry, Cathy. It's over.'

'What do you mean – over? Just like that? You're leaving me without a word? Why? Why, Paul? At least tell me, to my face, why you're going?'

'There's nothing to talk about. I'm sorry,' he said again in a terse, harsh voice, and picked up the case, moving towards the open door.

She couldn't just let him go without trying to hold on to him, she needed him too much. She kept remembering their nights together, their bodies moving in hot desire and then, when they had exhausted themselves with love, how they had slept closely entwined, arms and legs around each other, skin to skin, breathing as one creature, totally at ease one with the other. He couldn't just have married her for her father's money: he had loved her, she could have sworn he loved her, or he was the greatest actor in the world.

She stepped between him and the door and threw her arms round his neck, clinging, pushing her body into his. 'Don't go, please don't leave me, I can't bear it, I need you.' She lifted her face to kiss him but he sharply jerked his head aside so she buried her mouth against his throat, kissed him with desperate urgency, her mouth moving, inviting, begging, breathing in the scent of his skin.

For a second she felt the surge of emotion rising in his body like sap in a tree. His hands gripped her shoulders, the fingertips moved, caressingly, he was breathing as if he were drowning, then he groaned, 'NO!' and suddenly thrust her away with a violence that sent her sprawling backwards on to the smooth white carpet.

By the time she had struggled back to her feet, Paul had gone. Cathy was crying by then, wildly, helplessly, her whole body shaking with the force of her sobbing. She ran into the bedroom and threw herself on her bed, face down.

Downstairs, Steve, Sophie and Vladimir were standing in the hall, beside the open fire, arguing. Steve had given Vladimir a brief sketch of the discussions with Gowrie which had gone on while he was waiting outside the gates of Arbory House. Vladimir listened, glowering, a large half-drunk tumbler of whisky in his hand. It was his second. After his first he had asked to be shown around the hall. He wanted to have a closer look at some of the pictures hanging on the walls.

As Paul came down the stairs, Steve and Sophie looked round, and immediately noticed the case he was carrying.

'Going somewhere?' Steve asked drily.

'Where's Cathy? Is she OK?' demanded Sophie anxiously.

'Why don't you go up to her?' He was brusque, unsmiling; she saw a darkness in his eyes and was afraid for Cathy – had they quarrelled? Surely to God Cathy hadn't been right? He wasn't leaving her because she wasn't Gowrie's daughter?

Vladimir, in his obsessed way, was still thinking about what they had been discussing. In Czech he burst out, 'I don't care what you two say, Sophie, unless that bastard

Gowrie is nailed and we tell the world just what sort of creep he is, he'll end up president of the United States – and God help all of us then! Doesn't that bother you?'

Paul harshly said, 'It bothers the hell out of me.'

There was a silence. Sophie and Vladimir stared at him, then at each other, with shock and surprise. He had spoken in Czech: fluent, unaccented Czech.

'You didn't say you spoke Czech,' Sophie said, in her own language.

'What the hell is going on?' Steve asked in English, looking from her to Paul.

'Do I know you?' Vladimir asked Paul slowly, eyes hard and thoughtful. 'I thought I recognized you earlier, when I first arrived, then I wasn't sure. But I was right, wasn't I? We have met somewhere.'

Paul laughed with an odd sort of defiance and recklessness. 'Maybe. Sorry, I have to go.' He turned towards the front door and Vladimir drew a sharp breath, staring at his face in profile.

'My God. Pavel.'

Paul turned to look at him again, not speaking.

Vladimir stared at him fixedly. 'It can't be. He's dead. But my God, you look like him.'

Sophie stared at Paul too. 'Looks like who?' she asked Vladimir, still speaking Czech.

Furiously Steve shouted, 'What are you all talking about? Will you speak English, please?'

But Sophie was remembering her own brief sense of familiarity when she saw Paul. Who was it he looked like? One of her photos . . . what had happened to them? She had had them last night when she talked to Cathy.

'My family photos,' she said in English, looking at Steve. 'Have you seen them around this morning? I had them last night. Could you look in the drawing-room over there, please, Steve?'

'I burnt them,' Paul said, and she looked at him sharply.

'Why did you do that? You burnt my photos? I . . .'

Vladimir had been staring at him all this time, his face confused, uncertain.

'It is you, isn't it? My God, it is!' he burst out. You aren't dead, you were never dead. You're alive. My God. I don't believe it. Pavel . . .'

Cathy started. Pavel? He couldn't mean . . . no, it couldn't be! Pavel was a popular name; there must be thousands of Czechs with the name Pavel. What was the matter with her, getting into a panic over nothing? Vlad must know a hundred Pavels. She knew several herself; there had been three Pavels in her first year at college, she remembered.

Then she thought: of course, Paul was the English version of the name Pavel. Vladimir must have met Paul before somewhere. Nothing to do with her father!

But what was all that about being alive, not dead?

Vladimir said hoarsely, 'It is you, isn't it? I'm not imagining things? My God, I can't believe it, although after the story your wife told me about Anya I'm almost past being amazed. Even if you tell me you're a ghost I think I'll believe it.' He grinned. 'Are you a ghost, Pavel?'

Sophie began to shake violently. She felt she was almost breaking apart. It couldn't be true. Her father had been killed by the Russians; she knew the story by heart, she had heard it all her life – how he had been in a car that didn't stop at a Russian checkpoint, they had shot the driver and the car had crashed, killing everyone in it, and her father had been a martyr to the cause of freedom, a hero of their country.

What was Vladimir talking about? He had mentioned Anya. Asked if Paul was a ghost. But he couldn't mean her father. Paul couldn't be her father. Her father was dead.

But she had been told Anya was dead. Her own mother had told her over and over again how Anya had died of measles before she was born. She had visited Anya's grave a thousand times, talked to her, taken flowers to her, even taken her own first communion wreath to her – but it hadn't been her sister in that grave; it was Gowrie's child. All those years her mother had been lying to her.

Had her father's death been another of her mother's lies?

Once upon a time Sophie had believed in something she thought of as 'facts', but now she was beginning to realize that 'facts' could be just as lying and manipulative as any fiction ever written. Her head spun dizzyingly. Everything was a cheat, you couldn't believe anyone or anything.

'What did you say, Vlad? What the hell are you talking about?' Steve asked, his eyes sharp as diamond cutters, whirring from Vlad and Sophie to Paul's grey, stony face, biting into them all.

Sophie was almost fainting. Vladimir saw the colour draining from her face, the wild shock in her eyes. He caught hold of her just as her body turned heavy, began giving at the knees, falling. He held her up, muttering roughly, anxiously, 'Sophie! I'm sorry, girl. I am stupid, a stupid fool. I forgot what it would mean to you . . . Steve, you better take her in that room. She should lie down, she's going to pass out, I guess.'

'No! I want to know . . .' Sophie took a long, audible, shuddering breath, fixing her eyes on Paul. 'It isn't true, is it?' She didn't believe it, yet she had to ask because she no longer knew what was real and what wasn't, and she had to know or she would go mad.

Paul looked at her bleakly. 'I don't know what to say to you. I'm sorry, Sophie.'

'You . . . you're . . . my father?'

He didn't say anything, but his eyes told her the truth.

Steve caught her as she fainted, lifted her bodily into his arms, her head on his shoulder, his arm under her slack legs. He was barely conscious of her weight, he was too

346

busy looking at her unconscious face, reading the pallor, the lines around mouth and eyes, and so worried about her he felt sick.

His ears buzzed with hypertension. He was beginning to guess but he didn't want to believe his own intuition. It couldn't be true. It couldn't be.

Poor Sophie, he thought, hasn't she stood enough over the last week? One shock after another. Now this. And then another thought hit him like a knife in the guts. Oh, my God, Cathy; what will this do to her? His stomach began to churn as he took in all the implications. He had loved Cathy passionately once, she had hurt him when she dumped him for this man, but Steve had forgotten all that now. It was just part of the past, whereas his lifelong affection for the girl he had known most of her life had survived their love-affair and even been deepened by it. How on earth could she cope with a discovery like this?

Vladimir said, 'Holy Virgin, I wish I'd kept my mouth shut.'

'So do I, damn you!' Steve said with bitter force, moving away. Behind him the other men followed in silence, each absorbed in his own thoughts.

Steve took Sophie through the first door he came to, into the elegant drawing-room, the calm formality of the room making an ironic setting for that moment. He laid her down on one of the silken brocade couches. She was already stirring, her lashes fluttering, her breath coming so lightly and shallowly that he could only just hear it. Steve slid a cushion under her head, knelt beside her, stroking her cold cheek with one finger, looking down at her compassionately.

She was beautiful and he had fancied her the minute he saw her, but his feelings for her now were deeper and far more complicated. Getting to know Sophie had been a helter-skelter ride these past few days, a mind-shattering experience. She had guts, this girl – he'd known plenty of men with less nerve than she had, less determination and tenacity, but she had had a tough time already. The strain of the past week must have eaten into her reserves, and now, just when she had managed to meet and get to know the sister she had come so far to find, now, just when Gowrie's threat to her was neutralized, this had to hit her!

How the hell was she going to be able to cope with this too?

He looked round and saw Paul, stared at him with new eyes – this man was Pavel Narodni? He must be a damn sight older than he had seemed to be.

Paul met his eyes and turned away, walked across the room to a cabinet, got out a bottle of brandy, poured some into a tumbler and came back, holding it out to Steve.

'Give her some of this.'

'Good idea,' Vladimir said. 'I could do with one of those, myself, but a little more than a finger, please.'

Paul gave him an ironic, angry smile.

'Help yourself.'

Vladimir came back with a large tumbler of brandy and swallowed a mouthful, sighing.

'That's better. Nothing like a good brandy to cure shock.'

Paul began to laugh hoarsely. 'My God. Vladimir. It would be you, wouldn't it? You were always a gadfly, buzzing around into every cesspit . . . but I never expected it to be you who would break my cover.'

Vlad nursed his tumbler of brandy, staring. He asked curiously, 'You mean nobody ever recognized you until now? You've been very lucky.'

'Very,' agreed Paul. 'I knew that some day someone would turn up, I was prepared to have to deal with it, but why is it you, of all people? For years I expected it every day, but it never came, and I suppose I forgot, in the end, that I was living on borrowed time.'

Rapid footsteps crossed the hall, then Gowrie walked into the room. 'What was all that shouting about? For Christ's sake, what is going on now, Paul?'

Paul looked at him with deadly calm. 'I'm not Paul Brougham. My name is Pavel Narodni.'

Gowrie, mouth open, like a fish stranded out of water, breathed noisily, staring at Paul.

'What?'

'My God, you've changed, Pavel,' Vladimir said.

'I don't understand . . . what are you talking about?' Gowrie sounded almost demented. 'Are you trying to tell me . . . you can't be him, he's dead, he's been dead nearly thirty years. Pavel Narodni was Cathy's . . . her real . . . father. What are you trying to pull?'

Paul's lips curled. 'The reports of my death were much exaggerated, as your Mark Twain once said.'

Gowrie staggered to a chair against the wall and sat down, looking as if he had been pole-axed. He had aged visibly; his face had fallen in on his bones, his eyes sunk into his head. Nobody now would think he looked strong enough, fit enough, to become president.

'Cathy,' he whispered, almost whimpering. 'Jesus, how do we tell Cathy? You're her father . . . you married . . . Jesus, that's sick.' He sat up again and almost screamed. 'You fucking bastard, you married her, your own daughter, did you know? All this time, did you know? She'll go out of her mind, she'll . . . Jesus . . .'

Paul closed his eyes, breathing audibly, his face ashen. 'Of course I didn't know. My God, do you think . . .? When I realized who she really was . . . and that was your fault, you lying bastard . . . when I realized what had happened to us, I felt as if a trapdoor had opened under my feet, it was like falling through space.'

'It's a lie, it can't be true, you can't be him!' Gowrie screamed.

'I wish to God I wasn't. Ever since I found out, I haven't been able to think straight. I had to be alone to try to think, and that hurt her, I knew I was hurting her, but I couldn't do anything about it, the whole world had just disintegrated but I wasn't ready yet to tell her, I didn't know how to do it.'

Gowrie sat back again, staring at nothing. There was a long silence, then Vladimir said, thinking aloud, 'I get it . . . the Russians lied? You weren't killed, they took you away to be interrogated – you poor bastard, how long did they keep hammering on at you? Were they trying to get the names of all the student leaders out of you?' He frowned, chewing his lower lip. 'But surely they haven't kept you locked up all this time?'

'I wasn't in that car when it crashed, Vlad,' Paul said wearily. 'I'd got out just before we reached the checkpoint. I was going to collect some petrol bombs we had made that afternoon – we were going to attack some Russian tanks with them that night once it was dark. We didn't realize the Russians had set up a checkpoint round the corner. God knows why my friends didn't stop. Too damned scared, I suppose. We had some printed leaflets with us in the car. You know the sort of stuff we used to hand out, we printed them in a cellar off Wenceslas Square, below a bakery. I did most of them myself, on an old hand press.' His face contorted in a grin of mixed amusement and bitterness.

'What's funny?' Vlad asked.

'Life. It's just so funny how things work out. I never thought when I was working down in that cellar, printing away, that one day I'd actually own a large printing works.' Then he shrugged. 'The leaflets were innocent enough, a lot of talk of freedom, that was all, but freedom was a dirty word after Dubcek fell.'

'A very dangerous word, too,' agreed Vlad. 'If the Russians had found your leaflets they could have used them in a show trial, called you traitors!'

'But they didn't need to, because my friends panicked and were killed. I was just sliding quietly down a side-street when I heard the shouting, then shots, and then the explosion when the car blew up. I ran like hell, of course.'

'But the official verdict was that you were in the car and were killed, too,' Vladimir protested.

'I know, I heard later. I went into hiding. An old friend had a tiny space under his roof, not even an attic, just a gap right under the beams. I couldn't even stand up, and after three days crouched like that I could hardly walk. My friend heard the news about the car crash and told me my name was on the list of those killed, when he brought me water and bread the next morning, but the Russians came for him later that day. He vanished into prison on some trumped-up charge, and died there of a heart attack, so they claimed. The bastards probably tortured him, but he never betrayed me to them, because nobody came looking for me.'

'How long did you stay hidden? Didn't anyone know you were there? Was the house empty?'

'No, his sister lived there too. She took care of me, brought me food and water every day, which was very brave and kind of her, because the body that had been identified as mine was that of her lover – a foreign student at Prague University, Paul Brougham. The irony of it was that he got into the car when I got out – that was why the authorities thought he was me. Nobody had seen us change places.'

'So that's where you got that name?' Steve said flatly, hostility in his face as he watched the other man.

He had always had him down as an opportunistic acquisitive bastard, building his empire by grabbing this and that, even grabbing Steve's girl, so he wasn't surprised to hear that the man had snatched his very identity from its real owner.

Paul turned his head to look with wry understanding at him. He had always known Steve hated him; it was mutual, he had detested Steve too. He had been jealous of his old relationship with Cathy. His stomach clenched. He must not think about her. Must not.

'Yes,' he said flatly. 'His girlfriend told me he was dead. She was heartbroken, but she still insisted on helping me. For his sake, for our country, she hated the Russians like poison. She brought me all his documents, including his passport, and told me everything she could remember about him, so that I would be word-perfect if I was stopped and questioned. He had been born in France, and had a French mother, but his father was English, so he had dual nationality and two passports. I got out of the country on the French passport.'

'And nobody suspected anything?' Vladimir asked with what sounded like admiration. Vlad was always impressed by daring and courage. Steve was too, and couldn't deny that Pavel Narodni had exhibited both, but he had other reasons for hating the man.

Paul shrugged. 'I grew a beard, because he had had one. We looked vaguely alike and his passport photo wasn't very good, it was fuzzy. Our colouring was very similar, and the shapes of our faces. At the airport they hardly gave me a second look. Thousands of foreign students were flocking out of the country. I was just one of the crowd. The Russians had closed the borders and the airports for some days. By the time they let people leave there was a terrific pressure for seats. They weren't interested in foreigners – just Czechs who might be trying to escape to the West.'

Steve coldly asked, 'Why didn't you let your wife know you had survived?'

Giving him an equally hostile look, Paul snapped back.

'You don't understand what life was like for us then. You Americans never do understand what life is like for everyone else. You live in a mental Disneyland. But life isn't like that outside America.'

'We're not so innocent any more,' Steve said. 'Vietnam and a whole host of other wars have taught us quite a lot. I wish to God they hadn't.'

Paul said curtly, 'Well, I couldn't risk letting Johanna know I wasn't dead.' He saw the contempt in Steve's eyes and bit out, 'As much for her sake as for my own. If the Russians had found out they might well have arrested her and tried to blackmail me into coming back.'

Vladimir grunted, making a face. 'I guess they would, at that. It was the way they always worked, Steve. He's right.'

'OK, but couldn't you have let her know later, when it was safer?'

'I waited too long. I was too busy to think much about her at first. I could only just make enough money for myself to live on, I couldn't have sent her any money for the first few years. By the time I did have a good income it was too late.'

'Oh, come on!' Steve snarled. 'What do you mean, too late?'

Paul gave him a look of deep dislike. 'I mean it was too late. Literally. I got a private investigator to go to the village to look for her. He told me Anya was dead, and Johanna had remarried, some schoolteacher. I knew the baby she had been carrying when I left had been another little girl and the detective got me a photo of her at her first communion, but I couldn't let Johanna know I was alive, could I? She had a new husband, she was expecting his baby – how could I wreck that for her?'

Steve didn't argue that one; by then it had been too late, obviously, but why had the man waited so long?

'I had you checked out,' Gowrie suddenly said, as if

slowly beginning to understand. 'I should have realized you were a phoney – I did wonder about you right from the start. You were far too vague about your past, but then I thought it might be because you were English and the Brits are always so tight-lipped. My people couldn't find out anything about your life up to the point where you showed up in Paris, but they got lots of details about your family history from the village your people came from.'

'I visited there, myself, just for a day, to look at the place. I had to go to France when I left Prague, because of the passport. I was only permitted to board a plane to Paris.' Paul smiled at Vladimir. 'My French was always very good – remember? Nobody suspected me for a second.'

'How on earth did you survive there, though? Did you have any money with you?'

Paul shook his head. 'A few francs. I got a job, of course, translating freelance for a Paris publisher – I had to sweat for hours to earn enough to live on.'

'And nobody realized you weren't this Paul Brougham? What if his parents had started searching for him, had gone to the police and reported him missing?'

'That was one of my biggest pieces of luck. He didn't have a family. His parents were dead and he was an only child. He hadn't lived in France for years.'

'But how did you get a job and somewhere to live so quickly?'

'Through the international student grapevine. I met up with some French students as soon as I landed. I just went to the Left Bank and hung around in cafés until I managed to make friends, some guys who had connections with our group in Prague. Because of the Russian invasion they were very sympathetic, they helped me out with somewhere to live and with introductions.'

'They didn't suspect you weren't who you said you were?'

'If they did they never said a word. They accepted me as Paul Brougham, no questions asked; they would have thought it was bourgeois to ask questions. The police ask questions – students didn't want to sound like policemen. They believed in individual freedom.'

'Freedom is one of those things that you don't even think about unless you haven't got it,' Steve drawled, and both men looked at him, nodding. He asked Paul, 'But didn't anyone you met know the real Paul?'

'I just told you, he hadn't lived in France for years. And I only stayed there for a year, and had to work so hard there was no time for much of a social life. I didn't allow anyone to get too friendly, and I went on to London as soon as I had saved up enough. I thought it would be safer to keep moving around, not stay anywhere for too long. I didn't want to be noticed by the police. I started doing some translating in London too, and then I got a job with a printer, but of course I didn't get a chance to work on the presses because of the unions. They said I was a foreign scab; if you hadn't served your apprenticeship you couldn't work as a printer. I just got a job in the office, which was when I realized I had a head for business.'

Gowrie burst out, 'But how did you get all that money? Where did it come from? You can't have earned it working in an office.'

Paul's eyes flashed. 'I did, though. I discovered something I'd never realized – that if you have the brains and the drive you can make money easily. Most people just don't have what it takes. I meant to move on to Italy after a while in London, to the sun – London could be very cold – but I found I liked living in England, I didn't want to leave – the atmosphere here suited me. I suppose I was getting older, losing my taste for travel and politics. It happens to us all, doesn't it?'

'You still haven't explained where all your money came

from – the money to buy this place, for a start!' Steve drily said.

'I was working for a firm run by an old man who died suddenly. I managed to talk his widow into letting me take over managing the company. She wasn't interested in business, had no idea what to do – I visited her every Sunday to show her the books and talk over my plans with her. She had no children, I had no family – we adopted each other, in a way. When she died she left her estate to me.'

Steve gave him a cynical smile. 'I see what you mean about having a head for business and knowing how to make money easily.'

Paul gave him an angry, white stare. 'Think what you like! She was a second mother to me. I was very fond of her.'

'Sure you were. So, why didn't you send any of this lovely money to your wife and daughter back home?' mocked Steve, and then from the sofa they both heard a smothered sob and knew Sophie was listening. Steve could have kicked himself. He quickly went over to her. She had turned her face away and was sobbing into a cushion, her body shaking with violent emotion. Steve sat on the couch next to her, lifted her up into his arms, although she tried to push him away, and turned her wet face into his shoulder, his hand on her dishevelled blonde hair, running his fingers gently through the silky strands.

She only fought him for a second, then he felt the warmth and yielding of her body settle closer. She's never been loved, he thought, holding her. Nobody ever made her feel loved. I will; she's going to be loved from now on and she's going to know it, be sure of me.

Paul watched them for a second, then said huskily, 'Sophie, I'm sorry. I don't know what to say to you. I can make excuses until the cows come home but it won't make any difference to the truth, will it? All I can honestly say is I'm sorry to have hurt you like this.'

She sat up, pushing Steve away. 'I heard your excuses,' she said in a grey, flat voice. 'You walked out on us and were relieved when Mamma married again and gave you an excuse not to look back. You didn't care a damn for us.'

He visibly flinched, but said quietly, 'I won't argue over how you see it. I can understand why you should see it that way, but try looking at it from my point of view. I was a boy, still only twenty-two when I left Czechoslovakia; I was pretty irresponsible, and although I loved your mother I wanted my freedom too. I felt trapped, we had got married too young. But I did love her when I married her, I was crazy about her. It was just that the responsibilities of being a husband and a father were too heavy for me then. I wanted to do so much, and my marriage stopped me. But your mother was very beautiful, and I did love her.'

His face turned to stone again and he fell silent, looking down, his mouth tight and bloodless. What was he thinking? wondered Sophie, turning her head to stare at him in mingled curiosity and disbelief. Her father. He was her father. She couldn't take it in, couldn't feel it, emotionally. It was too staggering.

He was Cathy's father, too.

The thought was like being knifed. She bit down on her lip to stop herself crying out. God. How was Cathy going to take this?

'Cathy is very like her,' she said aloud, harshly, and saw him wince.

'Yes,' he whispered. 'The first time I saw her, across a room, in Washington, my heart nearly stopped. I thought . . . it's Johanna . . . and for a second I almost believed it was her, but then I realized it couldn't be, Johanna wouldn't still look the way she did when we were young. She would be middle-aged by then, I was middle-aged myself – but here was this girl who looked like all my memories of being young, and I couldn't take my eyes off her. I fell in love all over again with the same hair, same eyes, same smile. How could I guess . . .? For Christ's sake, she was an American, from an old family . . . it never entered my head that she could be my d –'

He put a hand over his mouth, turning away, his shoulders heaving as if he was fighting sickness.

My God, Sophie thought, if she had never come here they would never have known. This was another mortal blow she had dealt them. She stared at the window and saw the wintry sky moving overhead, saw the pale wraith of the sun among the slowly drifting clouds, and thought of all the years that had passed since her father turned his back on his old life, his family, his country. He must have thought he would never see any of them again. How could he possibly guess that the young girl he met as an American heiress, the daughter of a leading American politician, was actually his own daughter?

He would never have known if she hadn't come looking for Anya. It all went back to that. She wished to God she had never started out on that quest.

At that instant she caught sight of a figure in a mirror on the wall opposite the open door. Sophie stiffened. Cathy was standing on the stairs. How long had she been there? Oh, God. Could she hear their voices? Had she heard what Paul had been saying?

As Sophie watched her, Cathy began to move, silently, stealthily, treading on tiptoe down the stairs. Sophie almost believed she was seeing something that wasn't there: a soundless vision. Only the faint icy tinkling of the magnificent chandelier which hung above the hall betrayed the fact that Cathy was there, her movements making the glass drops sway slightly and chime like fairy bells. Where was she going?

She had changed out of her elegant amber dress and was wearing riding clothes: crisp, pressed beige jodhpurs, a shirt and over that a duck-egg-blue sweater. The outfit suited her; made her look very English, very cool and collected. Preppy, the Americans called it, that look, it was as English as bluebells and roses, and cricket on a village green. Who would believe that this very English girl was really a Czech?

And then, before she reached the last stair, she turned to take one quick look into the drawing-room, and her face told a different story, paper-white with shadowy dark stains under the eyes, which had a wild, crazy look, her mouth colourless, trembling, a little tic going beside it.

Sophie's stomach plunged. She knows, she thought. Oh, God, poor Cathy, she knows, she must have heard everything Paul said.

Why did I come here, why did I insist on seeing her? This is all my fault. I did this to her. Tears began to steal down her face and Steve exclaimed softly, frowning. 'Hey, kid, not more tears. How much salt water have you got in there, for heaven's sake?'

A second later Cathy's image in the mirror vanished as soundlessly as it had appeared and Sophie gave a shattered sob, putting a hand up to her mouth to silence it, pushed Steve away and began to run after her sister.

'Where are you going?' Steve asked, coming after her, grabbing her shoulder to stop her. She gave him a frantic look, struggling against his hand.

'Let go of me! I have to talk to Cathy!'

'Leave her alone,' Paul bit out harshly, glaring. 'She's upstairs, resting. Give her a little peace, can't you? She's going to need all the strength she's got later.'

Breaking free of Steve, Sophie sobbed, 'She isn't upstairs, I just saw her going out of the front door.'

'What?' Paul's eyes leapt with fear and pain, a pain

Sophie flinched from, a pain that no one should ever have to bear.

'She was wearing riding clothes, she must be going to the stables,' Sophie said, but he was gone before she had finished speaking, his running feet very loud on the polished hall floor.

They all went after him, then stopped outside, under the elegant portico of the house, hearing hoofbeats on grass, staring as Cathy rode into view on her big chestnut horse.

'Cathy! Cathy, for God's sake!' Paul yelled, still running, then stopped and stared after her, shouting her name in a hoarse, strangled voice. 'Cathy! Cathy, come back!'

She didn't look back or even seem to hear him. Her body moved instinctively with the horse, her knees pressed into its shining flanks, the reins held loosely in her hands. The two of them were galloping full out now and Sophie's heart beat hard in her chest. She was so terrified she could scarcely breathe. They were covering the ground so fast; she suddenly saw that there was a stone wall, about twenty feet high, ahead of rider and horse. Too high to jump, Sophie thought, too high – turn, Cathy, turn!

'Don't, don't,' she muttered aloud, her hands clenched at her sides, trembling with tension and dread. 'No, Cathy, don't . . .'

Echoing her, Paul screamed it out, 'No, Cathy, don't!' and began to run again, over the flat green parkland.

Gowrie was white. 'If she doesn't pull up now she'll hit the wall of the rose garden,' he whispered.

At the last second the chestnut seemed to realize its danger; it sheered sideways abruptly, galloping along the wall instead of continuing on its path towards it.

Cathy was flung off, her body flying in an arc for a second before she hit the ground.

Paul reached her a few moments later and fell on his knees, bending over her.

Steve had been a reporter most of his adult life. He would have described himself as immune to shock, hardened by years of exposure to the sensational aspects of human life and human death, to murder and cruelty, cunning and crime – but he found he could still be knocked off balance. The sun was shining and birds singing in the green parkland; it was a beautiful morning. Steve was shaking so much he couldn't even move. Cathy had always loved riding, being out in the country whatever the weather, tiring herself out, exercising one of the Easton horses. She had had accidents before – but she had never been seriously hurt. Until now.

His heart sinking, he knew that this time was different. She wasn't going to get off with a few bruises this time, or even just a broken bone or two.

Paul got up, holding her in his arms, and began to walk back towards them.

Sophie was so terrified that she clutched at Steve to stay upright, and he looked down at her briefly, putting his arm around her. He opened his mouth to say something comforting, make some automatic, soothing remark like, 'It's OK . . . It will be all right . . . don't worry . . .' But he couldn't, because he felt the way she did; he couldn't lie about it.

They knew, before Paul reached them, that Cathy was dead. Her body was slack and limp. She lay in his arms like a doll, her head hanging down backwards over his arm, her dark hair swinging at every step he took. And Paul was crying silently, tears running down his face.

Steve went to help Paul carry her, but Paul knocked him out of the way, shaking his head, snarling.

'Leave her. Don't touch her. I don't want you touching her, get away from us.'

He sounded crazy. His eyes were wild.

'Get a doctor,' Steve said to Sophie as Paul staggered

past them into the house, his strong body beginning to buckle under the strain of carrying Cathy's dead weight.

She's dead, thought Sophie incredulously, not wanting to believe it. She's dead. Anya was dead, and came back to life. Her mind was whirling like a kaleidoscope. Death, life, death, life, they merged into each other, and which was real? She no longer knew.

'No doctor,' Paul snapped. 'There's no point now. She's dead, her neck's broken, she's dead, no heartbeat, no pulse, dead, dead, dead.'

Steve watched him warily. The man looked insane. He might turn dangerous, violent, any minute.

Softly he said, 'I think a doctor should see her, though. You never know. She may just be in a coma.'

Please God, let her be in a coma, thought Sophie, but she knew in her heart that her sister was dead. Life did not look like that. Eyes open, staring, but so blank, no expression in them at all. The sunlight glittered on those wide, glazed surfaces and Anya didn't even blink. She was blind to the sun, it could not wake her now, or penetrate those open staring eyes.

She was dead. Dead, her hands hanging loosely, palms down, fingers loose. A trickle of blood at one corner of her mouth, her neck at a strange angle. Her neck was broken, Paul had said, and you could see it. Her head looked like a flower on a snapped stem, the black hair streaming in soft petals down over Paul's hand as he sank down, breathless, legs shaking, on to the couch in the drawing-room, holding her over his lap, kissing her on the temples, the cheeks, the eyes.

He was mumbling incoherently, his voice breaking every few words. 'Cathy, Cathy . . . Oh, God, what have you done? What have I done to you? My poor little love, this wasn't how I wanted it to end. I'd have died rather than hurt you. Why did you do it? God, why?'

362

Steve turned to whisper to Vladimir, 'Despite what he says, we have to get a doctor and the police. There'll have to be an investigation and the police will need to talk to all of us. I'll go and ring them. Keep an eye on Sophie for me.'

As he turned to go he almost collided with Gowrie, who had been watching Paul and Cathy, his face the colour of melting cheese, a waxy yellow.

He had obviously heard what Steve said to Vladimir. He caught at his sleeve, urgently said, 'No, wait! Before you ring anyone I have to get out of here. I can't be here, I can't get involved with the British police. You mustn't even tell them I was here. Keep me out of it. Especially ... especially the past ... Don't tell the police anything about me. Now she's dead there's no story. You see that, don't you? No point in telling anyone all that stuff from thirty years ago. What's the point of raking up history? It's all over now. This draws a line under it.' He gave Sophie a glance, flinched from the bitter contempt in her face, then said hurriedly to Steve, 'My helicopter's waiting to get me away. I told them I was leaving shortly. Don't forget, we have a deal, Colbourne? You won't regret it.'

Paul made a sound deep in his throat, a fierce snarl of fury. He laid Cathy gently down on the couch and stood up, glaring at Gowrie, his eyes those of a wild animal in bloodlust, the whites red-flecked, the pupils huge, glittering.

'You aren't getting out of anything, you bastard – you did this to her! If you hadn't passed her off as your daughter I'd never have met her and married her. You ruined our lives. This was all your fault, and you aren't getting away scot-free, so don't think it. You needn't start planning how to do some damage-limitation – your political career is finished. And so are you.'

Gowrie was afraid of him, but he had some sort of animal

courage, or was desperate enough to outface Paul. He backed, his lip curling in an answering snarl.

'Do you think I don't feel responsible? Of course I do, for God's sake, man! I have feelings, too. Do you think you're the only one who loved her? She may have been adopted, but I loved her as my daughter for most of her life. This has shattered me. I can't believe she meant to do it, she wasn't the suicide type, she was so full of life, this was just a tragic accident. I'll never get over it, and God knows how I'm going to break the news to my wife and her father – this has been the worst day of my life. But if I stayed, what good would it do? I'd just get embroiled in a big scandal, the newspapers are going to have a field-day over this – God knows what they'll invent, or guess. I can't be here when the shit hits the fan. Where would be the point of chucking away my own future, my own life? That won't bring her back, will it? And I'm sure Cathy wouldn't want that. She was always right behind me. I can do so much good, don't you see? If I get elected I could do so much good.'

Paul took him by the throat and shook him like a dog, glaring into his face.

'You lying bastard – all you're thinking about, all you've ever thought about, is yourself! You don't care about Cathy, you never have. I'm going to kill you.'

'Please don't!' Sophie cried out. She hated Gowrie too, she would like to kill him herself, but Cathy's death had used up all her emotions. She wanted no more death, no more grief, no more violence.

Paul looked at her for a long moment in silence, then said gently, 'Sophie, we never got a chance to know each other, and I think I would have loved you very much . . . you look just like my mother when I was a little boy . . . He destroyed that chance too. It's all too late, time just ran out. And why should he get away with that? She's dead. He ought to die.'

'He doesn't deserve that much luck,' Steve said very quietly, and Paul's head swung his way, staring into his eyes. Steve smiled ironically. 'Leave him to me. I'll make sure Cathy gets justice. When I've finished telling the world the whole story, Gowrie will be finished, believe me.'

'You'll break the story?' Paul asked, and Steve nodded.

Gowrie went white. 'You can't do that. You made a deal with me. Are you crazy? You don't think the network will let you put this out? Have you forgotten how much influence I have? My friends won't let you do it.'

'What friends? What influence?' Steve mocked him. 'Now Cathy is dead, so are you, Gowrie. Your wife's father will be the first to hear the whole story, and after that you're finished. Nobody will lift a finger to save you once the Ramsey family turn against you.'

Desperately, Gowrie caught at his arm, gabbling. 'Listen, Steve, don't be a fool, I can do a lot for you, name your price, the sky's the limit, you can't do this –'

'Watch me. You're a dead man, Gowrie,' Steve said, shaking him off.

'Why don't I just shoot him?' suggested Paul. 'It would be easier. It would make me feel better, too.'

Gowrie gave him a wild look, then turned and began to run. Over his shoulder he screamed, 'Don't even think about telling anyone, Colbourne, or I'll see you get yours!'

They heard the slam of the front door, his running feet on the gravel.

Paul began to laugh. 'Well, I'll leave him to you, then, Steve.' He held out his hand and with a surprised look Steve slowly took it. 'Sorry I didn't get to know you better,' Paul said with a friendly look. 'Too late now, but thanks. Crucify the bastard, for Cathy's sake.'

He walked back to the couch and picked up Cathy again,

before moving towards the door at an unhurried pace. The others all stood and watched. Sophie put a hand over her mouth to stifle a sob. She had never had a real chance to get to know her sister. Now she never would.

'Give me ten minutes alone with her,' Paul said as he walked out of the room. 'Then ring the police.'

Nobody moved or spoke as he went out into the hall, up the stairs. In the silence the creak of the floorboards upstairs sounded as loud as a shot.

Sophie jumped, opening her mouth to scream. Nothing came out. She felt as if her head was exploding. Nothing seemed real any more.

At last she managed to whisper, 'We ought to go with him. He's desperate, he might . . . do anything.'

'He's old enough to make his own decisions,' Steve said gently, looking with compassion at her white, drawn face.

Vladimir said, 'I need a stiff drink, I don't know about you.'

'I think we could all do with one this time,' Steve grimaced.

Looking at Sophie intently, Steve said, 'You're not going to faint again, are you?'

She couldn't even answer. He pushed her down on to a chair and held a glass of brandy to her white lips.

She pushed it away, shaking her head, but he put it up to her mouth again. 'Drink some. No argument, Sophie. You need it.'

She reluctantly parted her lips and took a swallow. The spirits made her cough, her throat growing hot as the brandy went down.

Steve made her take another couple of swallows, then he sipped at his own glass. She saw from his face that he was as shocked as she was; he needed the brandy.

'This isn't really happening. I'm having a nightmare,' Sophie murmured to herself.

'I wish to God you were,' said Steve heavily.

'I wish I was, too,' she whispered.

They heard the shot upstairs a moment later.

Epilogue

Eighteen months later, on a fine May morning, Sophie pushed open the gate of Arbory's medieval church and paused to look across the grass which lapped the graves in a green sea, looking for the grave which, last time she saw it, had been a raw, weeping wound in the earth, without a headstone to mark it.

It had rained the day they were buried. The gargoyles on the ancient grey stone walls had spouted water from their mouths, rain dripped from holly and yew, the very paths became small streams running downhill towards the gate.

Today the weather was very different. Sunlight gilded the stained-glass windows along the sides of the church, making the haloes of medieval saints glitter, robins and blackbirds were busy feeding their young in the ivy which curtained the wall around the churchyard, carrying caterpillars and moths to stuff into the gaping mouths waiting for them. The trees were all in full, green, glorious leaf, rustling and sighing around the churchyard. The whole world was full of promise.

'There it is, Anya, at the back,' she said, looking down at the baby she was carrying in a wicker carrycot, and as if in answer the pink starfish hands waved back at her.

The grave lay in a pool of dense shadow cast by a great, spreading yew. Sophie walked slowly along the path to it and put her free hand on the scaly bark, looking back across the years, remembering another churchyard, another yew tree far away, and another grave.

She had been back to the Czech Republic a few months ago to put flowers on her mother's grave. Johanna had died without ever knowing what had happened to Cathy. The joy of talking to her long-lost daughter on the phone had been too much for her. She had had a stroke a few hours later and been taken to hospital, where she lingered in a coma for several weeks before dying. To Sophie at that time it had seemed that death was all around her, she could not escape it wherever she went. It was months before she came out of that grim mood.

When she had visited her home again she wandered over to look at the grave which for so long had claimed to be the last resting place of Pavel and Anya Narodni. The stone had been removed, and so had the remains of little Cathy Gowrie. Her grandfather had had his only grandchild brought home to lie in the graveyard at Easton. The real Paul Brougham was still buried where he had lain since 1968, but no headstone proclaimed his identity. Sophie had knelt beside his grave and said a prayer for his soul, wondering if he would want to be moved. The little village was a peaceful place to sleep until eternity.

The real Anya and Pavel had been buried here, in England, a week or two after their deaths, once the local coroner had allowed the burial to take place. First there had been an inquest, held in a small hall locally, with a grey, stooped coroner listening to the evidence, asking polite, hushed questions with a sympathetic, appalled, incredulous expression on his wrinkled, tortoise-like face, while a great mob of reporters scribbled, whispered, stared.

They had waited outside to pounce on Sophie, Steve and Vlad when they left. Flashbulbs exploding, photographers jostling, reporters screaming questions. The story was already out in the States. Steve had done his weekly programme from London, via the satellite, and made sure with a few judicious leaks to major newspapers that the media were all watching that night. Next day every daily newspaper in America had carried the story as their lead.

369

Gowrie had been a front-runner for the Republican nomination. His exposure had been a major scandal. The world press had gone to town on the story: newspapers and television had been awash with photographs of Gowrie; his home; his wife; her father, old Ramsey; distant shots of the Ramsey family estate at Easton; wedding pictures of Cathy and Paul. From Vladimir's agency they were also supplied with pictures of the Narodni family and their home village.

By the time Steve had finished, Gowrie's tour of Europe had been cut short and he flew home a disgraced man, with no chance of getting the nomination as presidential candidate and no future in politics. The entourage that had flown out to Europe with him had all drifted away; he flew home alone.

Over the next few months his wife had divorced him quietly, unopposed, through the person of her lawyers. She, herself, was by then living at Easton with her father, and was never seen in public. For not contesting the divorce, old Ramsey agreed to pay him an undisclosed sum, but other than that he was cut off from the Ramsey money. During the same period, Gowrie gave up his seat in the Senate, on grounds of ill health, and went into hiding somewhere in Florida. Steve said Gowrie was quietly drinking himself to death there.

Whether or not there were going to be official proceedings against him only time would tell. The mills of God and the government ground exceeding slow. The Czech Republic had made a lot of angry noise about an American diplomat illegally removing a Czech child without official permission, but it had all happened so long ago that nobody seemed to know what should be done about it now, and the same applied to the American government. There had been rumblings of threats against him for bringing a Czech child into the country on an American child's passport, and threats of prosecution for fraud over presenting another child as the legal heir to the Ramsey fortune – but nothing had actually happened on either count.

After the funeral of Anya and Pavel Narodni, Sophie and Steve had flown back to the States, Vladimir had returned to Prague and slowly life returned to a familiar pattern again. Steve had been summoned to Easton and had told a frail and desolate Ed Ramsey the same story he had told the British police, the inquest and the press. Ramsey was a tougher audience, harder to convince, his eyes shrewd and cold, yet Steve had sensed that his grief for Cathy, as well as for the little granddaughter who had never come home from Czechoslovakia, had sapped his life already. He wanted to destroy Don Gowrie, he made no secret of that, but once that was done Steve had the feeling the old man would not last much longer. He had told Steve that his estate was now tied up carefully in an involved trust fund administered by a charity. Don Gowrie would never get his hands on a cent of the Ramsey money.

There had been no sign of Gowrie's wife. A friend of Ed Ramsey had told Steve one day that she had descended completely into senility now.

She didn't remember her own name or where she was; only occasionally would she ask for her father, never for Gowrie, but sometimes she would start to sob and call out, 'Cathy . . . where's Cathy?'

It had taken Sophie a long time to recover; she had made herself concentrate on her work, and had not wanted to see Steve at first. He reminded her of everything that had happened.

He didn't give up or go away. Lilli grew used to him turning up on their doorstep and usually asked him in, gave him her favourite Czech meal, a beef consommé with dumplings made from liver and garlic, and showed him her latest progress with the wheel of his family which she was creating.

Lilli was not in a hurry, but then neither was Steve. It gave him an excuse to come to the apartment whenever he was in New York. Worn down by his persistence, Sophie let him take her out to dinner in quiet restaurants and then to parties given by old friends of his who lived in Manhattan. Or they saw the latest films, went to opera at the Met, to premières of new plays. When Lilli finished his family wheel, he persuaded Sophie to come with him to present it to his parents. That was the first time she had met them and she had been shy with them. His father she found easy to talk to, but his mother intimidated her on first sight. Sophie saw that Mrs Colbourne was not happy with the idea of her precious son marrying a foreigner.

Sophie had felt like telling her that she had no intention of marrying Steve! It was true then; she was fighting how she felt about him, reluctant to love him, afraid of getting hurt. Her emotional skin had been so thin after the events at Arbory – for a long time she had only wanted peace and quiet, but slowly her grief had healed and Steve was there, patiently, inexorably, waiting for her. He was not a man, it seemed, who had ever heard the word no.

Kneeling beside the grave, Sophie put the carrycot down; her baby was blowing bubbles now, gazing up with those dark blue eyes at the sky wheeling overhead.

Sophie looked at the clear-cut names carved on the headstone. It seemed odd to see them here, in England. Pavel Narodni and his daughter, Anya. So far from the country where they had been born.

'I'm sorry I haven't been for a long time, Anya,' she said softly. 'But look who I've brought with me . . . she's a month old, and I've called her Anya Katherine – and she has your dark hair, Anya, but then Steve is dark, of course.' Lifting the baby out of her carrycot, Sophie held her up, the little feet in knitted white bootees kicking violently. 'I think she has the family face. She's a Narodni, all right, just look at her chin – obstinate and determined to get her own way. Steve says we're going to have trouble with her, and I think he's right, don't you?'

The baby gurgled, reaching for a fistful of the long grass which swayed so temptingly beside the grave. Sophie laughed.

'See what I mean? Grab, grab, grab! Steve thinks the sun shines out of her. He's already a doting father, he wants to give her the moon on a plate.'

She laid the baby back in her nest of blankets. 'We're very happy. I did have a problem when I was carrying Anya, I had to stop work for a few months – high blood-pressure problems, I had to rest a lot. It was so boring, and Steve probably found me even more boring, I kept crying for no reason, I couldn't help it. Steve thought it was the shock still working its way out, but my doctor told me pregnant women are often very emotional. I don't want to give up my career, mind you. I'd like to go back to work, but not yet, not until she's old enough to go to school. It costs a fortune to have someone else minding your baby while you work, and you miss out on all the fun stuff of the first couple of years, so I'm staying home with her for the moment. Steve's show is being networked coast to coast twice a week now, so we bought a lovely house in the countryside outside Washington and he commutes daily. At weekends we often visit his parents, but since Anya was born his mother is driving me mad. She thinks she knows it all, nag, nag, nag. Oh, she means well, and she does love Anya, but I need to keep my temper, and that isn't easy when you've been up all night with a grizzly baby.'

She looked down into the cot and smiled at the way her baby was watching the branches moving on the yews.

'She's on her best behaviour today, for you and Papa. You should see her some night on one of her crying jags! Last time we stayed with the Colbournes, Steve's mother said to me: leave her with me tonight, so I did, just to show her what it was like! I heard Anya yelling blue murder once or twice but I pretended to be deaf. I bet she doesn't suggest that again! His father's a darling, though. I wouldn't want to hurt him, and Steve can handle his mother. I guess it will work out, and it's good to be part of a family. I'm planning to have another baby once Anya is walking.'

She picked up a bouquet of red and white roses she had brought, unwrapped them carefully and laid them loosely on the grave.

'Smell these! Isn't that scent gorgeous? I bought them in the village. We're staying at the Green Man for a few days. Steve will come tomorrow, but he let me come alone with Anya today. He knows I'd feel self-conscious talking to you with him listening. I expect he thinks I'm crazy, talking to the dead. Oh, I miss you, Anya. And Papa. I wish I'd had a chance to get to know you both better. I hope Mamma has found you at last. I put roses on her grave too, last time I was there. It was so strange, her dying so soon after you both. As if it was meant. I visited Franz and my half-brothers while I was there, but really we don't have that much in common. I think *we* had, Anya. We would have had, if there had been time.' She sighed, looking at her watch. 'I'll have to go. It's nearly feeding time, and Anya won't wait, she'll go red and start yelling any minute. I'll be back with Steve tomorrow. I wish we lived in England and could visit you more often, but while we are here we'll come every day, I promise.'

She picked up the carrycot and looked once more at the quiet grave. Sunlight glinted on the carved stone, a speckled mistlethrush sang among the rustling grass, there was a scent of roses and honeysuckle on the air, and even in the brightest sunshine the yew trees cast their dark shade over this fine and private place.

It was hard to believe how violent the deaths of those

who slept here had been. All the uncertainties, the grief and anguish, had ebbed away. The world's heartache and glory meant nothing to them any more. Unseen, their dust slowly merged in the warm earth, yet she would not have been surprised to be told that they walked together under the silent midnight moon or in and out of the shadow of the courtyard yews, pale flitting ghosts like summer moths, their spectral voices whispering secrets all night long.

O SIGNET

By the same author

In the Still of the Night

Annie Lang, star of the top TV police drama *The Force*, is a character known to millions. But, in the real world, the actress with the innocent face harbours her own terrible secret. Why do those who get close to Annie have a habit of dying – suddenly and violently – in the still of the night?

Two very different men dominated Annie's past. Both vanished nearly eight years ago. Since that fateful night, ambition has driven Annie to the top. Now at the peak of her success, she has everything she has ever wanted except love – the one thing she would trade it all for.

Bestselling author Charlotte Lamb – the Queen of Romance – turns to crime with a darkly compelling tale of obsession, desire . . . and murder.